crooked little heart

also by anne lamott

HARD LAUGHTER

ROSIE

JOE JONES

ALL NEW PEOPLE

OPERATING INSTRUCTIONS

BIRD BY BIRD

Crooked
Little
Heart

BY ANNE LAMOTT

 PANTHEON BOOKS NEW YORK

Grateful acknowledgment is made to the following for
permission to reprint previously published material:
Dutton Children's Books and Methuen Children's Books: "Disobedience" by
A. A. Milne, from *When We Were Very Young* by A. A. Milne, Illustrations
by E. H. Shepard. Copyright © 1924 by E. P. Dutton, copyright
renewed 1952 by A. A. Milne. Rights in the United Kingdom administered
by Methuen Children's Books, London. Reprinted by permission
of Dutton Children's Books, a division of Penguin Books
USA Inc., and Methuen Children's Books.
Random House, Inc., and Faber and Faber Ltd.: Excerpt from "In Memory of
W. B. Yeats" by W. H. Auden from *W. H. Auden: Collected Poems.* Copyright
© 1940, copyright renewed 1968 by W. H. Auden. Rights in the United
Kingdom administered by Faber and Faber Ltd., London. Reprinted by
permission of Random House, Inc., and Faber and Faber Ltd.
University Press of New England: Excerpt from *Times Alone* by Anthony
Machado. Copyright © 1983 by Wesleyan University Press. Reprinted by
permission of University Press of New England.

Library of Congress Cataloging-in-Publication Data

Lamott, Anne.
Crooked little heart / Anne Lamott.
p.   cm.
ISBN 0-679-43521-2
I. Title.
PS3562.A4645C7   1997
813'.54—dc21   96-47718
                                                       CIP

Random House Web Address: http://www.randomhouse.com/

Book design by Fearn Cutler

Printed in the United States of America

2 4 6 8 9 7 5 3

This one is for the Smiths,
Bill, Emmy, Nell, Luisa, and Sam,

and for Leroy Lounibos.

Last night, as I was sleeping,
I dreamt—marvellous error!—
that I had a beehive
here inside my heart.
And the golden bees
were making white combs
and sweet honey
from my old failures.

—Antonio Machado,
from *Times Alone*

sea change

one

Rosie and her friends were blooming like spring, budding, lithe, agile as cats. They wore tiny dresses and skirts so short that their frilly satin tennis bloomers showed. Into their bloomers they tucked an extra tennis ball to extract when it was needed, as with sleight of hand, like pulling a rabbit out of a hat, a quarter from behind an ear. Their days were spent honing their games in lessons and practice, playing in tournaments, and in between matches, watching each other compete, killing time, hanging out, playing Ping-Pong and endless games of cards. They were brown as berries, with feet as white as the moon; the sock lines at their ankles were as sharply drawn as saddle shoes. Rosie and her partner Simone Duvall were good, ranked number one in the girls fourteen-and-under doubles in northern California. Cocky and devoted, they loved to be watched by almost everyone but their parents, loved to be watched by other kids, by their pros, by the other kids' pros, and by members of the clubs at which they played—the weekend duffers who'd look at Rosie Ferguson, thirteen years old and seventy wiry pounds, hitting the ball as hard as almost any man they knew, thick black curls whipping, Siamese blue eyes steely, impassive, twenty bullets in a row, over the net and in, frowning almost imperceptibly if she missed.

The kids on this circuit could go to any club in the country, probably the world, and in simply rallying with one another draw a small crowd. Their parents sat in groups holding their children's knapsacks and sweats, unconsciously dandling them in their laps when the tension rose. The parents—tight-faced, vigorous, vibrating—sat in silences so grave and tense that except for the rampant whiteness and signs of wealth, they might have been waiting for disappeared children in Central American plazas.

Each tournament was played by dozens of these tiny pros, all watching one another play, all aware of each other's rank and seed. The girls would have loved to be watched by boys. For the most part, however, the girls watched the boys play but the boys rarely watched the girls. The boys were stronger, heavier, more aggressive, and most of the men preferred to watch them play—except for the girls' fathers, sometimes their coaches, and Luther.

There was a man named Luther who had started following the girls from tournament to tournament last year, arriving in Sacramento or Palo Alto or Berkeley or Stockton, wherever that week's tournament was. Luther came by bus with no suitcase, no gym bag, no nothing. He looked like one of the men who stood by the side of the road at intersections, holding up a sign saying they were hungry and homeless, had babies or AIDS, would work for food. One day in Modesto he just showed up and started watching some of the girls play. It quickly became clear that he had favorites—and that Rosie Ferguson was one of them.

People guessed that Luther was in his late forties, although he could have been much older or younger. He was white but sometimes dirty, and big, with rounded shoulders and a close crew cut. He may have been handsome once, with a good straight nose and rugged jawline. He wore old worn pants and jackets, black wing-tip shoes. His eyes were dark brown, often rimmed with red as though from drinking, although you never saw him with a bottle. His teeth were strong looking but the yellow of old linoleum. The slow smile was the worst part. When he was sitting on the lowest bench of the bleachers, as close as he could get, and he leaned in to watch when a girl had to bend low to the ground, and he smiled, a current of fear and excitement would run through the girls, a dark thrill like they felt at scary movies.

The parents had tried all last year to get the police to make him stop watching their daughters, but because he wasn't doing anything wrong and was never publicly drunk, there was nothing they could do. The club tournaments were open to the public, and many tournaments were held at public parks; he was the public. He didn't push his luck, either, didn't walk or hitch rides to the lonely satellite courts where overflow matches were often played—junior college courts or cracked, dilapidated public courts with metal nets. He stayed right in the public eye, shuffling from match to match. Just watching.

Rosie's stepfather James tried to find out who this man was and whether he had a record. Everyone naturally assumed he was a child molester, and James hoped to discover that he was breaking probation. But no one knew his last name, and none of the police in any of the towns and cities James contacted had any information on him, except that the tournament officials there had also been calling to inquire about him. One old-timer from the Golden Gate Park courts—where Luther spent quite a lot of time, according to the kids who practiced there—claimed that Luther was a veteran, with a wound that had left him . . . well, as the old-timer put it, had left him Luther.

James was not crazy about Luther, although he was not convinced that the man was dangerous, but he actually hated Rosie's coach, her big handsome pro, J. Peter Billings. Peter was a man of fifty, handsome as a model in a toothpaste ad, with a shaggy blond head of hair and big blue eyes. He was the pro at the club where Rosie had a junior membership, a club to which only the seriously wealthy could belong. The only exceptions were three junior members who paid a small monthly fee in order to play there and be coached by J. Peter Billings. Most of the young people who took lessons from Peter were the children of rich parents, who either played tennis themselves or lounged around the Olympic-sized pool. Their family memberships cost nearly fifteen hundred dollars a year, and since this paid Peter's salary, membership included his effusive friendliness.

Rosie and Simone, on the other hand, each paid forty dollars a month for their junior memberships, and since neither could afford more than two lessons a month, they did not warrant a great deal of loyalty. Furthermore, he was coaching two promising boys who had been nationally ranked for several years now and who were sure—at the very least—to snag a couple of great tennis scholarships; he also had a female protégé who had gone from winning national singles tournaments at sixteen to being a touring pro who now won her share of international doubles tournaments.

So J. Peter Billings had no need of two teenage girls lacking the national recognition or wealth of his three main students, students who bought two and three and four rackets every year and had each of these strung every few months. The girls were doubles champions, that was true, but Simone was lazy, and Rosie had a tendency to "choke," to blow solid leads by spooking herself into a state of dread. Real champions entered matches assuming that they would win; Rosie played many singles matches driven by the terror of losing. Still, Peter had all but promised that if the girls kept up their games, they would get scholarships to decent colleges someday.

He rarely showed up specifically to watch either of the girls play, but if he drove to a tournament where one of his boys was playing, he might give Rosie and Simone a ride, and then would sometimes stand with a fatherly, proprietary air near the court where one of the girls was playing. Rosie basked in his attention and tried to play so well and so hard that he would stay. But James watched him watch Rosie with thinly disguised contempt. James said that you could never trust a man who parted his name on the left. And he hated Peter's sexy, stupid little jokes: "You know where they get virgin wool, don't you, Rosie? From the fastest sheep." When Rosie repeated the joke to her parents at the dinner table, they had just stared back at her blankly. Rosie found Peter impossibly handsome, with his movie-star hair and long, tautly mus-cled body, and he coached her well, worked her hard at lessons, pound-ing thousands of balls at her from a shopping cart at the net. She'd heard him bragging about her achievements, and sometimes that felt wonderful, like sunshine, and sometimes she felt like a pet rock in whom he had begun to lose interest. But she was grateful and relieved for any attention from him whatsoever, because she knew that she was not a true champion, not a singles champion. And no one cared nearly as much about doubles.

James also disliked most of the kids, except for Rosie and a few of her friends.

"I can't help it," he said. "All I see are a bunch of spoiled kids, raised in the lap of luxury. They're billboards for suburban perfection. Do you think they are really happy?" he asked Elizabeth once. "They have all the accoutrements, all the right clothes, and it all seems so lost on them."

Still, every so often, he came along when Elizabeth drove Rosie to wherever that week's tournament was, and he alone could exert a calm-ing effect on Rosie in the hours before important matches. He said funny things to make her laugh, let her play her awful music on the car stereo, and he censored his caustic commentary on the world for her sake. He surprised her with Baggies of trail mix or dried fruit to boost her energy, moleskin in case she developed a blister, a washcloth to tuck in the waistband of her tennis skirt, with which she might mop up her sweat or tears. And Elizabeth hoped each time that he'd come around, see the animal beauty and skill of the young bodies, the dedication, the joy. But it did not stir him, did not send him into the disciplined trance of the other parents, huddled in their unhappy groups.

One day in February, he and Elizabeth sat a discreet distance from Rosie and Simone, who were paired in the fourteen-and-under doubles final in the season's first tournament, traditionally held in Bayview, where they lived.

Once there had been Miwok Indian villages here, then dairy farms and fisheries, and in the 1880s, the railroad, with tracks all through town, a depot, a roundhouse, a pier on San Francisco Bay so that railroad cars might carry their freight and passengers by ferry to San Francisco and beyond. Now, wherever you looked, you found shops, boutiques, cafés. The railroad tracks had been converted into bike paths on which the tanned, handsome people of Bayview jogged, walked pedigreed dogs, or raced along on bicycles and roller skates. The railroad workers, the fishermen, and farmers could never have afforded to live here now. The Fergusons and James lived here only because Elizabeth's first husband, Andrew—killed in a car crash when Rosie was four—had bought an old ramshackle house fifteen years ago, before all the boutiques and coffeehouses, before three tennis clubs and four private schools had sprung up within five miles of each other. Outside the walls of these clubs and schools and boutiques, women, pregnant or with sad dirty children, and men huddled by the road at intersections, holding their signs, begging. James had heard them referred to once on the radio as the residentially challenged. He almost always gave them a dollar or two. Their numbers were growing: on the way to the previous season's last tournament, held in Palo Alto in late November, James and Simone and the Fergusons had counted twenty-eight people asking for money at traffic lights, seven with children, one with four all her own.

Still, Bayview was about as beautiful a place as you could wish to be, with its low rolling lion-claw hills and tree-lined streets, temperate weather and wondrous views. Two islands floated on the wide blue bay, Angel and Alcatraz; Angel green and lovely, peopled by hikers, picnickers, children; Alcatraz haunted, dark, abandoned, chill. Sailboats and ferries sliced through the rough blue waters; way over to the right was the Golden Gate Bridge, its arms outstretched from Marin on the north to the golden lights of San Francisco. And watching over the town's ten thousand people was their mountain, small and sublime, the mountain the Indians called Tamalpais, the sleeping maiden. You could see her verdant shoulders and head and breast from almost everywhere in the county, and the hills and slopes unfolded beneath her like big swells in the ocean. You could see her from the street where the Fergusons lived; you could see her from the bleachers where James and Elizabeth sat today, watching the match. Whenever Elizabeth drove the five miles from home to the base of the mountain, to its beautifully defined skirt around which Rosie had been crawling her entire life, she thought of the mother in the *Nutcracker,* with her huge hoopskirt and all her children pouring out from underneath.

Elizabeth sat watching her daughter and Simone play hard and fierce. She was mother to them both today, as Simone's mother had been unable to get away from the nail salon that she owned in town. The girls were concentrating on each shot, moving like quicksilver around the court, up and back and over in the ballet of girls' doubles. Simone played gracefully, steady and serene, with a powerhouse forehand and a slightly reserved topspin backhand. Rosie, on the other hand, looked like she was out to avenge the Holocaust. She was scrappy and pigeon-toed, moving about with unbridled energy like a shark. Their opponents never had a chance. One of the girls, who'd gained twenty pounds since last season, wore a baseball cap for a visor, with a thick river of reddish hair pouring out the back like a horse's mane. She had entered the court holding her racket carrying case like a briefcase, as if she had just come home from the office. Her partner was a very small black girl, nearly thirteen, with glasses and cornrowed hair, who hesitated coming up to the net and so kept getting caught in the no-man's-land between the T of the service line and the baseline, where it was ridiculously easy for either Rosie or Simone to pass her. Her name was Kaya, and she had been ranked in the top five of the girls twelve and under, but she wasn't doing so well in the fourteens. She played angry and erratic, like a colicky baby grown up.

An incredibly lucky return of serve had emboldened Rosie early on, and she simply wasn't missing. She and Simone, together at the net,

were an old married couple who knew how to finish each other's physical sentences. Rosie, for instance, playing backhand, knew that
Simone's backhand net game was more deadly, more precise, than her
own forehand volley, and she knew how to tell by the most minute ad-
justment in Simone's posture whether Simone was going to step into
the path of an oncoming ground stroke and try to put it away or
whether she herself should step in and take it. They did not have a
foolproof system though, and sometimes each would think the other
had the ball, and both would move out of the way, and then they
would get passed down the middle of the court. When this happened,
they would hang their heads good-naturedly, or roll their eyes, or smite
their foreheads. But for the most part, they were smooth, exciting
dancers, instinctive, brilliant in anticipation underneath the transparency of their also being best friends.

Elizabeth watched in awe and so felt disloyal when she laughed
under her breath at James's sarcastic comments.

James looked around nervously from time to time, scanning the
bleachers for Luther, who wasn't there, and taking in the opulence,
the luxurious landscaping—irises and early roses in the flower beds,
kaleidoscopic flower boxes everywhere, bursting clownlike with gardenias and purple African daisies. Sometimes he scribbled down observa-
tions in a little notebook he kept in the back pocket of his jeans. He
wrote down funny things she and Rosie said; he collected what he
called Simone stories to use in writing his novels. Just today, driving
over to the club, Simone had confessed that she was so afraid of being
buried alive that she'd written a note that she kept in her desk that said,
"In case of my death, make sure if they're going to bury me that you
shoot me in the head and heart first." James had whispered, "Whoa,"
and Simone had gone on to something else, and at the next red light,
James had extracted the little notebook from his back pocket, and
scribbled this down.

An arrogant rodent-faced boy of Rosie's age, playing singles on the
next court against a tall impassive Chinese boy, made a wheezing,
droning grunt with every shot he hit. It sounded like an approaching
mosquito. James shuddered.

"Is that some kind of mantra?" he said. Elizabeth shook her head.

"Neee-ow," said James.

"Nee-ow," said the boy, hitting a backhand.

"It's like the sound a kid makes when he's playing with toy airplanes. Maybe it helps him guide the ball in. Like air traffic control."

Elizabeth studied James, his wild fluffy hair, his beautiful green eyes, and he looked at her and smiled. She loved being with him; it was that simple. She felt happy when he was around. He loved her, he loved her child, he made them laugh. Sometimes when she called from the grocery store to see if he needed anything, he would cry out plaintively, "Come home! Why aren't you home?" She reached out now, at the club, and touched his cheekbone with the back of her fingers, and then moved her fingers down to his lips, and he opened his mouth, enough for her to feel his warm breath, and she felt him smiling, just barely, beneath her fingers. After a moment he kissed one of her knuckles and went back to watching the girls.

"You know what I do like about this place," he said, "is the sound of the ball on the racket and the court. It sounds like something is being accomplished. How often do you get to *hear* skill? I find it comforting.

"But on the other hand, this right here represents the end of white Anglo-Saxon America. The boats are unloading beautiful rainbow people onto our shores right now, whose turn it will be. Ah," he exclaimed, looking over to the right. "Speaking of rainbows."

Simone's mother, Veronica Duvall, had shown up after all, wearing a cotton dress of prismatic hues. She waved to James and Elizabeth and tottered over on high-heeled mules. She was very pretty, with dark yellow hair, ten years younger than Elizabeth, very friendly, full of innocence and New Age platitudes. She drank perhaps a little too much on occasion, but nothing like the quantities Elizabeth used to put away, after Andrew's death and before she got sober. Everyone exchanged quiet pleasantries as the girls played on, Elizabeth bending over to whisper into Veronica's ear that the girls were winning the finals easily. Almost all the other parents wore expensive tennis shoes and were dressed as if they might play a set of doubles together themselves after the children were done; Veronica looked as though she were off to serve cocktails at the harmonic convergence.

Rosie and Simone won, as expected. Elizabeth and James clapped loudly, proudly. The sun shone in the bright blue sky. So you would have thought, watching Rosie bask in the applause, in the glow of the on-court presentation of their trophies, that she was still a black-haired golden child, the child of last year who had played in ecstasy, in joy of motion, so fulfilled and happy moving that she could barely stand it, as if her inner camera were for the moment fully focused.

And there were times, like right now, when she still felt that joy, when she still felt wild. But in the last six months her body had begun trundling her into tortured, self-conscious adolescence. She felt she was on the wrong planet. She feared that all the other kids were drawn into life in a way that she wasn't; she observed the grown-ups and saw in their lives a lack of vitality and joy, saw a flatness in their faces. It gripped her with fear. She sometimes decided that she had been put on the earth among all these earthlings so that scientists might study her. She was afraid she would never have a boyfriend, breasts, periods. She was afraid because four years before, Mr. Thackery, the father of her best friend Sharon, had shown her his penis, made her see it, hard and purple, when she was only nine, and she was afraid that seeing it had infected her insides, had tainted her. She was afraid she would never forget. She was afraid of dying in either a nuclear catastrophe or a drive-by shooting, she was afraid that curious, staring Luther would find her and rape her, she was afraid she would end up poorly ranked, but more than anything else, she was afraid that her mother would die.

Her daddy had already died, nine years ago. Pictures of him hung on the walls of her bedroom, and so every day she remembered how tall and good-looking he'd been, with thick wavy brown hair and blue eyes, a shy smile, and a long nose that was almost too long but instead looked aristocratic. She remembered riding around town on his shoulders, and how he held onto her ankles with his large beautiful hands, how everyone said he had beautiful hands, and how safe she felt sitting on top of him, like they were one long person, a totem pole.

Sometimes when she could not fall asleep, her mind would lock onto the image of her mother drowning, those last few moments of suffocating underwater, looking up in panic through the frigid water of San Francisco Bay into the bright sunlight where her screaming daughter stood, unable to save her.

JAMES always took her and Elizabeth out for dinner when he came to watch her play. If she had played well and won, or played beautifully in losing to someone ranked higher than she, she found him funny and forgave him his terrible clothes. If she was disappointed, she listened to his jokes and sarcastic commentary with thinly veiled disgust. This time they ended up at a small Korean restaurant near home. There were big dreamy landscapes painted on the wall, bamboo mats and kitschy gewgaws everywhere. They were the only customers. They ordered sodas and studied the menu.

"Girl, you played so beautifully today," said James. Rosie squirmed, and Elizabeth smiled at her husband's soft touch, her daughter's look of dazed naïveté. He went back to reading the menu. He wore Ben Franklin–style reading glasses now, which he bought at Thrifty. "I suppose it's required that I get the octopus," he said. "You always make me get the octopus, Elizabeth."

"I've never made you get octopus, darling."

"Well, it turns out that I *desire* octopus tonight. That's what victory does for a man. In fact, I'm going to order both the octopus and the squid and stage an underwater fight."

Rosie was shaking her head. She was used to this and traded a look with her mother.

"James," she said. "Why would you order things you don't want?"

It was wonderful food, light and bright, hot and sweet, full of garlic, ginger, chilies, sugar. "I like that," said James. "I like a cuisine where they add sugar to everything."

"Better, of course, if they also add heavy cream," said Elizabeth. All of a sudden Rosie was blinking back tears as she stared miserably at the food on her plate.

"Oh, darling," Elizabeth murmured in surprise.

"Why can't anything ever be fine just the way it is?" Rosie said. "Why do you two always have to find fault with everything?"

James and Elizabeth looked at each other wearily.

"But I love this food, honey," said Elizabeth.

"You'd love it more with cream."

They ate in silence. From time to time Elizabeth glanced up and studied James while he ate. I love you, she thought, I do.

She reached out and rubbed Rosie's forehead. Rosie's eyes were closed. After a minute, two tears trickled out, which Elizabeth rubbed away. Rosie squirmed. "Okay?" said Elizabeth. Rosie nodded.

Elizabeth felt a wave of peace, of reconciliation. And when, for no particular reason, one of James's cheap wooden chopsticks suddenly broke in half, the sound made everyone smile. He looked around as if something awful had happened, then held out both broken parts to their waiter, who was hurrying toward them with two more courses.

"Do you have any wood glue?" James implored.

THERE were days and moments now when Rosie was as sweet and attentive and interesting as one could hope for in a thirteen-year-old girl, and there were times when, physically and emotionally, she was frozen, hard, full of blame and something bordering on hate. Five years had passed since the Thackerys moved away, Elvin—free and apparently unbothered by what he'd done—promoted at his company and moved out of the county. Now Simone, whom Rosie had known almost her whole life, was Rosie's best friend, but Rosie still grieved Sharon's departure. They had not spoken by phone or mail since the Thackerys moved, and Elizabeth felt sometimes, when Rosie froze up with derision and judgment, that she was secretly armoring herself against any more hurt, any more lost friends, any more lost dads. Rosie sometimes seemed to believe that if she didn't cause the lost connection, it would be done to her anyway, and so if anything more was going to be snatched away, she herself would do the snatching.

Tonight's small moments of connection, Rosie's pleasure in their company, filled Elizabeth with quiet relief.

THEN the next morning Rosie was so openly hostile at breakfast that James got up and left. Elizabeth looked at her sad fierce child, then tilted her head and studied her like a painting.

"Is it anything you can talk about, Rosie?" Rosie shook her head, staring into her bowl of cereal, as if on a phone call full of bad news where no one else could even see the receiver. Sun poured in on them, on Rosie's skinny little shoulders, brown stick arms, that face full of resignation, anxiety, questioning. She looked as if the angel of death were appearing to her. "Honey?" said Elizabeth, and Rosie glanced up with a now familiar look, a look that James characterized as saying, If you knew how tough it is for me, you'd realize why you make me so sick. The sun smelled warm, like laundry in the dryer, like melting yellow crayons.

two

I N the last couple of months, since turning thirteen, Rosie had undergone what her mother called a sea change and what Elizabeth's best friend Rae called the changeover from dog to cat, from friendly and engaged and doggishly attentive to mysterious and aloof. Elizabeth knew something had changed, that Rosie had crossed some sort of threshold, when Rosie stopped looking at her. Elizabeth frequently felt as if she were being looked past, and she found it deeply disconcerting, even more so because when she first began to notice it, she heard herself say one of the things her mother had said to her when she was young, something she'd sworn she'd never say: "I want you to *look* at me when I'm talking."

Then Rosie would suddenly, maliciously lock onto Elizabeth's gaze like a cat watching someone eat a tuna fish sandwich. So Elizabeth didn't say it anymore. She remembered avoiding eye contact with her own mother when she was Rosie's age. It was partly, she thought, because her mother might read her mind, and her mind was so seditious, plotting her mother's overthrow. She also remembered having had the superstitious belief at thirteen, twenty-nine years ago, that if she didn't look at her mother, drunk and dramatic, or out like a light at midday, or sick and shaky, her mother might just go ahead and disappear.

Also, she had been profoundly ashamed of herself, so big and busty and heavily eyebrowed, so huge and clumsy. Elizabeth knew that Rosie was ashamed of being small and undeveloped. Elizabeth had been so ashamed of her drunken disheveled mother, and even though she, Elizabeth, had now been sober four years, Rosie was still ashamed to have a mother who used to get drunk and bring men home from the bar, and who now had to go to her endless meetings. She did not understand why her mother could not control her drinking, enjoy a beer or two on a hot summer's day, like her friend Hallie's mother, like most regular people. She didn't understand why her mother couldn't act more normal, why she needed so much solitude, why she couldn't have a lot of friends and a job, and throw lots of fun parties, smile, wave to more people. Her mother was a little like a wolf, an outsider, strange somehow, like Luther. She was ashamed to think that, but it was true.

She was also scornful of her mother's clothes and her refusal to wear makeup. "Would it really kill you to wear a little lipstick?" Rosie cried when Elizabeth showed up at school to pick her up one day. And then, three weeks later, when Elizabeth did show up wearing a little foundation and some blusher, Rosie all but rolled her eyes. "Don't even bother, Mom," she'd said.

ROSIE was aware that the things she said hurt her mother, but why did her mother have to be so annoying, so weird? For instance, Elizabeth had a pair of ratty black loafers she was practically living in these days, as if the family didn't have enough money to buy her a new pair. From Rosie's perspective, those shoes might as well have been bloody rags, strapped to Elizabeth's feet with adhesive tape, advertising to the whole world that the family wasn't doing very well. Elizabeth promised not to wear them when she picked Rosie up at school or the courts, but then just last week she'd forgotten, and Rosie, spotting the shoes on her mother's feet, felt stung with betrayal. She had staggered to the car with humiliation.

"Darling, what is it?" Elizabeth asked as they rounded the corner toward home.

Rosie was scowling. "This will not do," she muttered.

SCHOOL was so confusing, seventh grade. The "campus" was very pretty, covered with trees that were now in full bloom and a huge green playing field, all the trappings of an upper-middle-class school for mostly white kids. Rosie belonged to the larger group of forty or fifty kids who got to think of themselves as the popular crowd. But within that group there were the top ten girls, the cutest, foxiest girls, a little more rebellious than the others, who smoked pot and spiked their drinks at dances and parties, who made out with boys and always had boyfriends. Rosie liked a number of the less-popular popular girls, girls in the second echelon of popularity, and sometimes went along with them to the mall or to their parties. She was included in gossip and parties because she was funny and famous for being a tennis star. Mostly, though, after school and on weekends, she and Simone were on a tennis court somewhere. Rosie found most of the really popular girls spoiled and sarcastic without being funny. The boys were not at all interested in her, and this was very painful. She remembered a dance last year, held right after school in the gym, where she'd felt so wild, so desperate to be a part of one of the happy dancing couples, that she'd leapt away from the sidelines and thrown herself at a couple who were slow dancing, as if she could be in the middle of all that affection, a part of it, or maybe bump the girl away like a billiard ball and take up dancing the girl part. They had looked at her as if a monkey had just tried to cut in.

Besides this, she didn't like some of her teachers. She sometimes had the feeling that they didn't really know or care about the subject they were teaching, as if instead they had just read up on it the night before. Mr. Allen, her science teacher, was funny, though, and seemed genuinely to love science and want his students to be excited too. Rosie looked forward to his class more than any other. English right now was terrible. She had always liked English a lot, because she was good at it, good at the verbs, the nouns, the pronouns, and of course she loved reading so much and writing little stories, but right now the class was reading *The Diary of Anne Frank,* and most of the class was really bored, because it went so slowly. Rosie thought it might be the best book she had ever read. The most popular girls were all passing notes back and forth to each other, and Rosie got into it too, she did not want to seem different, like she thought she was better than everyone else. But the class would be reading these entries that were so incredibly sad and hard, and the girls would be whispering, Does my hair look good? Do you have any lip gloss? I *hate* this jacket, I *hate* how my makeup looks. Even worse, the boys would be cracking up every time Anne mentioned breasts or bras or periods.

Even though these boys were so immature, she felt badly that none of them wanted to go steady with her. She kept waiting for one of her friends, like Hallie maybe or one of the other popular girls, to hand her a note that said, "Do you like so and so?" and if she said sort of, they'd write back, "Well, you better. Because he's going to ask you out." And then he would take her to the mall or a movie, be with her somewhere private like his house or hers, and kiss her. It would be a miracle, though—no one had ever asked her out on a date. She didn't look like the beautiful girls. She was a little stick figure. Simone was beautiful and had had boyfriends and sometimes this made Rosie incredibly sad. But then when Simone was in hysterics because maybe the boy didn't like her anymore, Rosie would feel old, and safe.

AFTER another solid week of rain, the sun finally came out and dried the courts. Peter had arranged for Rosie and Simone to play one afternoon with two sixteen-year-old girls at a nearby public park.

Riding their bikes to the court, Rosie and Simone passed a horse pasture and an old sawmill. Under the redwoods next to the bikepath, birds sang, squirrels darted out chattering onto the telephone wires, and the creek, swollen with the recent rains, burbled a wet drumbeat. The court lay in the dappled afternoon sunlight, and it smelled just as Rosie remembered it from the one other time she had played here—mucky, slightly mildewy because of the shade of the trees and the wetness of the creek. Under the redwoods, huge knotted tangles of roots hung like baskets over the water. She remembered the smell, a little like dirty socks, in a good way, salty, yeasty, breeding life.

Rosie lived in a world of smells. She always seemed to be sniffing things for information. All these things in her life filled her with confusion—her body, boys, how impatient she felt with her parents, her constant fear that her mother would die, thoughts of her future, memories—but smells, smells were clear, like a powerful radio station.

Simone did not go around sniffing things. She went around tossing her chest about, watching its effect on boys and grown men. She was already fourteen, so pretty and voluptuous, with shoulder-length blonde hair that looked great when it hung down, framing her face, her pretty full lips, charcoal gray eyes, and small straight nose, and it also looked great pulled back into a sloppy ponytail, with wavy little wisps and tendrils breaking free. Rosie already knew that beauty could save and protect you, that if you looked beautiful, people wouldn't poke around and go in too deep—if you looked the way they hoped and expected, they wouldn't look further into the dark parts that she read about in her creepy teenage horror novels. If you were pretty, the secret of your essential un-okayness would remain a secret.

The court under the redwoods alongside the swollen creek was hard and fast, like Rosie liked it, and both she and Simone served with utter confidence; they pounded back impossibly angled ground strokes, moving in together at the net to put away volleys or, with a flick of the wrist, to send over a tricky spinning little drop shot that the older, heavier girls simply had to give up on. Rosie could have played all day. She really wanted to be ranked number one again. She pretended they were playing in the finals at the state championships, the bleachers full of spectators, Peter watching proudly. Sometimes she liked when Luther watched her play, or she liked to pretend that he was watching; her edge, her focus grew tauter, like a string inside of her tightening, and she scrambled. She imagined him now in the shade of the redwoods, stepping out from behind the trunk, heavy-lidded and watchful as she skimmed over the hard court like a water skeeter. She got to everything that day, chased down the toughest shots and got most of them back, with no one really watching and nothing to lose. It was just a long hard game of doubles under the trees, in the crisp dappled sunlight of a late spring afternoon.

THEY pedaled home just as night began to fall.

Riding her bike made Rosie think of Charles Adderly, her mother and father's great friend. Years ago, he had kind of tricked her into learning to ride a bike; she hadn't wanted to learn at all, had only wanted to be able to *do* it. She was quite afraid of falling at the time. She had just turned seven and her dad had been dead a few years and maybe that made her more afraid. But Charles and Grace gave her a red two-wheeler for her birthday, with a rack on the back that you could clip things onto, hold your books with, and it had pink and magenta streamers pouring forth from the plastic grips of the handlebars, and one day right after her birthday, Charles said he would teach her to ride. He said, I'll hold on to the rack in the back and walk along beside you. Just pedal and steer; I won't let you fall. That's all he kept saying— just pedal and steer, I won't let you fall.

The next day, he came over after breakfast. He was tall and stooped and had gray hair that was receding at the temples, and he was handsome in the same way her father would have been if her father had lived long enough to grow old. Even though he had gotten too much sun over the years, hiking, sailing, bicycling with his wife Grace when she was still alive, Rosie thought he was very handsome for an old man. He looked like a retired astronaut.

They went out on the sunlit sidewalk together. She got on the new red bike and put her feet on the pedals, and he took hold of the rack and she started pedaling down the sidewalk. She felt so tight that her elbows were locked and even her knees were locked as much as they could be since she still had to try and pedal. She didn't really trust him, but he kept walking alongside her while she wobbled down the sidewalk. "You're doing fine," he kept saying, "I won't let go. I won't let you fall." They went all the way to the end of the block, turned around, and pedaled back home. She kept checking to make sure he was there behind her, and he was.

"Let's do it again tomorrow, Rosini," he said when they were back in front of her house. She didn't really want to. She thought maybe taking a few days off in between lessons would be a good idea, but he was there the next morning when she got up; he was in the kitchen with her mother, drinking coffee, reading the paper, waiting for her. He smelled of powder, like the medicine powder you might sprinkle between your toes, and he smelled like clothes in the dryer. He always wore the same things, khaki or corduroy trousers, worn plaid shirts, moccasins. She went over and leaned into him at the kitchen table while he told her mother how beautifully she had done on the bike the day before.

This time they went four blocks, two blocks away from home and then back. He held on to the rack, and she was still terrified. He kept saying, "Just pedal and steer. I won't let you go. I won't let you fall."

The third day he was in the kitchen again with her mother when Rosie woke up. He was wearing a red plaid shirt. They went outside, and she got on the bike and started pedaling. He took hold of the rack. She was feeling more confident, a little looser, and she picked up the pace a little, smiling finally, and he had to walk very quickly, almost trotting, to keep up with her. Then she started pedaling really fast, and after a minute she risked the quickest look over her shoulder to check in with him since he must have nearly been running, but he was gone, and she looked way back, and he was a whole block away, so far away that his shirt looked pink, and he was waving to her.

Now, pedaling home as the sky darkened, she remembered how

much fun Charles had always been before he got sick. These days he would just open his eyes and smile at her from his bed when they went to visit him. "Is Charles dying?" she'd asked Elizabeth the last time they'd been there.

"Oh, honey. Yes; yes he is."

ELIZABETH was standing at the kitchen window when Rosie and Simone pulled up on their bikes. She opened the window and called out a greeting, but Rosie either didn't hear or was choosing to ignore her. Simone smiled and waved. Elizabeth waved back. Finally Rosie deigned to look up at her and jutted out her chin in greeting. Then she looked away. Elizabeth sighed, shook her head, and closed the window. Having a teenage daughter was one's punishment for having been a teenage daughter. She went back to making dinner—chicken enchiladas and salad.

It grieved her to have given someone life who was now going to have to endure being a teenager. Some girls hit thirteen with gusto, filled with confidence, bursting through the door saying, "Here I am!" But not Rosie. Rosie was destined, just as Elizabeth had been, to edge through the back door with slouched, rounded shoulders, arms held in front of her chest. The heartbreak was huge, the sorrow of moving from the land of childhood, where life smelled like grass and earth and sap and berry pies—pies made from berries you and your best friend, scratched and stained, have gathered—to the steely metallic world of puberty, where everything smells like pennies, like sheared copper, and you still have friends but you all know now that you're really just trading cards: you have a certain worth and dispensability. A year ago Rosie still smelled like a child, of clean dirt and salt and shampoo and sweets. Now, mingled with the clean soapy smell of shampoo, came the sharp whiff of medication, dabbed on her skin every morning to prevent breakouts, and of a flowery spray deodorant that smelled like week-old leis. The scent of a locker room hung in her bedroom now, too, for Rosie's huge feet in the last year had begun smelling as gamey as James's, like salt and dirt and fur, like a moose's might.

Elizabeth remembered the sense of hopelessness she had felt at that age: the conviction that life was so tense and disgusting and false that she wondered how she'd ever survive. The deep disappointment

of realizing at thirteen that although she'd survived childhood, the re-
wards she'd hoped for—respect, autonomy, romance, thrills, belonging—were still out of reach. She remembered feeling glamorous and
aloof, like a twenty-six-year-old inside who was still stuck among all
these children. The boys around her were all absurdly tiny, and she was
alone, an outsider. She hung out with another misfit, named Jessie, and
they'd barricaded themselves in Jessie's room, talking conspiratorially,
trashing the in crowd as conformists, shallow featherheads with no
compassion. That she had to go home every night was a nightmare.
Her room, which had been a refuge all those years, was suddenly too
small. And everything was too real; life at twelve and thirteen, she remembered now, stopped feeling so cartoonish and instead started feeling steely and unpleasant. You couldn't use toys anymore to shift the
world through your imagination. Looking at her daughter, sad or sullen
at the dinner table, Elizabeth remembered that feeling—that half the
time the world was just there, life was just there, like a long dull irritating play, and the other half of the time it was fraught with danger.

When Rosie was six, smart as a poodle, and had just mastered tic-
tac-toe, the two of them sat playing in the kitchen one day. Rosie hated
to lose, as Andrew had hated to lose, and Elizabeth watched her
daughter's fierce competitiveness with some amusement. Rosie announced that the person who went first got to go twice in a row and
that she in fact would go first. And that she would be *O*'s. A few minutes later, she drew a larger grid than usual and drew an *O* with wavy
lines radiating out from it, like the sun. "That," she said, "is a fireball."
Then she took a penny, slid it under the paper, and made an *O* with a
pencil rubbing of Abe Lincoln's head, unrecognizable and evil. "That
is the devil warrior," she announced. Then she handed her mother the
pencil. "Your turn," she said.

Elizabeth looked all over the paper for some place to put her mark.

"Where can I go to be safe?" she asked. Her daughter, looking at
her with some pity, said softly, "There are no safe places for you,
Mommy."

THE girls were so luscious. Elizabeth had been watching them all
morning at a weekend tournament in San Francisco: out on the court,
where they both lost their first singles matches; milling around waiting

to play a doubles match; huddled together on a bench whispering their secret thoughts and language. Rosie wore a sweet little dress with lace trim around the neckline that Simone had grown out of over the winter. Now Simone wore women's tennis skirts and tight white scooped-neck T-shirts. Elizabeth glanced at her round sunny cleavage, the pale blonde milkmaid face. It was sometimes hard to take your eyes off Simone for her blossoming vanilla beauty, or Rosie, for that matter, so much smaller, but beautiful, raven haired, strong featured, like a fair-skinned gypsy, marvelously physical. Here at the tournament, Elizabeth observed their mix of unself-consciousness and hypercon-sciousness. And she watched spooky Luther watch Rosie, feasting on her, getting juice from that wonderful nubility of flesh, female with no traces of age, seamless and dewy.

Elizabeth sat as far away from Luther as she could but close enough so he would know a mother bear was watching. She kept glancing at him out of the corner of her eye, taking in the worn windbreaker, dark bristly crew cut, the wolf eyes watchful and patient. She imagined him stalking Rosie, talking to Rosie softly, hypnotizing her. Once she had begged Peter Billings to get him arrested somehow, to for God's sakes do something, and he had looked at her like she was a nervous case. He said Luther was actually a pretty smart guy, harmless, sad, maybe not so good to look at but certainly of no danger to anyone. She had seen Peter and Luther sitting together in the bleachers at the Golden Gate Park courts last summer, the sun glinting off Peter's Hollywood blond head, Luther in a tattered jacket on a warm summer's day, the two men—one so light, one so dark—watching Rosie play. Peter said Luther knew more about tennis than he did and that he just liked to watch the girls play. But was that all? she wondered.

She loved to watch the girls play, too. She loved their innocence but couldn't remember having felt it herself, doing something so full of joy that she completely forgot about the watcher. Especially the self-watcher who judges and finds fault. She watched the girls get lost in the game and saw with a rush of anxiety that they didn't stop to cover themselves. They were so naked.

Luther was, to Elizabeth, all that was wrong with the real world, all that was dirty and drunk and mysterious, all that was random and cryptic. She sneaked another look at him. He was ragged, a tree that the weather had whipped away at for too long. He was so dark, and he loved to watch her curly-haired girl in the tiny white dress. She watched her child deliberately avoid his gaze, almost meanly, seemingly not afraid, and the thought crossed her mind, Who is stalking whom? Did Rosie miss his dark attentions when he didn't show up? Her daughter was now playing out of her head, hard, focused, inflamed. Elizabeth, looking from Rosie to Luther and back to her daughter's bright body again, felt suddenly how thin the membrane was between order and chaos, how thin but there, real enough to palpate, like a fontanel.

three

$\mathbf{R}$OSIE looked at herself in the mirror all the time now, half to see how she looked, half to make sure she was really there. She saw in the mirror the world's saddest person. When she was eleven, she used to look in the mirror and imagine herself in the movies. Now, at thirteen, she saw herself all of a sudden as she imagined others saw her. Late at night, very late, when she explored the dark dangerous existential place where sleeplessness took her, she'd traipse down the hall to the bathroom, and look at her weird sick face in the medicine chest mirror. Under the awful humming lights she could see how *other* she was, could see the wrinkles and bumps and pores.

She had insomnia. Maybe it was hereditary; her mother had it too. The fear of not sleeping kept her awake until the early hours. Just last night she'd still been awake at midnight, and at one o'clock, and two—up and down, up and down, in and out of bed, to the bathroom, the kitchen for a bowl of cereal, finally to the TV room. She made a little rabbit bed for herself on the couch, with the pillow from her bed in its Raggedy Ann and Raggedy Andy pillowcase, and a quilt. It felt safer here than in her room. After a while her mother came downstairs and sat beside her in the dark. They were both vaporish with fatigue.

"What's bothering you, darling?"

"I can't sleep."

"Are you reading something scary?"

"No," Rosie lied. The truth was that she was always reading dark, scary books. Sometimes they were sort of racy and turned her on, although the only really dirty book she had ever read was *Candy,* which Simone had found in Veronica's room. They had read it in Simone's bed, in the dark, under the covers, with a flashlight, and Rosie had felt half crazy with fear and excitement. But most of the books she read involved young girls and women who were taken over by various dead beings. Some days when she was gawky and tense and weepy, it was all Rosie felt good for—to be a vessel for powerful dark spirits, a gravy boat for ghostly sluts. An empty keyhole limpet shell that a wayfaring psychic snail might decide to inhabit in a tide pool. She read lines like "Taken over and ridden as she felt by the sudden dark forces of sex, Adriana wondered if her enthrallment to Jasper's Ouija board was a way of not having to feel responsible for the sudden onslaught of evil sexual impulses and thoughts," and she underlined them, read them again and again, voraciously. They whispered a dark edgy truth to her. She had in fact just finished rereading her favorite for the fifth or sixth time, a sort of gothic teenage version of *The Group,* where five or so girls at a private high school fell under the spell of a new and charismatic teacher. At first it just looked like these were schoolgirl crushes. But then they were completely taken over by her, and hideous fates befell them all—all, of course, but one. And the one, the chosen, knew by the end of the book that one day she'd grow up to be a teacher too, at a private girls' school, and get to choose her own first batch of girls . . .

"Let's go to your room. I'll lie down with you," her mother said.

"It won't help."

But it did. Elizabeth lay down beside Rosie in the dark and told her stories until finally around three o'clock, Rosie fell asleep.

JAMES woke up when she finally crawled back into bed with him.

"Rosie couldn't sleep," she told him. He yawned, burrowed up against her.

"Do you need me to be awake with you?"

"Would you? For just a few minutes?"

"Okay. Do you want to talk about anything in particular?"

"Tell me what you were like when you were thirteen."

He didn't say anything for a minute.

"This is something you really want to talk about now?"

"Uh-huh."

"Okay." He half sat up in bed, rubbed his face, yawned, shook his head, sat thinking. "I remember being politically insane. I dabbled in right-wing politics. I was in grief."

"Over what?

"I was in grief because I was turning out small. That was incredibly defeating. And then another huge myth died around then, the one about my father. I'd thought he was perfect and knew everything, until I was thirteen, and then it turned out he was a total fuckup—that is, he was an ordinary person. And I always held it against him after that."

"Were you as sullen as Rosie is?"

"Yes. Worse. And I was terrible in school."

"Why?"

"Everything was so heinous to begin with, and then at thirteen I started getting hard-ons every morning, every single morning in class right between third and fourth period. I'd have to get up and walk out of the classroom with my binder held in front of me and try to be nonchalant about it, but I might as well have had a blue spotlight on my dick."

"Why did you get so many hard-ons?"

"Because that's the nature of being a boy. You're woozy with hormones. At thirteen, girls start giving off mysterious hormonal smells from their scalps—this is just my theory—and they wash their hair all the time. Don't they? Rosie washes her hair all the time. It's her life. That is my strongest memory of being thirteen. The smell of girls' hair and the smell of cherry lipstick. The girl I was kissing at the time wore lipstick that smelled like cherries, and her hair smelled of Prell and hormones. That smell really threw me off. Up until then, up until thirteen, I had a mind. And then I do not remember having a clear thought for the next fifteen years."

HE and Lank first became best friends in second grade. Twenty-seven years later, five years ago, they had gone backpacking to Pretty Boy Meadow on the same weekend that Elizabeth's friend Rae had managed to convince a deeply skeptical Elizabeth to come along for her first outing. The four of them had met that night under the stars at adjoining campsites. Lank, who was now an elementary school teacher but who had once aspired to a professional singing career, sang them "Stranger in Paradise" under the almost-full moon. Elizabeth, who had earlier claimed that given a choice, she would rather spend a weekend having her gums scraped than go backpacking, had wept. Lank was family now. He came over a couple of times a week for dinner or to drop James off after basketball. He was the sort of man who at first seemed soft and bearish, with a broad forehead and big bald spot and slight double chin, a broad nose and a small mouth. But when people loved him, like Rosie loved him, he became very handsome; then they saw his kind old blue eyes that stayed on you when you were talking, that never looked away, and lovely soft fair English skin, roses in the cheeks. His heart was huge; he had raised his big mutt from a six-week-old puppy, and Bruno was so sweet and calm and eager to please that this couldn't help but reflect well on Lank. He spoke of the children in his elementary school classroom with tenderness, humor. They called him at home sometimes, sad or confused. His answering machine said, "Operator, I accept all collect calls from children."

He was not lucky or wise in love, though.

Neither was Rae. Hilarious, kind, ten pounds heavier than big-boned and ample, with brown almond eyes and thick chestnut hair that was always piled on top of her head like an off-duty Gibson girl, Rae lived in a world filled with light and color and religion and distressing relationships. People paid thousands of dollars for her big earthy weavings, mostly in shades of bricks and browns—black browns, soft bear browns, terra-cotta, the soft tawny brown of a lion's fur, the amber of its eyes. But she took men the way Elizabeth used to take drinks, obsessively, sneakily, and usually showing bad judgment. She had been in love off and on for two years with a therapist named Mike, who was very tall and tan, with a plump face. If pressed to describe him in two words, Elizabeth might have suggested "supercilious" and "obsequious," which made for a particularly unpleasant combination of fawning, groveling arrogance. Rae had told her things that made Elizabeth's stomach ache for her friend. He didn't like to come during sex, for instance, believing that it robbed him of strength. He'd gone away at one point to Colorado for a month, six months ago, left her one phone message the whole time, and brought her back an odd little hippie candy ball of nuts and honey and God knew what; it looked, as Rosie pointed out, like a little round golf ball of poo.

"That's very touching, Rae," Rosie had said, who loved Rae like a second mother. She studied it from all angles, holding it up to the light. "I hope when I grow up I have a boyfriend who brings me nice things like this."

"Do you like him at all?" Rae asked Elizabeth the next day over the phone.

"Well, I like that he's so bright."

Rae snorted. "Of course, so was Hitler." Elizabeth smiled. She was staring at the weaving that covered most of the living room wall; Rae had given it to them on their first anniversary. Her eyes always traveled to it, relaxing in the coarse wools and yarns, the lumps and holes; it was muscular with browns and mossy greens, a patch of indigo blue. "And so was Roy Cohn," Rae continued.

"What?"

"You were saying you thought Mike was smart, right? And I was saying, Well, so was Roy Cohn. But do you think Mike's good-looking?"

"Yes, I do," she said, although she didn't. The plumpness of his face bothered her. It suggested someone who couldn't forbid himself anything. Also, she suspected that he dyed his glossy black hair.

"But what is your overall impression?"

"Honey, I don't know. He mentions his Ph.D. quite a lot, doesn't he? I guess I'm never going to think there's anyone out there who's good enough for you."

There was a silence. Then Rae said, "You hate him."

"No, I don't," said Elizabeth, although she did. "I just love you so much."

"But you don't even know him," said Rae.

"You've told me some terrible things about him."

"I shouldn't have told you, then."

"But they would have still happened, even if you'd kept them a secret."

Rae wove secrets into her designs. In the living room weaving, she had hidden a bit of a twig from a cherry tree, which you could feel with your fingers if directed to the spot above the brown mountain's sloping breast. She had let Rosie in on the secret a year before she told Elizabeth. "The cherry twig," she said, "was from the countryside in France. Once, a hundred years ago, or so the story goes, some schoolchildren playing in a grove of trees in the dead of winter saw an apparition of Mary, the mother of Jesus. But when they told their parents, they were punished for lying. Some were beaten. So they returned to the barren cherry trees, called out their plight to the cold winter air. Suddenly, they heard voices in the wind, telling them that they must go home and return the next day with their parents. And when they did, leading their skeptical parents up the hillside to the grove, they saw the cherry trees glistening and pink in the sunlight—they were in full bloom."

Rosie was ten when Rae had told her this story and shown her where to put her finger in order to feel the bit of twig. Rosie at ten still believed a cherry tree might bloom in winter. Now she knew better. Now, at thirteen, she seemed to feel that if the miracle really occurred, if you came up that hill and looked too closely at those flowering fruit trees, you might discover that their pits were full of poison, their branches full of worms.

Fʀᴏᴍ time to time Rae would break up with, or try to break up with, Mike. Recently, on Groundhog Day, she had broken up with him again. "No shadow, no Mike," she had announced over the phone. Elizabeth had the feeling Rae might really pull it off this time. Mike had phoned once, and asked her to call him back, which she hadn't. Instead, she had called Rosie and asked her to come over for dinner and a video.

There was nothing Rosie liked more than visiting Rae on her own. There was just the one big room filled with antiques, and then a bright, spare bathroom. It felt very private, on its own little piece of land, surrounded by trees, mostly pine with a few redwoods and a couple of pear trees. One side looked out across an empty meadow to a ridge. Rosie loved this cottage so much. There were windows in every direction so you got all sorts of light at all times. The big bed was the centerpiece, even more so than the loom, smack in the middle of one wall, with everything important within reach, so you could lie in bed and look at the fire in the woodstove during winter, buds on the trees in the spring, the light on the ridge whenever you wanted. The wood-burning stove was a black iron box on legs, set in front of a convex copper heat shield, which sent out heat when the fire was lit, glowed like soft flames when it wasn't. There were little containers everywhere, tiny glass jars, framed photographs, handmade paper boxes holding more little secrets: a folded-up poem, a rock from the beach, a tiny ceramic house that Rae thought might once have been a hash pipe.

Sometimes Rosie read Rae's fashion magazines while Rae worked on deadline; she watched in awe as Rae, bent over the loom, took all that long skinny thread and yarn, which had no substance yet, and made things with which you could cover your walls or yourself. She sometimes crossed her eyes slightly so she could imagine Rae cave-painting, lost in those ancient rhythms. Rosie often got to help her make the dyes for her yarns. Sometimes they'd go out and pick things from fields or beside streams on the mountain and boil them: elderberries made lilac blue, prickly pear made a purplish pink, rabbitbrush made yellow. Sometimes what you plucked was a different color from the dye it produced: the red flowers didn't necessarily make red wool. Beets made gold dye. Coffee beans made a dark yellow tan. But most of all, Rosie loved to hear the sounds of Rae's deep rocking squatting labor, as she wove herself into the yarns, always weaving one tiny secret in between the threads.

four

ELIZABETH had believed for years that Rae and Lank would make a good couple, but there was one real hitch in her plan: neither of them was interested in the other. Lank pursued young beauties who loved his gentleness and sweet face and always left him for more dashing men. Rae did not care so much what her men looked like just as long as they possessed certain qualities, which Rae listed as intelligence, humor, soul, and a love of oral sex—and which, if you asked Elizabeth, meant tendencies toward inconsistency, passive aggression, and a charming, jovial ability to be sadistic and noncommittal.

"Don't you *ever* entertain sexual feelings about Lank?" Elizabeth had asked a few days after the tournament in San Francisco. Elizabeth had become a Democratic precinct worker, and Rae had come over after lunch to walk around the neighborhood with her. They would go door to door like Girl Scouts, registering voters, soaking up sunshine, getting in some exercise.

"Look, honey," Rae said. "On slow days I have sexual feelings for waxed fruit. But I don't feel anything romantic toward him. He's family. Besides—I'm dating a flock of Bedouin now. Many of them are very thoughtful."

"Lank's available," said Elizabeth. "That's why you're not attracted." They set out down the sidewalk. Bayview glowed, sun shining on all those greens—lawns and low hillsides, maple and pine and eucalyptus, the bay jade green in the distance. Rae turned to smile at her as they walked. A strip of bright green sour grass grew at the edge of the sidewalk, like a baseboard at the meeting of fence and sidewalk, a seven- or eight-foot stripe with brilliant yellow flowers, bent at the root after a wild wind the night before, lying forward on the pavement as if in obeisance—an English crowd bowing low while the weary monarch passed.

THE next morning, the last day of February, an unusually warm blue day, Charles Adderly came home from the hospital for good. His cancer, which had begun in his bones, had spread to a number of organs. He'd been admitted for an experimental course of chemotherapy but had been too sick to tolerate it. He was getting worse quickly and now had a full-time hospice nurse at home. One day not long ago he had been just fine, seventy-six years old but hale and animated, visiting friends, working on the house, driving to the library, bookstores, hardware stores, hiking with the Fergusons, resting every afternoon, swimming laps before dinner. Rosie felt that he was her real grandfather, and when they hiked and swam and browsed at the library, she acted like his granddaughter, basking in her closeness to such a distinguished and amiable old man. But then his stomach began to hurt, and he went to see his doctor, expecting a prescription for ulcer medicine. He gave some blood to the lab, and five days later was in surgery, "slit," as he put it, "from gizzard to zatch." The surgeon had closed him back up without taking anything out. There was cancer everywhere, cancer like little cauliflower buds. James had been with Charles in the hospital room two days after Thanksgiving when the doctor had said that there was nothing they could do, that Charles might live at most for a few more months. Rosie and Elizabeth had been at home reading together on the sofa when James called with the news. Rosie had answered the phone, and James said, "Hello, honey," and Rosie could hear that he had been crying.

"What happened?" she said.

He did not answer right away. Then he said, "I'm with Charles."

Well, they already knew that, she thought. Her head started to feel funny; Charles must be very sick. She waved for her mother to come to phone, scooping armfuls of air toward her with her free hand.

ALL the next day at school Rosie felt little lurches inside her, like when you fall asleep at the movies and suddenly pitch from your dream back into your seat.

She and her mother drove to San Francisco late the next afternoon; James had already spent all day and the previous night there, reading magazines while Charles dozed. It had been stormy in the morning, but the sun had shown up at the very end of the afternoon. Rosie cried for a while in the car, and on top of that she had a cold; her throat ached, and she could not get any air at all into her nose, and the only way she could disguise her bloodshot ugliness was with a pair of horrible harlequin dark glasses she'd found in the glove box, a set that Rae must have left behind. They actually had rhinestones framing the lenses.

Lost and sad and scared about Charles, Rosie obsessed instead about her red blotchy skin, about how ugly she was. It was five o'clock when they got to the Golden Gate Bridge. A low strand of clouds lay just over the water, lit by the sunset—small round gray clouds connected in a line like a baby elephant walk. Rosie lowered her dark glasses and looked in the mirror on the car's sun visor. Her lips and eyes were red and swollen, and there were tiny pimples on her forehead. She put the harlequin glasses back on.

In the hospital parking lot, Elizabeth handed Rosie a pack of gum and some tissues and then got out of the car. "You okay, baby?"

"Uh-huh." She wouldn't take off the dark glasses even though she knew that they looked ridiculous. Ridiculous was better than hideous.

"I won't be long."

Rosie sat in the passenger seat chewing gum, noticing how stuck her breath was, staring out the window at sad people coming and going. Charles was going to die. It was too painful for words—even worse, much worse than when Grace had died three years ago of Alzheimer's. Everyone had said how wonderful it was that she got sick with the disease and died within a year; oh, thank God, people said, but it was not wonderful at all. Charles sat by Grace every day and told her stories of their past together—alone with no children, just the two of them.

Under the light of the street lamps in the parking lot, Rosie thought now of Charles dying, and a sudden terrible glee filled her, that he was old and dying and she was young, practically a child, her whole life in front of her while his was about to end. His candle flame was about to be blown out, and she felt the vigor of her own, the heat and light she gave off. She felt a rush of something like ecstasy that she wasn't dying.

But you couldn't tell anyone this, this horrible meanness of yours, toward someone so kind, someone who always took you to the circus, to the rodeo. The car and her nose were so stuffy. She looked around the parking lot wildly, looked around at the eerie golden spaceship light the street lamps cast. Where was her mother? Why was it taking so long? Please, please, God, she prayed, don't let my mother get cancer; please, I'll try to believe in you. I'll try not to be so mean to her. She rolled down the window and stuck out her head, like an Irish setter. The cold wet air bathed her face.

RAE had visited Charles a lot since his diagnosis, but even more so in the last few weeks, since she had broken up with Mike. "It gets me out of myself," she said, but sometimes she called her machine from Charles's, hoping Mike had called and had changed his character. But he never did. Sometimes Elizabeth came with her, but though she loved Charles so very much, she couldn't help him like Rae could. Rae was not afraid of dying people. She had moved in with her mother when she lay dying three years ago of heart trouble, and she had helped Charles take care of Grace when she was dying. Now she would show up just to hang out with Charles, sitting silently some-times, rubbing his feet, being alive together.

"The more often you visit Charles, the better your life will be," Rae had told Rosie when he'd first gotten sick. "It will be hard, but it will be worth it." But when Rosie visited him now that he was bedridden at home, she felt awful. She hated his smells, she hated how hard it was to think of things to say, how phony she felt saying them.

Charles's nurse, a big boring blonde named Arlene, usually left his visitors alone once her fierceness and fussiness had made it clear that he was hers, her prize rosebush or show dog: clean, fresh, fed, combed. Elizabeth, so much taller than Rae or James or Rosie, always bent down low to him, peered into his fine handsome face, smelled the hint of decay that no amount of sponge baths and bedside tooth brushing and lemon glycerin swabs could cover.

Rosie had had a strange thought come to her the last time she'd vis-ited Charles, the first weekend in March. He'd been sitting up that day in his wheelchair in the living room, in a broad band of sunlight that accentuated his paleness. Despite his emaciation, he looked like the pictures of the Buddha Rosie had seen in some of Rae's books: so peaceful and yet also so focused. Rosie burbled on about her exploits on the tennis court and, during silences, picked at her cuticles, and while Rae or Elizabeth spoke to Charles, she studied him. Later in the car, with Rae driving and Elizabeth in the backseat, she said to no one in particular, "He's like orange juice concentrate now. Like all the water is gone."

Rae searched in her rearview mirror and met Elizabeth's eyes.

"Why do you think that is, Rae?" asked Rosie, her head tilted back against the headrest of the car seat.

"Well. We're in these watery, confused states so much of the time . . ."

"Maybe it's our way of swimming through life," Elizabeth offered.

"Yeah," said Rae. "But Charles is starting the plummet. So he's stripped everything down, because there's enormous specific gravity in that. If you see what I mean."

"Well, I don't," said Rosie.

"Think about swimming, about diving from a high dive. When you do a dive, to protect yourself and to be economical, you pull everything in: you curve yourself. You concentrate, you don't leave parts sticking out. And you don't let your attention wander, because it could be fatal."

Rosie thought about this. She had her tennis racket with her, a Wilson graphite that cost over two hundred dollars. She needed two of them when she went off to tournaments, in case the strings broke on the one she was using. The strings cost seventy-five dollars. She got her rackets strung very tight, like the boys, like the men.

Sitting in the back seat with her mother and Rae in the front, she pushed the strings around as much as they would go; they creaked. Passing a grove of redwoods, Rosie opened her window to peer up at them, breathe in their primeval scent, squint at the canopy of leaves so that they blurred into a great doily of green.

Rosie and Simone got to play with two older boys at Golden Gate Park that afternoon. It was very foggy, as usual in San Francisco. Peter had arranged the match with the boys' pro. He was going to meet them there after his lessons were over and watch them play. Veronica drove them to the courts and then left to go shopping in the old Haight Ashbury district. One of the ex-tournament players who still hung out at the Golden Gate Park courts had told Rosie about what these courts were like in the sixties, when a constant parade of hippies passed by on their way to the Polo Grounds, where the Grateful Dead might be playing, or the Airplane. The women who played here as girls, some of northern California's finest, said there used to be perverts just outside the gates of the carousel, sitting in the grass or on benches, bottles of Midnight Express in brown paper bags beside them, seeming to pet small birds or puppies that sat in their unzipped laps. Now these girls were women who played hard hot doubles with the men, hanging out all day on the court, in the clubhouse, like outlaws who played tennis.

Luther was a regular here, Golden Gate his home turf. Rosie imagined him out by the carousel gates, all those years ago, fondling himself, but the woman who told her about the sixties said no, no, Luther was just a spectator, just a burned-out old guy. He had not been there to watch them in those days, but the women here sat with him sometimes now and said that he had a great eye for tennis, that he loved the tennis of the public parks. He was never seen playing, but these people thought he used to from the insightful way he spoke about the game. The players waiting for a court here wore much rattier clothes than you saw at the clubs; there was a woman who looked like a hooker and who could beat any of the men at Rosie's club, an old Asian man in chinos, great players who looked like bikers and maybe actually were, people smoking—smoking! Every time Rosie noticed Luther, for instance, he was smoking. People came over and sat with him or near him, hung out for a while, and then after a while pushed off and went elsewhere.

Rosie kept looking up from the court, expecting Peter. The boys, who were fifteen and sixteen, played hard with the girls, hitting ground strokes that cleared the net like bullets, which the girls whacked back over the net using the power of the boys' shots. The boys looked at each other, amused, impressed. Rosie, watching an overhead smash come at her at over a hundred miles an hour, kept her racket in close, met the ball early, way out in front of her, barely swung, blocked it hard and low so that it tore down the middle of the court and split the space between the two boys; both thought the other would get it, and neither did. One of them wolf whistled.

Rosie felt thrilled, like an Alpine skier must, going almost too fast,

right on the edge of being out of control. She looked up to the bleachers, longing for Peter to see her playing like this, smiling his lazy
pleased smile. But he was not there. Luther was. He was sitting by the
court next to the one where Rosie was playing, and he was smoking,
and smiling, and Rosie knew why: she was on fire. She had nothing to
lose, nothing to fear, and so was playing at the top of her game. Once
she looked up after she'd put away an overhead smash, angling it so
wide that the boys didn't even bother running for it, and Luther was
laughing, nudging an ancient Asian woman in the ribs, as if he had
taught Rosie the shot.

She felt sparklers in her stomach.

At one point she raced after a lob that went over her at the net, and
she lobbed it back so brilliantly, sending it over both boys at the net,
that even Simone looked bashful and victorious when the boys shook
their heads with amazement, and Luther laughed a loud throaty laugh
of appreciation and something like joy, as if she had just done a magic
trick, and when Rosie looked up and accidentally met his eyes, he took
her picture with an imaginary camera.

It made her afraid she had gone too far.

Afterward, Simone bought everyone Cokes at the snack bar, and
the boys hung around her. Is she giving off something? Simone was so
entirely girl, so busty and juicy, like there was mercury inside her. Rosie
couldn't believe the stupid things Simone said and how the boys acted
like they were pearls of wisdom. Simone said, "I might want to be a
chef. I love to cook. But I hate food," and Rosie watched the boys go
Uh-huh, isn't that interesting, watching her intently.

Simone, Rosie wanted to say, you've never cooked a thing in your
life! You can't even toast Pop Tarts right. They're always burned or
cold and uncooked. But the boys were squirming with fascination. It
made Rosie feel vaguely sick. The boys smiled at her from time to time,
as if she were Simone's homely little brother.

"I just go nuts if someone mistreats an animal," Simone was saying.
Rosie watched the boys try not to gape at her tight T-shirt over those
swollen breasts, the succulent plump thighs and arms, her pouty
mouth. "Like, it really bothers me when people kill wolves." Wolves?
Rosie could hardly believe her ears. "Wolves are really incredible. They
have a secret kind of thing about them." Rosie looked into the faces of
the boys, who were both so handsome, so tan, and she wondered if ei-

ther of them might ever dance with her at one of the dances, with her, with her, with her.

The boys had a secret kind of thing about them, and Simone had it, too. Rosie did not have it and was not even sure what it was, unless it was sex appeal— if that's what those words meant: you talked to a boy about wolves—warm, shaggy, mysterious, dark, golden-eyed and dangerous—and it made you want to dance with each other. Rosie only had the cravings, the fantasies. "I totally hate poachers," Simone continued, and it turned out one of the boys hated poachers, too. Rosie felt torn between trying to memorize exactly what Simone said so she could tell James later and wanting to stay here with Simone and the boys, so close and salty and masculine.

Finally Rosie had to turn and walk a few feet away so she wouldn't burst out laughing at how ridiculous Simone could be—like Veronica, so flirty and cheap—and as she whipped around, she walked right into Luther. He was standing there like a wall, like something that had risen up out of the sea. She hadn't noticed him before, or maybe he had just arrived, and she smacked into him, bumped back and peered up into his face, like you look up the trunk of a redwood, and he smelled like a tree, like bark and sap.

"You played like Billie Jean King out there," he said. His voice was soft and sounded rusty with lack of use. She could smell cigarette smoke on him, too—like a tree in a mist of cigarette smoke. She worried that she was weaving like a cobra in a basket being hypnotized, partly because it was so great he didn't say she played like a boy. People were always trying to give her the ultimate compliment and say she'd just played like a boy, and it made her furious. But now she felt like Luther's words were an attempt to touch her, and her first thought was to scream so that Simone's new boyfriends would see that she wasn't his friend.

And then she remembered him in the bleachers, watching her play, and without meaning to, she flushed pink in the hollows of her cheeks, up through the brown baby skin.

five

—————

Who was it who said that God created man because he loved the stories? Elizabeth relished the stories one heard in AA. No one came in on the wings of victory; everyone had terrible stories to tell. Many, if not most, people's stories were far worse than her own. For instance, at the last meeting, Elizabeth had met a woman who had rowed her children out onto San Francisco Bay with a thermos of apple juice dosed with Demerol so they would be out like lights before she dropped them off the boat and into the cold sea. But she hadn't gone through with it and had gotten sober two months later, twenty years ago. She had grandchildren now and still went to meetings nearly every day.

Sometimes, sitting on one of the metal folding chairs in the basement of the church, Elizabeth felt a hot dry lump in her throat. Her story was so tame, the worst things pretty run-of-the-mill. Right after Andrew died, she had gone through men like paper towels, some married, some not. She had drunk whiskey every night until she was able to sleep, and so was hungover most mornings when she went to get Rosie up for school. She had driven a thousand times under the influence, putting strangers and even Rosie at risk, as well as Sharon, Simone, and children whose names she no longer remembered, picking them up, dropping them off, chewing peppermint gum, sucking on Sen-Sen, willing herself to concentrate. She could remember driving Rosie and Sharon around one night when she was so drunk she had to close one eye to focus. So when Thackery jerked off for her daughter, touched her arm with his erection, Elizabeth was busy with her own guilty secret. And Elizabeth was so out of it that she was almost useless to her child: it was Rae to whom Rosie turned for help.

Rosie worried that her mother used to be addicted to alcohol and now was addicted to these meetings. She came along sometimes to keep her mother company, but there were a number of things she hated about them. More than anything she worried that they would run into people they knew, parents of kids from school or the club, and everyone would know her mother's secret. And Rosie hated sitting under the fluorescent lights in dingy church basements. The incessant clapping wore on her nerves, and the earnest missionaries with their Styrofoam cups of coffee and little sayings embarrassed her. She didn't like that they called their book the Big Book, like they were all at the teddy bears' picnic. In the early days of her mother's sobriety, Rosie was just relieved that her mom didn't have boozy breath and pass out anymore. James had recently moved in, and not long after he and Elizabeth had gotten married, at City Hall, and Rosie had spent the whole day worrying that her mother had a bottle hidden in one of the closets, that her mother would blow it again like she'd been blowing it for so long, promising to be somewhere or to do certain things and then drinking too much instead. Rosie was afraid James would leave them. But he didn't.

Rosie had gone to a meeting with her mother a year ago where her mother "shared"—told stories of what it was like to be drunk all those years, what it was like to be sober. And it was so strange for Rosie to watch her odd, shy mother up at the front of the room. Her mother twisted her long thin fingers as she spoke, as if she were working on a Jacob's ladder, about to pull her hands apart to show you the final construction of yarn. Her mother would stare down at her feet like she had an outline of her speech written on her shoes, and then she'd look up from time to time, smiling like some smart, bashful little kid. In front of all those people her mother said that though she felt afraid sometimes that there wasn't quite enough money, being Rosie's sober mother made her rich. Then she pointed at Rosie, so everyone could see. Rosie stared down into her lap, although this pleased her very much. And Elizabeth said one thing at the very end that really blew Rosie's mind, about how when she first got sober, she felt as if the mosaic she had been assembling out of life's little shards got dumped to the ground, and there was no way to put it back together. It was a whole life's worth of little mosaic chips. So she simply began to pick them up, shard by shard, getting to know each one. And week by week, life began getting better.

When Rosie and Elizabeth had gotten into their car that night, Rosie turned to her mother. "Mom," she whispered, in the dark of the car, staring at her mother's profile in the flickering streetlight. She felt like a spaceship was trying to land on their car, and her mother leaned in close to hear better. And then Rosie couldn't think of how to say what she was feeling, so she just sat as close to her mother as she could, in silence. She first noticed that night that her mother's breath smelled like tea, real tea, English breakfast tea, and even now, it still smelled like tea—so maybe her mother *was* addicted to the meetings now, to all the corny little sayings and the rest of it, but anything, anything at all was worth this sweet tea breath.

EVEN though Elizabeth had been sober all these years now, she still had not discovered what she wanted to do with herself. So almost everyone had stopped asking her when she was going to figure out what she wanted to be. She took care of her family. She was a Democratic precinct worker for her neighborhood. She loved gardening, she liked reading James's manuscripts and helping as much as she could; she had a good editor's eye and the ability to be both tough and full of consolation. She liked puttering around the house. She liked cutting things out with scissors, although she joked with Rae that it was only one symptom of her undiagnosed autism. But these days she found the world so bright and loud and untrustworthy that it hurt her nervous system. She might look composed, but she'd always understood people rocking or tapping the sides of their head for hours on end, putting the world in order, giving it a rhythm. She missed the days when she and Rosie could spend hours together sitting on the floor cutting out paper dolls, paper pueblos, paper forests. Nowadays she clipped all the write-ups from the local paper about the tournaments in which Rosie played. She found the sound of the scissors delicious and calming, the sharp blades closing with metallic precision; it reminded her of the huge paper cutters from her school years, the whooshing forest sounds of all that paper falling away, the beauty in those executions. No wonder Madame Defarge sat there knitting as the aristocrats

were killed by the guillotine. It was fun listening to the sound of lop-
ping.

Elizabeth smiled at her own odd, dark mind. She sat in the garden
by the new cactus Lank had given her for Christmas, studying the
plant's long reptilian fingers. Such ugliness, yet out of them had
already come such surprises: elegant red silky flowers. She had spent an
hour tending her roses—apricot brandy roses, white roses, Joseph's
Coat roses—spent some time smelling the fragrance of the antique
purple roses. She cut off the dead heads, weeded around them, saw
that they needed a little drink. Well, she thought, don't we all.

Roses took so much work. She sifted snail poison into the soil
around them. "You kill snails?" Rosie had once asked weepily, as if
they were little kittens. "Yeah," Elizabeth said. "I killed about thirty
this morning, and I feel great about it. They were killing my favorite
plants. I see this as war."

Time started in a garden, James liked to remind her. Studying the
old plants and new growth in their yard, she thought again of how sur-
prising James was to her. They had been married four years now. He
was not what she had had in mind. As a lonely teenager, Elizabeth had
longed for a certain kind of man, someone big, someone like Louis
Jourdan in *Gigi,* to come along and find her, recognize her as a good
person. He would be elegant, quiet, gentle and adoring, a great dancer.
James was none of these things, except gentle and adoring. He was a
terrible dresser. But he had come into the bathroom just this morning,
while she was brushing her hair, and he had stood behind her, with his
arms around her waist, his chin buried in her shoulder, and together
they had studied their reflection. Elizabeth, so much taller than he,
looking younger at forty-two than she had five years before, pale with
hazel eyes and a long straight nose, a tousled bob of thick black hair
now flecked with gray; and James with his crazy Einstein hair and eyes
as green and clear as the scent of pine, somewhat wrinkled and maybe
a little tired. He liked to say of them that they were both in very late
youth. He would be thirty-seven on his next birthday. He wore a
derelict T-shirt, shapeless and torn; she wore a fresh white one, with
pearls. Looking at each other in the mirror, they had narrowed their
eyes at the same time, as if staring into the sun, and smiled.

James had left the bathroom to go back to work, and Elizabeth had
stayed a minute longer to run a comb through her hair. She looked all

right for forty-two, she thought, good enough for now at any rate. There were times when she fretted about having married a younger man, who looked younger than she did, who'd had a taste for pretty young women before they married; there had been two or three lapses during their courtship—or at least, she believed there had. She mostly tried not to think about it now. That had been so long ago. Today she looked in the mirror and could see the worried beauty of both the girl she had been and the marvelous crone—God willing—she would become one day.

She used to love looking at Grace's aged face before she got so sick, the wrinkled skin like crevices and landscape, land whose weathered bones Elizabeth could see. Grace had shone with a wonderful rude health in her midseventies, the life force that was still in there shoving past all the outdated need to look pretty. Elizabeth especially admired Grace's steady gaze, the look of someone who had lost so much over the years—her youth, best friends, her health. She saw that in many ways Grace was off the hook of yearning. She had had a good look at the impermanence of things and so was not clutching at much. There was beauty—beauty and freedom—in that.

Elizabeth longed for this freedom from fear, but lived with a constant low-grade anxiety that she would somehow lose Rosie. Images of Rosie came to her all day: Rosie on the court, Luther watching, Rosie at school, Rosie in her room, Rosie dead or dying. Ever since Rosie's birth, Elizabeth had been half-expecting her to die. Visions floated into her head of the ax falling. She pictured herself holding Rosie's lifeless body and screaming in white-hot silence. She loved her with desperation, with heartsickness, with a kind of lust, and she saw how vulnerable Rosie was, her skin so soft and thin, her bones so rubbery. And she saw the meanness of the world, saw the world aquiver with menace. Elizabeth always fell in love with her daughter all over again on vacations or one-day trips out to the ocean or up to the mountain. There she got to watch other people fall in love with her child, too, her shy but engaging daughter, away from the inbred day-to-dayness of the house, away from the mother's boredom of spending so much time alone with a kid. She hated herself for this boredom, imagined she was the only mother who did not thrill constantly to her child's long, involved monologues, the pelting of questions, the lagging behind on walks, the tedium of playing Crazy Eights. So she loved to watch her daughter dazzle other people with her shy beauty and quick mind. She loved to be away from the exasperation of daily life, Rosie's provocations, the tension she felt as a result, her voice spiraling out of control, her hand itching to strike.

Over the years she had watched Rosie splash in the waves out at Stinson Beach, joyful among the pelicans and gulls and sandpipers on that long rural stretch of sand. But with her mind's eye Elizabeth could see rogue waves sweeping her away, and when they hiked on mountain trails, she could imagine Rosie losing her footing, toppling off a cliff or tumbling down the hillside. Almost anything could set off a projection of Rosie dying or dead. In the wrong mood, mention of dinosaurs could trigger a movie in Elizabeth's head of Rosie being torn apart by raptors. Sometimes Elizabeth retreated to the image of a perfectly sterile environment, a luxuriously appointed laboratory, with locks on the doors and security guards, where she cradled Rosie in her arms, safe from killers, snakes, cars, white water, cliffs, airplanes, pedophiles, pit bulls, burning houses, trains, eddies, sharks, fallen electrical wires—only to watch as her angular, sturdy daughter, draped over her arms like an infant, grew wasted and blue with leukemia.

"Honey," Charles Adderly had told her the day after Rosie was born, "you'll never draw another calm breath as long as you live. That blissful amniotic unconcerned state of people without children is a thing of the past."

"Why is that?" she'd asked, looking at the baby girl sound asleep on the bed beside her.

"Because you're a monkey," he answered. "And monkeys care."

six

Iт rained the entire first two weeks of March, and Elizabeth began to feel both anxious and melancholic. She started waking up in the middle of the night for no particular reason and found herself staring at the walls, the shadows, her sleeping husband, her stomach taut with a nebulous tension, unable to fall back to sleep. In this strange twilight time, her thoughts spun with images of Charles, Luther, Andrew, Thackery. She would get up, and crawl into bed with Rosie, and lie in the dark listening to her daughter's quiet breathing; after a while she would go downstairs, where she sat in the window seat with a cup of warm milk, reading, a blanket wrapped around her.

One night when Simone had slept over, Elizabeth stayed up until three in the morning. She finally dozed, but bolted awake from a dream about her garden, a violent frightening dream where the garden looked like a jungle, where snails were eating everything and cats were stalking birds, and a twenty-foot python lay sleeping in the overgrowth. The house was in deep stillness. The night was so dark and she felt so alone, sad and scared like she used to feel as a little girl when she'd wake up in the middle of the night and not be able to fall back to sleep, haunted by shadows, by the insistent silence of dark forces; she used to sneak into her parents' room just before dawn, and lie on the wood floor beside their bed, and sleep there until it was time to get up for school. She was not allowed to sleep with them; if they discovered her in bed with them, they would make her go back to her own room, and so she lay on their floor, covered with whatever clothes her father had left on the chair when he'd undressed that night, and she'd always be cold and afraid of whatever snakes or spiders or men might be waiting for her under the bed. But alone in her own room in the middle of all that silence was worse.

She started to recite a poem she knew by heart, which Andrew used to read to Rosie at bedtime, "James James Morrison Morrison Weatherby George Dupree." She tried to meditate, she tried to slow down her heartbeat. But she heard this terrible sound, a descending tone deep inside her, thin, high, and empty, all of the wetness squeezed out of the sound, like a last gasp of long skinny sorrow. God! Maybe she was going crazy, maybe there was something wrong with her mind, maybe it was broken. She got up, wrapped the blanket around her shoulders, and went back upstairs to bed.

James woke up when she crawled back in between the sheets. "Oh, honey," he said tenderly, laying his head down on her chest. "My sleepy wife."

After a while, she sighed. "James?" she asked. "Do I seem different in the last few days?"

"Different how?"

She thought for a moment. "I get up now before I used to go to bed." They lay back in bed and cuddled, and she smiled at herself, at how crazy her mind could be all alone in the dark, and after a while she began to doze. When she woke again an hour later, the girls were tearing around, trying to get ready for their tournament. She joined in their preparations, drinking some of the rich coffee James had made, and somehow found herself, just an hour later, driving along on the Golden Gate Bridge.

She had almost no memory of having gotten in the car, of having driven for twenty minutes on 101. She simply came to on the bridge. She was daydreaming about her courtship with James, how strange it had felt at first to have fallen in love with a man who was several inches shorter than she was, with a chipped front tooth and terrible clothes, so unlike Andrew on the surface. In a way Rosie had accepted him first. She'd looked past the package to what lay underneath. He was funny and he was deeply loyal, except . . . She looked around at the sun breaking through the fog on the bay, a tugboat pulling a freighter out to sea.

Except there was a memory like a faint headache pressing in on her, of calling him late one night in the early days of their romance; he had been saying he loved her for a while, and she had finally called to say she loved him too. It was midnight, her heart was full of love and acceptance, and she couldn't wait to tell him. But a woman with an English accent had answered his phone. She felt an internal lurch even now, on the bridge, and she closed her eyes for a second to close the drapes on the memory, then looked off in the distance at the red cast on the hills, on the skyscape, on the sea.

ANDREW is walking beside her on the beach at Aptos, in the middle of Monterey Bay, and the water, the waves, are red with plankton, salmon red. The beach is called Potbelly Beach because of the stoves in the tiny houses up past the sand, up past the emerald ice plant dotted with spiky purple flowers. Andrew and Elizabeth have been married eight months now. They are both tall, young, shy, tan from their days in the water here, hugging and holding in the water, silky as seals. They are walking along the sandy beach at dusk, they have had two martinis each in paper-thin glasses and are holding hands, looking in wonder at the redness of the water, the otters bobbing out a ways, past the breakers. Elizabeth sneaks secret glances at her new husband's face and feels like they are kids, best friends, playing house. He has the bluest eyes anyone has ever seen. They are so happy that they stop to talk to other people who are walking along the beach, discussing the plankton that floats and drifts so intensely red on the tide, and everyone is smiling as they speak, everyone is watching the red water. There is a breeze coming off the sea, and Elizabeth's hair, which is still long, flowing several inches past her shoulders, whips around her face. Andrew does all the talking to the other people walking on the beach, and as he talks, he nonchalantly tries to hold her hair back, brushing it off her forehead although it blows back right away. She feels like a child he is tending to, and it feels so lovely, so loving, so sexy, for this big patrician man to be trying to hold the hair out of her face so she can see, so she can be seen. Her long dark hair is getting into her mouth, and he pulls it out and it is wet from her mouth. Cliffs made of fossils loom above them like churches, beyond the ice plant, beyond the tiny houses with the potbellied stoves and the potbellied owners, and she looks at her husband's big wide inviting young face, serious blue eyes, the salt in his brows. When he smiles shyly at the people with whom they stop to talk, he presses his lips together so that the corners turn down slightly in amusement. They keep on walking, they've been walking nearly an hour, and the breeze keeps whipping her hair around, and finally he stops and stands behind her, gathering it up and away from her face, weaving it into a braid that he holds on to. Then they start to walk again, Andrew holding onto her rope of hair, and she can't stop smiling. At first she believes he is doing this because it is so strangely amusing, but his eyes search the wet beach as they walk, as if he's looking for precious metals, and his eyes don't meet hers for the longest time, and this somehow feels like a deeper form of looking at her than if he were staring right into her eyes. After a while, he finds a long strand of beach grass and tries to use it to tie her braid, but it doesn't work. Finally he finds a piece of tattered kite string half-buried in the sand. He bends down low to pick it up and pulls her down with him so he won't have to let go of her braid. The string is about a foot long, unraveling and dirty, and he uses it to tie the end of her braid, tightly and then in a bow, as if it is a length of satin. She lets go of his hand so she can reach out and stroke the golden hair on his carpenter arms, the sparkles of silver sand on his skin, and she feels she could die right then and there, climb up the reddish copper cliffs, the seashell-embedded cliffs, hold hands and fly off together so she can live with him forever.

THE memory stopped playing in her head at the toll plaza, and she had to ask Rosie twice to get the money out of her purse, which was on the floor in the backseat at Rosie's feet, and you would have thought from Rosie's annoyance that Elizabeth had asked her to run back home to Bayview for Elizabeth's wallet.

THE girls won their match that day and, eventually, the trophy for the girls' fourteen-and-under doubles. There was almost no room on Rosie's bookshelves for any more trophies. There were already fifty or so, and she was only thirteen. Simone, nearly a year older, had just as many, maybe more. Rosie talked Simone into giving these latest trophies to Rae. "We don't need them," said Rosie. "And Rae is very sad." Simone hadn't thought twice before saying okay. Kids at school whispered behind her back that Simone was stupid, but Rosie thought she was just extremely innocent, even though she was also so boy crazy.

Another thing besides her kindness that Rosie loved about Simone was that she didn't care about material stuff, not like some of the girls in school who only cared about things like their hair and their clothes. But practically all Simone ever thought about was boys, boys, boys— oh, he's so cute, oh, he's such a fox, oh, he'd be a good boyfriend for you, Rosie—like all the movie-star boys in their class were going to fall in love with a skinny, ratty little tennis jock. But Simone was incredibly generous. She was like a big goofy dog with huge paws and eyes full of longing. So when Rosie explained that Rae was sad about breaking up with a man, Simone thought it was a great idea for them to give her their new trophies. They rode their bikes over to Rae's as the sun fell slowly to earth, and they peered in the windows of her wonderful fairy-tale cottage, but Rae wasn't home.

They left their trophies in the mailbox, on top of the day's mail.

"Maybe she'll think her boyfriend left them."

Rosie's shoulders sagged. "Why would she think her boyfriend would leave two girls' tennis trophies? I mean, *God,* Simone."

EARLY in the school year, in a development bordering on the miraculous, one of the popular girls had asked Rosie to eat lunch with them. In Rosie's eyes, this girl, Hallie Randall, was perfect, with long straight chestnut hair, dimples, a pretty white smile, and a huge trampoline in her back yard. At lunch, the girls talked mostly about the models they hated the most, and the music they loved the most. Rosie craved their company like Elizabeth used to crave Jack Daniels. Elizabeth, picking her up one day after school, found her waiting with them on the steps of the office building, attached to them like a barnacle. She watched Rosie, with downcast eyes, say something, at which everybody laughed. Then they looked over her head at each other, like amused royalty, and Elizabeth was filled with distress at the sight of Rosie's transparency.

Hallie invited her back for lunch the next day. But after that it was on and off and on again, and Rosie never knew what to expect. Then she called and invited Rosie to come over after school and play on the trampoline. Elizabeth wanted to forbid this but did not see how she could. Her own mother had had a fear of trampolines that bordered on the pathological. The family across the street from the house in which Elizabeth grew up had owned the town's first trampoline, and this was the most popular house in the neighborhood. All the kids played there, waiting their turn to jump—all except Elizabeth, whose drunken mother never let her go. She had read an article in *Life* about a valiant young girl who was learning to live a full life in a wheelchair, after having broken her neck while doing a back flip on a trampoline, and from then on Elizabeth's mother viewed the apparatus as a springboard to paraplegia. Her father was not around enough to stand up and fight for Elizabeth's rights. And when Elizabeth, who had one long black eyebrow spanning both eyes and was lonely as a manatee, begged to join in, the mother looked at her with scorn, as if, at eight, Elizabeth wanted to borrow the car.

So Elizabeth gave Rosie permission to play at Hallie's, and then found herself holding her breath off and on until Rosie came home again, whole and mobile.

So it went all year, with Rosie praying for inclusion with the popular girls. Sometimes she was invited, sometimes they just waved gaily and passed her by. Then one day in February Hallie had brought Rosie to the table for lunch, and conversation stopped.

The girls looked worriedly at one another until Hallie began to chatter about how awful their gym teacher was, who had a huge mole under one of her arms that made them all sick to their stomachs.

"But there's something happening, I just know it," Rosie had confided miserably to her mother that day after school.

"What do you think was going on?" Elizabeth asked, who remembered the same girls—the exact same batch but with slightly different hairstyles—from twenty-five years before.

Rosie looked around jerkily, as if the answer were flitting about the room like a moth. Her nostrils flared. She shrugged.

"It's probably nothing," said Elizabeth. "You'll see."

But it turned out to be something big. One of the girls was throwing a Valentine's Day party at her house, catered by her mother, a sit-down dinner for the six girls and their boyfriends or dates. Hallie explained apologetically that the only reason Rosie was not being invited was because it was for couples. Rosie came home and went to her room, slamming the door. Elizabeth went upstairs to investigate. Rosie wouldn't let her in, but two hours later, when Elizabeth encountered her in the hallway, her eyes were nearly swollen shut with crying. Rosie let her mother hug her, hold her, in the hallway, but wouldn't explain the source of her grief. Finally she told Elizabeth and James at dinner.

"Oh, that's hateful," said Elizabeth.

"They're despicable," said James.

"Hallie's really nice," said Rosie.

"Fuck Hallie," said James. "I wouldn't even watch her commit suicide."

Rosie hung her head. She felt like she might be about to black out. The pain inside her mind had a sound to it, but it was so sharp you could hardly discern it, like a dog whistle, pitched that high.

So she ended up back with Simone. They practiced together almost every day after school, spent countless hours in each other's rooms, speaking in a private language somewhere between pig Latin and the "Name Game" about boys, their weight, their mothers, the dogs they would have one day. Elizabeth rarely came to pick Rosie up at Simone's anymore, since the girls lived within six blocks of each other and were big enough now to walk home, even at night. But a few times a year, she came by and always exchanged a few friendly words with Veronica, although most frequently they were just firming up arrangements about which one of them would drive the girls to their next tournament.

Elizabeth and Veronica had thought about being friends when the girls had first begun to play at the park together, over nine years ago now. Elizabeth had been widowed six months earlier. She had been drinking at the time and had come inside one afternoon to pick up Rosie after a play date. The two mothers had ended up having a couple of beers in the kitchen as they compared notes about the raising of daughters. Veronica had only been eighteen when she gave birth to Simone five years before, against the ferocious wishes of Simone's father, who was happily married. Rae had asked once, "Why would a *happily* married man sleep with Veronica?" Elizabeth thought the answer was obvious: she had a certain 1920s beauty, an arrogant sauciness, a waterfall of thick black curls, and a round, succulent bottom.

Veronica had made them both coffee, and into their second cup they each poured a healthy slug of brandy. The girls ended up having cereal, popcorn, and tomato soup for dinner in front of the television, while the women moved on to sangria, and then on to more brandy.

Veronica was intense and earnest. Elizabeth knew by dinnertime that there was no real basis for friendship, yet she kept pouring herself another drink. While Simone practiced ballet leaps around the kitchen, Rosie watched the mothers out of the corner of her eye and finally gave her own a look of flat sternness, a face such as you might encounter in an aged and deeply religious Dane. Elizabeth rolled her eyes and poured herself another Drambuie. The girls were put to bed in Veronica's room, and the women stayed up well past midnight, talking.

Simone's anonymous father had given Veronica a lump sum to leave him alone, and she had used it to open the first facial and nail salon in Bayview. Women, especially married women, loved her ditzy maternal attentiveness, the soothing New Age tapes that always played while she and her girls worked, the candles, the incense, the cooing sympathy. Her business thrived. Men, especially married men, loved the intensity of those round black eyes, loved her tiny clothes, and she was forever flying off with Simone and her beaus to places like Vail and Cancún.

Elizabeth did not remember driving home that night, although in the morning her car was parked perfectly in front of the curb. She had even turned the lights off and locked the doors, which she discovered when she went outside, squinty and stiff, unbalanced by seasickness and a pulsarlike headache, to investigate: Was anything unpleasant embedded in the grille or dangling from the fenders—antlers, for instance, or worse?

Over the next few months, Elizabeth had wiggled her way out of any more social evenings with Veronica, but she was always grateful and relieved for Veronica's hospitality toward Rosie. Among other things, she couldn't imagine being friends with someone who collected mystical New Age chotchkes—stars, moons, whales—made of clay and metal and glass. There were always lots of angels represented, as well as candles so artistic you would never think to burn one: candle stars, candle angels, candle women dancing in a circle.

Elizabeth was always amazed by the amount of stuff in other people's lives. On their shelves, tables, counters, on every smooth shiny space in their homes, little artifacts sat, passively protective. Even Rae's home was filled with religious kitsch. Elizabeth understood the need for fairy tales and happy endings, but she also suspected that everyone was trying to fill up and decorate the white space out of fear that the white space was the abyss. James said that Veronica, with her crystal star charms, her dancing women candles, and—as he put it—all those fucking angels, was practicing a form of idolatry and that this worship saved her the pain of being responsible, of being aware and alive and grounded.

Lank and Veronica went out a few times, and even to bed, but Lank, with his pre-Mayan figures, and Veronica, with her God's-eyes and wind chimes, did not have much to talk about.

"She's kind of a—I don't really know the word," Lank confessed.

"Mindless twit?" said James.

Lank nodded gravely. "She's got those crazy black Rasputin eyes. They made little Lank very tense."

Veronica gave Elizabeth a petulant little angel paperweight after their one long night all those years ago. Elizabeth had guiltily thrown it away. Several months later, when Elizabeth stopped in at Veronica's one morning to pick up Rosie, she'd seen the same angel paperweight on Veronica's little altar by the front door. Veronica was upstairs helping Rosie get her school gear together. There was usually New Age music playing, or disco exercise tapes blaring from the den, but that day the only sound had been Simone's little cat batting a pushpin around on the hardwood floors. Elizabeth, who had a mild hangover, found the sound annoying. She felt like she was inside a bowling alley. She wondered if Veronica had been going through her trash or if she bought them in bulk, to give as door prizes. At any rate, Veronica was now using the angel to hold down an eagle feather on a scrap of sky-blue silk, so neither would blow away.

seven

EASTER was early that year, the third Sunday of March. Rae had made Rosie a small woven picture for Ash Wednesday, the first day of Lent, the day when Jesus was baptized by John in the river Jordan. The picture was of the river, blue and green with golden satin threads to show the shimmer, and with a smear of ashes on it, real ashes from her wood-burning stove—ashes to remind us, as Rae said, that this is all a passing show.

Rae had become a Christian two years before, which was a source of great consternation to everyone. It was one thing when she had believed in God in a general, ecumenical kind of way, another when she began making space in her chair so that Jesus might sit down beside her. They all hoped it would pass, like a cold, but it showed no signs of doing so. She also remained a left-wing activist, but now she went to church every Sunday, began every morning with prayer and Scripture, and tried to see Jesus in everyone—even Luther, even Republicans. She had not yet begun referring to God as "the Lord," but Lank had said bitterly just the other day that this was right around the corner.

Rosie went to church with Rae on Ash Wednesday. She was expecting this big gospel choir, because Rae always talked about this beautiful choir at her church, with all these black people singing, and Rosie knew that black folks had something special because the few black girls at her school were always the first to start off the dancing at the school dances and they were so *so* much better than the white girls, so much bigger in their dancing. She didn't really know how to describe the difference, because a lot of the popular girls were technically very good dancers. But that day at Rae's church, the guy who played piano was terrible; even Rosie could pick out all the wrong notes he was playing, mistakes that threw the choir off. And instead of bleachers onstage filled with swaying singers in choir robes that Rosie had been half-expecting, there were only eight people, singing, "Pass Me Not, O Gentle Savior." This one black woman was crying even as she sang: "Hear my humble cry," she was singing, "while on others you are calling, do not pass me by," crying, crying, so it came out as kind of a warble, and the pianist was playing notes that didn't even sound like they were part of the same song, and Rosie felt very uncomfortable with the lack of competence. Then she noticed Rae swaying slightly in her seat, listening, her eyes closed in this way that made you think she was seeing some huge vista inside her head, a view she was trying to memorize so she could use it in a weaving someday.

Rosie hung Rae's small unframed piece above her bed between a photo of her dad and a photo of Peter Billings with one muscular bronze arm around her and one around Simone; they had been at the indoor courts in San Rafael, fifteen minutes from Bayview, practicing at night. Peter held a membership there that allowed him to bring a van full of students at night whenever it rained. Rosie didn't like playing there very much. The club reminded her of an airplane hangar, eerie with purplish light from long tubes that hung from the ceiling and that swayed when hit by a lob. Each light was like an elongated sun, and every time you looked up, you had to squint or be blinded. And the smell was mucky, like hot wet dirty shoes. She liked being with the boys, though, the older boys, who teased her and laughed at her jokes. She remembered the night the photo was taken, during Christmas vacation last year. Now she was already at least an inch taller. In the photo she and Simone both looked like silly kids. Simone's breasts were much smaller in the picture, but Rosie remembered that Peter made a little joke when he gave Simone a dollar for a soda; he said to please get him change in nipples and dimes and then he pretended not to have done it on purpose.

That made her feel just the opposite of the way she felt with Rae in church that night, when she too finally closed her eyes, and she heard why Rae was having joy—because something was happening in spite of the incompetence of the pianist and the singers. Something was happening in spite of how funky the surface of the music was, like spirit rising up through all the dreck of the world.

On the night before Easter, Rae stretched out on the couch in the living room after dinner as if she were at her psychiatrist's. James and Elizabeth sat in easy chairs beside her. Rosie was lying on the floor working halfheartedly on a report for social studies.

"Are you comfortable down there, Rosie?" Rae asked.

"Pretty much."

"Because you could always try to shove a huge, foul, arthritic old woman over to one side of the couch."

Rosie smiled at Rae affectionately. "It's okay."

"I'm missing Mike so badly this week. I can't believe how I still feel after all this time—I mean, it's been almost two months, right? I still feel like I'm in nicotine withdrawal. In fact, Rosie darling? I'll do anything if you'll run to the store and get me a pack of cigarettes."

"Rae, you don't smoke. Remember?"

"I don't? Did I used to? Did I quit?"

"Uh-huh. A few years ago."

"Do you think you will call him?" James asked.

"I don't know," said Rae. "Maybe. Probably."

"He doesn't have much to give, Rae," said Elizabeth. "Meanness, and crumbs."

"Well," said Rae, "it's better than nothing." Elizabeth smiled gently. "I was so comfortable with Mike, because I'm so good at fending off sadism. It's what I learned to do well as a child. And to thrive on turnip juice—emotionally, it was all my parents had to offer. It's a little bitter perhaps, and dehydrating. But it tastes like love to me. And that's what Mike has to offer. Turnip juice in a beautiful goblet."

"Do you hear how crazy that is? To give your heart to someone like that?" Elizabeth said.

"Uh-huh," said Rae.

"You want him to be tuned into you, and he keeps saying, 'Hey, honey, turn on the radio and twiddle the dials.' "

"I know," said Rae. She closed her eyes.

"He's a narcissist in delusion," said James.

"And what's the delusion?"
"That's he's not a narcissist."

THE next day Rosie went over to Lank's in the afternoon to work on her report, a five-page paper on any topic she pleased. She had chosen the history of women's tennis, and so far her report, which Elizabeth had read over breakfast, began:

> The history of women's tennis is that for a long time, there were some great women tennis players, touring the world with the great men. This was long before Billie Jean King played Bobby Riggs, who was a sexist little jerk, and who lost to her. Helen Wills Moody was one of the early greats, Suzanne Lenglen was another. But they were amateurs, just as the men were. If you played at Wimbledon, you just won a trophy, unlike now when you win hundreds of thousands of dollars. Of course there was also a sexist period when the men started winning prize money but the women won toaster ovens. Things could not have been less fair, although of course this was the case in "all walks of life," so you'd hardly notice one more little thing. But even before this, in the 1950s and part of the 1960s, there were some touring pros, like Rod Laver, and Ken Rosewall, and one of these was a woman named Maria Bueno, from Brazil, who was an extremely great athlete. These touring pros traveled around the world playing each other in exhibitions, and were paid under "the table."

Rosie adored Lank. He was the first man she had loved in a romantic way, when she was ten and found him so sexy she could hardly breathe, with his cherubic face, that soft fair skin, and his big body like a friendly bear. He was so different from the other boys and men she knew—the tennis boys mostly, and Peter. He was the exact opposite of Peter, partly because he was so uncoordinated but also, he was so sweet and regular. Peter was like a movie star who happened to be a great tennis player. Her mother said one of the things she loved about Lank was that you could still see his baby self—the animal self, the dreaming self, the self that didn't have language, the self that was fluid and full of appetite and satiety and frustration, that could not cover its nakedness with motor control.

Lank was lacking in motor control.

He was one of the least coordinated men Elizabeth had ever seen. James, who played basketball with him and a few of their friends once a week, said that Lank was the Pee-Wee Herman of the sports world, simultaneously stiff and rubbery. And even Rosie, who watched him with basset-hound eyes, had to admit that he wasn't much of an athlete. She had played tennis with him the summer before, because he'd said he played, and on the first shot he lifted his back leg like a garden statue and hit a backhand so stiffly, with his back leg still poised behind him, that it looked like a stream of water was about to spout from the top of his head.

But he knew how to be a friend, and he knew how to get kids to want to do well in school. Whenever Rosie had a report due, she'd take all of her notes and research over to Lank's for an afternoon. He always made her describe the report in one or two sentences, "as if you were writing copy for the TV listings," so she'd know exactly what she was and wasn't writing about.

Now Rosie was bent over Lank's cluttered kitchen table, trying to figure out what else she could say in the report. She cared passionately about her subject: she and Simone and all the other girls on the junior circuit talked about the history of women's tennis the way Democrats used to talk about the civil rights movement. Just the other day at breakfast, Rosie had been discussing the women's long march from the early days of Helen Wills Moody, Althea Gibson breaking the race barrier, to the great Maria Bueno, to Margaret Court and Rosie Casals and the pivotal moment when Billie Jean King whipped Bobby Riggs, "that froggy little butt," as Rosie called him. Her eyes were flashing as she recounted the *miracle* of Chris Evert's transformation from goody-goody to one of the leaders of the movement, like Martin Luther King, and when James volunteered gently that perhaps he wouldn't go *quite* that far, Rosie stalked from the table and shouted down from the top of the stairs that James was a froggy little butt, too.

LANK loved Rosie in much the same way Rae loved Rosie, in the unabashed and spoiling way of godparents. He loved her company, the warm quality of the companionship she was able to show to people who made few demands on her, who took her as she was, unlike the bottomlessly annoying and judgmental way of her parents. They sat at his table today, side by side, Rosie writing her paper, Lank correcting homework and answering her questions. Bruno slept on the floor beneath the table as they worked, pressed against Rosie's ankles like a warm furry log. She inhaled Lank's smells, the saltiness, his maleness, like soil.

Lank's last girlfriend had been fifteen years younger than he; she spoke in a little Kewpie-doll voice.

"She's a lot smarter than she looks," he said when James and Elizabeth were rolling their eyes about her one day. "And she's very sweet, and very honest."

Dust motes danced in the flickering gleams of sunshine that streamed through the kitchen windows.

"Lank," said Elizabeth. "Honesty does not mean telling a couple of strangers about your urinary tract infections over dinner."

"First of all, you're not strangers, you're my best friends. And second of all, she was just explaining why she wasn't having drinks that night—because of her medication."

"She pronounced vagina 'pagina,' " Elizabeth said. James smiled. Lank looked away.

"All right. Maybe she's not Susan Sontag." He rubbed his eyes, then turned to Elizabeth. "How did she work it into the conversation?"

"It was just some throwaway line. Some passing reference. To her cat's pagina."

Lank stared off into space for a moment, mulling this over. "So she wasn't actually talking about her own, then. It could have been worse."

James actually brayed with laughter. Elizabeth reached over and took Lank's hand. "Lank," she said sternly, "it was bad enough."

"It's so easy for you guys to make fun of me, because you have each other. But James, you had that girlfriend who pronounced spaghetti 'basketti,' " said Lank.

"But the point is I have a brilliant, handsome grown-up now, a woman who—"

"Well, you lucked out," said Lank. Elizabeth turned to James and nodded vigorously.

"But you could have Rae," said James. "She's pretty, she's smart, she's hilarious—she's funnier than either of us."

"But she's fat. She needs to lose fifty pounds. And now she's religious. So into Jesus. It makes me edgy. And anyway, she's not interested in me."

Elizabeth had to admit that this was true. Rae liked him as a best-friend-in-law, but she didn't find him attractive. Also, as she confided to Elizabeth one night, she thought he was a tightwad.

"He's not a tightwad, he's a teacher. He doesn't have that much money," said Elizabeth.

"Besides, Rae," added James, "you two could have the most beautiful children."

"You guys never give up. And besides, I don't think I like children."

"But you adore Rosie."

"Rosie," said Rae, "is God."

ROSIE did not sleep at all the night before the last big dance of the school year, the May Day dance, the most special one of all, when seventh and eighth graders danced till ten in the gym to music videos playing on a big screen onstage. Some of the kids would be sneaking beer, she knew; some of the kids would be smoking outside—the big kids, eighth graders, smoking in the shadows.

Rosie wore long black shorts and cowboy boots. Simone had outgrown the boots and had given them to Rosie, along with her training bra, which Rosie wore underneath a tiny white T-shirt. Elizabeth had nearly cried when she saw Rosie dressed for the dance. There were the smallest of all breasts pushing against the shirt, like beautiful gardenias, and those long legs widest at the knee, and those camel-colored cowboy boots that seemed three sizes too big. Rosie wore a little blusher and some lip gloss, her hair pulled back in barrettes. She appeared downstairs when she was ready to go, standing against the wall like a mouse, watching for her mother's reaction.

"You look so beautiful, Rosie. Like a model in a magazine."

Rosie scowled, pleased; she appeared to be grinding out a cigarette with the toe of one cowboy boot. She went out to the living room, picked up a magazine, rifled through it, waiting for Simone, who finally showed up wearing a short white skirt, new cowboy boots, and a black tube top filled to bursting. Rosie looked at her with wonder and desolation.

"You look great," Simone said. "Those shorts are totally cool."

"You do, too." Rosie's voice was hollow, flat.

They sat a few feet apart on the couch, with their heads dropped all the way back so they could stare at the ceiling. When Elizabeth came in to offer them some juice before they left, both girls rolled their heads from one side of the couch to the center, rolled their vision across the ceiling, so that their eyes might meet.

THERE were two strobe lights set up, and picnic tables with benches, the tables covered with black-and-red-checked paper tablecloths. Not all the lights were on, so it was dim enough to dance like real people, not like the little kids dancing midday under bright school lights. Watching the music videos gave your eyes something to do besides stare at how beautiful all the other girls were. Simone was talking to a group of boys and girls who were clustered around the screen, and Rosie stood there and listened to the rhythm and blues video blaring now. But it was too loud; she felt blanketed in its thrum, in its river of loudness, instead of being able to hear what was great about it. She could smell Simone's horrible rose toilet water, like incense from Mexico that would be sold in a tube with a picture of Mary on it looking depressed. Being able to pick out her smell was like having a fishing line connecting them, and this relieved her. She started missing her mother. She stared off into space, hating herself because she was at a dance with music videos on a huge screen and strobe lights and all she could think of was needing to call her mother and make sure that she was okay; the fear was like Ajax cleanser sprinkled on her insides. The bejeweled flickering colors of the strobe light made her feel off balance, like when you spin too long, unwinding, on a rope swing.

The black girls started doing their dances, the Tootsie Roll, Butterfly, so fine in their movement and style that you wouldn't be surprised to see them dancing in music videos someday. And then only a few guys had the nerve to ask a girl to dance, and these same five boys and the five girls they asked kept changing partners among themselves.

Simone was one of them, but Hallie wasn't, and Hallie locked on to Rosie, and Rosie let her, trying not to think about that bad business with the party, and Hallie told her about who liked whom, who had gone how far with whom, and you had to shout to be heard. The crashing music and strobe lights enveloped her, but Rosie couldn't discern a pulse in the music, just sound, like she was inside too much energy. She looked at the boys who were dancing, and she felt both desire and hopelessness; her pelvis tingled and tightened inside her. Simone was dancing like a stripper in a nightclub Rosie had seen on TV once, and Rosie could not take her eyes off her. She was dancing with an eighth-grade boy named Dylan, and after a couple of minutes he bent forward to whisper into Simone's ear, and Simone stopped dancing and stood there not moving but somehow looking like she was about to shimmy. Then she and Dylan pushed past the other dancers and ducked through the open back door.

Rosie watched, hoping they'd pop right back in, but they didn't. Simone had been letting boys feel her up practically since she first got breasts. She liked to kiss; she *loved* to kiss, but she told Rosie it wasn't enough for boys. Boys liked the other things too. Her pelvis tightened again, like it was holding its breath, and she turned toward the stage to watch the music video. Now there was footage of seals, popping their heads out of the surf as if to the beat, cheerful and sad all at once. At first she thought they were the seals who lived in the bay, the ones you saw from the ferry or who sunned themselves on the piers of San Francisco or at the beach on the Hospital Cove side of Angel Island. In the video there was an old one sitting by himself on a rock above the water, and maybe it was his wet doggy eyes or the tatters in his coat, but he made Rosie think of Luther.

And she saw Luther watching her, there at the dance, from the screen, hidden inside the seal.

Simone loved dolphins, but Rosie loved seals. She thought dolphins were smug and fishy, with their skimpy little eyes. It was hard to imagine truly snuggling with dolphins, but seals seemed made to snuggle, they were boneless and floppy like sofas. Around her more and more kids were dancing, but she was locked into the seals on the screen. The sweet dog eyes of the old one were looking right into the camera, right into her. The music was too loud. One of the seals came splashing out of the surf onto the sand, this guy who had been so speedy and graceful in the water but was so clumsy on land. There was something in its lumpy wigglishness that made her think of herself—not of her athletic outsides but of her secret, private self. She looked around for Simone but could not find her. One of these days Simone is going to go too far, she said to herself—it was a line from one of her favorite novels, uttered by the angry mother of a teenage girl as she raised a cup of poisoned coffee to her lips . . .

On screen the most amazing thing was happening: in the shadows of the beach, one of the seals was pulling off its seal suit, pulling the wet brown rubbery skin down past its head, to reveal a sad and beautiful woman within, and the tight suit slipped down over and past her shoulders, the way you'd slip out of an off-the-shoulder evening dress. Oh, Mom, she thought, missing her mother again, I wish you could have seen it; it was exactly what it feels like to be me. Where you mostly think you're one shape but deep inside you know you're many. So awkward here at the dance, but so fast on the court, like the woman who had been inside the sealskin—one skin, another skin, same stuff. She pictured Luther watching her swim, Luther with his wet brown eyes.

"Hey!" said Hallie. "Earth calling Rosie." Rosie looked away from the screen, from the seals. She smiled at Hallie and the other girls. "Do you see Simone?" she asked, and Hallie looked around and then jutted her chin toward the door. Simone was stepping back inside, all discombobulated, tugging at her tube top, sweeping blonde hair away from her eyes, wiping away smeared lipstick. *God,* Simone, Rosie thought, why don't you be a little bit more obvious? Simone looked over and tried to catch her eye, but Rosie looked away, back to the stage. Another music video was starting, with three men in grass hula skirts playing electric guitars. She wondered if the woman would ever wriggle back into the seal suit. Hallie jabbed her in the ribs with her elbow and smiled in exasperation. Rosie closed her eyes tightly to clear her mind. When she opened them, a whole lot of girls had started dancing together side by side, and Rosie began to move with them in one spot, weaving like a cobra, slowly at first and then faster, and her cowboy boots began to move beneath her, and lead her around the floor like a partner.

eight

One rainy night in early May Elizabeth was vacuuming the living room rug, since the girls planned to sleep on it later. They had gone off to the indoor courts for an evening of practice with Peter and some of his better boys. They would be home by nine or so. James was upstairs working in his study. He had offered to help her clean, but she had not wanted his help. She did not even want music on the stereo. She just wanted to be alone in the silence, and clean.

The floor of their living room was honey-colored wood. When she and Andrew first moved in, it had been varnished brown and deeply scarred, of no distinction. He had spent a week on his knees sanding it with a small hand sander, blasting off the ugly brown shellac until beautiful amber pine appeared. Hag to princess, he said, when the surface dross was gone, the gouges and scratches and discolorations. Elizabeth called it their second-chance floor. They bought a thick green rug, sea-foam green, just big enough for the two of them to lie on. Sometimes on sunny afternoons they put pillows from the couch on their little rug, and they read. They read poetry, books on the Renaissance, novels with no plot, on the quiet green island that was their marriage.

They are lying on their rug with Rosie, who is four years old and asleep face down on Andrew's chest. He is sleeping too. Elizabeth studies them for a moment, listens to them sleep. Then slowly she reaches out and touches the distinct arch of Andrew's dark brow. She strokes it with the lightest touch. She feels like a mother wiping away sorrow, or headache. After a moment, he opens his eyes, blue as a Siamese cat's, blue as Rosie's. There is nothing more intimate, she thinks at that moment, than tracing a loved one's eyebrow. Those delicate hairs, so close to the vulnerable eyes; one is saying, tracing the brow, I am right next to your unprotected place, and I am blessing it. Rosie makes an impossibly loud snore, like an old pug, and they both smile, and Elizabeth just keeps tracing the one eyebrow with her baby finger, without taking her eyes off his.

THAT rug was no longer there. Elizabeth had thrown it out a few years after Andrew's death. There had been too many other men on it. She had never really wept for Andrew; there had been Rosie to tend to, and besides, she felt somehow protected by the newness, the unbelievability of it all, of having gone from being totally married to being a widow. The stabbing sense of loss never caught up with her. She'd kept it at bay, night after night at the bar, drinking Scotch and water, bringing home that night's suavest available man, anyone semihandsome who could make her laugh. She had been through a lot of carpenters, businessmen, poets, painters, writers, some cowboy types, even a biker or two. And when this stage had come to an end, more or less of its own accord when Rosie was seven or so, Elizabeth had gotten a new mattress for her bed and replaced the sea-foam rug with a handsome dark green dhurrie. James had courted her on this rug four years ago. They used to lie on it in front of the fire. Now Rosie and Simone slept on it in sleeping bags whenever Simone stayed over, because Rosie's single bed had grown too small for the two of them.

It seemed lately that Simone had spent every weekend night here with them; Veronica was dating someone new, and perhaps that partly explained things. But whatever the case, James and Elizabeth had fallen asleep most nights recently to the sound of the girls in late-night whisperings of boys and tennis, of the places they would live when they were older.

Rosie never had insomnia when Simone spent the night. They slept side by side in their separate sleeping bags, huddling against each other like puppies.

James had always maintained that there was good crazy and there was bad crazy and that you just had to make sure you stayed good crazy, but it seemed to Elizabeth that Simone was in danger of teetering off toward bad crazy. "No, no," said James. "*Boy* crazy, not bad crazy." But Elizabeth wasn't so sure, and the more time she spent with Simone, the more she worried that bad things were in store.

She was so lovely, fair as early morning sun. She was a powerful child, though—perhaps the natural result of her having started school a year late. Elizabeth had always been aware of her power to hurt. Even at five, Simone had had the ability to turn men's heads, with her pouty lips and long thick yellow hair and plastic high heels. Yet she could also be surprisingly loyal and tender. Elizabeth could remember driving home after a day on the beach, not too long after Andrew died, Rosie and Simone side by side in the back seat of their old station wagon. Simone still had half a bag of potato chips left, while Rosie had eaten all of hers. Simone took one small bite of a chip and then handed it to Rosie, who took a tiny bite also, and they did this until it was gone, a potato chip communion.

Even at that age she could make the world stop turning with her will, her games. Elizabeth and Rosie used to drop by her house on their way to the park and stand waiting on her doorstep while Simone tried to make up her mind about whether to go with them or not. Head down, toeing the ground, clinging to her mother's dresses, refusing to commit—she exerted the power of the held breath, the power of not taking anything or giving anything away. It was a very quiet tantrum, and it must have been such hideous fun to watch the parents fling themselves around trying to get her to do what they wanted.

The girls had played together nearly every day that year.

So it came as a shock when, after Veronica had dropped Simone off early one morning, Simone announced primly, "This is the last time I'm coming over, Mrs. Ferguson."

"But you two have so much fun together," Elizabeth protested.

"I need to make new friends besides Rosie," said Simone.

But, Elizabeth wanted to cry, you are her only friend, and her daddy has just died. And she only weighs forty pounds in this heavy world! Elizabeth wanted to shout, "Get out of here or I'll set the dogs on you!" But they had no dogs.

Rosie was trying very hard to stay cool. Once she had cried when she had to say good-bye to Simone, and Simone had said, "This is very disappointing, Rosie."

Now Elizabeth said, "Simone? You will always be welcome at this house." She did not mean it for a second. What she did mean was— You don't want us? Well. We don't want you. In fact, we hate you.

Rosie looked stricken but did not cry. "Honey?" she said. "Everything's going to be okay. I honestly don't think Simone means it."

"Yes, I do," said Simone.

It was so painful to endure your child's pain, especially a broken heart.

She took the two children to preschool, although Rosie had barely blinked in the last half hour. Then she spent the morning reading the paper. She wondered if Simone was just panicking because Veronica was talking about their moving to another state. Or maybe the tiny cruel part of her heart had started beating all of a sudden. There are so many reasons why a small child's heart turns hard.

That afternoon, Elizabeth and Rosie were reading on the floor in the living room, when Veronica called to see if Rosie could come over to play at their house.

Oh, I'm sorry, Elizabeth wanted to say. Rosie's a little booked up. Maybe next week—no, no, wait, next week's no good . . .

But instead they met Simone and her mother in the park ten minutes later. Simone's announcement was never mentioned again.

S{OMETIME} later, before kindergarten began, Simone and Veronica moved to Vail. They came back for visits from time to time, but by first grade Rosie had become best friends with Sharon Thackery. Then when Rosie was eight and a half, Sharon and her family moved out of town. Rosie's heart was broken. She began taking tennis lessons, and at ten years old she entered and won her first tournament. She started looking around for a doubles partner. She had a new best friend named Tina, but they were not completely dedicated to each other, as Rosie and Sharon had been. And Rosie still missed Sharon.

Charles Adderly had given Rosie a magic set for her birthday that year, and one morning Elizabeth was cooking a cheese omelette with parsley and mushrooms for herself and James, when Rosie called to her with some urgency from the living room. Elizabeth turned off the heat on the stove and went to investigate. She found Rosie sitting on the dark green rug, hunched over her black magician's hat to hide its contents from view, fiddling with something secret inside.

"What do you need, honey?" Elizabeth asked.

"I'm doing something magical. It's about missing Sharon. Watch me."

"Okay."

Rosie appeared to go into a trance. Her eyes fluttered. She felt about on the dark green rug, pulling up invisible things that she then dropped into the black cone of the hat. "I am dropping dust," she intoned in a spooky voice. "Dust and air." Then with her eyes still closed, she moved her hands like a sorcerer's over the space above the hat, casting a spell, massaging the magic into being. She opened her eyes and lowered her head down into the magician's hat, then held it on with one hand while she slowly raised her head. Elizabeth was stunned to see that Rosie's eyes were brimming with tears. They spilled over and trickled down her cheeks. Elizabeth sat down on the green rug with her daughter.

"Honey!" she said. "You're really missing Sharon, aren't you?"

Rosie nodded without looking up. "I want her to move back."

"Of course you do." Elizabeth looked at her child, and she believed that the Buddhists were right—that if you want, you will suffer; if you love, you will grieve.

"Mama?" Rosie pushed her fists against her eyes.

"Uh-huh?"

"Does anyone love Mr. Thackery?"

Elizabeth slowly tilted her head, stunned.

"You mean, besides Sharon and her mom?" she asked gently.

"Uh-huh."

"Probably," said Elizabeth. They were both silent for a long moment. "Do you want people to love Mr. Thackery?" Elizabeth asked.

"Yes," said Rosie.

"How come?"

She didn't answer right away. "He must be so lonely," she said.

"Oh, Rosie," said her mother, reaching for her, feeling a capsule of pain in her own throat. Rosie did not answer, and Elizabeth tried to lift her daughter into her lap, but Rosie resisted, drawing back, hunching her shoulders forward. Elizabeth let her cry for a while. I know you feel lonely, too, she wanted to say, but she knew better than to try to fix her daughter. Her daughter wasn't broken—just in grief. She heard James walk softly to the living room door, but she did not look up at him, and then she heard him walk softly back to the kitchen. Rosie took her fists away from her eyes, which were bleary and sleepy and wet, and looked up at her mother. "So *do* you believe in magic?" she asked, and she looked shy and defiant all at once, even though her face and fists were wet from crying. Elizabeth nodded, although the truth was that she didn't—not really. Then, poised, mischievous, wise, head held high, Rosie closed her eyes again, drew herself up very tall, as if going into a yogic pose, smiled, and shook her head gently. And from beneath the magician's hat a dozen pennies rained down.

THREE weeks later, Veronica and Simone moved back to town. And magically, Rosie pointed out, Simone had become nearly as good a tennis player as Rosie: a thousand miles apart, rarely in contact, each girl had become a tournament-caliber player.

Simone had been taking lessons since she was six, because Veronica had been living with a tennis pro. Simone was a natural player; to no one's surprise, she practiced little and did not particularly care if she won or lost. She was ranked number seven in the twelve-and-unders her first year of tournaments, one notch beneath Rosie. They were ranked number two in the doubles the first year they played together.

At eleven, she was, as James put it, as fresh and delectable as a newly opened bag of marshmallows. With tennis, Elizabeth hoped, Simone was learning to move with her wild side, her dark side, rather than be ruled by it. She flung herself around with an incredible physicality, throwing herself at everyone but mostly at boys, pushing and jabbing and grabbing things from them, her body in all ways saying, "Hey! Come play with me!"

When Simone was twelve, with breasts budding, all that energy went subterranean, much weakened in the body but still powerful in the spirit. This year, at fourteen, she regained her fierce athleticism. She had the champion's blithe sense of assurance, the belief when she stepped out on the court that she would probably win. When she lost, she seemed fascinated, more than anything else. Rosie, on the other hand, stepped out onto the court filled with dread at the thought of losing, and when she won, she felt more often than not the purest relief that she had once again escaped the hunter.

JAMES was spellbound by Simone, by her husky voice, her insolence, her sexuality, but he kept—or at least tried to keep—a grip on himself.

The first time he saw her sunbathing in her bikini out in back with Rosie, Rosie still built like a beautiful boy, Simone already like a woman, Elizabeth saw his eyes narrow in cunning, a predator spotting his prey—a predator who seemed to be grasping that nothing could be done now, but maybe later.

He shook his head to clear it, shuddered.

"Don't leer at Rosie's friends, darling."

James had the decency to hang his head.

"Men can be so embarrassing," Elizabeth told Rae later. "Can you imagine lusting after a twelve-year-old boy?"

"No. I guess not. But only because I can't imagine craving anyone who has never hated LBJ."

There had been times since when Elizabeth had seen James have to pull his nose out of emotional confusion, like a cat will suddenly sit down and wash, when Simone appeared in one of her tiny outfits, bursting out of the top, her flanks glistening with dark tanning oil. Elizabeth sensed that he wanted to strut and flirt, that he was suffering the basic conflict of civilized man.

"This is how she affects us," he explained. "We can't help it. It's automatic. This wave of feeling passes through us. We don't act on it, but we think it. She's a warm little sexual jewel."

"This little fourteen-year-old girl can whip you all into slavering servitude? Leave you all looking like Luther?"

"Pretty much."

"Doesn't this embarrass you at all?"

"Now, now, Elizabeth," he said primly, mocking her. "I'm hearing a lot of anger today."

Perhaps, she considered, she was more aware of his admiration for Simone's beauty because of those times before their marriage when he had been with other women. But why was she dredging this up again, after all these years? It made no sense. Still, she looked off into the middle distance sometimes, remembering how much it had hurt—how scared, how betrayed she had felt.

He had begun to tell her he loved her after they had been together a few months. She had not been able to say that she loved him, too. He said, "I love you"; she said, "Thanks."

So finally, when she felt like she could say it she had called him at midnight to tell him, to say the words out loud. But a woman with an

English accent had answered, and Elizabeth had hung up. The same
thing had happened a second time with another woman. Once again
it had been late at night and this time someone had quickly hung up
the phone. She was still drinking at the time, and when she'd accused
him of faithlessness, he had used the drinking against her, insisting
that she must have dialed wrong. But she knew she hadn't. And the
only time in the ensuing years when she had brought it up, as casually
as possible, he had said that he honestly hadn't slept with anyone else
since falling in love with her. That she must have misdialed. Remember? he had asked. You were drunk. But she'd never been convinced.
In any case, this was years ago; she had been sober and he had been
faithful since their marriage, and there was no reason for her to be fix-
ating on it again. Unless perhaps Simone's flowering sexuality, which
had captured her husband's attention, was rubbing against that old
abrasion.

Actually, everyone seemed to be ogling Simone. Even Rae joked in
sexual terms about Simone, about how she had recently begun pranc-
ing about like an athletic stripper. Just tonight Rae had made a crack
when she'd called, full of craving for Mike, shortly before Elizabeth
began vacuuming the living room rug.

"Oh, you," said Elizabeth. "I know just how it feels."

"How? How do you know?"

"I quit drinking, remember? And smoking. I *know* from withdrawal."

"I think if I call him, we could talk everything through, and he'd understand that I was worth fighting for."

"And it would turn out that he was all well!"

"Yes, yes!" cried Rae.

"Oh, honey. This makes me think of something I read somewhere
once—that certain kinds of people present themselves to us like huge
erect penises. And we stand enthralled and cowed and afraid before
them, while they throb and wave from side to side. Mike is like this,
honey. You need some very primitive nurturing. You need the breast.
But Mike can't provide that. He can just come over and sway wienielike
at you."

"But I love that in a guy."

"I know."

"Well, all I can say is, it's *Panic in Needle Park* over here right now.

Maybe I'll stop by your house later, and we can all have sex with Simone."

Elizabeth kneaded her forehead wearily. "You can't tonight, as it turns out. They're at the indoor courts."

PLAYING tennis indoors under stark lights was like playing inside a spaceship. Sounds echoed and hid, boomed forth, then were vacuumed up by all that space. There were five boys and Rosie and Simone tonight, and Peter was doing ground-stroke drills with them as one group. All the kids were playing as hard as they could, raising each other's levels of play by their sheer force of concentration. Rosie felt enveloped in a fierce dreamy vapor of belonging. They were one, the seven of them laughing at Peter's jokes about the fat middle-aged ladies drop-shotting each other to death five courts away. The women belonged to Peter's club, too, but they played here in a league one night a week. He waved affectionately to them and then called his kids by the ladies' names if he thought they were slacking. "Get off your duff, Ruth Ann," he had just said to Jason. Peter was up at the net hitting forehands at the kids as hard as he could. When the shopping cart full of balls was empty and the kids stopped to gather them up again, Rosie felt as if she were one of the popular girls. Everyone was working so hard, concentrating, laughing and sweet, even though Peter kept making little jokes, like why do mice have such small balls? Because not very many of them know how to dance.

Peter really poured himself into the practice, but out of nowhere it began to trouble Rosie that he was mocking the ladies. During the mornings when he gave them group lessons, he flirted and joked and complimented them; he actually sort of sucked up to them. She felt worried suddenly that he made fun of her and Simone, too, when they weren't around, that he joked about them with other men and with these same boys. She thought of something James had said to her mother the other night at dinner. Elizabeth had been talking about Mike and how strange it was that he did so many good deeds in the world and then acted so stingy with Rae. And James said that lots of nurses and therapists and priests were secretly sadists; being so giving and helpful in the world helped them avoid the truth that they didn't really give a shit about anyone but themselves. They were takers, but they got to look and feel good about themselves because they were doing such compassionate work. James said that they were lifeless rocks in beautiful settings. That line had stuck with her.

Peter and the kids played for almost three hours; then Peter bought them all sodas and, driving home, told them about his glory days at college, where he'd played doubles on the tennis team. Rosie suddenly understood that he must have believed for a while that he could really be someone, ranked in the world, living on his winnings, traveling all around to tournaments. But here he was, a pro at a cheesy little club in the suburbs, spending all day teaching ladies to play and then mocking them behind their backs—to *kids*.

On the trip home Simone sat in the way back, and although the van's last seat was designed for two, she was squished between two sixteen-year-old boys. The handsomest one was named Jason, and Simone seemed to have a crush on him. She sounded wiggly, warm. Rosie tried not to listen, tried to hear instead what Peter and another boy in the front seat were talking about. She watched Peter's handsome face in the rearview mirror, lit by streetlights they passed. He was reciting one of his stupid little poems: Jack and Jill went up the hill, each with a dollar and quarter; Jill came down with two dollars fifty—who says they went up for water? And she saw that he loved being with his best seven kids, so young and gifted and eager, driving along in his brand-new van, which still smelled of leather—and she saw that in the center of all this he was a rock, and her heart brimmed with grief for him.

Elizabeth and James, lying in bed that night, both with books propped open on their chests, listened to the two girls downstairs trying to go to sleep in the living room. They had come in from practice, plopped down at the kitchen table with James and Elizabeth, eaten gigantic bowls of cereal, and then set up their sleeping bags on the dark green living room rug.

James was listening now, hoping for a classic Simone moment. Elizabeth started to ask him something, but he put his fingers to his lips and tilted his head toward the open bedroom door.

"Do you ever think about being crucified?" they heard Simone say.

"*God,* Simone."

"But you know, think about Jesus. I was thinking about him yesterday. See? You'd just hang there like this—pooping all over yourself until you died, with people watching."

"Oh God, Simone," said Rosie. "That's so disgusting."

"Wait! This is really incredible—you need to tell everyone this. You should definitely tell Rae. You know how Jesus's life from nineteen to thirty-three is missing? And no one knows where he was? Well, I found out. He was in Budapest."

"What on earth was he doing there?"

"Learning Buddhism."

Elizabeth and James began to laugh, with their hands clapped over their mouths. Elizabeth rolled closer to him and buried her face against his chest.

"I'm not going to marry a Christian, though," Simone continued. "I want to marry a Mafia guy. They're cute. But unfaithful."

"I'm going to go downstairs and tuck them in," she told James, who shook his head.

"Just let them be. They'll fall asleep soon." Elizabeth glanced at the clock. It was nearly eleven.

"Hey, you two," she called down. "Go to sleep!" The conversation in the living room stopped for a moment; then the girls dissolved into helpless giggling. When they were together, they could get lost in full-on absurdity, in the wonderful headiness of recognizing absurdity everywhere. It was like emotional surfing for them—the vigorous laughter right on the verge of tears, both riding the waves of pure intensity. And it was safe. Because when you played with such intensity, you had to do it with someone else; by yourself it led to total craziness, and you might not find your way back.

Finally the girls settled down. There was silence, except for the sound of James turning the pages of the book he was reading. "I'm going to go down and tuck the girls in," Elizabeth said again, but as it turned out, they did not need her to. They were tucked in against each other. In the golden, old-fashioned light of the street lamp, they looked like girls in a daguerreotype. Their sleeping faces were lovely, so terribly open that Elizabeth nearly moaned, wanting to put up a shield around them. Simone stirred and rubbed one cheek against her shoulder, like a deer rubbing its antlers, her lips in the pout of a sleeping toddler, not the saucy sulky lips of adolescence. Elizabeth looked up at the living room windows and went to pull the curtains. Images of teenage boys, Luther, Peter Billings, flickered through her head. She rolled her eyes at herself: What were you going to do, hire a bodyguard for your kid? Rosie cleared her throat and flung an arm over her head like a ballerina, then settled back in against Simone. They were so still in the lamplight, pure unconscious children, so free of the isometric tension of wanting to be noticed and wanting to be invisible, and Elizabeth watched them sleep for a while longer before going back upstairs.

nine

ROSIE did not think her mother was doing very well this spring, and it filled her with a deep concern. Her mother seemed more distracted, sadder. She seemed to be looking around all the time, like you do when you first hear the drone of approaching mosquitoes or planes. She kept this to herself for as long as she could. Then, late in the afternoon on the first really hot Saturday of the year, when Veronica was out dancing at Stinson Beach, playing with her grown-up friends under the hot chalky sun, Rosie discovered her mother lying in bed beneath plain white sheets. The curtains were drawn, and her mother's face looked as though all the parts that were juicy and alive were gone. When Rosie asked, from the doorway, if she was sick, she said no, no, she was just having a bad day.

Rosie did not want to go into the dark lonely bedroom. She remained at the door trying to figure out what to do.

"Want me to open the curtains?" she asked. Elizabeth shook her head. "You sure?" Elizabeth nodded. Rosie frowned. "Where's James?"

"He's taping his radio spot in the city."

"Mommy," Rosie implored after a moment of silence. "Veronica put on a tie-dyed dress and went out to Stinson *Beach. Dancing.*" Her mother rubbed her eyes wearily. Rosie scowled and looked to the ceiling for help. "What could have happened, Mommy, that's so bad you have to go to bed?" She walked slowly into the dark still room and sat down on the bed. She felt for her mother's long skinny shin under the top sheet. "You weren't depressed at breakfast."

"I stood up Charles," Elizabeth said finally. "While you were gone. His nurse just called a little while ago to remind me that I was supposed to have come for a visit this morning."

"God, Mom. Lighten up. I'll go visit Charles later—I'll ride my bike over, okay? And James always says we appreciate mistakes in this family. Right?" Elizabeth nodded. "Right, Mommy?" Elizabeth closed her eyes. Rosie sat calmly beside her for a moment, smelling the stale air of the bedroom. She watched her mother for a moment, staring at her unseen eyes. She imagined herself a hypnotist, able to command her mother in perfect silence to get out of bed, to wake from the trance, put bright floral sheets on the bed, and get up and cook. She rubbed her mother's slender hand until Elizabeth opened her eyes. Rosie looked at her sternly; then, wearing a look of wounded virtue, she got up off the bed and went to open the curtains, the way you would for someone who was lying in bed hungover—the way she used to in the old days. Below, the garden glowed with color. "Here's what I think we should do," she continued from the window. "I'll go visit Charles today; you can go by tomorrow. I think maybe you should get up, put on something nice, and go garden." She felt bossy and slightly foolish, but she also felt that she was doing the right thing. So she turned away from her mother's amused gaze, threw open the windows, and with her shoulders thrown back, chest puffed out like Patton's, she took a noisy breath of the fresh air that wafted in.

ELIZABETH sat outside, working in the garden in the late afternoon sun. There was a lot to do, a lot of cutting back and weeding, cutting off dead heads in the rosebushes. You need a garden you can fuss with, she thought. Otherwise, what is the point of having a garden? She studied an outrageous bearded iris, white with a purple border, breathed in the musky perfume of her antique roses, traced the geometric pattern of a fern with a dirty finger, these ferns like exotic doilies. She smiled at her poppies that grew pell-mell near the fence. Leave us alone, she imagined them saying, we'll be fine.

She stared off into space, missing James. One good thing came as a result of his first book's good press: a gig on the local public radio station, a five-minute essay once a month on any topic of his choosing. There were drawbacks, the main one being that he had to work with a difficult producer, whose name was Mel. Also, the three-page essays usually took a week to perfect. But they were bringing him a small following, and a few stations up the coast rebroadcast the show via satel-

lite, and besides, it paid two hundred dollars a shot. So he wrote his essays and some articles and book reviews for some magazines, while
waiting for the stamina to begin a new novel.

Her azaleas came in colors from snow white to violet. She had read
that the Japanese love azaleas, love the explosion of color, and that lots
of Japanese gardens have very old azaleas in them. And therefore,
Elizabeth thought, I respect azaleas, because the Japanese know things.

She loved her dark brown irises, so statuesque and velvety, like
Eleanor Roosevelt. And she loved her reeds and bamboo and
grasses—because this garden was not all about flowers; flowers fade.

But Elizabeth's real love was and would always be her roses.
Sometimes she came out and set up a folding chair, just to sit with
them. She experienced a tremendous feeling of force from them, like a
low hum or silent white noise—almost a sense of sitting in the middle
of waves of rhythm and color. In the morning, wet, the garden felt
crisp and clean and new, and in the afternoon, tired; like the rest of us,
it had to get through the whole goddamn day. And toward dusk, you
could actually feel the garden wind down.

She weeded around a perfect red rose called a Mr. Lincoln, thinking
for a moment about how briefly he blooms and how that was one of
his most beautiful qualities. And then she blinked, looking up, puzzled
by movement across the street in Amy Haas's empty old house—a blur
on the porch, big as a human, disappearing around a corner.

She stared, craning her neck as if this would let her see around the
corner, and after a moment she saw a hulking brown shape in the back
of the house. Whatever or whoever it was appeared to be bent over at
the waist. She couldn't see well in the fading afternoon light, but she
thought she saw someone dark or light brown step out like a shadow
from behind a wall for the briefest moment, before disappearing again
even deeper in the beams and scaffolding. And suddenly she thought,
it's Luther, stoop-shouldered lumbering Luther. That's him across the
street, watching. Fear flooded her, and she gaped at the deserted struc-
ture. Now there was no movement in the building, and—her mouth
dry with anxiety—she stood stock-still wondering if she had been
imagining things. But what if she had seen him, here, on their street,
fifty yards from their home, watching?

She got up slowly, unsteady, not breathing, and went inside to watch
from her kitchen window. But there was nothing. Now she was no
longer sure. She stood there watching the silent empty house for over

half an hour. No one appeared. Licking her lips, pushing the hair away from her face, she stood watching vigilantly, telling herself she was crazy, but unable to pull herself away. She locked the front door and waited for someone to come home. When, after half an hour, no one had, she picked up Rosie's racket and, holding it like a club, walked over to Amy Haas's old house to investigate. There was no sign that anyone else had been there that day, unless it was a deer, for there were only long hoof marks in the new grass behind the house, in the green furring over of the yard.

ROSIE felt so clumsy and afraid sitting next to Charles while he slept. His nurse had been surprised to find her at the door and expressed dismay that because it was so late in the day, she didn't know if he'd wake. But Rosie had thrust her bouquet of yellow tea roses at the nurse and gone in to sit by his bed.

She sat watching him sleep, trying to will him awake by the sheer force of her stare. He smelled so different since he got so sick—of medicines and alcohol, of old clothes like something from the as-is department of a secondhand store. Boy, talk about as-is, she thought, studying his face, his emaciated body under the blanket; he looked as torn and worn as some terrible tweed jacket Luther might wear in early spring, when it was still cool out. Charles seemed barely alive. He smelled like the stuff old people put their teeth in. He smelled like the inside of an electric shaver. He smelled like old hair and soap and toenails. Once she had spent the night here with him after Grace had died, and she had found his electric shaver plugged in to the socket next to the bathroom sink, but the top was off the metal shaver part, and she could see and smell his old hair inside the metal part, and she felt like she was spying on one of his most private places.

There was a plate of orange wedges on the little hospital table by his bed, oranges on an aqua blue saucer, and a number of memories popped into her head all at once, like bubbles—memories of going to the Petaluma dump with Charles all those times over the years, ever since he moved back to town and bought the old Ford pickup. They'd fill the back with garbage and magazines and head up to Petaluma. He liked to put country music on the radio for their dump runs. He drove slowly because he was old even then. It would just be the two of them. Who else would even have wanted to go? After driving on the freeway for half an hour, they'd leave the main road that ran into Petaluma and head up the little two-lane through the woods that led to the bumpy dirt road that led to the dump. You could smell the sweet decay and smoke way before you got there, and Charles would roll down his window and look over at her with glee. "There it is, doll," he would say, and they'd inhale it like it was fresh bread baking in the oven, smiling at each other, pantomiming delight. It was the smell of a thousand oranges going bad, a thousand oranges and always some smoke and something strange like ether or a combustible that the dump people must pour all over the garbage to get it to burn or to kill the little brown rats you'd see scuttling in and out of the piles of garbage. The guy at the booth would tell them where to pull in—or rather, where to back up the truck—and Charles would back up to the pit and get out slowly, the way he moved with a little arthritis and just generally being old and no spring chicken, as he was the first to say. And he'd open the back of the truck and he and Rosie would start pulling out stuff, pitching it down into the pit, working alongside other families who were doing the same thing; you'd see an ancient *Life* magazine go tumbling by, one you really wished you could look at, and an old Snoopy doll, or one old brown wing tip with mildew on the toes. There would always be all these odd people, besides the regular dumpers like her and Charles and the other families. The other people were like the dumpees; maybe they were vets or something, she wasn't sure, but there were always all these mysterious people in Budweiser hats, like rag people who came out of nowhere to paw through all the stuff people were throwing out and load it into their own crummy dumpy cars. And the thing was, Charles would always stop and talk to everyone, like it was right after church, just the way her daddy used to talk to everyone when they'd walk into town together. Charles didn't go to church very much. But he'd stop and admire something one of the rag people had salvaged, a hubcap or an old toaster, as if he were at the hardware store in Bayview, helping someone pick out just the right crescent wrench.

After a while she had to get up and take the plate of orange wedges out to the nurse, because the smell was making her feel too weird. "I don't think he wants these," she explained, handing the plate to the puzzled woman.

"Is he awake?" the nurse asked, with surprise.

Rosie looked helplessly into her face for a long moment. "No," she said finally. Shrugging, the nurse took the plate off to the kitchen without another word.

He slept the whole time she was there. She kept clearing her throat loudly, but at the same time she was secretly glad she could just watch him sleep, not have to try to think of things to say. She thought back to that first time he let go of her when she was riding her red two-wheeler and how when she turned back and found him waving to her, she was so afraid because she didn't know how to turn the bike. She was sure that if she turned the wheels at all, the bike would fall over, so she slowed down as far as she could and kept on pedaling straight ahead, praying for there to be no cars in the crosswalk, which there weren't, and finally she came to the cul-de-sac at the end of the street where she lived, and she braked gently and slowly turned the handlebars. It had felt like trying to turn a wagon train around, but she hadn't fallen over.

ELIZABETH was walking across the street swinging Rosie's racket and looking discouraged, as if she had just lost an important match, when Rosie came riding up on her bike. Rosie braked to a stop next to her mother and glared.

"What are you doing, Mama? Why do you have my racket?"

"I . . . I thought I saw someone hiding over at Amy's house. I—"

"You were going to hit them on the head with my racket?" Rosie said incredulously. "Why didn't you take James's baseball bat? That costs like twenty bucks. And Mommy, if you see someone you think is a bad guy, you call the police. Don't you even know *any*thing?" She pulled the racket roughly out of Elizabeth's hand, pedaled across the street to their house, lay the bike on its side in the front yard, and stalked up the garden path, swatting at thin air.

ROSIE was so unpleasant at dinner that Elizabeth stopped feeling guilty about having gone to bed. James had gotten home from the city, where he had taped his essay for broadcast sometime the following week, and he had bought Thai takeout with part of the check Mel had given him. They talked about their days. Rosie told him about Charles, how he had slept all day, but she made sure not to include her mother in the conversation.

The food was all so delicious, pork with spinach and peanuts, pad Thai, chicken to dip into spicy sweet-and-sour sauce. Elizabeth savored each forkful, the friendliness of her husband's voice. Rosie glumly pushed a bite of pork around on her plate with long slow strokes, as if mopping something up, but James and Elizabeth were so glad to see each other that they mostly just talked about nothing in particular.

"Can I come to the tournament with you tomorrow?" James asked Rosie. A tournament had started in Fremont, and Rosie wasn't scheduled to play until the following day.

She shrugged. "If you want," she said.

"Hey, baby," Elizabeth said sharply, "you are sitting on my *last* nerve now." Rosie gave her a long sideways look. Why do you have to be such an insolent little shit? Elizabeth wondered, looking away: this guy's willing to give up a whole Sunday to cheer you on. And you're so lucky to be loved by him.

And he did love Rosie so. He loved her even when she was stomping around; he loved her even through the tears and hysteria, the grief caused by feeling left out at school or losing a match on the circuit, by unrequited love or raging hormones. He loved her even when he whispered to Elizabeth that she was the she-devil. He loved her tonight, when she squeezed all the lime on her own pad Thai, leaving none for anyone else.

And he even loved her the next morning when she didn't return his greeting. She was sitting catatonic at the table and staring off unseeing, the posture and mood he called Tar Baby in Bayview. Coming upon her this way, James peered down, positioning himself in the path of her gaze, Brer Rabbit first laying eyes on the beautiful creation.

"And how," he asked with panache, "is your disposition situated, O lovely lady?"

And when Rosie glowered and said nothing, James drew back and said with a strong Southern accent, "Your shyness stirs my heart."

"Why are you in such a good mood?" Elizabeth asked, watching him, feeling his happiness. After breakfast she had followed him upstairs into his office, where he had pushed around piles of paper and notecards until he found a small notebook. He tucked it into the back pocket of his jeans and sat down in front of his computer.

"I cannot work with you today," he told it. "Rosie has a tournament." Elizabeth stood behind him smiling. She began to rub his neck, and he let his head drop onto his chest. "Me and my computer finally know how to start our new book," he said.

"You do? Honestly?"

"Yep," he said. "Me and my computer, we are ready for love."

It had been months since he had gotten any decent work done, months since his first novel hit the stores, garnered some good reviews, and sold less than two thousand copies.

"When are you going to start?"

"Monday." She stroked aside some of the soft brown hair that covered the collar of his shirt, rubbed the pale skin underneath, pushing her thumbs against the taut ropy muscles that betrayed the tension he carried, the tension of being a writer, a husband, a dad. "Oh, don't stop," he moaned.

"We need to go in a minute," she said, but she rubbed his shoulders anyway, and he groaned. There were notecards taped to the wall by his desk, notecards on which he'd written little messages to himself, notecards he didn't want to lose in the lovely chaos of his desk. She read them now as she stood behind him, rubbing his shoulders. Some she had read before, but there was a new one. "Fiber adds bulk to the stool," read one piece of newsprint taped to an index card, "and among Finns stool tends to be three times larger than among New Yorkers."

"Honey," she asked, stopping her massage to point to the card. "How on earth will you use this?"

He raised his head slowly to see what she was reading.

"Writing," he said rather primly, "is an extremely mysterious process."

HE helped Rosie pack for her match that day, bringing her a washcloth, sunscreen, a waxed paper bag of cashews and raisins mixed together. And he brought along a tape to play in the car as they drove to the East Bay, an old Phoebe Snow tape he knew she liked.

TWO days later, the morning was socked in with fog. Children were milling around the Fremont Golf and Tennis Club, studying the draw, watching the matches, brooding, playing cards, playing Ping-Pong.

Simone had lost the day before; Rosie was in the quarterfinals. Rosie and her opponent had been sent to the junior college courts to play, and she had forbidden James or Elizabeth to come along. So they sat on the sidelines at the club with the other parents, watching the match on the nearest court, where a boys' fourteen-and-under semifinal was in play. In the hour since they'd arrived, James had already called his answering machine twice. There were no messages.

Dane Williams, seeded number one in the boys' fourteen-and-under draw, had been the unrequited object of Rosie's affection the year before. He was playing a boy no one had ever heard of, a kid half his size, who stood on the baseline and returned everything that came over the net. Dane won the first set easily, but the smaller boy was holding his own in the second, and at three games apiece, he broke Dane's serve. Two games later, Dane left the court hunched over, wiping at his eyes. He went and sat under a tree and cried.

"Oh, I can't bear this," said Elizabeth.

"But, honey. The little kid deserves to win," said James. "He's playing the top seed, someone forty pounds heavier, and he's just playing his little heart out."

"But there always has to be a loser, doesn't there?" said Elizabeth. "Oh, well. I wonder how Rosie's doing."

Rosie was seeded fourth, which meant she had been expected to get to the semifinals, and this was the round she was playing. Her opponent was an eleven-year-old named Marisa DeMay who'd won her quarterfinal round by default—the second seed had come down with leg cramps during the match. Rosie had been relieved just to get to the round she was expected to make, but now she was dismayed to discover that this unseeded girl, who'd gotten into the semis on a fluke, was actually very good. Rosie was so anxious about losing—even before they'd started keeping score—that it threw her game off. She and Marisa were playing long hard rallies, and Rosie had just barely won the first set, seven-five. Mrs. DeMay was doing needlepoint on the sidelines (an eyeglass case with a picture of teddy bears) and rarely looked up. Rosie was spooked. Her usual strategy and strength were consistency and infinite patience. Other players—Simone, for instance—lacked the patience for endless rallies and would try to put the ball away out of sheer boredom, but Rosie could wait all day for an opening if she had to. She didn't care. She just wouldn't miss until, like a break in the weather, a corridor opened down which she could discharge a lethal ground stroke.

But today, against tiny little Marisa, she was in trouble. It was like playing Thumbelina, except that Thumbelina hit as hard as a boy. On top of it all, she bounced around a lot and made an annoying squeaky noise. Rosie, a foot taller, two years older, was unnerved. She wanted the trophy so badly she could taste it, the trophy she'd get for playing in the finals, and here was this runt on the other side, chasing down every shot like a crazy little Chihuahua. She thought of her mother in bed the other day, depressed and overwhelmed.

She began patting in her second serves, like the old people did at the club—"Hey, nice serve, Ruth Ann," Peter would have said—and chanting to herself in an incantory way, "Head down, head down, one two three one two three." Tiny Marisa flitted around the court making squeaky sounds of effort, a little cat toy that just wouldn't miss.

Both of them held serve until four all, and fear beat inside Rosie. She could hardly manage a forehand, while little Squeak-jump on the other side batted the ball from side to side. Rosie served a puffball forehand at thirty all, and Marisa put it away down the line. Adrenaline flooded Rosie like a sudden fever. Her hands were shaking; one more point and Marisa would break serve, be ahead five to four, zipping along on a roll, with her irritating mother stitching away, maybe humming. Rosie began to fixate on Marisa's mother and whether she was in fact humming or not. She was about to serve, but stopped and tilted her head toward Mrs. DeMay, straining to hear.

"What?" said Marisa.

"Nothing," said Rosie.

It was hard to catch her breath. She served a deep loopy backhand that miraculously dropped in, and Squeak-jump lobbed it back, and Rosie pushed back a forehand that barely landed over the net, and Marisa tapped it back, and they rallied for this critical point like that—dinking, pushing, patting endlessly, until Marisa hit a ball near the baseline. And it was not solidly on the line, but it was definitely in, touching half an inch of white. It was the most basic rule of tennis sportsmanship that you always gave your opponent the benefit of any doubt. If her ball was so close you honestly couldn't say for sure whether it was in or out, you played it as in. This ball was definitely, though barely, in, and time became thick and vacuumy and so silent that it was almost noise, and Rosie turned as if to hit this backhand, saw that Mrs. DeMay was reaching for something she'd dropped, and without really thinking about it, Rosie caught the ball on her racket and called it out.

Nonchalantly, heart pounding, she whacked the ball over the net to a stunned Marisa and walked to the forehand court.

"That wasn't out," said Marisa. "That hit the line."

"No," said Rosie innocently. "It was just barely out."

Marisa looked over at her mother. Her mother looked up kindly at Rosie.

"It was out," Rosie explained.

"I saw it. I looked at it," said Marisa. Rosie shrugged sympathetically.

"Why don't we take it over?" she offered.

"But that was my game!"

"Look, I'm sorry." Rosie walked to the alley and pointed with her racket to a spot just outside the line, a spot where a part of her was now convinced the ball had landed. "It was right here. But you can take two if you want."

Marisa looked with despair at her mother, who shrugged and held up her hands.

"Sorry," said Rosie. "Want to take two?"

After a moment of fidgeting, Marisa walked to the baseline to receive the serve. Rosie felt strangely calm, even cold, calculating: after she tossed the ball, she suddenly glanced away, as if distracted, and Marisa was thrown off by the sudden movement. She hit Rosie's easy serve into the net, and began to fall apart. She was fighting back more tears, while Rosie stood there waiting nicely, almost encouragingly. Then she nonchalantly aced her. On the next point, at ad-in, she once again glanced away after the toss, which so startled and distracted Marisa that she hit the ball over the fence.

"Four-five," said Rosie. A strange maturity filled her, and excitement. She felt terribly sorry for Marisa: when they changed over, Marisa was staring at the ground, so teary as to sound asthmatic. Rosie broke her serve for the match in four crisp points.

The mother made everything okay, gathering up her embroidery as she gushed over both of them: what a wonderful match, she said, and they'd both played so well, and to Marisa, wouldn't her father be proud that she had gotten so many games off a seeded player? She had cold cans of orange soda in an ice chest she kept in the trunk of her car, and Marisa began to cheer up, standing by the car, and Rosie looked at her proudly, for getting so many games off a seed, and then Mrs. DeMay leaned forward to tug at a loose button at the neck of Rosie's shirt, and it came off in her hands, as if she had just produced a coin from behind Rosie's ear.

"It was just about to drop off," Mrs. DeMay said. Rosie reached for it apologetically. "You sit down," she instructed Rosie. "I am going to sew that right back on."

"Oh, no," said Rosie, reaching again for the button, which Mrs. DeMay had already dropped into the pocket of her sundress. Rosie watched with disbelief as Mrs. DeMay began threading an embroidery needle with white thread. Give me the fucking button, Rosie wanted to cry. This could not be happening. Marisa was sitting in the dirt, taking off a shoe and sock to check for blisters, and Rosie looked around for help and, seeing none, saw herself smashing nice Mrs. DeMay over the head with her racket. As if in a dream, Mrs. DeMay led her to a chair beside the court and had her sit down, while she stood bending over Rosie, holding Rosie's shirt out by the collar, with hands that smelled of soap and lotion, hands that moved close to her and then away, close and away, as Rosie sat there hardly breathing, her head level with Mrs. DeMay's stomach, smelling a faint womanly underwear smell and con- nected by a long white thread to the mother of the girl she had cheated.

THE cold clamminess of the fog soothed her. It covered everything, erased the world, the colors and shapes. Sitting in the back seat on the way back to the club, Mrs. DeMay and Marisa bubbling away in the front, Rosie saw in her mind the Walt Disney paintbrush that magically washes color into the world and felt now the relief of its opposite, the fog. In the fog, ships hit icebergs and sink. She liked the mystery, the shroud. It meant you got to wear jackets at night, blankets when you slept. It surrounded her now with silence, a silence she didn't hear any- where else, and she realized how profoundly in this car with two other people, she was alone.

baby baby

one

THERE was a part of Elizabeth that was relieved that the friendship with Hallie had suffered such a setback when Rosie was excluded from the dinner party, not because of the company Hallie kept—girls who were said to drink, girls who had dates with older boys—but because of the damn trampoline. It would be too much if after forty years of sneering at her mother's fear, it swallowed up Rosie, the way the surface of a pool swallows a diver seamlessly. She lived in fear of ironic endings.

But early this morning, Simone had come by at breakfast to say she'd been invited over to Hallie's to use the trampoline. There was no school: it was "staff development day," whatever that meant. And the question was did Rosie want to come.

"You're going to Hallie's?" Rosie asked in disbelief.

"What's so strange about me going to Hallie's?"

"You've never been there before, right?"

"Well, I'm going to go there today. Is there something wrong with that?"

And Rosie said no, no thank you. She said with great dignity that she would see Simone the next night, when Veronica picked Rosie up for a dance at a nearby club, where the next big tournament began the following day. Then Simone insisted they go into Rosie's room to talk privately. Elizabeth kept expecting the two of them to reemerge and leave together for Hallie's, but Rosie, who had been acting distant and odd since the tournament in Fremont, prowled behind as Simone walked out the front door, waving good-bye as if forever. Elizabeth coaxed Rosie into the kitchen, where it was light and warm, but Rosie did not feel like talking. She sat looking bored and long-suffering, until

Elizabeth said she could go. Then she went upstairs to her dark smelly room and put on a rap cassette.

"I STILL want him to call so badly," Rae said over the phone sometime later. "I mean, I know it's like wanting Norman Bates to call. But I still do."

"Of course you do," Elizabeth said. "Look. The way you feel now—betrayed, strung out, abandoned? It will look like fucking *heaven* compared to what it would be like if he got into therapy and married you. He'd come home from his important work, and he'd be completely indifferent to you. There'd be nothing left for you. If you asked for any love and assurance from him at all, he'd look at you like you wanted him to go retile the bathroom that night."

"Tell me what to do."

"Just don't. Don't call. Then you get to not debase yourself. That's a lot."

Rae cried for a few minutes over the phone. Elizabeth listened quietly, breathing soft sounds of condolence from time to time. When she finally heard Rae sigh with exhaustion, she spoke. "The good news is, Rosie needs you," she said. "Hallie and Simone are spending the morning together, and Rosie feels very left out. Can you take her to her tennis lesson this morning? And then maybe help her shop for something to wear to a tennis dance tomorrow tonight?"

"Of course I can," said Rae. "And I am going to fill my house with votive candles, praying all morning for Jesus to slather those snotty little jerks who were mean to her with acne. And tsutsu gamushi for Hallie."

"What's tsutsu gamushi?"

"Dreaded Japanese river fever."

ELIZABETH sat with her daughter on Rosie's bed while they waited for Rae's arrival. Rosie picked at the calluses on her palms with great annoyance. She was wearing the same huge black shorts she'd worn to the last school dance and a voluminous brown T-shirt of James's. She looked as scrawny and bewildered as a wet cat.

"Do you want to talk about it?" Elizabeth asked delicately.

"What's there to talk about?" asked Rosie. She stretched out on the unmade bed and shielded her eyes with one cupped hand. "Mom? Why did you even have me?"

Elizabeth stroked Rosie's skinny shoulderblade. "I know exactly how you feel," she said. "Honey, it's horrible being a kid. Don't let anyone tell you differently."

"I thought these were supposed to be the best years of my life."

"Whoever said that?"

"It's something you hear."

"Well, it's the great palace lie. These are the hardest years. Sometimes you just have to find some great company and wait for a little time to pass. I felt like a total misfit, too. I used to feel all this homicidal envy and loathing for people who seemed to be doing so well, the beautiful popular people. My first year in college, I was so obsessed with the sororities—I hated them and felt completely wretched and rejected by the girls in them. I felt like I wanted to die when they didn't pick me during pledge week."

"How could they not want you?" Rosie asked.

Elizabeth shrugged. "I was an oddball. And I *hated* them—why would they choose someone who thought they were scum of the earth? But then it got better. And it's gotten better ever since. Now maybe I'm still kind of a mess sometimes, but I have great company now. I have you, James, Rae, Lank, Simone."

"Charles."

"Charles. And this makes all the difference in the world."

"I hate being an oddball. I hate that I don't fit in. I hate that I'm kind of a loser."

Oh, her mother wanted to say, you're a lot of things, Rosie. We all are. You're good and caring and accomplished, you're ambitious and lazy, selfish and greedy, dark and light. And you're more beautiful than anyone you compare yourself to. Just different—the worst thing at thirteen to be. And I look at you sometimes, and I feel like you're also the bird who just flew by.

But what she said was "I know, baby."

Elizabeth watched Rosie waiting out on the street for Rae to arrive, skinny little frame, stick arms. She longed to rush out and hold her but could see that what she needed was space to breathe and regain her dignity. James had said during a recent bad patch with Rosie that because everything was such a big deal with her, it taught you that nothing really is. But what Elizabeth saw now was her daughter standing slumped and pressed, as if up against an invisible wall, her social life and self-esteem a wasteland, her neck as long and thin as a bird's. She wanted to explain it all to Rosie—that we're all yearning for something, for there to be a meadow somewhere, and that you can miss it by a mile or, even worse, discover that it's not really there, but still not be destroyed. Hurt, shocked, even annoyed, but not destroyed.

She watched her through the window until Rae pulled up.

Rosie spent the night with Rae. She started out in a sleeping bag on the floor, but in the moonlight the loom towered over her like a woolly monster. He stared at her, smiled. She tried to think of other things, things that didn't scare her, but her mind turned to thoughts of hugeness. Charles had told her last year that the world weighed two hundred million million tons, and it was just too huge to think about when you only weighed eighty pounds yourself. Also, Rae was weaving a piece of cloth that had dragonflies in it, and Rosie remembered learning in fifth grade that the insects that spiders eat every year weigh more than the entire human population of the earth, and it disturbed her to death. She lay in the dark fearing the size of outer space. After a while she got up and tiptoed over to Rae's bed and gently shook Rae awake.

"Rae," she said softly. "Rae."

Rae opened her eyes.

"What's the matter, sweetheart?"

"I wondered if I could sleep here with you."

"Of course you can. Here." Rae pulled down the blanket and sheet next to her, and Rosie crawled in, feeling as shy as a deer.

"Better?

"Um-hmm."

"Good night. I love you."

"Love you, too."

The bed was so warm, and it smelled like bread. She listened to Rae falling asleep, breathing slowly, quietly. The cloth with the dragonflies was for a rock star in San Francisco. A friend of Rae's would sew it into a jacket for him, and they would sell it for a thousand dollars. She had watched Rae weaving for a while that night, taking thin air and some yarns and making something you could wrap yourself in on a cold foggy day. The cloth Rae was weaving seemed almost alive, full of light, soft mossy green, camel-colored birds and the palest yellow drag-onflies. It was like having a landscape inside, like a painting, but with fibers. Rosie had been here a few weeks ago when Rae was just begin-ning the piece, with all of her yarns on the floor, and Rosie and Rae had gotten down on all fours to move them around, feel the textures, and try out colors side by side. It was funny, how there could be colors you didn't like very much, like the pale yellow, because you didn't look good in it, and you put it side by side with something else, like the camel, the lion-colored yarn, and like Rae said, you made a marriage, a third color, and it made you like the first color for giving you the third.

Sometimes Rosie thought Rae was the most beautiful woman she had ever seen, with that thick auburn hair piled on top of her head and those rich warm almond-shaped eyes. She loved the little pinches at the end of Rae's nose. They made her look like an English fashion model. When she was younger, she and Sharon Thackery used to call those little indents Rae's proton nobulators. It was the best phrase they had ever invented. This made her smile to remember. She lay beside Rae and imagined the creaky little sound of the treadle, the mechanical, rhythmic thump of the beater, the murmur of the yarn, the whisper of Rae's busy hands. Thinking of that rhythm, breathing in that warm smell of bread, she fell asleep.

two

VERONICA picked Rosie up after dinner the next night and took the two girls to an oldies dance at the club. Simone was immediately asked to dance by one of the eighteen-year-olds. Rosie watched them dance to an Elvis song, and then another, and then slow dance to the Beatles. Her heart longed to slow dance. One boy she knew asked her to dance on the next song; she loved every moment, especially afterward when they stood together waiting to see whether they felt like dancing again. Rosie would have danced to the national anthem, but the boy deemed the next song too slow and walked off the dance floor. She followed along until he hooked up with some sixteen-year-old boys, who swallowed him up in a circle, leaving her outside. Her heart sank. She felt a little as if she were a runner in a relay race, passing him off to these new runners, standing there on the track watching them run the next lap.

She flushed, seeing herself through their eyes—skinny, flat, homely—and she tried to say good-bye to the boy with whom she'd been dancing, but he was talking to another boy. She went looking for Simone.

Some of the other thirteen- and fourteen-year-old girls were standing in a pack against the display case full of club trophies and plaques, looking over each other's shoulders, pretending not to care. Most were chewing gum.

"Hey," said Rosie, shouting over the noise of the band.

"Hey yourself," said Deb Hall, one of the girls Rosie and Simone faced most often in doubles finals. "Want some gum?"

"Sure. You seen Simone?"

"She went off with Jason Drake."

Rosie was shocked. He was eighteen, one of Peter's best players, although not one who was nationally ranked. Rosie thought back to that night when they'd all gone to the indoor courts together, when Simone and Jason had been all warm and squishy in the way back of the van. He was cute enough to be in the movies. A lot of the tennis girls had crushes on him. She remembered that once last summer he and his old doubles partner had drunk a bottle of peppermint schnapps behind the bushes of the clubhouse during a tournament dance in Sacramento, and when they came back inside Jason's doubles partner had thrown up all over a candy machine near the dance floor. He had been expelled from that season's tournaments and hadn't been back.

"Where did they go?"

"Out that door," said Deb.

Rosie studied the exit. She held up one finger, as if she needed a moment to think or was trying to figure out the direction of the wind. She burlesqued a look of befuddlement, at which everyone laughed, and then she left.

A bunch of juniors were milling around the lawn, talking about their matches, both the ones they'd played last week and the ones they would play tomorrow, and Rosie saw an older girl named Natalie, one of the best of the eighteen-year-olds, who'd always treated Rosie like a younger sister. She was totally cool, like a beautiful blonde hoodlum, someone you'd see on a street corner smoking cigarettes with guys on motorcycles. She had even given Rosie one of her old purses last year, the coolest imaginable purse, worn brown leather with fringe and a silver Indian button. Rosie loved it, although she did not really need a purse yet.

Natalie was standing around tonight with a mixed group of older teenagers, drinking Cokes from the can. She was so friendly that Rosie could hardly believe it.

"Hey," said Natalie. "Why aren't you dancing?"

"I was looking for Simone."

"Yeah? She's in one of those boats over there," she said, pointing with her Coke can.

"With Jason Drake?" Rosie said, feigning nonchalance. She felt like a hummingbird vibrating next to a beautiful flower, suspended with nowhere to land. Natalie smiled. Her face was very soft when she looked at Rosie, almost maternal. She cocked her head when Rosie spoke, sensing her discomfort. And she nodded almost apologetically.

"You want some of this?" Natalie said, holding out the can. The other girls looked at her skeptically. "Maybe you don't."

"Actually I would," said Rosie.

"Let me go get you a can of your own. This is—fortified." Rosie gulped. She couldn't help it. The older kids laughed. Rosie felt faint.

"I've got a nine o'clock match," she said, as if otherwise she'd be slamming down a few drinks with them right there on the spot.

"I guess Simone doesn't, then," said Natalie.

"Why?"

Natalie looked around to make sure no one could see her and then pantomimed taking a drink.

"Oh, man," said Rosie. "This is great. We've got a doubles match at noon."

"Well. She's out there on one of the boats at the end of the dock. I'm not sure she's in the mood for company right now, though."

Rosie trudged toward the water. Boards groaned beneath her; the water smelled like sweat and eucalyptus and gasoline. The mooring lines between the boats and their berths creaked, and a loose clamp on one boat banged against the mast. Foghorns mourned. "Simone?" Rosie called out in a half-whisper as she got to the last three boats. "Simone?" No one answered. Most of the boats were locked up and dark. In the second-to-last boat, a low light shone, and Rosie stood on the dock trying to decide what to do. "Simone?" she asked quietly. The hatch leading downstairs to the galley was open, the lock hanging in the darkness of the space above the stairs. "Simone?" She smelled the stench of dried-up old starfish on the pilings. Then she heard whispering, giggling, a boy and a girl, Simone. The boy said, "Oh, shit, you're kidding."

"Rosie?" Simone called out. "Is that you?"

Rosie glowered in the dark, now thoroughly exasperated.

"It's time to go, Simone," Rosie said, feeling like someone from the Old Testament. She poked her head down into the hold, saw shadowy shapes in the back, and once again the smells caught her, mixed her up. In one instant she smelled mildew, too much wet wood, paint and turpentine, faint smells of rotting food and old beer. She thought she smelled rat urine, she thought she smelled a place where people had once been sick to their stomachs, and it all smelled like the metallic edge of a toilet tank when people take off the lid to see why it isn't working. She saw a flash of skin in the back of the boat.

"I'll meet you there in a minute, okay?" said Simone.

"Okay," said Rosie. She stood on the dock with her eyes closed, imagined herself in the arms of a boy, in the arms of Jason Drake, slow dancing, kissing him, being kissed, held, loved, and she opened her eyes to gaze at the stars, stood gripping her own shoulders against the cold, hearing a wind indicator whir from the top of a mast, seeing in the cold starlight the starfish on the pilings.

THE next morning, Simone played worse than Rosie could ever remember, swatting easy forehands out, whacking backhands into the net, serving either aces or double faults. Luckily their opponents were terrible. Simone looked like she hadn't gotten any sleep. She yawned and snapped her gum as she walked petulantly around the court. There was no rapport between them. Rosie felt miserable, like an angry nagging mother, and on top of this she had to cover almost the whole court, running for shots that got past Simone at the net, keeping the ball in play at all costs. They won, but barely. When they walked to the net to shake hands, beginning with each other as always, Simone shook hands as if they had just had the most fun imaginable, and Rosie started to cry. She shook hands hastily with the girls they had just beaten and walked alone to the far edge of the club; there she sat on the side of an old oak where she couldn't be seen.

There was a pine tree just a few feet away, and the needles smelled as fresh as Christmas. She picked up fallen acorns and thought about living out here, under her oak, on acorn mush. Everything felt green and growing, like leaves and seeds and grasses and flowers filling the early summer air, and she smelled like sweat and fear, and she hated herself and she hated Simone. God, Simone was so stupid—what had she done with that boy on the boat, how far had she gone? First base, for sure, the kissing, wet kissing, but second base? Maybe. She thought so. She felt like a little rashy stick-figure person whom no one loved and a few people felt sorry for so they were nice to her—people like Natalie. She leaned her face forward into her knees, which were drawn up to her chest, and tried not to cry. She heard the chorus of birds in the trees above her, and every so often one bird made a chirp like when the battery on a smoke alarm gets low. She heard footsteps in the grass coming toward her. She thought for a moment that it might be Luther. She saw herself look up the length of his body, past his knees, past his pelvis, up to his dark bloodshot eyes. She imagined him smothering her, strangling her with his dirty-fingernail hands, raping her. Then she smelled Simone's cheap rose toilet water.

"Hey," said Simone.

"Hey."

Rosie slowly looked up from the ground where she sat with her back against the trunk of the oak. Simone stood there looking just like she did when she had to face the music with Veronica. Rosie's heart hardened.

"At least we won, huh?" Simone sat down Indian style in the grass, facing her. Rosie shrugged. "I feel really terrible," Simone continued, reaching for a big pine cone, and Rosie thought she meant because she'd played so badly, but then she whispered, "I drank with Jason. He wanted me to drink with him." Rosie felt sirens go off inside her chest, and she looked into Simone's face. Even hot and sweaty she was so pretty that you just wanted to stare at her. Wisps of fine blonde hair escaped from her ponytail and framed the heart-shaped face; there was a dusting of freckles across her small nose, and then those sleepy charcoal-gray eyes—Rosie had heard one of the men at their club call them bedroom eyes. Simone would not look at her. She picked a cigarette butt off the ground and tucked it into one woody scale of her pine cone, picked up a bit of green glass and tucked it higher up in the spiral of woody leaves; the cap of an acorn went into another slot, a bit of tin foil another. "We did things," she said.

She took out her gum and put it like a star at the top of the cone.

Shame flooded Rosie, and fear. "What things?" she asked in a tiny little voice. She held her breath and studied Simone's hands, gently draping grass over each scale, blade by blade.

"He didn't exactly put it in me, if that's what you mean. I mean, he didn't put it in all the way. Sort of more around the outside." Rosie's heart pounded like a sewing machine.

"Sort of more around the outside?" she asked. Simone nodded.

"Well, a little bit in for a second," she said. "One or two seconds." They looked at each other and then closed their eyes. Oh, thank you, said Rosie silently to God. Simone had not crossed over, or had not crossed over entirely. It was like someone who is a few breaths away from being dead, who could go all the way over into stillness, but who at the last second gasps and comes back. Rosie felt like she was taking the first breath after you've had the wind knocked out of you. She wondered what things would be like now, now that Simone had done this thing with the boy—whatever that thing was—that was almost sex. The thing that was almost going all the way, which maybe Simone was saying she hadn't exactly done. But how long could it last? She thought about the dreaminess on Simone's face when she described this stuff, how she seemed to sway slightly and gaze off like she was under a spell. But maybe it was because she didn't want to look at Rosie. Maybe, thought Rosie, she feels *guilty*. She imagined all the stuff Simone didn't tell her, about what she had done last night, the parts she wasn't ashamed of because you were supposed to be doing them now—the parts she might have, must have, loved. She wondered if they could still be best friends or if Simone needed older girls now who did this sort of thing too. But Simone said she hadn't crossed that line, and this made things much less hideous than they could have been. Rosie sighed with relief; in that moment the air was warm and the birds were singing in the middle of all the silence, and Rosie felt a little like she'd been alone on a desert island for a while, and a bottle with a message had floated up, and even though you might not know exactly where it came from, at least you knew that someone was out there.

three
_____

ELIZABETH, standing at the kitchen sink, watched Rosie get out of the front seat of J. Peter Billings's van one afternoon several days later. As he drove away, Rosie waved as gaily as a little kid watching a boat pull away from the dock, but as soon as the car had disappeared from sight, her entire bearing changed. Her shoulders caved in, and her head dropped almost to her chest. She came up the walkway looking like a depressed hunchback.

Peter was leaving, as he did every summer at this time, to accompany his two best boys to the nationals back east. Elizabeth watched Rosie whack a rock out of her way with the racket, the two-hundred-fifty-dollar racket. Then she stopped and looked around, as if someone had called to her, her face filled with resignation. Elizabeth rinsed the dish soap off her hands, dried them quickly, and smoothed some lotion into them as she walked to the front door to meet her child.

She paused with her hand on the inside doorknob. Something had been troubling Rosie lately, and Elizabeth had no idea what it might be. Was it Charles, growing weaker day by day? Was there a boy Rosie loved who didn't love her back? Rosie had spun away from Elizabeth into a barren place of her own, and Elizabeth wondered for an instant if she was up to the task of helping her slog her way back. She stared at the closed door and heard the soft shuffle of footsteps on the pebbly walkway. Her daughter's depression filled Elizabeth with bewilderment and despair. There's no hope, she thought, slowly opening the front door. We're all doomed, we're all being ground down by slime. And the sun is burning out.

"Hi, honey," she said brightly, opening the door.

Rosie stood on the doorstep with a searching look on her face, as if she were not sure this was the right address.

"How'd your lesson go?"

"Good."

"Can I make you a little snack?" Rosie looked into her face with such an odd expression, as if the word *snack* was not ringing any bells. She yawned, and then sleepwalked smack into Elizabeth, like her mother was a wall against which she had come to rest.

ELIZABETH steered her toward the kitchen for a glass of orange juice. "I need you to help me plant some bulbs today," Elizabeth said, "while there's still sun." Rosie shook her head wearily. "Please, honey. I really need you. You help me out, and I'll give you your allowance early."

"Mommy," Rosie said with some exasperation, "I don't get an allowance. You or James just gives me money when I need it."

"We do?" Elizabeth exclaimed. Rosie rolled her eyes.

Lank gave them paper bags full of bulbs every year, dried-up balls with no visible life left in them. Last year she and Rosie had planted them—his daffodil bulbs—in pots, covered the dirt on top with rocks, and put the pots on a place mat in the middle of the kitchen table. In February they'd begun to poke their noses out. This is hope, she'd said to Rosie, this is life, poking its nose out through the dirt and rocks. It had worked then. Maybe it would work again.

They worked together side by side in the garden without talking much. Elizabeth felt less odd, less other, than she'd been feeling lately. She kept sneaking glances at her girl sitting beside her in the dirt with a trowel, sleek and brown and glossy as a mink, and she thought of her over the last thirteen years, sitting beside her in the rich soil of the garden. Rosie dug with ferocity at first, as if she were trying to save something before it smothered, and then in the silken gold afternoon light, she began to loosen, unbind. The furrows in her brow disappeared, and a dignified ease replaced the grim concentration. When she was finally able to look over at her mother, she smiled rather shyly.

They dug, added potting soil, buried the bulbs, covered them up, and watered. By the time they went inside to wash up, Rosie was asking if she could help with dinner and seemed disappointed when Elizabeth said it was made, that all she had to do was pop it in the oven for an hour. She even gave Elizabeth a quick hug before disappearing upstairs to her room. Through the kitchen window, she could see that the fog was coming in over the mountain, but the table was still dappled with sunlight.

"DARLING, will you please set the table?" Elizabeth asked Rosie that night. Rosie had stretched out on the couch with a book before dinner, but of course suddenly there were reasons she couldn't do it right then. "Just a minute," she said, "I have to finish this paragraph," and then, "Wait, wait, I will, but I promised Simone I would check in with her before dinner." But James was already on the phone with Lank, so Rosie stood beside him crossly as if he were tying up a pay phone. So Elizabeth waited a few more minutes, then shouted at everyone in general and no one in particular, and began to set the table herself. James tiptoed into the dining room and took the silverware out of her hands.

"Why do I always have to ask for help? I'm making the goddamn dinner."

"Lank is sick."

"Well, I'm sorry Lank is sick. But he's not always sick, and I always have to ask you or Rosie to set the table."

"No, you don't, Elizabeth. I almost always set it."

"But I have to ask half the time."

"Because when you ask, I know it's time for dinner. That's how I know it's time for me to set the table."

"Why can't—"

"Elizabeth? Just stop. Let's choose our battles more carefully. Okay?" After a moment, Elizabeth nodded and sighed.

"God, Rosie can be such a pain in the butt."

"Yes," he said. "She can."

Yet during dinner she was so friendly, so really interesting, that Elizabeth shook her head in wonder. And when Elizabeth got a headache that night out of the blue, it was Rosie, not James, who noticed first that she was not quite right. As usual Rosie was frustrated that this mother who was supposed to be taking care of her was such a mess, needed in fact to be cared for, but she came through with such maternal caring and sweetness that it left Elizabeth close to tears.

"Mommy, you need to lie down," Rosie said. Elizabeth stretched out on the couch. Rosie wiped the sweat off her forehead with a napkin, took off the hated ratty black loafers without a word, and rubbed her feet. She brushed some stray hairs off Elizabeth's face, was doggedly protective when the phone rang. She picked it up and listened for a moment. "No, I'm sorry, Rae," she said into the mouthpiece, "she's lying down right now. I'll have to have her call you later. You can talk to James if you want, but not to my mom. Okay, then; she'll call you later. Okay, okay, that's very funny. I'll tell her that," she announced stiffly, and hung up.

"Rae says to tell you she saw a bumper sticker today that said, 'Real women don't have hot flashes; they have power surges.' Are you having hot flashes, Mommy?" Elizabeth shook her head. Rosie was watching her with the concerned, proprietary look that Elizabeth recognized as her own. Her heart was stirred with tenderness and once again with a sense of Rosie's wounded psyche, of the corrupt government inside her daughter's head that accompanied and protected and condemned her, was stirred again by this most familiar of strangers.

SHE drove Rosie to a tournament over at a park in the East Bay several days later. Simone had the stomach flu. At the park, Elizabeth sat down on a folding chair near the closest court, while Rosie checked in at the tournament desk. Elizabeth watch Natalie Reynolds draw Rosie aside, confer intently for a moment. Rosie looked over, slid her eyes off Elizabeth twice. Elizabeth wondered if they were talking about her for some reason. She felt very old in the unforgiving sunlight and looked around for shade.

But Luther had seized the shade. He was sitting down on a folding chair at the other end of the court, in the shadow of an alder tree. Oh, God, she thought anxiously. She was frightened by the fact that he wore a black windbreaker on this hot summer day, by the sadness and tension in his vagabond face. He doffed his Giants cap at her when he noticed her watching him, and something inside her wobbled, like a gyroscope inside her had just tipped over off its string.

Rosie came over to say hello on her way onto the court.

"You're playing right here?" said Elizabeth. Rosie nodded. Her opponent, no one Elizabeth recognized, walked up from behind, and the two girls stepped onto the court.

Rosie moved about the court as seamlessly as a trout. Elizabeth watched Luther watch her. His dusty dark eyes were narrowed in pride.

He looked over to the side suddenly, caught Elizabeth studying him, looked like he was about to wink. She glared at him. She didn't mean to, but she glowered with reproach. You were there, weren't you, she thought, across the street from our house. He looked at her kindly, and she was sure he shook his head. Yes, she thought, you were; you rolled in, like an unexploded bomb, and you rolled away. But how did you leave hoof marks in the grass? She glanced at his shoes, high top black sneakers, like shoes that a flasher would wear. I'm losing my mind, she thought. Maybe I have tumors. Maybe I'd better go call James.

"Hi, he said when he picked up the phone. "Why aren't you here?" She smiled. "Is everything okay?" he asked.

"I'm so afraid of Luther, James. It makes me feel crazy."

"Oh, honey. He's such a creep, but I actually think he's harmless. You know, I think he functions like some desk organizer for all of your fears: your fear of Charles dying, of losing Rosie, of Rosie being a teenager. It's like the way some little kids are afraid of dogs; all the terror and mystery of the world can be laid on anything with four legs and fur."

Elizabeth thought this over for a minute. What he said made sense. She glanced over at where Luther had been sitting, but no one was under the alder tree now.

"Well, he's gone again," she said. "Maybe I like it better when I can at least keep an eye on him." It was just that there were so many ways to lose your kid, so many threats, so much evil. She stood at the pay phone, slightly embarrassed, and James gave her a cool glass of affectionate small talk: there had been a deer in the garden, nibbling at her wisteria! And he had chased it off in the most manly possible way!

"Oh, my brave honey," she said. She said good-bye and settled back into watching Rosie play. She was slaughtering the other girl, as the kids would say. But she had gone from the thing with Mr. Thackery, from his shadowy study, to the world of tennis, of clubs and lessons and matches and practice and pretty, accomplished children—and then Luther appeared, and Elizabeth could see again that the snake was everywhere.

He was watching the match again. She felt as though a Peeping Tom were watching her child, putting her at psychic risk, and there was nothing she could do. She noticed Rosie avoiding Luther's gaze, concentrating fiercely, but then flouncing past him during the change of sides in a way that made Elizabeth wonder if her child was finding power in ignoring him. She felt scared of her having any connection with him at all. She wondered again if Rosie missed Luther when he didn't show. She wondered if Rosie felt more drawn to him now that Peter was away, now that Peter had left her for his national boys. Maybe it felt like he was abandoning her. Elizabeth licked her lips and scowled, then looked over to discover that Luther was gazing at her with worry, worry and kindness. Then he turned back to the match, where Rosie moved in to the net like a skier, dipping down on a backhand volley and chipping the return back over the net crosscourt, so low and crisp and unexpected that it got lost on everyone's radar for a moment—everyone's but Rosie's and Luther's, who watched it catch the line on the other side of the court. Rosie grinned, Luther smiled, and then they looked at each other for a moment. As Rosie bent down to tie her shoe, a chill raced up the back of Elizabeth's neck. God almighty, how rich children's dark sides are, beautiful and slinky as coral snakes. She looked over at Luther again, sitting in the shadows, lost in thought, and she felt that somewhere an invisible noose was tightening.

THAT night after dinner Rae was sitting in the old easy chair, wearing a worn denim jumper with nothing underneath, and she looked tan and ripe and beautiful. Her hair was loose, spilling down her back in waves of dark light, and she wore black espadrilles that tied at the ankle. James and Elizabeth had gone for a walk. Rosie and Rae had declined their invitation.

They were playing catch with a roll of toilet paper that Rosie had secured with rubber bands so that it would not unfurl. They had been throwing it back and forth in silence from ten feet away without missing.

"Do you want to talk about it?" Rae asked eventually.

"Talk about what?"

"Is anything troubling you? Besides Charles?"

"Are you spying for my mother?"

"Uh-huh."

Rosie tossed the toilet paper roll at Rae. "Simone told me about something she did the other day, I can't tell you what, but I'll tell you this. It is *not* very good news."

"You're sure of that?"

"Yep. But I really cannot tell you what it is."

"Okay," Rae said finally. She seemed to ponder her own knotty weaving on the wall; the room was silent, as if waiting for something. Finally Rae gave Rosie a long sideways look. "Can I tell you *one* quick story?" she asked. Rosie, watchful, nodded.

"Long ago," Rae began, "there was a farmer who lived in the hills of China. And one day out of the blue, several wild horses crashed through the gates of his farm, causing a great deal of damage. 'Oh, no,' cried the neighbors. 'This is terrible news.'

"The old farmer shrugged. 'Bad news, good news—who knows?' "

Rosie closed her eyes and smiled, seeing in her mind's eye the ancient Chinese hillside, the nosy chickenlike neighbors.

Rae continued. "The next day the horses came back, and the farmer's twenty-year-old son managed to capture one." Rosie saw it—a stallion, fiery and exquisite. "All the neighbors ran over to admire it," said Rae. " 'Oh, how wonderful,' they cried. " 'What good news.' "

" 'Good news, bad news—who knows?' shrugged the farmer. And then, several days later, the farmer's son, attempting to break the steed, was thrown and his leg badly broken. The neighbors rushed over, peering in at the young man in bed. 'Oh,' they cried. "This is *awful* news.' "

"The farmer shrugged," Rae said. " 'Good news, bad news—who knows?' " Rosie blinked. "And then? A few weeks later, the Chinese army came by, conscripting all the area's young men for a war raging in the south. And of course, they couldn't take the young man with the broken leg."

" 'Oh,' " Rae cried. " 'This is *wonderful* news.' " Rae glanced at Rosie, who nodded, as if in surrender. "The story goes on—but maybe it's time for you to tell me what your not-good news is."

Rosie shook her head, seeing Simone. "No," she said finally.

"But you're positive it's not good?"

With a sidelong glance at Rae, Rosie shrugged. "Good news? Bad news? Who knows," she muttered to herself. She tossed the roll of toilet paper back and forth from her left hand to her right, then looking up impishly, she heaved it to Rae.

four

ELIZABETH asked James to change the lightbulb in the kitchen one morning in late May, because she had so many things to do to get ready for the picnic with Rae and Rosie that day. He sat at the table still reading the paper. She was doing half a dozen things at once, trying to get everyone ready for the day, and besides, she hated changing lightbulbs in this one particular fixture. You had to do it by braille, unscrewing unseen screws that held the glass globe in place, while your arm started to fall off and your neck got stiff. And then, when the screws finally came off, there were all those dead flies glued by sticky dust to the underneath brim. She felt like she was doing almost everything around the house but this one thing that would illuminate her work area so she could do even more for everyone else. James, sitting there reading the paper, could see just fine and so did not think to leap up and change the bulb. But Elizabeth knew that by the early evening the room would be filled with shadows, and preparing dinner would be hard and annoying, and so she said this to James, who said with slight irritation that he was going to change the lightbulb in a minute.

"Please will you just do it now?"

"You want me to leap up onto my little stepladder with my toolbox and coveralls and change it? Right this very second?"

Elizabeth nodded.

He sighed and wandered off, and she thought he would return in a moment with the ladder. She watched him out in the front yard on his way out to his shed to get the bulb. But first he stopped to unscrew something on the manual lawn mower, and amazingly, he got distracted. She swallowed her annoyance; he would eventually get around to the lightbulb. He liked to fix motors, to putter with his car, or take

apart the lawn mower. He liked to do things outdoors, in his manly do-
main. It was part of his hunter-gatherer legacy. He didn't like to change
lightbulbs. Don Knotts could change lightbulbs. It occurred to
Elizabeth, as she prepared the picnic basket, that she liked to put
things away, while James liked to haul things out and create huge
projects over which he could then look so serious; it seemed to her
that James liked projects that, as someone had once said about arti-
chokes, looked like there was more when they were done with than
when they were begun.

He finished with the lawn mower, and went out to his shed, and still
had not reappeared by the time Rae stopped by to pick up Elizabeth
and Rosie. Elizabeth, for everyone's sake, had stopped by the shed on
the way out, and reminded him with extravagantly good-natured no-
blesse oblige to please change the bulb before they got home from
their picnic.

They had the loveliest day at the national park, stretched out on
towels on the banks of the creek, reading, talking, wading, eating, dozing again, and Elizabeth tried not to think about the morning. But
when she and Rosie walked into the kitchen that evening and she
threw on the light switch, holding her breath, nothing happened. She
looked at Rosie, who shook her head.

"Men," she said to Rosie.

Rosie rolled her eyes. "Should me and you do it?" she asked.

Elizabeth considered this. "You and I," she said. "Let's not let him
off the hook so easily. Besides, it's too dark in here to do it now."

"Then how will he do it when he gets home?"

"That's not our problem. Our problems are blood sugar and world
peace."

They were both tired and hungry and yet so wanted to continue the
sweetness of the day that they set about good-naturedly in the dimness
to make themselves a simple meal. They sat down together at the table
to leftover soup and bread and cheese and ate by candlelight.

"Mama? Do you mind if I read my new magazine while we eat?"

"By what, flashlight?"

Rosie shrugged and nodded.

And so they ended up together, Rosie with her *Seventeen,* Elizabeth
with a book, reading in silence with flashlights. The only sound was the
turning of pages, like waves lapping the shore. Elizabeth looked up

from time to time to study her strange silky daughter in the candlelight, staring solemnly at page after page of emaciated beauty, with the baby finger of her free hand hooked over her bottom lip just as she had when she had read fairy tales at eight in the window seat, horse stories at ten, Nancy Drew mysteries at eleven, and now advice on weight control and boys.

A MOMENT later, there was a horrible sizzle and stink; Rosie, slumping, had gotten a bit of hair singed in the candle flame. There was a sudden pinch in Elizabeth's solar plexus, a sinking feeling, a rage at James. He must have assumed that she was going to change the bulb herself; he must see her as his mother, his nag of a mother. It was all hopeless. It meant that there was something really wrong with the relationship.

Elizabeth opened a can of mandarin oranges for dessert and knew that the syrup was spilling down the side of the can and onto the counter, as she tried by flashlight to spoon some into two bowls. It would be sticky soon and bring on ants, and all she wanted was to clean everything up and go to bed. She had lost her bearings in the dark. The kitchen was her territory, and it was supposed to be appetizing. But because of James's dereliction, it was a mess. She found herself lurching here and there, tripping, knocking things over, smoldering with resentment.

"Mommy? Why don't you sit down?"

THEY read their magazines and ate their mandarin oranges by flashlight and candles, a parody of an elegant dinner party. Good cheer and improvisation were burbling again in the visible world, but a roiling feeling had begun in her gut. She felt tired and short in her chair, as if she and Rosie were hunkered down in a cave.

They carried their dishes to the sink. Rosie, in bare feet, could feel crumbs and stickiness.

"How pathetic," she said to Elizabeth. "Men can be such slobs." And she wandered off to the ruins of her room.

. . .

AFTER a while Elizabeth went upstairs to read but found herself back in the kitchen two hours later, still waiting for James to come home. Rosie was up in bed with her latest teenage gothic. Elizabeth peered down into the nearly empty can of mandarin oranges, holding a flashlight on them with one hand, spearing segments one by one with a fork in the other. She hated leaving a mess for the morning; it always felt like part of you was still outside your body. Besides the threat of a bug invasion, there was the fear that the mess, the stickiness and crumbs and dirty dishes, could grow by themselves in the dark. Smells, growths, moss and mold, furry mold like troll hair, fuzz with fur on it. It could start composting. A miasma of smells would rise.

She shuffled around the house, went back to the dark sink, where she closed her eyes in the dark, and then went back upstairs, where she sat miserably for a while on the toilet. She could feel the seat embossing her butt. It was one of the stations of despair.

JAMES was still not home at ten, by which time she was livid. She got in bed and read for a while, and eventually turned off the light. A little while later, she heard him tiptoe in.

"Are you awake?" he whispered in the dark. She grunted softly. "I want to hear about your day; I want to tell you about mine. It was so great. Please don't be asleep." But she lay there like a smoldering log as he took off his clothes and dropped them softly on a chair. She heard him yawn, heard and felt him crawl into bed.

"Are you really asleep?" he asked. She yawned, made the smallest possible sound. He put his knees in the crook of her knees, and where there was usually a yielding, she was stiff. Straightening her knees would be too overt. He flung his arm over her, as he did every night in the presleep position, in that fitting together, the key in the hole. But she pretended to be asleep, breathing as shallowly as possible, trying to breathe out as little as possible; otherwise, who knew what might burst out—tears, invective, molten fury. If he didn't offer anything, she wasn't about to. "You always . . . ," she wanted to cry out. "You never . . ." You don't listen to me, you don't care—you only care about yourself. She felt like she was in a bunker, and she listened to him sigh, clearly now getting that she was annoyed, punishing him, but he didn't want to blow his day or his sleep.

And when he was asleep, Elizabeth lay in the dark for two hours, her eyeballs as rigid as her body, listening to his soft snore; then she got up and read in the living room until nearly four in the morning, and finally, finally she fell asleep.

JAMES was reading the paper and drinking coffee when she got up at nine. "Hi!" he said.

She could barely look at him. There were crumbs and snail tracks of stickiness on the table. He had not bothered to wipe it all up before sitting down to read.

"What is it, Elizabeth?"

"Remember the lightbulb?"

"Ah!" He smote his forehead, gripped his head as if being pierced with migraine, beat the table. "Oh, I'm so sorry," he implored. "Sit down; let me get you some coffee."

"Just change the fucking lightbulb."

"Do you want me to do it now?" he asked, surprised. She nodded. "I will. But have some coffee, let me finish mine."

"No."

"No, you don't want any, or no, I can't finish mine."

"No, you can't finish yours."

James stood there, as sullen as one of the teenage boys on the tennis tour. Elizabeth cleaned off the table, poured her own coffee, and sat down with the paper. There was always that feeling in her soul that the bottom could drop out of their marriage. There were so many areas where things could go irreparably wrong. And the jacket was always waiting in the closet, the jacket of being a martyr and a bitch, the jacket she was now wearing.

JAMES worked with great concentration, as if changing the dressing on a burn instead of a lightbulb, and when he was done, he walked to the wall switch and turned it on. The kitchen was flooded with golden light. "Watson," he cried, "come quickly. I need you." Elizabeth glowered at the paper. James turned the light off. She gawked at him. He turned it back on with a flourish, and then off. Elizabeth looked away. He turned the light back on with a gasp, a happy intake of air, like a child playing peekaboo. And then he turned it off. Elizabeth buried her face in her hands. The light went on again, and then, a moment later, off. Finally she smiled, and he turned the light on and left it.

THAT night when he bent his knees into the crook of hers, she yielded, melting into him, and they made love. Life was normal again, life was good—Bosnia to Paris in twenty-four hours.

He turned over with a big schlumpy male plop, now out of the presleep position and getting ready to drift off. He rearranged himself like a gull, shimmying his ruffled feathers back into place after landing.

five

CHEATING was much easier the next time. It was at a tournament only twenty minutes from home. She arrived in a great mood, having driven over with her mother and Rae for a ten o'clock first-round match. She was slated to play Deb Hall, who was unseeded in singles, although a frequent and ferocious rival in doubles. And after studying the draw, she realized there was a good chance that she could actually win one of the singles trophies, either the one for first place, which was a marble desk set with a fountain pen, or the runner-up trophy, a tall garish figurine mounted on fake marble, which looked just like the Statue of Liberty about to hit a forehand volley.

Rae bought her a Coke and they sat with Elizabeth waiting for Rosie's name to be called. Rae always made such a fuss over her whenever she came along to a tournament, making sure Rosie was warm or cool enough and that she had eaten just long enough before so that the food would not cause stomach cramps, ogling Rosie's name on the posted list of seeded players. It was sort of embarrassing. Rae didn't believe that Rosie was really just one of the pack on the junior tournament circuit. Still, when the tournament director called her name and that of her opponent, Rosie stood up, feeling for the moment like a championship thoroughbred, long-legged and muscular, raring to run.

LUTHER was sitting behind two ten-year-old girls, watching their loopy rallies. Rosie, walking behind him with Deb, smelled slightly sour BO. She turned once to look back over her shoulder at him with a slight sneer, and he smiled at her and winked.

"God," she said out loud and shivered

A dizzying number of balls were going back and forth across the nets as she and Deb walked to their court. She had breasts that bounced a little when she ran, and Rosie could not take her eyes off them. Deb never put one away, and she didn't take any practice shots at the net, but by the same token, she didn't miss very often either. She chased down everything, patted each ball back, and before they had even practiced their serves, Rosie had psyched herself out.

Her breathing changed. She could hear her pulse. Movies were playing in her mind where she saw herself leave the court in disgrace, losing to this bouncing girl, no ranking, no seed. Rosie took a dozen practice serves, made about half of them, felt a crick in her elbow. Deb took only two practice serves, hard and flat, both well in.

"I'm guess I'm ready," she said.

Rosie had won the toss and had chosen to serve first, which to her amazement she did well. She won the first game. But after the change of sides, she found herself patting Deb's serves back; she panicked that she was hitting so many out, and after several long patty-cake rallies, she somehow managed to lose the game. Her pulse raced as she headed back to the baseline, one ball tucked inside her panties, one ball gripped too hard in her talons.

Breathe, she heard Peter say, use your *head*. She closed her eyes and breathed deeply, shook her head, opened her eyes, and served an ace. But on the backhand side, her first serve missed by an inch, and the panic returned. When she went to toss the ball for her second serve, her left hand jerked up like the claw of a ball machine, and she actually tossed the ball two feet behind her. She had to chase it down. Hysterics mounted. The next toss was just as jerky and went only a foot or so above her head; the panic made her swing at it anyway, and she hit herself on the top of her head with the racket. But the ball somehow went in, and the two of them pushed it back and forth until finally Deb tapped it into the net.

Rosie felt unhinged. Breathe, she ordered herself. *Hit*. She watched the ball come off her strings and tried to will it across the court, but it hit the top of the net and dropped back on her side. She gulped some air, quavering. Twenty minutes later, the score was tied at four games all, Rosie serving at deuce. Unable to concentrate on her toss or on the destination of her serve, her head throbbed with excuses and explanations to her mother as to why she had lost so badly to such an average singles player. She squinted back tears of disbelief and embarrassment.

Deb hit a drop shot and brought Rosie up to the net, and Rosie ran her heart out and got to the ball on one bounce, scraping her racket along the court and digging the ball up and over a split second before it would have bounced again, and Deb lobbed the ball over her, and Rosie took off like a terrified jackrabbit for the ball, as it soared slowly overhead. She raced toward the baseline, but the ball was going too fast to retrieve, and then, miraculously, it seemed that it might go out.

If it went out, the score would be ad in, a huge advantage. If it went in, she would be doomed. *Doomed.*

She dashed toward it, running straight back toward the fence so that inadvertently her body was blocking the ball from Deb's view, and she watched the ball land and, to her horror, catch the line by maybe half an inch, maybe even less, by so little it wasn't fair, you should get to call a ball like that out, the ball was meant to go out. Rosie was a foot away from where it landed, and in a swirl of fear and disappointment, she shouted, "Out!" before she fully knew what she was doing. "Out," she said again calmly. She stopped to catch her breath, and heard the ball hit against the back fence, and looked up at the sound.

Luther, dark and clear, lit by the morning sun, stood on the other side of the fence and smiled. Then his eyes met hers and held. Her heart lurched. She whipped around to face Deb, who was peering around her, trying to see Rosie's baseline.

"Really?" Deb said, friendly as could be. "It was out?"

Rosie nodded sympathetically.

"I couldn't see it," said Deb, "because it was between you and the fence."

Rosie held up her fingers and thumb to indicate that the ball had landed an inch past the line. Deb scowled down at the ground and talked to herself silently and with great animation for a moment. Then her shoulders slumped. Rosie let her brood. She almost asked if Deb wanted to play the point over, but the relief was too sweet. She could breathe again. When Deb finally got into position to return serve, Rosie pushed Luther out from the inside of her head, so she could feel his darkness become part of the ace she served, and went on like Rommel to conquer the space before her.

S HE's the daughter of the devil," said James with disgust the next morning after a bad breakfast with Rosie. Upstairs now and since eight o'clock this morning, rap music had been blaring, with the bass turned up and Rosie screaming the words. It was so incongruous, coming from someone who could go into that trance of quiet concentration on the tennis court. At breakfast she'd sat at the table with a look of such wild unhappiness and judgment that all James and Elizabeth could do was stare at each other. Screaming rap music lyrics seemed to be how she medicated herself.

Elizabeth got up from the table, as Rosie wailed upstairs. "I think I'll take her for a drive. She doesn't have a lesson till early this evening." When Rosie was like this, hard and angry, and Elizabeth found herself missing her, she'd take her somewhere, up on the mountain, out to the shore. Often Rosie would revert and for a few hours be her old self again. This morning—against all odds—Rosie, still full of hostility and disdain, consented to go for a drive.

"James, do you want to come with us? I think we might go see the Meyers' goats. The Meyers won't even be there, we don't have to be social."

"Lozenge-eyed, yellow-eyed goats," James said rather dreamily.

"Is that from a poem?"

"I don't think so. I think I just made it up."

"Do you want to come with us, then?"

"No, I hate goats."

Elizabeth smiled. "Why?"

"They're repulsive is why. If they had the body of an African lion, or the grace of a running gazelle, or the rotund beauty of a hippo . . ."

"I would have sworn you liked them."

"No, I hate them. I don't mind sheep so much, in the proper setting. Which is to say, distant. But I hate how goats waddle around with
those distended bellies, looking like a bunch of bigoted old Finnish
peasants. I prefer the sight of a bunch of manly, dangerous-looking
bulls wandering around small crowds of heifers. It's sort of—stimu-
lating."

"James!"

"You two go without me."

THEY took the old Saab up past the Petaluma River—still a working
river, filled with barges and dredgers—past Black Point and over the
old road to Sonoma. They stared out opposite windows at low, flat,
deeply green hills, at horse pastures, trees, tractors, cows, sheep. When
they rolled down their windows, the smells of manure, of summer, of
grass no longer new filled their nostrils. Elizabeth loved the groves of
oak, solid as citadels, and the lines of eucalyptus and poplar, sinewy
and protective as old longhaired warriors, still with their long swords,
still in command. Rosie saw mostly electrical poles and wires, saw them
as huge corrals holding in giant animals you couldn't see. She sighed
with such annoyance that an observer turning on the channel right
then might have thought he'd just missed an argument.

"What is it, darling?"

Rosie did not respond right away. She stared out the window.
Finally she sighed again. "Nothing," she said.

"Tell me."

"No."

"Are you worried about something?"

"I'm worried about James coming to watch me play next week."

"Why?"

"Because it's embarrassing, he's such a terrible dresser. He looks
like a poor drug addict. Everyone will stare at us."

"What if I make sure he wears Levi's, and a T-shirt?"

"He'll wear zoris, with socks. One sock will have holes. His baby toe
will be sticking out. Like he should be by the side of the road with a
sign that says he just lost his job."

"Maybe someone will give us money, and we can go out for
dinner."

"It's not even funny."

Elizabeth shook her head.

THE huge field where the Meyers' goats grazed was emerald green, dotted with wild buttercups, tiny purple wildflowers, and dandelions. It smelled of feta, and mint, and a faint hint of goat manure, tiny turds everywhere but so mild and clean; Elizabeth always said that a goat field was the ultimate case for vegetarianism. Fifty goats milled around, in clusters and alone, balancing on fallen logs, rushing up to Rosie and her mother—billy goats, mothers with their young, white goats, black goats, black-and-white goats, two-tone brown goats, male goats with stubby rounds where their horns had been removed, some bloody from recent fights. Some had little hairy tufts hanging tonsil-like from their necks, and the littlest ones bounded around with their front feet together, like deer. All of them cried their goaty cries except for the younger ones, who crowed like roosters as they swarmed around Rosie and Elizabeth.

"We were here when you were little," said Elizabeth. "With your daddy. It must have been in the spring, because some of the goats were pregnant. It was . . . the spring when you were four, not long before he died. None of the mothers had had their babies yet. Only me."

ANDREW and Rosie sit by the creek, Rosie in Andrew's lap. Elizabeth sits on the other side, smelling the sour goat-milk smell of feta, mint, wet grasses. She watches Andrew hand Rosie twigs and pebbles and grasses to toss into the current. He buries his face in his daughter's black hair, closes his eyes, smiles. Rosie has just turned four. She'd said to her dad on the drive here, "When I grow up, and we get married, where will Mommy go live?" Andrew teases Elizabeth all afternoon, bending over to whisper, "Vermont is nice," when they first get out of the car and start walking into the field. He slipped his arm through hers as Rosie ran ahead and whispered the names of other places where Elizabeth might be happy one day. They'd walked slowly, lan-guidly, to the barn, into which Rosie had raced; there it turns out all the dozens of goats are milling, and for a terrible moment they can't find Rosie. They separate to look for her and find her by her sudden laughter; she is barely visible, surrounded by goats, like Ulysses escaping the Cyclops's cave, hidden in sheep.

"THAT s pretty funny, what I said to Daddy. Did he tease you with it all day?"

"Oh, for a week. One morning when you crawled in bed with us, he was holding you, and you were asleep, and he said to me, trying to be very helpful, 'Tomales Bay is lovely. Ross, I think, is a little steep.'" Elizabeth smiled shyly at the memory.

"Tell me more about him."

"Your daddy loved goats' goatness," said Elizabeth. "He said they had a great attitude."

"Yeah?"

Elizabeth nodded.

"He said they take humans as their equals—other animals dominate or have to be dominated. But not goats."

"He did?"

"Uh-huh."

"Our whole lives would have turned out differently if he hadn't taken that trip. Wouldn't they?"

"Yes," said Elizabeth. Rosie put her hands on top of her head and then folded her elbows down around her face, like a bat. She looked very sad, but her mind was only partly on her father. Memories of cheating kept popping up, and she could force them away by thinking of great rallies played fairly, rallies lasting three and four minutes, which she won; and then another memory would surface, like a Whack-a-Mole arcade game, scenes just kept popping up, of cheating Marisa and Deb, of Luther gazing at her. How had this, the cheating, these dangerous feelings, started? It was as if she'd been plodding along in the tennis world, everything bouncy and smooth, and then it suddenly felt like what she had been walking on had shifted entirely. Shame came in waves now. After a minute she began to walk toward the creek that ran down the hill from the top of the property to a pond.

She was wearing ratty jeans and a huge old black T-shirt of James's. She looked so much older than she had in the spring, less like a child, more like an angry teenage boy.

Elizabeth followed some distance behind her. They went to different spots along the creek, twenty feet apart, squatted in identical stances down close to the water. There was silence, except for the cries of the goats.

Elizabeth watched the water cascade past her, looked upstream a few feet to where it ran through flattened grasses, heard random noises for a while. Then she heard the individual voices in the water, the muted sound one ribbon of water made as it ran through the flattened grass above, the low roaring undervoice a few feet downstream where it fell half a foot, a small waterfall of creek that landed in a pool on rocks and twigs, grasses, bugs. She listened, oblivious to the goats, and the breeze, and her daughter dropping tiny twigs into the creek above her, letting the current carry them down as messages to her mother—oblivious to everything now but the voice of the creek where she was closest to it, tinkling as it hit tiny pebbles in a shallow shoal before her.

seven

JAMES and Rosie went to visit Charles. He was lying in bed dozing when they arrived, pale as could be, as if the vampire of life had sucked out all his blood. It made his hair appear darker than usual. James pointed to a chair near the bed for Rosie and pulled up the wheelchair for himself. These quiet sounds woke Charles, and he stared off into the distance before noticing he had company. "Hello," he said, soft as light.

Rosie looked on the verge of sneezing, and she tried to smile and to imagine what her mother would do.

"Hey, handsome," she said, pigeon-toed, chewing on her baby finger.

"Rosie. You should be outside on a day like this, not cooped up inside with a sick old man."

"This was Rosie's idea," said James.

"Mommy's going to meet us here," said Rosie, braiding her bangs.

Charles closed his eyes. Please, Mommy, prayed Rosie, please come right now. All she could smell was too much soap over the smell of something going bad in the refrigerator. She remembered swimming with him so many times, his trim old washboard body in navy blue shorts, him taking her to his club, throwing her into the Russian River when she was small. She remembered clamoring onto his back in the river, holding on like a drowning cat, holding her breath as he dove underneath the surface and swam around like a dolphin. She vaguely remembered nearly drowning once, but that was with her daddy, and she was only three or so, and what she remembered was being under the water, and the sun trickling through so that it all shone, and she remembered closing her eyes, and then opening them with her daddy blowing air into her, his mouth almost completely covering her face, and how her chest had felt it would burst, and how he'd cried when she opened her eyes. And she remembered hiking all those times with Charles, up on the mountain, how he always brought salami, how sometimes Grace used to come along and slow them down but made him so happy, and sometimes it was just Rosie and Charles, and maybe sometimes Elizabeth, but not always. And how he brought himself one beer to drink when they stopped for lunch, and one Coke for her. And he always had awful cookies, fig bars or perforated raisin flats, but sometimes he brought beef jerky, which she loved, and beer nuts. He was so patient, so calm.

And sitting there listening to James discuss his work, Elizabeth's garden, whatever, so much sadness welled up in Rosie because Charles was going to die soon that she felt her heart collapse inward. She tried to keep the tears from spilling over by widening her eyes alarmingly, while the men kept talking, blah blah blah, and her face was burning and she blinked like mad and tried to get old tennis matches to play in her head, but even though her eyes were as wide open as they would go, the tears pooled and dripped down onto her face. She got up, smiling like mad, like a crazy person. In a silent vacuum she saw James and Charles staring at her, but no one made a move. She escaped, hurrying down the hall like a hamster, into the bathroom.

She sat on the toilet for a while.

After some time she washed her face with cold water and tried to go back down the hall, but the tears started again, and she ducked back into the bathroom. She sobbed in absolute silence. Then she sat for a while and replayed long and specific rallies in her head, imagining her father watching her, marveling at her skill, Andrew with his wonderful long legs and beautiful quiet eyes, silently cheering her on, and then in his place she saw James on the sidelines, leaping up to go check his message machine, her mother staring off into space as if hearing distant melodies, her pro on the East Coast with the boys who were national champions. Leaning against the wall of Charles's bathroom, staring at the screen in her mind, Luther the only adult around really paying attention, sitting there on the sidelines like a dirty skeleton but almost handsome, too, in a dark, bloodshot way, like a medicine man, like some yogi. Like he knew things. She saw him give her long sideways glances, she saw that he knew who she really was, she watched him watch her cheat, watched him smile his smile of love. She covered her eyes with one hand until she stopped crying. But she remained on the toilet, small with fear, like a girl of five looking around for her parents, suddenly gone, and then, without actually planning to, she stood up and went to the medicine chest.

There were dozens of bottles of pills, but Rosie stared at a big bottle of aspirin. She saw herself taking them one by one, using the little aqua glass in the toothbrush holder, saw herself crumple to the floor. She closed the door of the medicine chest, studied her ugly, swollen red face, opened the chest again, stared at the aspirin. She couldn't go back into Charles's bedroom looking like this, and she couldn't leave the house on her own. She might as well kill herself. Near the aspirin was a box of Doan's pills, for backache. There was a girl named Sandy in her homeroom, who already (everyone said) slept with boys, who bragged about getting high on Doan's pills, Doan's pills and glue that she'd poured into one of her mother's boyfriend's socks and sniffed and sniffed until, she proclaimed, she passed out and woke up a few minutes later, floating and spinning through space, through jewels, through time.

Oh, it sounded like heaven. Heaven.

Rosie found herself wondering where Charles kept the glue. And what kind of glue were you supposed to use, anyway, she wondered. Surely not white glue. Wouldn't it soak through the sock and drip all over everything? Not Crazy Glue. Maybe rubber cement. There was probably rubber cement in Charles's great old desk in the study. But what about a sock—how could she sneak one of his socks out of his bedroom without his noticing? She could use her own sock. But she was wearing a Ped, a half-sock that only went to her ankles. Could you use a Ped for a glue-sniffing sock? Fill up the toe area and then clamp the whole thing over your nose, like a gas mask? She closed her eyes and imagined swooning, imagined coming to, swimming through space, through a light show of tropical colors, smiling weakly.

And then there was a voice. "Rosie?" Elizabeth was outside the bathroom. Her mother had finally come.

"What?"

"Are you okay in there?"

"Yes! God!"

She quietly closed the medicine chest, caught a glimpse of her reflection. Her face was still red and blotchy. Then slowly the bathroom door opened, and her mother stepped in, so tall and gentle, smiling sadly.

They sat on the toilet together for twenty minutes, Rosie on Elizabeth's lap, crying quietly. Elizabeth held her, amazed by her new weight, nuzzled her daughter's neck with her lips, blowing soft warm air on her skin through her nose, staring off into space.

JAMES had given Elizabeth his spot in the wheelchair and gone off to make them all tea and, Elizabeth surmised, to check his messages. Rosie had gone with him. Charles whispered to Elizabeth that he was distressed to see how unhappy Rosie was to be here, and Elizabeth nodded and tried to explain that of course it was painful for Rosie, and that it was important, and that it was right.

Charles had on his face the look of terrified age, of eyes that will never close. His lips, in the days since Elizabeth had seen him, had fallen into his mouth, and his mouth had all but disappeared into a thin pursed line, choking back expletives and sorrow. His face was exquisitely asymmetrical. Everything on the left side was bigger—the eye, the ear filled with hair—as if when age strikes, everything we've hidden with animation gets exposed. It's all *sanpakku,* Elizabeth thought; when things were totally screwed up, out of alignment, hopeless, James always said they were *sanpakku.* And when the whites of your eyes show below the iris, and they hadn't before, you were definitely all *sanpakku*—all fucked up.

They held hands and talked of nothing in particular, Elizabeth breathing slowly and calmly, filled with grief, with terror, with a sense of there being no comfort.

"Is someone coming in to touch up your hair these days?" she asked, and he smiled. Then they were silent for a while. There was an extraordinary and chaotic vigor to his eyebrows, but it was clear that he had lost a great deal of ground. You could tell that he had always worn glasses and that now he couldn't see her very well. James and Rosie were gone a long time. Charles's stark flat gaze seemed to stare at a wall that was coming at him. Elizabeth felt that his eyes were not looking out at the external world but rather at this wall of his life coming to an end. His thin hair was combed so touchingly, neatly framing his face. But Elizabeth had the sense that his mind had begun to fall to pieces, that his time now was full of trying to remember, that Charles's amazingly agile mind was now a moth trapped in a jar, and every time it tried something vigorous, more powder fell off.

eight

ONE day at the beginning of June, when it was so hot that the only things moving outside were the crickets and the anorexics, Elizabeth drove Rosie and Simone and Rae out through the valley past a number of tiny rural towns, dairy farms, and hippie campgrounds, between low golden hills and pastures, under the redwoods beside the long winding creek, to Samuel P. Taylor Park. It was so beautiful here, under a canopy of trees so airy and rich that you felt almost inside a cave of green. The park was five miles inland, five miles away from the fog and tumultuous surf of the coast, and it was a momentous day: at the age of nearly thirty-six, Rae was wearing her first pair of shorts out in public.

She had always described her legs as if people would scream upon seeing them. On hot days she had always worn gauzy pants or skirts. Elizabeth had never actually seen Rae's legs, and they had been best friends now for seven years. As it turned out, they were chubby but quite presentable—not too long or firm, but not, as Rae had suggested, stumpy and cadaverous.

Rosie and Simone walked around in the creek, studying water skeeters whose shadows on the water looked like mouseketeer ears or boxing gloves. The stream made everyone more monkeylike; you couldn't stride through the streambed purposefully, like a human. You needed to grip with your toes, duck away from low branches. There must be thousands of such beautiful streams in the country, Elizabeth thought, with huge trees, dappled light, big rocks, but this was theirs. The sunlight shone down through the canopy of trees on them all, sparkly with pollens and seedpods, held as if in the glass ball of memory, a snow dome in summer. Rosie's legs were like pipe cleaners, brown as walnuts, not so changed from last year when she played in the water by herself. She was not yet wearing the glasses of puberty that would allow her to see all the flaws; she was still able occasionally to get lost in what was right in front of her. Simone's legs were pinker, fleshier, sexy, in tiny shorts out of which the cheeks of her rear end showed. But, Elizabeth thought, she did not look as sassy as usual.

Elizabeth looked over at Rae, who appeared to be sleeping. "With us, the sassiness is mostly gone, isn't it? But in its place, in the place of a young girl still looking for a mate, your beauty, for instance, has to do with having gotten comfortable at being so skilled at something. And there's a lot of grace in comfort."

Elizabeth found Rae's legs lovely, womanly, even though she was aware that her own were so long and tapered—what legs were supposed to look like according to all the current standards set by movies and magazines. "The world's sense of beauty is so destructive to women, Rae. Your legs are great. All these years you should have been wearing shorts when it was hot."

Elizabeth, watching the two girls in the stream, saw Simone suddenly grip Rosie's arm in the frigid water, as if she were about to lose her balance, and joy filled Simone's face, and relief. She looked down over her shoulder, down toward her butt, and then over at Elizabeth and Rae, on the riverbank. Something very secretive was going on. Elizabeth looked away, then surreptitiously back again. Now Rosie was examining Simone's butt and shaking her head. Simone appeared crestfallen.

"Something's going on with Simone," said Elizabeth.

"Yeah?" said Rae, not opening her eyes. "What do you think it is?"

"No idea."

"Maybe it's hard to be that beautiful. I bet the boys are all over her at school. Do you think she's had sex yet?"

"No. I'm sure not. She's only fourteen."

"Elizabeth. Fourteen is not what it used to be."

Elizabeth opened her eyes to all the green light pouring off the trees. "You know, I was thirty before I knew that a person just being herself is beautiful, that contentment is beautiful."

Rae rolled over on her side and stared at Elizabeth.

"What started all this—this thinky thinking?"

"I don't know. Here we are, four females, no one else around. You in shorts for the first time, and Simone looking like Lolita, and Rosie . . . well, to me of course, Rosie is as beautiful as Simone."

"Please. It goes without saying. Rosie is an orchid."

"But to almost any man in this country, Simone is the beauty, right? Look at her over there by the tree stump, fixated on herself, unhappy. James gets around her for a few minutes, and it's all he can do not to start talking baby talk. Now look at Rosie, walking around like a puppy looking at things in the water. Rosie is so much younger inside. She's all caught up in the river, the guppies, the current. She looks like a little kid."

"I'm falling asleep," said Rae. "Will you tell me all these interesting things later? I really love hearing them."

Rae was so beautiful to her, her smooth face in repose, the soft brown skin with pink in the cheeks, the full pink lips. But she knew this face, which she so loved, was not considered desirable by most men. Elizabeth sometimes wondered if Rae would have been as gifted and successful an artist if she had been. She looked again at the girls, their young bodies, so different and so exquisite. Simone would have an easier life than Rosie, she thought. Beauty is a form of radiance that sets up a shield so people can't get in. Did Rosie know this yet? Rosie already knew how badly you can be hurt and betrayed. Simone didn't seem to. Looking at the two girls in the river, Elizabeth realized that it was going to be years before Rosie became aware of what she did have, instead of obsessing about what she didn't. It was going to be years before she saw that she was not the universal disaster she'd been assuming she was these last two years.

"Do you feel sad that no one is talking to you?" Rae asked, opening her eyes and turning her head to look at Elizabeth.

"No. I brought everyone here for a spa day. Everyone gets to do what they feel like."

"I'm going to wake up in a few more minutes."

"Okay, honey."

She propped herself up on her elbows to study the river. Downstream, in the folds and convolutions of the water, young people waded, some carrying each other, some alone, and the stream accepted them all, swept them along. There was room for everyone in the gentle force of the water, room for the teenagers, babies, children, room for Simone, so perfect, so fresh and voluptuous, who now sat on the far bank of the stream, sobbing, and Rosie, who watched in shock, as if Simone were melting before her very eyes.

AFTER dropping Simone off at Veronica's salon, they drove along bu-colic streets to Charles's little Spanish-style house, white stucco with soft green trim, all arches, old roses, camellias. Rae turned off the en-gine, and they looked toward Charles's front door, as if waiting for him to come out and join them.

"It's so scary for Charles to be dying," said Rosie. She was in the front seat with Rae. "It would be for me. It would be the worst thing in the world for me, because I really don't like the dark. It would be like everything going dark on you and you'd be all alone in it. Like all alone in a black sack. And everyone would cry for about one day."

"I would cry for the rest of my life if you died, Rosie," said Elizabeth.

"There's just nothing good about it. It's not like your good news, bad news story, Rae."

"But we don't know that," said Rae. "We're just sad because we'll miss him. But I notice one thing that is good. He's gotten good at knowing what really counts, and asking for it—a ride out to the living room in his wheelchair, a glass of cool water with a thin slice of lemon."

"It was different for my dad," said Rosie. Elizabeth, in the back seat, stiffened. She leaned through the space between the two front seats and reached her left arm across Rosie's chest. Rosie dug her chin down into her mother's arm, rubbed it hard, like a deer rubbing its nubs against a tree. After a minute, she continued. "He just got smashed into and died. That's what scares me, everything going dark on you all of a sudden. One moment, like 11:08, my dad was cruising along, thinking about me and Mommy and listening to the radio and thinking about what he was going to do the next morning, and then at 11:09, he was dead. Boom. At 11:08 I had a daddy, and then at 11:09, I never did again."

"Well, you do have a daddy," said Rae. "But not Andrew."

"I have James," said Rosie. "I have a James. Not a dad."

Elizabeth, in the back seat, closed her eyes, trying to breathe back in all the parts that were suddenly spiking out of her.

THEY sat in Charles's room beside his bed. Rae rubbed his feet. He wanted to know about Rosie's tennis and James's book.

"I heard him on the radio again," he said, in his soft reedy voice. "He was talking about something important. I can't remember what now. But he was very clear, very caring. You can't hope for much more than that."

Elizabeth watched Rae rub Charles's feet. His nurse had manicured them perfectly, cutting away calluses and doctoring corns. The nails were trimmed and buffed. They looked like God's feet, smooth and pale as alabaster, but at the end of spindly wasted legs; because they were so lovely, Charles didn't wear socks anymore. It was one incongruous frivolity in a man who had seemed to care so little about his physical package. Elizabeth saw his newly realized feet as something he had grown briefly, a new way of being in the world, almost like little feathers that he couldn't fly with yet because they were too new, but that he could preen.

ROSIE fell asleep in the back seat on the way home.

Elizabeth started to think of Charles's feet again, as they drove along. She found it hard to breathe. "I keep thinking of the physical part of Charles that isn't going to be here anymore," she said. "Like his feet." Neither of them said anything until Elizabeth pulled up in front of her house. She shut off the engine and hung her head.

"Can we just sit out here for a while?" Elizabeth asked.

Rae nodded, her eyes downcast, grave.

"Lank is inside with James. It's their basketball night. Look. They're peering out at us." The men stood at the window in the living room, waving. The women waved.

Elizabeth turned back to Rae. "I'm thinking," she said, "about the shoes that aren't worn anymore, and the feet that don't walk anymore, and yet how delectable they are. Feet in repose. Not transportation, not support. They're like beautiful perfect clay feet. And oh, Rae. He loves your massages."

They looked out through the car windows for a minute and then back at the men who still stood at the window, still waving.

"We don't make any sense to them," Elizabeth said. "Here we are, a couple of white women sitting in a stuffy car, talking about a dying man's feet."

For a minute, Rosie's snores from the back seat were the only sounds in the car. Then Rae smiled at Elizabeth.

AFTER a while the men came out of the house, James in his basketball clothes and high-tops, with a basketball tucked fiercely under his arm as if it were someone's severed head. Lank wore khakis and Birkenstocks.

Rae rolled down her window. "Lank. They'll never let you play like that."

"I left all my stuff at Linda's. I forgot it was basketball night. I promised I'd go for a walk with her. I'm supposed to meet her in town." He sighed. "Maybe she'll take cyanide instead."

"I thought you liked her," said Elizabeth. He had been dating Linda for three weeks.

"Maybe she'll hook up her garden hose to the exhaust."

"Lank!" said Elizabeth, but she was laughing. James bent down and peered in at his wife.

"Hi," he said plaintively.

"Oh, James."

"How was Charles?"

"He's okay, isn't he, Rae?" Rae nodded. "You need to see him soon if you want to say good-bye."

"Okay."

James peered in at Rosie sleeping soundly in the back, looked in-quiringly at Elizabeth, and pantomimed tossing back drinks. Elizabeth nodded, and they smiled at each other. Lank studied Rae.

"Is Jesus in there with you now?" he asked.

"He's always with me, Lank."

"Why don't you guys come inside," said Elizabeth, "and I'll make you a quick cup of coffee?"

"No," said Lank. "We're going. Don't even try to slow us up. We're going now." He started to walk away, and then turned back to peer in at Rae again.

"Is Jesus like your little shadow, Rae?"

"He's like my own little sun." Lank stared at Rae for a moment, and then he smiled, like a good sport, as if she had won and he understood this.

"You're great, Rae," he said.

"Hey, thanks."

"But we've given up on girls, me and James. Right, James? Girls confuse us." James nodded one nod of great finality, and they turned and walked away.

nine

Rosie was playing Colleen Morgen in the round of sixteen, in a tournament in Stockton, on the last court in a row of eight. She was seeded eighth in the tournament, Colleen not seeded at all, and it was five games each in the second set. Rosie had won the first set, but Colleen was playing hard now, with confidence, and Rosie was afraid. Her stomach ached with anxious thoughts of losing. Colleen needed one point to win the game.

Rosie looked around.

No one was watching the boys in the match on the next court, and they were consumed by their own play, and at first she thought no one was watching her and Colleen until she noticed Luther alone under a tree, reading a newspaper. She watched him for a moment. He did not look up. So when Colleen served a weak pouffy serve that landed on the intersection of alley and service line but just barely, Rosie, almost without meaning to, called it out.

She caught the ball on her racket, stopped it, and nonchalantly began walking to the backhand side of her court, to receive serve.

"What?" said Colleen, gawking.

"It was out," Rosie explained, continuing toward the other side of the court. She cocked her head, smiled gently. "Really," she said.

"It caught the line," said Colleen.

"Sorry," said Rosie.

Colleen continued staring and then laughed with derision, shaking her head, looking off over her shoulder as if for an unseen referee. After a moment, she served to Rosie's backhand, and Rosie hit a crisp winner down the line, winning the game.

Rosie was all but whistling as she went to pour herself some ice water from her thermos. Colleen came up to where she stood drinking but did not seem to see her and poured herself water in stony silence. An airplane passed overhead, but it did not entirely drown out the grunts of the boys on the next court, in the midst of a long baseline rally. Rosie walked to the service line. She turned slightly, all of a sudden sure that someone—maybe someone from the sportsmanship committee, maybe Colleen's parents or coach—was watching and had been watching all along. But there was no one. No one except for Luther. He was looking right at her, his brown eyes crinkled ever so slightly around the edges. She felt an incredible jolt of shame and amazement and fear. And felt also that without wanting to, she was sliding into him. She felt the way you do when you stick a plug into an electrical outlet, and turn on the machine—the blender or the vacuum—and are startled by the noise. She did not know what to do with her eyes, and so she glared at him, vibrant with distress.

In her mind, she saw herself running up the stairs toward him and pulling a knife from the waistband of her tennis skirt, stabbing him through the heart with it, killing him with her knife, and then she saw herself dying too. In this horrible moment she wanted obliteration. But turning back to the net, she realized that all she needed was to win four of the next six points—and she did, easily.

Colleen would not shake her hand at the net when the match was over. She appeared to be in a trance. Rosie smiled nicely and went to put her racket in its case.

People could be such bad sports. Colleen bolted away, and Rosie felt sorry for her, but mostly she was excited to be in the quarterfinals.

She lost in the quarters, as she was expected to do, to the number two seed, who went on to upset the number one seed. She did not mind losing at all as long as she was expected to. And still no one but Luther and a few of her opponents knew Rosie's horrible secret.

It was not until early the following week, while practicing with Simone at the public courts in town—there was a round-robin tournament for the adults tying up the courts at their club—that panic set in. People were sitting in the chairs next to the court, watching her and Simone with loud and obvious admiration, and that was almost the best of all feelings, and so she was shaken when her mind began to race with bad images. There she was, running Simone all over the court, vaguely amused by the skill of her performance, when she suddenly and for no reason went from ruthlessly pelting the ball from one baseline corner to the other to watching a slide show in her head of future disgrace. Click: she saw Colleen notify the sportsmanship committee of the junior tennis association, saw herself called before them, charged with cheating. Click: she was playing in a tournament, center court, when out of the audience steps a tall dour man in a suit, like someone from the FBI, who whips his wallet open to show her a badge. Click: she opens the front door and Peter Billings is standing there, brokenhearted, looking at her with pain and contempt. Click: she's standing in front of a closed door with SPORTSMANSHIP COMMITTEE stenciled across the pane of smoky glass, and she knocks and hears a friendly familiar voice she cannot place, a voice that says, "Come in"; flooded with relief, she pushes open the door, and there is Elvin Thackery sitting behind the desk, looking at her with disappointment, holding the little pocketknife he showed her that time when he put his dick on her arm, and he's so unhappy with her now for having cheated that all she can do is hold her breath and try to look cute and harmless so he will take pity on her.

"I have to go home now," she said to Simone, who was always glad to cut a practice short. The spectators clapped as they walked off the court, and Simone bowed at the waist, like the star at curtain call, while Rosie dipped her head down close to her chest as if someone had just spritzed her with cold water.

Rosie began watching the mail, watching her parents for any sign that they had been contacted, but whenever she studied her mother's face as she read or ate or thought, her mother would just look up and smile gently, in her sad and slightly spaced-out way, and then go back to her business. There was no indication anywhere that anyone knew, and she swore she was done with cheating for good, was starting over, starting now. But secretly, in some outlaw part of her psyche, she felt like she had discovered the secret of the universe.

God, she thought. You spend all this time trying to do right but always feeling wrong, and you wonder why you never get ahead and why it takes so much energy, like tightrope walking. And then here she was getting away with cheating, and for some reason in that she found a huge relief. She'd stopped being so good, and she no longer worried so much about falling off the tightrope.

She felt an electric thrill nowadays when she walked past Luther. It was sort of like when she woke up from a dream of kissing boys, or in real life, when Simone told her about kissing boys, about boys kissing her breasts, or how Jason Drake had put his thing into her underpants but not into her. Not really, not all the way. She met Luther's eyes. His gaze was direct and even warm. She turned her back on him and walked away.

SHE told herself it didn't matter if you called a few balls wrong. And the grown-ups were so stupid not to catch her. It made her feel smarter, like she thought Simone must have felt smarter at first, having gone so far with Jason all those weeks ago. Her period was late this month; she had been so desperate for it to start since that day at the river. Natalie had told Rosie something odd the other day, when Simone had the stomach flu and had to default her match. Natalie said to Rosie, "Tell her to give me a call if she needs me," and Rosie had passed it along when she called Simone that night. She asked Simone what that really meant—and how they would know what to do next—but Simone had been so cross with her that they ended up hanging up on each other. The next day, during a close match, she had tried so hard to be good and not cheat, because Simone was so stupid and cheap to let Jason go so far with her, and Rosie wanted to start over, to be a good person who could look down her nose at Simone. But at the same time, she was desperate to win, and wanting to win so badly made her feel like a kite pinned against a wall by a hard wind. And she cheated again, as if she were unable not to, as if she no longer had any choice in the matter.

ONE week later, midway through the next tournament, playing in the round of sixteen late one afternoon, she played a girl who was seeded. Rosie wasn't and it was okay to lose when you played against people who were better. And so she almost didn't cheat, and then she did, at the last moment, as an afterthought, and it was so strange because the seeded girl didn't even seem to notice. But Rosie had the sudden sense that a shadow had just crossed the moon, that someone was watching closely, judging. So she played with great sincerity and didn't cheat again, rallied as well as she could, her brain filled with fear like the piercing sound of a dog whistle, until, walking back to the service line, she could discern by his general shape that a man now sat on a folding chair, watching her through the wooden slats in the chain-link fence. She looked up to see who it was. It was Luther, and she was flooded with relief. *Oh,* my God, thank you, she whispered, it was just Luther. Meeting his eyes for a moment, she felt that sliding-together feeling, that plugged-in sense of connection, the prong sliding into the outlet, but then no rush of fear, no jolt, not much of anything but boredom, nonchalance. As she felt how close victory was, her concentration returned, and euphoria poured through her like a watercolor wash, and she played so well that she took the girl to three sets, and then lost six-three in the third.

For the next week or so, the fear of being caught returned, and she couldn't or wouldn't breathe deeply. It was a form of invisibility. The less air you use, the less beholden you are. She began acting outrageously, like a clown, like a whole circus, on and off the court. Elizabeth and James thought this was out of joy, out of moving so beautifully in your body, connecting with the ball and your partner and the air and the ground—the dance through the air. And sometimes it was; and sometimes she'd forget herself and play like she was dancing; and then Luther would turn up to watch her play, and she'd feel a shifting inside, a door slowly swinging open.

She had read a lot about the darker parts of people; her books were full of darkness and lust, people possessing you, dark forces penetrating your soul, your old good soul. She knew things. She knew he had entered her.

Whenever he came into the clubhouse or the bleachers where she sat watching others play, she felt his gaze on her like when the sun comes sneakily into a room and heats your hand. She found herself deeply aware of him. She kept her back to him, but she went near him more often, showing herself to him all the time without looking at him, without seeing his smirk, as if he had the goods on her, on her body. Someone watching her might have thought this was an offering. But she was just trying to keep tabs on him by always knowing where he was, so that she could see that he wasn't off telling the authorities, telling someone from the sportsmanship committee, whispering Rosie's secret into someone's ear. And yet she also believed, or knew, that he would never betray her.

There was no hiding after the anointing of his gaze. Each time, his eye slid over her and left an oily trace of knowledge.

ten

Simone came over to get Rosie one day at the end of June, in shorts and a tight little T-shirt. Veronica was outside in the car; she was driving the girls down to a tournament in Modesto. The skin of her arms was warm brown; her nipples showed through the thin cotton, like something delicious hidden in cream. Elizabeth stood at the sink, washing dishes.

"My mom heard you on the radio," Simone told James, licking her top lip, and wriggling in her chair as if her clothes did not quite fit right. "She said you were really funny." He sat a bit straighter, a jauntier tilt to his chin, listening closely, as if Simone were dissecting postmodern comedy. "You must be getting famous, to be on the radio," she said.

"Let me put it this way, Simone," he said, amused, avuncular. "Soupy Sales is more famous than almost any writer in this country besides Norman Mailer." Simone's gray eyes opened in indignation.

"I love Soupy Sales," she said.

James slumped back down in his chair. He was silent for a moment. Then he nodded. "I know you do, honey," he said mournfully.

Rae called just after the girls drove off.

"I'm worried," said Elizabeth. "They're so big, and Simone is so sexy, and they're going to be so far from home and I'm sure Luther will be there. Maybe I'm just hormonal. Tell me not to worry."

"Don't worry, Elizabeth."

"Okay. I won't. How're you?"

"I'm doing okay," Rae reported. "I'm actually having stretches of time where I forget to think about Mike at all."

"You sound a little depressed," said Elizabeth.

"I am. I've got a birthday coming up, you know. It's making me sort of sad. Six months ago, I thought I had a boyfriend in place this year, old awful Mike, and that maybe we'd go up to Mendocino or something for the weekend. Now it's just me again."

"And us."

"And you. That's true. I'd sort of forgotten. I just asked myself about fifteen minutes ago how I thought I should spend my birthday, and I thought, Well, I could always take my Visa Gold card, charge it to the max, and then jump off the bridge with my *nicest* gifts."

"Yeah. Or you could come over here for dinner and a movie. Rosie's gone for the week."

"All right, then. But next year, the Gold card."

IT was all going by too quickly. Was there even any point in caring so deeply when it all spun past like ticker tape? The last thing Elizabeth could remember, Rosie had been three years old, naked in sandboxes, painting the walls with poster paints, sitting skeptically on Santa's lap. "And what do you want for Christmas?" Santa asked her that year. "A tree," Rosie replied in a tiny trembly voice. "And what would you hope to find underneath that tree?" Santa asked. "Guns," she said. Now she was off for a week two hundred miles away, staying overnight with strangers, "housing" with people during the tournament, calling in every night to report on how she'd done—so far she'd won two singles matches and was in the quarterfinals, up against the fourth seed. She and Simone were seeded first in the doubles and so were expected to win.

Rosie had called that morning before playing; she hadn't slept much, and she sounded as squeaky as an eight-year-old. Elizabeth listened and made sympathetic sounds.

Rosie had a terrible time sleeping when she was away, and she often showed up to play morning matches on two or three hours of sleep. One time last year, before the finals of the state championships, she had called Elizabeth at four in the morning, scared out of her wits. She and Simone were housing in a dusty old mansion in San Jose, and Rosie was so afraid that she thought she might go crazy. Earlier that night, she had found a stack of old magazines on a shelf in the bedroom. Some were from the sixties, and when she was unable to fall asleep by midnight, she'd ended up thumbing through an ancient issue of *Time*. Simone was sound asleep, and at first it was good company, but then she had come to an article about a killer, a man with pockmarks and greasy hair named Richard Speck.

"Oh, no, honey," Elizabeth said over the phone. "I hope you didn't read it. Tell me you didn't read it."

But she had. At first she'd turned right past it, terrorized by the headlines—about the eight student nurses he had killed in Chicago— but it got me, she said in a hushed voice.

Elizabeth had imagined Rosie in her nightie in a strange house, reading of the murders, riveted, her mouth open, not moving her head, the way she did whenever she was darkly entranced—her eyes hooded and flickering from one photo to another. Elizabeth remembered the story well, how Richard Speck had entered the little townhouse in Chicago, holding a gun on the nurse who answered the door; how he had bewitched the eight student nurses who lived in that little townhouse, beguiled them with his quiet jokey seductiveness, his greasy pockmarked power like a paralyzing freezing gas from an aerosol can. Elizabeth had closed her eyes, as dread drained through her. She remembered the eight young women who sat with him on the bedroom floor, almost as if at a tea party, mesmerized, thinking their magical thoughts, clinging to the shore of happy endings. The fear must have frozen or curdled their blood, for no one thought to try and overpower him.

"Let's think what we can do to help you through the night," Elizabeth had said, turning to look at the shape of her sleepy husband who was yawning in bed beside her in the dark. A pulse raced in her head, "Honey," she said. "This will not happen to you or to me. This happened years and years ago, in Chicago. Okay? And in two or three hours the sun will be up again."

"Mommy," Rosie had asked, quavering, tremulous. "Mommy? Why didn't the nurses even try to gang up on him? The article said he sat around with them for a while, talking and smiling, before he tied them up. He smiled, that's what the girl who lived said. Then they had to listen to each other being killed. Mommy? Do you remember that?"

"Yes."

"But the one girl hid. He must have lost count," Rosie said. "Like on Halloween when you're done with trick-or-treating, if someone hid a candy bar or two, there were still so many others you wouldn't even notice."

They talked about it on the phone for half an hour, both in the dark, quietly, and Elizabeth steered the conversation to sweet ordinary moments, as much for herself as for Rosie. Finally Rosie said she was going to crawl into bed with Simone and see if she could get a little sleep.

But later that morning, when the sun had indeed come up and James and Elizabeth had driven down to San Jose to watch the girls in the finals of the twelve-and-under doubles, Rosie had been so defeated by the nightmarish night that she almost didn't care if she won or lost. Not caring had freed her. Simone had leapt around the court like a long-legged African cat, while Rosie moved as little as possible, quiet and broody as a gaunt young buffalo; still she'd played out of her head. Bleary and cross, she whacked backhands down the line, fired in aces, made impossible winners off their opponents' best shots, and they won the finals in straight sets.

She had not brought up Speck and the nurses again.

Now, she and Simone were housing in Modesto. Elizabeth sighed as Luther shuffled once again unbidden into her mind. Her hazel eyes shrunk as if with strain; she wondered if he was a real threat to Rosie, this dark ruined man. Maybe, as James said, he was not evil, like the greasy satanic Richard Speck. And yet he cast a shadow, a penumbra, on their lives. In his psychic intrusion, his fascination with Rosie, he was looking for something on the other side of her beauty and health, on the other side of her clothes, her skin. And so she hoped that Luther was not in Modesto, watching the girls in silence, biding his time.

It was still hotter than hell at ten o'clock. Nearly one hundred degrees all day, there had been several hours after dinner when the temperature had dropped twenty degrees, and Rosie and Simone had hung out all evening with the Doyles, the childless couple housing them. The heavily landscaped street where they lived was filled with life, couples of all ages sitting in beach chairs out on their lawns, children tearing around through sprinklers, racing past on bikes, tossing water balloons at each other. There was a lot more energy out on the streets than in Bayview, where in early July it seemed like everyone stayed inside, behind their gates, or went to clubs or up to the mountain. But the parents didn't sit in lounge chairs on their lawn, and they didn't let their kids play kick-the-can at night either, out on the street. Their children stayed behind fences with them.

The couple who lived next door to the Doyles were young and blond and had Southern accents, like they were from Georgia or something, and they got the girls cans of Mountain Dew from the refrigerator in their garage. Two men who lived in a bungalow across the street invited the girls to play Ping-Pong out in their driveway, and the girls trounced them.

"One more game," they begged at 9:30, but Rosie explained that she and Simone had to be up at 7:00 for their matches. Please, please, they wheedled as Simone looked eagerly over her shoulder at Rosie, Rosie who had so much more sense, and Rosie shrugged.

"How 'bout I get you girls another Mountain Dew?" one man asked, and Simone said no, she didn't think so, and looked to Rosie, who shrugged and said well, okay, sure, thanks. It was not until she'd finished the second can that she remembered that this lemonadey clear yellow soda was actually full of caffeine, and she closed her eyes, knowing that another night of despair lay ahead.

BECAUSE the Doyles' old Tudor house was still so hot, the stucco and brick holding in the day's heat, the girls chose to sleep in sleeping bags out on the screened-in porch. They were still awake at eleven, talking about their matches tomorrow and, in the same tone, about Simone's period, which was now extremely late.

"What do you mean?" Rosie had asked that day on the river, her face knotted with anxiety, a feeling like a clenched fist in her stomach. "You're late, but . . . wait . . . What do you mean, you hope you're not pregnant? How could you be, when you said he didn't put it in?"

Simone had not answered for a minute.

"I told you. He didn't put it in *all* the way."

Now, here in Modesto, with Simone's period six weeks late and Simone already several pounds heavier, Rosie was trying to be supportive, listening to Simone go on and on about what if she was pregnant, and if she was, then maybe she'd keep the baby, and Rosie could be the second mother. It was like she was talking about getting a puppy. Rosie's eyes were hooded in the dark. She would not really get to be the baby's other mother; she would be the baby's mother's little thirteen-year-old friend. But she murmured to Simone yes, yes, discussing how great it would be. Simone would still get to play tournaments some-how—there were still a few details to work out. They yawned in the heat of the night, sweaty, dusty, tired. You could hear crickets, the river moving slowly through the town. Big moths sunned themselves on the dim porch light, a delta breeze wafted in through the screen, smelling of vineyards and almond orchards. The Modesto night was moonless, black, the stars at their brightest.

Rosie's heart was pounding with fear and caffeine. She looked at her watch. It was after midnight. She looked at Simone. Simone's eyes were closed and her mouth a little open.

"Simone?" she whispered.

"Yeah?"

"Are you falling asleep?"

"Uh-huh."

"Okay. See you in the morning." She had not brought anything to read. The porch light was still on; moths were still worshiping at it. She desperately wanted to hear her mother's voice. She heard the whine of a mosquito and searched the walls and screens of the porch until she found it, a whiny black spot on the wall. She tiptoed to it, holding her slipper, and whacked it.

Simone opened her eyes. "Sorry," Rosie whispered. "Mosquito." Simone nodded, yawned, went back to sleep, and Rosie got back in bed. She had not been there but a minute when she heard another whine, started scanning the walls and air slowly until she found it on the ceiling above her. She picked up her slipper and tried to hit it, missed. It flew away, and she scanned until she found it again and killed it with her slipper. This time Simone did not wake up. Rosie lay back in bed for a second, until the next mosquito appeared, and she got out of bed to track it and kill it, stealthily, and then there was another, and Rosie bounded around feeling like a wired little rat on its hind legs.

Finally she thought she'd killed them all. Simone snored like an old pug. Rosie's skin prickled and stung with heat and sweat, and she couldn't get back in the sleeping bag, and she couldn't turn off the

porch light because she was too afraid, and she lay on top of the sleeping bag in her tiny baby-doll jammies. Her heart beat, frogs croaked
from one of the nearby irrigation canals that crisscrossed the town,
and she thought she heard footsteps; out on the sidewalk, she thought
she saw spaces darker than night.

"Simone?" she whispered. No answer. It felt like a jungle inside the
porch. One of her hot sweaty legs lay across the other like a boa. She
imagined snakes slithering around the floor. She said the Lord's Prayer
and, on finishing it, said it again. "Mommy," she whispered out loud. It
scared her to have said it out loud. "Mommy," she whispered again.
She watched Simone sleep, and she cried for a minute out of loneliness. It was nearly one. They had to get up in six hours. She said the
Lord's Prayer again and had the sudden urge to jam her elbow into
Simone's eye socket. She saw herself sinking her slightly bucked front
teeth into Simone's pearly forehead. She cried because Simone might
be pregnant and because she was afraid she might be crazy and because her mother was going to die someday. Finally she closed her eyes
and began to count backward from six hundred by threes, like Lank
had taught her to do, and a few minutes later a sleepy waking dream
filled her head, and she drifted off.

eleven

A
‎T eight o'clock the next morning, Rosie walked
onto the last court in a row of six at the Modesto Swim and Racket
Club, walking with her opponent Donna Brooks, a lovely young player
who moved like a ballerina and hit as hard as one of the older boys.
Dressed in a little skirt and tight white tank top, she streamed onto the
court like sunshine, head held high, while Rosie, squinting against the
few rays of morning light that broke through the dark foggy day,
moved like an abused whippet.

She was wearing huge shorts, which weren't really for tennis, and
one of James's big white T-shirts. She tried to calm herself as she
walked to the baseline for warm-up. But she watched in disbelief as the
first ball she tried to return sailed past Donna and hit the fence. She
laughed nervously. Nice shot, she said to herself, and hit the remaining
ball over the net. Donna pranced after the two balls like a little cartoon
unicorn.

Donna hit hard, but if you kept getting the ball back, eventually
she'd miss, and Rosie tapped one ball back after another, not breathing
in between rallies. Never had she played so poorly, so tight and defensive. Nowhere were her trademark shots, long deep crosscourts, hard
flat down-the-line backhands, and her serve was so constricted that she
looked like Lank serving, or Rumpelstiltskin.

Her face felt enflamed. She was ahead now, three games each but
her ad, one point away from a definite psychological advantage; this
seventh game was the most important in any close set. All she had to
do was win this one point, and she'd be halfway home. A fresh shot of
adrenaline flooded her, and she balled up her fist, coaching herself:
come on come on come on. She looked around for the extra ball.
Instead her gaze was lifted to the top bleacher, where Luther sat alone,

hunched over, his head barely raised high enough to see. He wore his raggedy black windbreaker, darker than the dark foggy day surrounding him. And he was smiling.

Rosie could have cried. There was Donna's nice mother, in good clothes, and there was Donna's nice coach, handsome and tan in tennis whites, talking quietly as they waited for play to resume, while her own mother was home acting spaced out and odd, and J. Peter Billings was three thousand miles away. And in their place was Luther.

She served as hard as she could, a beautiful hard spinning serve, but it missed by an inch, and she sent her second serve over as if it were an egg she didn't want to break, and Donna smashed it down the line for a winner. Deuce. Rosie served hard again, out of control, and it somehow went in—it surprised Rosie as much as Donna—who muffed the return. Donna swung petulantly at the ground. Luther clapped. The hairs on the back of Rosie's neck stood up.

She served another hard first serve, and they rallied for a while. Then Donna hit a drop shot, which Rosie got to, just barely, and Donna lobbed the ball over her head, and Rosie set off running toward her own baseline, chasing it down, but she couldn't get to it. The ball landed on the very outside part of the baseline, mostly on the red but definitely catching a quarter inch or so of the white line. She knew instantly that her body was blocking Donna's view, and looking up she saw Donna's mother searching for something in her purse, and Donna's coach was peering in too, as if it went down a very long way, like a well. Luther alone was watching. He smiled. She stared at him. She turned to Donna, who was up on her toes, trying to see around Rosie, as if the ball had left a spot on the court that she could see from the opposite side, and Rosie said, "Just out." Donna hung her head and then looked up.

"Are you sure?" she asked. "It felt good." Rosie, holding both balls now, walking toward the net to change sides, nodded.

"It missed," she said. "By a speck."

She was in the semis now. It was a good win, not an upset, because she was seeded higher, but a necessary win. Donna shook hands after her loss like the prima donna she was, and Rosie left the court without making eye contact with anyone.

After reporting the score and returning the balls at the tournament desk, Rosie went to the locker room and sat on the bench. She was alone, so tired she felt like crying, but happy about her win. And now when she thought about that one point, she could almost imagine that the ball really had landed out, that there really had been a tiny patch of red hard court between the ball and the baseline—past the white paint of the baseline, a thin red line, like the last thread of a sunset.

twelve

I'VE begun dating a twelve-year-old," Rae announced over the phone the next morning. "But he's very mature."

"Well, then, that's wonderful, darling."

"Why shouldn't I call Mike again?"

"Because if you call him, after going for all these *months* without calling, he'll feel great, but you'll feel like shit. If you don't call, you'll feel great, and he'll feel like shit. You get to decide."

Rae sighed. "You know what I hate, Elizabeth? I hate that men know, they learn, that if they just wait, the woman will almost always come after them."

"That's right."

"But as soon as you appear available, their interest lags."

"Unless they really want to develop something with you. And Mike made it clear over and over that he didn't want to. Or wasn't able to."

"You know another thing I hate?"

"What's that?"

"That any man who's even fairly attractive has twenty women who want to fuck him."

"That's right."

"I don't think I'll call."

"Good."

"But stay by the phone all day anyway, in case I need you."

"I will, Rae. What are you going to do today?"

"I'm going to drive the owner of this new gallery out to the airport. He's flying to New York, and he's taking slides of my stuff with him. Then I'll be right back, unless I meet a bunch of fancy strangers at the airport—and then who knows when you'll hear from me again."

"This woman is really something," Lank told James and Elizabeth a few hours later, referring to the waifish art student he had found in the personals. James was on the phone in his office, Elizabeth listening in the kitchen, the phone cradled in the crook of her neck while she weeded the utility drawer. "We cooked together the other night, me braising some meat for the stew while she did the vegetables. The two of us chopping away, like a little salt-and-pepper set."

"Have you gone to bed yet?" asked James.

"Oh, yeah."

"And?"

"She comes like a flock of birds."

"What does that mean, Lank? She had crows in her pussy?"

Elizabeth looked at the floor and smiled.

"I think you would both be happy for me if you could stop wishing for Rae and me to fall in love," Lank retorted. "We're not going to. It's simply not going to happen."

"We know that," said Elizabeth. "We don't care."

"I care," said James. "I want you to. I hate for both of you to be so lonely when a great, available person is right in front of you."

"It's the chemistry, James. Come on, man. And the God thing drives me crazy. I can't believe someone so smart believes in Jesus. Once she told me how she feels his love in the tenderness of her friends, the beauty of the earth, the warmth inside her heart. I said yes, I feel all those things too, but why do you have to drag Jesus the friendly ghost into it?"

Elizabeth stared at a spiderweb on the ceiling. It was so strange to have a close friend who loved Jesus. Rae saw poor people, she thought of Jesus; she saw wildflowers, grapes on the vine, full moons, and she thought of Jesus. Rosie asked her recently why she used to see friendship and nature as just being friendship and nature and now she called it all Jesus. And Rae told her the story of a pastor asking his Sunday school first graders, "What's gray and has a long bushy tail and collects nuts in the fall?" And a small boy answered, "I know the answer is probably Jesus, but it sure sounds like a squirrel to me."

Elizabeth studied the small brown spider who sat in the center of the web, and after a moment she said good-bye to Lank, hung up the phone, and went to get the broom.

ROSIE called not long after, and James listened patiently as she described yesterday's win against Donna in great detail, including the lob at three games each, how it had landed one inch out.

"Good girl," he said. "Way to go. Did Simone win too?"

"She hasn't finished playing yet. Is Mommy there?"

"She's in her room, cleaning our closets."

There was silence on the other end. "Mommy's cleaning the *clos-ets*?"

"Yeah. She's on a bit of a tear. When I came out of my study, I discovered she'd gone through that big catchall drawer in the kitchen and sorted out all the thumbtacks and paper clips and doodads. Now they live in little tiny baby-food jars, each labeled, all in a row. Like a little nursery."

"James? Is she okay?"

"I think so. Do you want me to go get her? She's going to be so proud of you."

"No. Tell her I'll call later. Simone just came off the court."

SIMONE's face was red and blotchy, and her tight, blue nylon dress clung to her. She had lost in straight sets to Mandy Lee, who was ranked way below her. Rosie felt anxiety radiating off her like sun-beams. Rings of sweat darkened the dress beneath her armpits, like a grown-up's. Rosie longed for those womanly rings. "Didja play okay?" Rosie asked, her eyes opened wide with hopefulness. Simone answered in a voice at once quavery and petulant that Mandy Lee had just pushed every ball over the net, even serves, never hitting hard and low, dinking and lobbing and spinning and doing whatever it took to keep the ball in play.

"I hate that so much," Rosie said. Simone stood staring at the ground, twirling a strand of hair like a little kid. Then she stalked off.

Rosie found her around the corner standing with a group of fourteen-year-old boys, watching the fathers of two sixteen-year-old girls push and shove each other in the parking lot. The father of a girl named Gail Smith, whose ranking had gone from number one in the fourteens to number eight in the sixteen and unders, was poking his finger into the chest of Jessica Paul's father, who had his fists up. This was not an entirely unusual experience: two or three times a year the tennis dads went at it, usually the fathers of teenage girls who had been ranked one or two in the younger age divisions and who were maybe not going to go on to national rankings or tennis scholarships. One time Jessica Paul's father had beaten up Mandy Lee's father in the parking lot of a club where the state championships were being held, and another time Mandy Lee's father had leapt out of a bush and nearly broken Deb Hall's father's nose, after Deb's father accused Mandy of messing with Deb's concentration during a semifinal match.

There were twenty or so kids standing around in clusters, just like at school when two kids squared off on the blacktop. Luther stood a little ways off, wearing his crummy black windbreaker and a visor, because it was nearly a hundred degrees. Rosie watched Luther watch the two men square off as if it were just another match. She felt both thrilled and stricken, smelling the blacktop on fire and oily with the heat of the long hot day; it smelled like grime, like cannons, like cars. Simone seemed enthralled, feeling the heat, the two angry men, and the cluster of boys, the sun pouring down on them all, and she glanced from one boy to another.

"Don't make a mistake with me," Gail's father said to Jessica's father.

"Yeah? Yeah? What does that mean?"

"I'm the wrong guy to fuck with."

The time Mandy Lee's father had beaten up Deb Hall's father, he kept saying, "You got bad eyes, Herb, weird eyes—psycho eyes," and for days afterward the kids who had witnessed the scene went around telling each other, "Hey, you got weird eyes—psycho eyes."

Gail Smith's father eventually yelled at Jessica Paul's father that he was going to have to take things up with Deb Hall's father, who was on the junior tennis association sportsmanship committee. He walked off the parking lot with both arms raised in the air, giving Mr. Paul the finger, the *double* finger, and the children in their tennis finery and Luther in his ragged jacket stood in the parking lot spellbound and watched him go.

. . .

AFTER both men had left, the boys hung around Simone, who looked like someone who should be in a television commercial for Swiss chocolate milk, except that her hair was not in braids but hanging loose, framing that sulky milkmaid face. Rosie remembered last summer when Simone was going out with Andy Gold, how often they had just started necking like newlyweds on TV, even though Rosie would be standing right there on the curb beside them, shuffling her feet, trying to act nonchalant. It always made her feel like some dried-up old praying-mantis auntie. Now Simone was telling the gathering of boys about having lost to skinny awful Mandy Lee, whom they all secretly hated anyway for being Chinese and wearing glasses. Rosie didn't hate her at all. What was to hate? Mandy Lee was shy and driven and had an awful father who coached her from the bushes. Rosie just felt very sorry for her, because she wasn't all that good and her father wanted her to be great, but the boys' faces were twisted with derision and sympathy as they listened, snatching occasional looks at Simone's breasts. Rosie stood beside her, looking at her like a golden retriever, adoring and loyal. None of the boys said hello to Rosie, but she did not expect them to. She could smell them, eyes closed. They smelled of many things all at once, and then, slowly, the smells sorted themselves. There was Absorbine Jr. wafting up from their feet. There was the same deodorant that James wore when he went out—Old Spice stick. And there was a faint trace of ammonia, and of sweat, and rain. She felt like a boat at sea, out of control.

Simone no longer looked like she had lost. She swayed ever so slightly as she stood there, silky, sinewy, luring the boys in. Rosie felt a fluttering in her groin, that tightening—as if she might start swaying, too. All at once both girls noticed Luther watching them from twenty feet away, in his windbreaker and scuffed wing tips, leaning against the building, looking at them all, at Simone, who looked up at him as if across a crowded dance floor, slowly pushing her chest forward and then, slowly, incredibly, tracing her lips with the tip of her tongue, right at him, to him, to Luther.

The boys, wired and hot, turned as one to see whom she was being so seductive with. Everyone but Rosie began to laugh at Luther standing there staring back. Rosie felt a warm flush of sorrow at his being the object of their ridicule and at their not being able to see the tiny piece of light in his face, the pathetic part that wasn't scary—the yearning. And she was so glad the mockery wasn't directed at her that she finally joined in the laughter. But she could not take her eyes off Luther as he walked away, across the black asphalt, through shimmering waves of heat.

dusk

one
_____

Rosie studied the sunlight streaming onto Natalie's long blonde hair. She usually wore it in a ponytail for matches, or clipped to the back of her head, and even sometimes in a ballerina's bun, but today it fell loose down her back like drapes. Flaxen was the word, like someone's hair in a fairy tale, thick and straight, four or five colors of yellow, from yellow white like early morning sun to the yellow of a parakeet or a lemon's deep yellow. It was the most beautiful hair Rosie had ever seen, multicolored like those skeins of yarn going from white through each shade along the way to the darkest hue. The sun sparkled in all of those strands of yellow, like it was dancing with its own family.

Rosie was sitting in the back seat of Natalie's car, an old powder-blue Mustang. They were listening to oldies on the radio, although Natalie kept pushing the buttons, trying to find better songs.

In the passenger seat next to Natalie, Simone sat staring straight ahead, so teary and grave and full of herself and her hardship that it was almost like bragging. It was like they were taking her in to find out if she had cancer, instead of for a pregnancy test.

They had told their mothers that Natalie was taking them down to Menlo Park for the day to practice with her and her doubles partner at the convent, which was so lovely you could hardly concentrate at first for the beauty of the trees and the old buildings. Of course the mothers had said yes. Veronica always just needed for Simone to have somewhere to be so she could work at her salon, and Elizabeth had gone back to bed that morning, claiming to have a headache. But a lot of mornings lately she had gone back to bed with one excuse or another.

Natalie had a wonderful father, a tennis pro of great renown who loved his daughter so much; they always stood together at tournaments, watching his students, like Natalie was his wife, so tall and well developed, so tan, so accomplished, so pretty.

"Trust me," said Natalie. "You're not going to be pregnant."

They drove the ten miles to San Rafael to the local Planned Parenthood office. Natalie had had an abortion here a few years ago when she was fifteen, and her boyfriend, who had been ranked number one in northern California, had been with her. They had gone steady for three years. He was as handsome as a Greek statue, but tan, really tan, beautiful as Natalie. They always were the first to dance slow dances, and you could see they were really in love and that you would never be in the arms of such a handsome guy who loved you so much. His name was Bill Shephard, and she called him Billy, in this way that sounded like she had a slight Southern accent. But he went back east to college on a tennis scholarship and had stayed there for the summer.

She had been on the pill ever since her abortion.

"We're going to get you taken care of," she said to Simone after she'd picked the two girls up this morning. "If you're pregnant, I can help you get the money together. Don't even worry about it now. Jason will contribute, I give you my word on *that.*"

Simone had gotten it into her head that Jason would come today, be there with her, be there with her next week if she needed an abortion. But he was heading up to the Pacific Northwest in a few days for the circuit there, which was for the kids who were not quite good enough for the eastern nationals but too good to hang around playing the lesser tournaments here. And he couldn't take time off from practice.

So Rosie had been dragged along, like a pet hunchback, in the back seat behind these blonde girls—not really girls but not women yet either—who sat in the front seat of the Mustang, talking about birth control pills and abortions like Rosie and Simone used to sit in back seats and talk about their lessons and the dogs they would have one day.

THERE was no one outside the clinic when the three girls went in, Simone with an artichoke-hearts jar of the morning's first urine hidden in her purse. Rosie and Natalie sat in the waiting room with three black girls and dozens of old magazines. Natalie was reading an old *Mademoiselle* with such poise you could picture her waiting for her hair to dry at a beauty salon. Rosie's stomach was racing, like it was filled with lightning bugs, like she was about to get diarrhea. Mostly she was praying for Natalie to be right, for Simone not to be pregnant. But there was a part of her, too—the mean narrow-eyed part, the demon-field part—that hoped she was, that said she deserved to be, that said she was bad and deserved an abortion, deserved to have sharp cutting things inside her. And Rosie squinted back guilty tears, tears of hating herself, of being sorry, so when Simone came out, white as a ghost and weak like after people give blood, holding some papers, Rosie's heart both sank and soared in guilty flight. A middle-aged woman walking with Simone touched her shoulder gently, pointed to something on one of the pieces of paper, and reached into the pocket of her white jacket for Kleenex. She handed the tissue to Simone and disappeared.

Rosie and Natalie stared at Simone, who wouldn't look at them, and walked out the door of the clinic without saying anything. Rosie and Natalie looked at each other.

"God," Rosie whispered.

There were protesters shouting outside the clinic when they left, protesters with enormous signs, one woman holding a huge photo-graph of a tiny fetus, the size of your thumb, attached to the umbilical cord, so perfectly humanly formed that it might have just been born. Natalie took Rosie's hand like she was her big sister and pulled Rosie past the crowd to the car.

Rosie felt wild on the inside, jazzed, like she was on something, al-though the only thing she had ever been on was a cup of Veronica's leftover coffee, lukewarm with lots of cream and sugar.

When they caught up with Simone, she wasn't crying, but mascara was smeared like shadows below her eyes. "I'm going to have an abor-tion in a couple of weeks," she said. "I think." Rosie put her arms around her. They hugged for a long time, while Natalie got in the car and reached over to unlock the passenger door. When Rosie had climbed into the back seat and Simone into the front, Natalie reached into her purse for something and handed it to Simone. It was a hundred-dollar bill.

"I got it for graduation," she said.

"I have eighty-seven," said Rosie.

They both looked at Simone. "I have thirty," she said.

"We're halfway there," said Natalie. "We'll get the rest."

"Do you have to tell your mom? Does she have to sign—like—a permission slip?"

"Rosie, duh. You don't get permission slips for abortions."

"Ask Jason for two hundred," said Natalie.

SOMEHOW Jason got the money a few days later. Simone called Rosie to tell her in a whisper one morning, and Rosie felt her heart sink with disappointment. She felt ashamed and dirty to admit it, but she was mad at Simone for lying and saying she hadn't gone all the way, for making it seem like if the guy only put it in an inch, it didn't count as going all the way. Rosie had finally figured it out. Simone had gotten drunk and *gone all the way*. And they could never again be as close as they had been. There was something more important to her than Rosie, their friendship, and their tennis life together. Now Rosie was like this little kid with skinny little legs, and Simone *was* half like a woman. Simone had crossed over. And Rosie felt she should be punished. Natalie had crossed over too. She was on the same side of the river as Simone. They should both be punished. Rosie was standing on the bank alone, a warty river gnome.

So Rosie rode her bike into town with Simone to meet Jason in front of the pharmacy on the boardwalk. The girls got off their bikes and sat waiting on a wooden bench. There were flower boxes everywhere, with geraniums and every color of impatiens. You could see the mountain, the slope of the Indian maiden's breast. Jason had said he'd be there at two, and Rosie imagined him getting out of his dad's car, walking into Simone's arms, telling her how sorry he was that he couldn't be there, but he loved her and would call. And they would embrace like newlyweds, while Rosie sat on the wooden bench, acting vaguely bored while they kissed passionately, and she would stare at the mountain and watch the fog roll in. But people came and went in a parade of tanned faces, well-dressed little children, mothers mostly in tennis clothes but a few in business suits, men mostly in suits but a few in tennis clothes, teenagers on bikes and skateboards. Finally Simone asked someone the time. It was 2:35, and she turned to Rosie, looking like a dog you're playing a trick on with hidden cheese, and a moment later Jason's tennis partner, Mark Evers, pulled up on a mountain bike. "Hi!" said Simone. "Is Jason with you?" Mark shook his head. He was trying to be cool, but his eyes looked fearful or angry. He reached into the back pocket of his perfectly faded jeans and took out a folded-up envelope. Simone cocked her head and peered into his face.

"Isn't Jason coming?" she asked.

He flung the envelope at her, but she was too surprised to catch it. It fluttered to the ground like a paper airplane and landed at her feet. She bent forward to study it, as if something alive had fallen from the sky. Rosie looked into Mark's sharp brown face, and before her very eyes, his face softened.

"Pick it up, Simone," he said, but she didn't.

"Where's Jason?" she asked in a scared, small voice. Mark sighed, got off his bike, lay it on the ground, and retrieved the envelope. "Here," he said, not unkindly. Rosie's heart pounded in her ears. After a long moment, Simone took it out of his hand. Mark stared down at his sneakers and then looked over his shoulder. Simone started to say something but stopped. Rosie watched Mark get back on his bike and whip the handlebars around, as though he were riding off on a horse.

"Could you tell him to call me?" Simone asked, and Mark said sure, and pedaled away without looking back.

two

O N the seventh of July, James celebrated his thirty-seventh birthday, and they decided to spend the day at the Russian River—James and Elizabeth, Rosie, Rae, and Lank. Simone and her mother were out of town for the weekend. Rosie had been out in the garden all morning weeding; she charged her mother four dollars an hour and had been working a lot all week. She was apparently saving for something.

James came into the kitchen and kissed the back of Elizabeth's neck as she stood at the counter making sandwiches. He kissed the top of Rae's head as she sat at the table stuffing celery sticks with cream cheese. She sang him happy birthday. He bowed and went to the freezer for an ice cream sandwich. He held one out to Elizabeth, who shook her head, and to Rae, who drew back, a vampire recoiling from the cross.

"Please, James. I feel like a pike today. Before they gefilte it."

"So whom were we talking about?"

"I'm sort of interested in this guy at the gallery."

"Is he available? Is he straight? Does he speak English?"

"I don't know. We went for coffee, but I didn't end up knowing all that much about his circumstances. But clearly he adores me."

"Well, we like that," he said and handed her the ice cream sandwich he was working on. She absently began to groom the borders with her tongue. "Did you ask him if you could come over and watch him dance in the shower?" Rae shook her head. "Isn't that what you usually ask on a first date?"

Rae nodded happily and handed the ice cream sandwich back to him. She had brought a paper plate of homemade meringues flecked with dark chocolate, because it was James's birthday and because Rosie had always especially loved them. But when Rosie finally lumbered in and slid down into Rae's lap, wearing the remains of a pair of cutoffs, a tank top, and a Giants cap, she looked askance at the meringues, as though they were laced with strychnine. Her fingernails were ringed with black crescent moons of soil from the garden. She finally picked out a meringue and ate it in tiny bites. Elizabeth, at the cutting board, opened her mouth like a baby bird, closed it for a moment to make peeping sounds, and Rosie got up, ambled over, and put the last bite on her mother's tongue like a host.

LANK was standing on the grass outside his house when they pulled up a while later. The sun shone directly on his bald spot, which was surrounded by lovely reddish hair. There was so much forehead now, smooth as a baby's; it gave him a gentle look. His eyes were closed and his head was bowed as if he were hearing the national anthem. But when they honked, he looked up, clutched his heart with passion, and walked with his arms outstretched toward James in the driver's seat.

ROSIE sat between Lank and Rae all the way up to the river, her knees drawn up because of the hump; she wore a headset, listening to rap music. She could feel their sides and shoulders against her, and Rae's thigh. Rae smelled like soap, Lank faintly of dog. Rosie wished they could have brought Bruno. He loved to chase sticks even if you tossed them way out into the river. Lank called him his Adirondack-log dog. She would rather have had a dog to play with instead of all the grown-ups. She hadn't slept very much the night before. She'd lain there in the dark filled with visions of handsome boys taking her face in their hands to kiss, or leading her out to the dance floor, looking back over their shoulders at her as she walked in slow motion in their wake. Half the night she'd watched matches in her head, rallies she had memorized without meaning to and rallies that might happen one day—endless, deep, hard, heroic. Whenever she saw one of the rallies in which she'd cheated, she blinked hard until a new rally began. The rest of the time she thought about Simone. She tried to imagine Simone having sex, and she thought about the abortion Simone was going to have in five more days, the details of the procedure as Simone had described them to her—the rod with the suction vacuuming out the little blob of stuff. They almost had enough money now, with Natalie's hundred, Jason's two, the money Rosie and Simone already had, a hundred or so they had earned since. Rosie remembered last summer when she and Simone were saving to go to Marine World.

Finally near dawn she had drifted in and out of sleep, into an altered state that felt like she kept entering the chambers of an insect's eye, those dark bejeweled catacombs. And then she would lounge there, dozing in those burrows, until she jerked back awake.

In the car on the way to the river, she heard the grown-ups talking about Charles, and she turned up the volume on her Walkman and watched the passing view—the dairy farms and golden fields and oak trees on either side of the highway and then the vineyards. When she turned it down sometime later, they were talking about politics, so she turned the volume back up. The next time she turned it down, she heard Lank telling a story over the sound of the rap. She listened like a spy.

"It was one of those dates that was life scarring. These mutual friends of ours thought we were made for each other. 'Hey, yeah, they both like to read! That'll work!' We're both single, almost the same age, and they tell me how great she is. She's supposedly got this glorious black mane of hair. Her name's Gloria, right? They make her sound like the best thing since beer in cans. And she's got a voice on the phone that makes you want to rush over and start licking her. So I arrange to pick her up at her house. I drive over, full of hope and expectation, and she opens the door, and I almost gasp—'No,' I want to scream, 'no, no—where's the woman I was talking to on the phone, with the velvet voice?' Well, she opens her mouth, and it's her. 'Hiii,' she says softly, and I swear to God, I think about faking a heart attack, about falling to my knees and grabbing for my chest: 'Oh, Jesus, Jesus, my heart—no, don't call 911, I'll be okay; I just have to get back to my car. I'll crawl, I'll crawl, I'm fine.' "

"What did you do?" asked James.

"I said, 'How nice to meet you, Gloria. Gee, you have a glossy coat.' "

Elizabeth turned to give Rae a look of disgust. "Imagine what they would say if we weren't here."

"Men are pigs," said Rae. Lank smiled.

"Look at James and me," said Elizabeth. "I was looking for someone my height or taller. I was looking for David Niven. Or at any rate I
had a picture in my mind, and it did not include chipped teeth and
polyester shirts and smoking and Einstein hair."

"I don't wear polyester anymore."

"I know you don't, darling. All I meant is that you did not exactly fit
the fantasy I'd been carrying around my whole life of a Ken doll
grown up. I mean, by the same token, I don't think you were looking
for a tall drunk, with a kid and a dead husband and no idea what she
wanted to be when she grew up."

James smiled at her. "Right?" she asked. He shrugged. He wore
white T-shirts and Levi's these days. But now they were the kind cut
for slightly older men, with extra room for a bigger belly and butt, and
he seemed to be somewhat offended by the accuracy of the fit.

THE river was wide, gray green nearest the shore, deeper and darker
little by little until the water on the other side, reflecting the overhung
trees and bushes, glowed jewel green. Elizabeth studied the wall of
redwoods that towered above a lower wall of willows and bay and
buckeye trees, ash and sycamore. An osprey hovered overhead. The
water was striped by beams of light, dotted with children in inflatable
rubber ducks, grown-ups in black inner tubes floating lazily along.
Redwoods rose straight as sentries all along the low hills that framed
the river, behind and above every bend, row after row in both directions, like mirrors full of trees reflecting mirrors full of trees.

Elizabeth stretched out on one of the woven mats Rae had
brought, and after a minute, Rosie lay down beside her, on her side
with her back facing Elizabeth so that even through the baggy clothes
her hipbones and shoulder blades jutted. Elizabeth rubbed her back,
tracing the bony lines of her girl's developing body. There were rented
green-and-white beach umbrellas everywhere, shading a middle-class
crowd of families and bikers, retirees, burnouts. She heard James and
Lank talking together on another mat, splashes and cries from the
river, dogs barking, sticks being thrown and retrieved, a breeze, babies,
bugs. Rae was asking if anyone wanted something to drink, and
Elizabeth shook her head and inhaled her daughter's smells—those
doggy feet in the first moments out of their shoes but her hair just

washed. It would never cease to amaze her that she had given birth to such a creature, who once nearly ten years ago had been wading here at this very spot with her father. Rosie in underpants, four years old, thirty-five pounds of bird bone and ringlets and blue Siamese eyes, standing in a radiant shaft of sun, right where the water seemed to change from gray green to the dark emerald. Andrew was not even ten feet away, in the darker band of river. Rosie had waved to her mother, taking one more step toward a bouquet of trees on the shore directly behind her, lit by the same beam that made her look like a vision, and then suddenly she was gone—in the literal blink of an eye, vanished. Andrew's eyes had veered away for just a moment, toward some ca-noers, until Elizabeth started screaming. He sloshed through the water toward the flat still surface of the river where his daughter had stood moments before, halfway between the two shores. He started pulling up empty handfuls of water while Elizabeth splashed toward where he stood. They gathered armfuls of water to them, crying for others to please help them, please, please, and after a minute or so, Andrew's arms drew Rosie up and out of the water—Rosie blue and still. They bounded to the dirt beach, Elizabeth keening behind them, Andrew breathing into Rosie's mouth as he ran with her to shore. And then the miracle happened. Rosie threw up water, gagging, choking, breathing.

Now Elizabeth lay thinking about Andrew, his lovely deep blue eyes, how he had given her Rosie, saved her here, and then died six months later. "There are holes out there," Elizabeth called to Rae, who was walking around in the river up to her knees, big voluptuous chubby Rae in a black tank suit and baggy shorts. "Watch your step."

"I stepped in one," said Rosie. "When I was little I nearly died."

"Yes."

"Tell me the story again, Mama." So she did, and this time a wave of something way deep down and long ago quivered inside her when she got to the part where Andrew's arms found Rosie, and she swallowed it back and shuddered, stopped rubbing her child's winglike shoulder blades and just gripped them, not breathing. She rolled over to look at James, like Rosie used to look back at her, making contact before she would venture further away. James lay on the mat with his eyes closed. She felt a wave of tenderness, looked over his head for a moment and imagined meeting ghostly Andrew's eyes. She could almost feel him standing there on the other side of James, smiling approvingly at her, and she smiled back at him. But then something like revulsion rose inside her. Memories rose out of nowhere like whales, coming to the surface for some air. First Luther broke through the water, smiling, shy, and then Elvin Thackery's face appeared behind him, looking pasty, arrogant, amused. She couldn't take her eyes off him for a moment—it was as if she were hypnotized—but she knew suddenly that there was something behind him, ducking down, hiding, and she tried to see around the corner. And she saw a pretty young woman with soft white skin, saying hello on the phone, letting the curly coils of the cord twist around her finger like a snake. The way Elizabeth always pictured the woman with the English accent at James's that night—young, sexy, playful, all the things she herself had stopped being long ago.

She lay on her towel and fended off waves of distress. Maybe she had called the wrong number both times, like he claimed. But she didn't think so. What was amazing was that after the ensuing fights, Elizabeth drunk and close to hysterics, James defensive and disparaging, they had stayed in love, he had kept on loving her, *wanting* her; and they had married six months later.

And as she lay baking in the sun, she listened to the silence and the sounds of the river, until like onions cooking so long that they caramelize, sharp turned to sweet. The billows of green hillsides here at the river went back behind each other like countless backdrops, always another behind the last one, slightly taller, back as far as you could see.

SHE opened one eye and studied the two men, who sat side by side. Lank was sitting up with one hand rather shyly on his little beer belly, in pale shorts, watching Rae, who was halfway out now, up to her thighs, with her head tilted all the way back, staring up at the sky. Nearer the shore two girls not much older than Rosie but buxom and brown, in bikinis, were just getting used to the water, and Elizabeth watched James watch them, taut and predatory. She watched Lank watch Rae and her soft droopy butt, in worn rolled-up khaki shorts, with her beautiful breasts and auburn hair, and his face was blank at first. She looked absolutely radiant, like a rose, plumpness filling in the lines of her face, giving the skin a newborn smoothness. Still in the water, she stepped out of her baggy shorts, revealing the whole of her raggedy black tank suit underneath. She stood there in her swimsuit, her shorts tucked under one arm, and she drifted over toward the shore. She came up to where the rest of them lay, wincing at pebbles that dug into the soles of her feet.

"Hi, cutie," said James. She ducked her head down, bashful.

"Come wading with me, boys," she said, and Elizabeth smiled when the two got to their feet and followed her as she led the way back to the river.

LANGUOROUS in the afternoon heat, comforted by birdsong, Elizabeth was drifting off when Rosie whispered, "Mommy? I need to talk to you." Elizabeth was so close to true sleep that she could barely open her eyes. But when she did she saw that Rosie's were closed, her face full of pain, as if a tooth had been aching too long. Rosie looked so tired that Elizabeth almost believed she had been talking in her sleep.

"Shhhhh," Elizabeth whispered, like a wind, the way she had soothed Rosie to sleep as a child.

"Don't shush me!"

Elizabeth reached for her shoulder, but the moment her hand touched the soft brown skin, Rosie stiffened, as if about to arch her back.

"What did you want to talk about, darling?"

Rosie glowered. "I hate it when you shush me. Don't you think it makes me feel like a baby?"

"I'm sorry. Please tell me."

Rosie shook her head.

What could she do? She looked up at James on the river, and so did not see that Rosie's forehead was furrowed with the effort of holding back tears. James looked over his shoulder, knee deep in the river, and waved to Elizabeth like a child. No, he did not look like the grown-up handsome man she'd imagined as her husband, the husband she had had in Andrew. But she loved him. Lank was talking to Rae a few feet away in the green water, dappled sun, and she studied his sweet un-veiled face, the transparency of those pale blue eyes and all that fore-head. You felt like you could rest in all that brow. Maybe, Elizabeth thought, it helps to stop longing for huge significance, meaningful new memories; maybe it helps to be satisfied instead with these little mosaics of connection. That was all she wanted right now, but after a moment she turned back to see how her child was doing. Rosie was sitting up, staring at an empty stretch of slow-moving river. Her bottom lashes had been combed together with tears into thick black lines.

"Honey, honey," Elizabeth whispered, reaching out to touch her daughter's impassive face. "Please tell me now. I'm sorry I wouldn't listen before," but Rosie just stared off at the green river, hard and distant as the rocks on the other side.

three

_____

JAMES and Lank flew off for a few days on the Green River, as they did every summer. James loved camping out, he loved the roaring river, the rock faces scrolling past. Elizabeth suspected that he loved being away from them, too. She couldn't blame him, especially this year, when she was feeling so odd, ingrown and strangely haunted, and Rosie was acting so hard and furtive, except when Simone was around. And Elizabeth had hoped that James's absence would give Rosie the space she needed to trust her again, to take her into her confidence, but so far, Rosie had deftly skirted every effort to tell Elizabeth what was troubling her. She was gone a lot, off with Simone to the mall, the club, the boardwalk, and when she came home, she went to her room and listened to rap on her headphones. Sometimes she deigned to lie in bed with Elizabeth, each reading her own book, but on one such occasion, when Elizabeth had asked her directly what she had wanted to talk about at the river, Rosie said it had not been important.

"Is it something you've done?"

"Mommy. Just drop it. It's not important."

"Is it about Luther?"

"Luther? God!! Is that what you think?"

"Is it about Simone?"

"No."

"Why is she gaining so much weight?"

"Why is Rae gaining so much weight?"

"I don't think Rae's gaining weight, is she? But Simone is."

"Well. Why don't you ask her yourself?"

So one afternoon, when Simone had stopped by, Elizabeth decided to bring it up. The three of them were sitting at the kitchen table, folding laundry together, listening to the Beatles on the tape player. Sunlight the color of butter poured in through the lace curtains. Simone wore one of the gigantic T-shirts she had taken to wearing, and Rosie was wearing one of the tiny tube tops Simone used to wear. Elizabeth looked at them, brown as nuts, and she practiced her opening line: Simone, I noticed that you've gained a little weight, and I'm wondering if there are more problems than usual at home? Simone, I'm wondering, does your mother have some horrible new man, and is the horrible new man too attentive to you? Is the new flesh a way of putting a wall around yourself, between your body and his? Simone? I was just noticing you've gained a little weight.

"Elizabeth?" said Simone, holding up one of James's tattered black T-shirts. "I guess you've noticed I've gained a little weight."

Elizabeth nodded, startled. "Yes, you know, I have."

Simone folded the black T-shirt carefully, smoothing out the wrinkles. Rosie picked absently at a tiny bump by the side of her nose, feigning nonchalance.

"Simone? Is there something going on that I could help you with?"

Simone looked at Rosie, and Rosie almost imperceptibly shook her head: No. No. Both girls turned to the dust motes floating in the broad current of sun, little specks of dust revealing the brilliance of the light.

"I really would like to help somehow if I could."

"You do help me, Elizabeth."

"I do?"

"Uh-huh. But sometimes I get afraid. I have bad dreams. And sometimes I'm just totally freaked out by all the things in the world."

"Oh, honey. But is that why you're eating more? I mean, I assume you're trying out new things with boys, and that must be scary, even though it also probably feels good. Right?"

"Right," said Simone. Rosie gave her a long sideways look.

"Why do you look so sad?"

"I don't know," said Simone, setting down the pair of shorts she was folding. Her eyes narrowed. "I can't believe anyone has a good life."

"Oh, darling. Listen. You know—"

"Please, Mom," said Rosie wearily. "Please don't give us a little talk."

"I just want Simone to know, and you too, that if and when you need to talk to someone about birth control, then that someone can be me."

Simone blushed, lay the folded T-shirt down on the proper pile. "Okay, Mom."

Simone lifted up a pair of Elizabeth's baggy, ratty old underpants out of the laundry basket. She held them up, and Elizabeth for one awful moment thought she might be checking for stains. Simone looked first at Rosie and then at Elizabeth with innocent curiosity. "Do they even *make* bigger underwear?" she asked.

W HEN the girls went upstairs to change for their match, Simone pulled Rosie into the bathroom and locked the door. She stood looking at Rosie and panting as if she had just had a terrible fright. Her cheeks were flushed and a thin sheet of sweat covered her face and chest.

"You have to help me," said Simone. She took a long deep breath. "I want you to cancel my appointment at the clinic."

"What?" Fear began to go off inside Rosie like a steeple bell, ringing low, swinging in silence to the other side of the steeple, ringing, silent, swinging.

"I can't go through with it."

"What do you mean?" Rosie felt like slapping Simone across the face. What are you *talking* about? "You'll feel different by the end of the week. You don't have any choice."

"Oh, yeah? I do have a choice. I can have the baby."

"You can't have a baby, Simone. Are you stupid?" Panic flowed through her, and she remembered kids at school who said Simone was dumb, and she wanted to scream, force Simone to come to her senses. "That's ridiculous," she said, shouting.

"Shhhhhh," Simone pleaded, glancing at the locked door.

"Don't you dare shush me." She imagined shaking Simone like you'd shake some kid who'd been drinking at a dance, slap them across the face, get them to gasp back to consciousness in the moments before their parents came to pick them up. "This is so unfair," she hissed. "This is so unfair of you to do this. This is a total fuckup, Simone."

"Rosie, I need some time!"

"You don't have any time when it comes to this, Simone. Don't think! There's nothing to think about."

But a few minutes later, scared and confused, Rosie stood at the phone in the hallway, whispering the words "Planned Parenthood" to the voice on the other line and then dialing the number she was given.

"I have to cancel an appointment for Friday," she began. "Something's come up. Duvall? Yes, Simone. No," said Rosie. "You can't call me here; I'll call you."

Just before four, at a club half an hour from Bayview, Rae and Elizabeth watched the girls walk away through the parking lot and toward their first doubles match of the tournament. Simone had developed a walk somewhere between a flounce and a lumber, while Rosie moved like a wild animal with a slight injury. Elizabeth saw that they were very close, their shoulders touching as they moved, almost without ever losing the connection of their skin.

"The girls are so beautiful today, creamy, like pearls, aren't they? Look at them," she said.

"Oh, God, yeah," said Rae. "They're like little warm puppies. That's why the perverts love them."

Elizabeth felt a sudden darkness insinuate itself into her field of vision, like the shadow in the darkest forest or deepest water, a shadow of such hardness and depth as to be like a mirror. And she knew without turning toward it that it was Luther.

"Speaking of which," she said. "Look." He was sitting with his back to the car just outside the entrance to the club, like a cat staring out the window at the rain. The girls were about to pass him, and Elizabeth held her breath. Rosie, walking with Simone, moved past him with her eyes straight ahead, while Simone turned to look at him askance, as if she'd never seen him before. The girls looked over their shoulders, Rosie grim, Simone blasé, and they waved again to the women.

Luther turned, noted the two women in the car, and remained half turned toward them, smoking with his eyes closed, as if he were sitting in a nightclub listening to a long dreamy saxophone solo. Then he opened his eyes and got up to go inside.

Elizabeth swayed as if in a trance and wanted to moan and sway, to ground herself, soothe herself—moan and sway like poor people in church. Something was coming back to her—something she hadn't quite gotten until now: that Luther was watching her girl's innocence, her unself-consciousness, but was also watching the new depravity, the hideous adolescent. And this was the parent's privilege. He was horning in, and that was why she was so scared; he was loosening their connection. Watching Rosie flounce into the clubhouse, she could see a childlike purity still intact; it had been protected since the thing with Thackery, because no one had been looking at her—until now. And now that someone was watching her, it felt as if some deeply personal privacy were being breached. She wondered if he was stalking Rosie or something that still existed deep in Rosie's soul.

R$_{AE}$ put the car into gear, and they headed off toward Charles's house.

"Rae? Do you think he's stalking her?"

"Oh, I don't think so, Elizabeth. Is that what you think? He just feels—well—strange and lonely to me."

"Maybe. Maybe. Oh, Rae, do you ever feel like you're going crazy?"

"Of course I do. All the time. But I feel like the good news is that they couldn't institutionalize either of us on the evidence they have so far." Rae smiled and glanced over at her.

"I feel so odd these days. Like something is trying to rip out from deep inside me. All these stuffed memories, all this stuffed stuff. Way below the words. And now it wants out."

"Maybe Luther is its poster boy."

"It's very dark, it's big, it's bigger than me. It's like the Mississippi River—swollen, black. It wants to wash me away."

"Maybe it wants to wash you clean."

"I don't think so."

"What do you think it is?"

"I think it's sadness, and fear. A whole life's worth."

"Could it be loneliness?"

"I guess it could."

"Because I have felt loneliness as huge and white and flat as the Kalahari Desert. And that can be quite scary."

"Why now, though, Rae? Why is it so acute for me now? Is it because Charles is dying?"

"I think that's a part of it."

"But crazy? I feel so strange. Remember Joyce's Mr. Duffy, who lived a short distance from his body? That's how I feel."

They were nearly to Charles's house. It was warm and quiet in the car. Elizabeth shook her head. "I don't really want to see Charles."

"Why don't I take you home? We can see Charles another day."

Elizabeth stared out the window. "No, it's okay," she said. "It's worse if I don't go." She closed her eyes for a moment. "I'm scared that I'm so crazy, Rae."

"Oh, we're all crazy, honey. But most of us don't have your style."

CHARLES looked like a corpse, gray and motionless. His mouth was open, his eyes were closed, and he did not wake up while they waited. Rae rubbed his feet. Elizabeth sat in a stiff-backed chair near his shoulders and studied him patiently, as if he might wake up in a moment. He crystallized all that free-floating sadness inside her. She imagined Andrew's cold empty body in the morgue back east, nearly ten years ago. She hadn't seen his body, only the urn of ashes. Charles had taken her out on a borrowed boat, and he sailed them under the Golden Gate at sunset one night. They tied up at a little cove beneath the headlands, and they drank from a bottle of Bushmills, Andrew's favorite drink, and Charles poured most of the bottle into the ocean in the moments after Elizabeth poured out Andrew's ashes. Rosie had stayed home with Grace. Elizabeth hadn't cried. She had comforted Charles, who read the Twenty-third Psalm and sang sea shanties—"The Golden Vanity" and "One-Eyed Reilly's Daughter." He had wept all the way back to the harbor. The stars were very bright that night, she remembered that, like diamonds in the black sky. She watched Charles sleep now and thought about James coming home in a couple of days, and having to tell him how Charles was fading; she thought about holding James in bed, making love, being held, and she looked over at Rae, who was motionless now, holding Charles's feet, eyes closed, stricken. She thought about the abyss of Rae's loneliness, the dignity she managed to muster. Charles groaned, shifted. She tried to imagine the effect that their being around for his dying was going to have on her and Rae, and Rosie. She didn't know what that effect would be, because it was like a tiny green shoot whose flower was growing in the dark. But sitting with him today gave her this hard gift: it let her acknowledge one incandescent part of the world that would soon be gone, extinguished.

four

ELIZABETH had woken up full of hope the day James was coming home, and opened her eyes to the sound of the mockingbird out in the sycamore tree. She called to Rosie down the hall, with a fantasy in her mind of Rosie bounding in, dressed in her tennis gear, ready to go yet glad to stretch out on the bed with her mother for a moment. Instead, she had to call out a second time before Rosie finally appeared in the doorway in tattered cutoffs and a T-shirt from the ragbag. She lumbered in, her head jutting forward, her arms dangling down long and monkeylike: Australopithecus in shorts.

"Hi, honey."

"Hi, Mom."

"I thought you had a match today."

"Uh-uh. I don't play my first match till tomorrow. I got a bye." A bye meant you automatically moved past the first round, where almost everyone else started out. Often the seeded players got a bye.

"What round are you in?"

"Round of sixteen."

A lot of kids were gone now, playing tournaments out of state, some up in Canada, some off with their families for summer vacation.

"What are you going to do then?"

"Go to Hallie's. To play on the trampoline. See ya!"

Elizabeth watched her leave.

"I love you," Elizabeth called. "Wave to me." Their old first-grade parting: I love you—wave to me. Rosie turned and waved.

EMPTINESS descended. She made herself a cup of coffee. Streams of slanting sunlight poured in through the kitchen window, and she considered the incredible soup of particles illuminated by the shafts of light, the dust and fibers and fuzzes. She pushed herself up from the table, not sure where she would go once she was standing. She idly cleaned up the kitchen, watching movies in her head of James coming home, making love, Rosie on the trampoline, breaking her neck, Rae at the loom, weaving.

The phone rang, and assuming it was Rae, Elizabeth picked up the phone and said, "Hi, honey."

There was silence on the other end. Elizabeth's eyes widened. "Hello?" she asked.

After a moment, a gravelly male voice said, "Rosie's late."

"What? For what? Who is this?"

"For her match."

"Who is this?" asked Elizabeth. "I thought she had a bye."

"No. She's late."

Her mouth opened as an image of Luther appeared in her mind and seized her. It was Luther's voice, the voice of a shade, of a dirty white spook. She looked around quickly, as if he were hiding in her kitchen studying her. Her heart raced, and she couldn't catch her breath for a moment; he had looked up their number, felt bold enough to call. She felt like she was tipping over, like she might fall to the ground; she sank into one of the kitchen chairs.

"Leave us alone," she cried, but heard only a dial tone. Terror lapped at her like little waves. She felt violated, as if a Peeping Tom had been watching her go about her business. Neither the old wooden walls of this house nor the love of their friends could protect them; the walls could be scaled, the house invaded. She looked at the phone in her hand until it went dead. She got up and went to the kitchen window with a sudden conviction that he was across the street, watching her through binoculars in a phone booth that had sprung up like a mushroom overnight. But no one was out on the street at all, and there was no phantom phone booth. Elizabeth tried to think, tried to figure out what to do next. She wanted to hear Rosie's voice, be sure she was okay. She called Hallie's house. Hallie's mother answered.

"Hi, it's Elizabeth. I need to talk to Rosie."

"Well, you've just missed them. They've already left."

"What do you mean? Left for where?"

"For the city, remember? They were taking the ferry in."

Elizabeth froze.

"Rosie went to the *city?*"

"I thought you knew. I thought you'd given permission."

"When are they due back?"

"I said I'd pick them up at the 2:30 ferry."

"Let me pick them up instead," said Elizabeth, beginning to tremble. She said good-bye and hung up the phone. Goddamn lying little shit, she thought. God almighty.

She peered back out the kitchen window, surveying the picture-perfect neighborhood, the sun on the trees, brilliant gardens. How had this horrible man become a part of their lives, watching her daughter—dark and smelly, leering, silent—how had things gotten so out of hand that he felt emboldened to call them at their house, as if he had the right to keep tabs on Rosie? It was open season on children these days, especially girls. There was no safety out there anymore. A girl in the next town over had been missing a week; she'd left to go visit a friend one day after her swimming lesson and hadn't been seen since. A little boy from Kentfield had been found dead, stuffed in a kiln, last winter. Anxiety covered her like sweat. She called Rae, whose answering machine was on, and hung up. She walked upstairs to Rosie's room, just because it was the only contact she could have right now with her, and opened the door. It looked like a cross between a rummage sale and a homeless camp under a bridge, and it smelled like the latter, vile beyond all imagining. It stank; it smelled like sweat and decay, dirty concrete, like rain on the sidewalk. She took Rosie's racket out of its case and looked up at the wall, bright with newspaper photos of great women players, framed pictures of Andrew, inspirational sayings culled from magazines over the years, little weavings Rae had made her, dried flowers, and a bumper sticker that said, "Oh, lighten up," which finally caused Elizabeth to snap. Before she knew what she was doing, she had lifted up the racket and smashed it against the wall so hard that it left a gouge in the Sheetrock. She gaped at the hole, tottered, then smashed the racket on Rosie's unmade bed, the smelly wrinkled sheets full of crumbs. They bounced when struck, like water on a hot skillet. She stared at one of the pictures of Andrew; he was barefoot, in khaki shorts, his long, long legs dangled over the side of a broken-down chair. He was laughing, squinting a bit crazily in the late afternoon light. Tears sprang to her eyes. After a moment she shuffled out raggedly, holding the racket over her shoulder like a hobo's stick without the bandanna.

She went downstairs to the kitchen. She sank into a chair at the kitchen table. Trying to slow down her breathing, she tipped her head back to stare at the ceiling. Finally she located the number for the tournament desk and called to say that Rosie was sick with the flu.

"Well, I wish you'd let us know earlier, then," said the voice primly. "Her opponent has been waiting for twenty minutes." And Elizabeth saw herself threaten the person with the racket she now held poised like a blackjack.

She gripped her forehead as if suddenly stricken with migraine. The corners of her mouth twitched downward.

OUTSIDE the kitchen window, her roses, the valiant old girls, still blooming apricot and lavender and red, looked funky and worn out, as if after having produced so many magnificent flowers, they just wanted to go to sleep. The harvest is past, she thought, remembering words Rae had read them once from the Bible. "The harvest is past, the summer is ended, and we are not saved."

After a while, she began to wander from room to room, straightening things up, sitting down and staring dazedly off into space, getting up again to arrange books on the bookshelves. She worked her way upstairs, where she put clean sheets on her bed, and then without actually meaning to, she climbed in and pulled the sheets over her head. She lay in the dark for quite a while, dazed, and then dozed off and on until noon.

HE was walking toward her on the beach. They were each wearing a pair of his Levi's, even though she was five months pregnant. He was walking toward her from the Bolinas end of Stinson Beach. His hair was windblown, and his nose was a little sunburned. The sun was going down, and she had fallen asleep after sharing a bottle of wine with him in the late afternoon. No one knew back then that you shouldn't drink when you were pregnant. He had brought along a book of poems, Auden, to read to her. "You shall love your crooked neighbour With your crooked heart," she remembered all day, and it gave her such relief. Andrew was as good-natured as an easy baby. Walking toward her from the spit at the far end of the beach where the water in the channel rushed back out to the sky, where gulls cried and pelicans skimmed by impossibly low and graceful, he held out his fists to show her he was hiding a treasure from her, something he'd found on his walk. It was early fall, and the beach was almost deserted because everyone else was back in school. He walked toward where she sat on the blue blanket in the sand with the sun going down behind her, and you would have thought she was an apparition or at least a movie star by his look of entrancement. He sat down beside her with his hands closed around the treasure and he asked her to pick a hand, and she picked the left, and he uncurled his finger to present her with a sand dollar. She smiled and began to study it, shake it to hear the sand inside; it was perfect and whole, the size of a silver dollar. "That's the one I found for you," he said, and she went back to studying it, smelling its salty sea smells, but he cleared his throat to get her attention and jutted his chin toward the right hand, which was still in a fist, and she tapped it too, and he opened his hand to show her a second sand dollar, this one the size of a quarter, the one he had found for the baby.

THERE was an hour left before Rosie's ferry was to arrive, and she drove into the downtown area to do errands. She felt deeply confused, eager to see Rosie alive yet filled with a need to punish her for lying, for giving Luther an opening into their lives. It took her nearly twenty minutes to find a parking space, and once she did, she needed to sit there collecting herself before she could go into the hardware store, the nursery, the market. Car engines revved, sirens tore through the steady drone of traffic. A woman with a large, serious-looking baby in a backpack opened the passenger door next to Elizabeth's car, hoisted her daughter out of the backpack and into the child's car seat. While the mother went to get into her own seat, the baby girl frowned at Elizabeth and banged the front of her car seat, like a Supreme Court justice, a rattle as her gavel.

Nothing was in stock anywhere; everywhere she went, all the petty functionaries of the world conspired to thwart her from behind their counters, behind the bulwarks they'd established against encroaching chaos, real and imagined, serving their long lines with grim self-importance. She bought the makings for chicken cacciatore, which she could cook and heat up for James when he finally got home. And then at the checkout line, she happened to glance out the window of the Safeway as she waited for her total, and she gaped as Luther, or someone with Luther's exact shape and shuffle, walked into the convenience store across the street. Her mind spun, and she thought about bolting; then she turned slowly to the sound of the checker's voice, telling her how much she owed, and as if under water, she handed him two twenties and checked back to make sure Luther, or the man who looked like him, had not escaped. She imagined Andrew talking to Luther, firmly but respectfully telling him he must leave their little family alone *entirely*. James should be here, taking care of them. Did Luther know he was away? She was going to have to go talk to him herself; no, she was going to threaten him with arrest or grave bodily harm, she was going to shout into his face that he must stay away from her child.

Stepping toward the doorway, she looked across the parking lot to the convenience store on the other side of the street. She could see Luther's dark shape at the checkout counter, and she stood taller, drawing herself up to give herself courage. She also noticed a young Mexican couple on the pay phone just outside where she now stood, and she saw their child in ragged clothes, a boy of three or four, hanging on the little divider between the automatic door and the phones, waiting for them to finish. She stepped toward the area rug by the exit door just as the boy stepped down onto a four-inch strip of pavement to the left of the door's arc, and without registering what he had done, because she was hurrying to confront Luther at the cash register, she stepped onto the rug, and the door swung open and smacked the child on the side of the head.

Elizabeth and the child both yelped. The child covered his head with his arms, folding his elbows around his face as if to ward off further blows. Elizabeth cried out apologies and finally thought to step off the mat. His mother flocked to him, talking softly while waving to Elizabeth not to worry, not to see them, look away, look away, and the little boy wept. When they lifted him off the mat and stepped away from the door, she rushed out to their side.

The mother lifted her stunned child into her arms, gentling him, as Elizabeth kept saying again and again how sorry she was, and then they turned and walked away quickly, almost running.

Elizabeth stood there feeling skinned. When she finally looked across the street, Luther, or the man with Luther's shape, was gone.

ELIZABETH stood in the shadows at the far end of the dock, watching people pour off the ferry. Finally the girls came traipsing toward her, both of them now in Hallie's tube tops, both wearing Hallie's makeup, Hallie looking like a thirteen-year-old hooker, Rosie trying to. Elizabeth felt afraid in the cool salty breeze.

When Rosie looked up, expecting to see Hallie's mother but seeing her own instead, the color drained from her face. Elizabeth shook her head with disgust. Rosie craned forward almost imperceptibly to take a reading, and Elizabeth looked away, as if it pained her too much to look at her own daughter.

"Hi?" Rosie asked when she drew near.

"You're in disgrace, Rosie Ferguson. You blew off a match—"

"I had a bye!"

"No, you didn't. And I know you didn't. How? Because you know who called me? Guess."

Rosie shrugged. Hallie was looking around for a means of escape. "Guess."

"Mommy, I have no idea."

"I'm so angry! I'm as angry as I've ever been."

"Mommy, what's the matter with you? Why are you being like this?"

"I want to smack you!"

"Mommy!" Rosie looked with profound anxiety from her mother to Hallie and back to her mother.

"Luther."

"*Luther* called?"

"Yes. To tell me you were late for your match. Let's go," she said to the two girls. "Let's start walking."

"I have to wait for my mother," said Hallie.

"You wish," said Elizabeth.

THEY drove along the main street of town across the bay from San Francisco, past the waterfront, past the old railroad yard. The girls sat in the back seat, looking furtively at each other from time to time, long sideways glances, and then out the window, and then at each other again.

"I hate it that you lied, you rotten little shit," said Elizabeth, gripping the wheel with both hands, avoiding the rearview mirror because she did not want to see her daughter's eyes, full of deceit, and she did not want her daughter to see her own, full of hate.

They pulled up at Hallie's house, and the girls looked at each other. After a moment, Rosie waved. Hallie held an imaginary phone to her ear, and Rosie nodded.

"Forget it," said Elizabeth. "Rosie's not going to be on the phone again for about six weeks."

"Mom!"

"Thank you for the ride, Mrs. Ferguson."

"Call me Elizabeth," she sighed.

WHEN they got to their own house, Elizabeth got out without saying a word and slammed the door.

Rosie got out and ran after her. "What are we going to do now?"

"You're going to clean your room. I really don't want to see you."

"When is James coming home?"

"After dinner. Go, go. Get started, Rosie."

"I honestly didn't know I had a match. I thought I had a bye." Rosie stood before her, hanging her head, pawing at the ground.

"I'm so angry with you. I want to smack you," Elizabeth repeated.

"Why do you keep saying that, about smacking me? You never smack me."

"Because you lied. Because you betrayed me. Now go away. Go clean your room."

ELIZABETH spent the next couple of hours puttering, allowing time to pass, trying to keep her expectations low. Expectations are resentments waiting to happen, she told herself. But finally loneliness and remorse overcame her, and she went upstairs and opened the door to Rosie's room. Rosie drew back, as if Elizabeth's fist were raised. The windows were open, and the room smelled fresher. Most of the clothes were up off the floor; Elizabeth lay down on the bed, which Rosie had made.

She stared at the hole she had made in the wall with Rosie's racket. Rosie went and got her a cool wet compress from the bathroom and lay it on her forehead. Then Rosie went back to straightening up her room, singing songs she knew her mother liked, ballads Joan Baez had sung, folk songs from the sixties, softly, off key and sweet.

SOMETHING opened like a kaleidoscope inside her when James walked in the door. He hadn't shaved in nearly a week, and he was tanned and tired. They stood in the doorway holding each other, until Rosie bounded down the stairs to see him, threw her arms around his neck, and dragged him upstairs to see her newly clean room.

Elizabeth didn't really want to hear about his trip, she wanted to be in bed with him, done with talk, not needing to share him with Rosie but having him all to herself, holding and kissing and making love. But after he'd checked his messages, complained about their insignificance, opened his mail, complained about feeling abandoned, he wanted to tell them everything, and Rosie felt like listening. So Elizabeth sat as close as she could on the couch without actually straddling him and listened with her eyes closed; like a teenager she breathed him in, sweat and dirt and exhaustion. She did not want him to shower. She just wanted everyone to go to bed.

"I don't really understand the concept," said Rosie. "You just race down the river, and try not to drown, right?"

He nodded. But then after a moment, he added that he *loved* the muscularity of the water, like watching wild horses, he said, or Rosie play tennis. He loved the feathery vegetation along these rivers. But maybe most of all he loved being away from the phones. Elizabeth inwardly rolled her eyes. Yeah, *right,* she thought.

"Yeah, *right,*" said Rosie. "How many times did you check your answering machine?"

"Once," said James. "No, twice. No, a little more than that."

"A hundred times?" said Rosie. He nodded guiltily, pulled her to him, tickled her ribs, and then held her.

ELIZABETH started to doze, her head now on his shoulder. She heard him softly from far away, still talking to Rosie.

"Can I go with you next time?" Rosie asked.

"Yeah. Of course you can."

"Rosie can never go anywhere ever again," Elizabeth said with her eyes still closed. "She's permanently grounded."

"What'd you do, baby?"

"Lied."

"Blew off a match, too," said Elizabeth.

"I thought I had a bye."

"Luther called me to tell me she didn't."

"Luther called here? To talk to Rosie?"

"No, just to tell us she was late for a match."

"Oh, man."

"Mom, I'm not really grounded forever, right?"

"I am not raising a liar!"

"All right. *God.*"

THEY talked for a while in bed. She told him about her horrible day, Luther and the little Mexican boy, and she said she felt like there might be something wrong with her mind, that it felt rogue and scattered, forgetful and violent and weird, like it was spinning out of control all the time. Maybe you were missing me, he said. I was, she said, but it is more than that. Maybe you're too worried about Charles. I am, she said. Oh, never mind. It was so good to have him home, to lie in bed beside him, basking in his heat, his gentle voice. Then he began to make love, and she wanted to and responded, but more than that she wanted it to be over, for them both to have come, so the cell membrane of intimacy would envelop them in quietness and love. Lying in bed, entangled in each other, smelling of the sea, talking softly in the dark—it was as close to nursing as you could get at this age. But afterward he fell asleep, apologizing as he drifted off that he and Lank had gotten up at dawn to be here on time tonight. She wanted to splutter, No! I waited a week for you to comfort me, hold me, listen, be here to help. But soon he was snoring, and as she stroked his soft fluffy hair, the feeling of resentment passed. Charles had once remarked that holding on to a resentment was like eating rat poison and waiting for the rat to die. She was glad he was home, and she smiled in the dark. A feeling of calm returned as she rubbed her face against his, breathing on him softly, warm as a mother horse. Patch, patch, patch, she thought, life and her friends kept putting patches and Band-Aids on her. Patches, and layers of repair, like the couch in the living room, the frayed back covered with a Navajo blanket, the frayed parts of the old blanket covered with an exquisite shawl Rae had made for Rosie years ago—a shawl of Rosie's colors: light blue, deep lavender, mossy green—and covering the holes in the shawl, a worn antimacassar of the finest Belgian lace.

five

_____

THE next day, under the gloss of a white-hot sun, James and Elizabeth sat in plastic garden chairs on the deck of an elegant club in Alameda, watching Rosie's semifinals match on center court. Simone had defaulted again, after having entered the tournament months ago. She had called this morning to tell Elizabeth she wouldn't be coming after all, that she had some sort of doctor's appointment. She had been whispering. Elizabeth had asked if she had laryngitis. She had said sort of, and Elizabeth couldn't get any information out of Rosie at all. She was just so glad that James had come along today to cheer on their daughter. She felt centered in a way she hadn't in weeks, as if his company gave her some sort of rod inside, like the armature sculptors use so that their long clay forms won't topple over.

Rosie was playing Renee Mettier, the second seed, and so was not expected to win. Both girls were playing with raw aggression, hitting deep angled shots in endless rallies, and Rosie, who had nothing to lose, was making winners off shots that other players could never have gotten to. Renee's coach nodded respectfully from the sidelines. J. Peter Billings was still gone, now on vacation in Maui.

They were tied four games apiece in the first set. Several dozen people sat on the deck watching, while others milled around and studied the draw or chatted with the tournament director. Luther lay on a knoll on the far side of the court so that only his shoulders and head showed. The heads of the other spectators swiveled back and forth during the endless rallies, but Luther, loyal Luther, watched only Rosie.

At five all, thirty-love, with Renee serving, Rosie returned serve down the backhand line but missed by several inches, and she swiped lightly at the court with her racket as she walked to the backhand court to receive, looking arrogant and petulant.

"Knock that off, you little snot," James whispered.

"Good shot," said Renee.

"Oh, come on," said James. "Rosie's shot was out by a mile."

"Excuse me?" said Rosie. "That was out."

"No. It was right on the line," said Renee, and walked toward the corner to retrieve the ball. Rosie looked over at Elizabeth, checking in. Elizabeth shrugged.

"It really was out," said Rosie. "I got a good look at it."

"So did I," said Renee, smiling. "It was right on the line." Rosie looked at Elizabeth again, catching her eye; she looked puzzled and unhappy. Elizabeth shrugged again. Rosie stared off into the middle distance, slouching now, mouthing words no one could hear.

"What's going on?" asked James.

"I don't know. Renee just called an out ball in. She gave Rosie the point; and it was an important one. She'd be ahead forty-love now."

The tall lovely girl smiled a secret smile at the baseline and served, a hard forehand with a lot of spin. Rosie barely got her racket on it. She squinted at Renee and then over at her mother. Then she walked to the forehand court to receive serve at forty–fifteen.

James looked over at Luther for a moment to see what he was doing. Luther's eyes were closed, his great derelict head bobbing with admiration, and all of a sudden James said, "Ah!"

"What?" said Elizabeth.

"I just got it. That was a very sophisticated use of power on Renee's part."

"What do you mean?"

On the next serve, Renee aced Rosie.

"Game, six-five," Renee trilled. Both girls walked to the bench for water.

James turned to Elizabeth. "Renee just assumed the power in this match. Don't you see? She just told Rosie, when she called that ball in, 'I'm in charge now. I'm going to give you a point here because I choose to, but I am going to beat you anyway; and that is how it is. So play on.' "

After the changeover, Rosie, shaken and anxious, stood at the baseline like a tourist trying to figure out if she should get on this streetcar

or not. Renee waited, bouncing on the balls of her feet, confident
and businesslike, as if she might have a month-at-a-glance date book
in her back pocket. Rosie whispered something to herself. Elizabeth turned to study Renee. She hated the girl, so full of herself. In
twenty years she'd be in charge of the PTA, putting down all revolts
the way she was putting away volleys today. Elizabeth cast an evil eye
on her.

Then she watched her daughter look at Luther, who held his palms
two inches apart to show how far out that shot had been. Her look was
beseeching, his full of knowledge. Elizabeth's heart lurched. "Stop,"
Elizabeth hissed at Rosie. "God," she said, turning to James, "look
at—"

But Rosie just squinted grimly, and then smiled, and served an ace.
Then she aced Renee again. James smashed a fist against his palm.
Rosie tried a drop shot on the next point that landed in the net, but she
won the fourth point when she tried another and made it. James
clapped.

"That drop shot took balls as big as cantaloupes," James said to
Elizabeth, who shushed him. She was still buzzing with adrenaline; she
heard an inside whine of confusion and fear. She closed her eyes to
quiet it. Then Rosie hit a winner down the forehand line, and the set
was tied at six games each.

During the tiebreaker, each girl held serve until three all, on Rosie's
serve. She hit a low-angled forehand, a beauty that hit the top of the
net and hung in the air for a second, then rolled over and down Renee's
side of the net. Renee looked as if a cow flop had just dropped onto
her court.

"Come on come on come on," James whispered.

With Renee serving, a long tense rally ensued. Rosie hit another
fantastic drop shot that Renee somehow got to one split second before
it bounced again, and she continued up to the net. Rosie lobbed it over
her head, and Renee got to the lob and lobbed it back, but her shot
landed an inch or so past the baseline. "Yes," said James. "All right."
Rosie stopped the ball, caught it, took a long deep breath. Elizabeth
breathed a sigh of relief.

But Renee tilted her head quizzically at Rosie. "You're not serious,
right?" she said.

Rosie froze. James leaned forward.

"It was out," said Rosie, pointing with her racket to a spot on the court.

"No, it wasn't," said Renee.

Rosie looked over at James and Elizabeth. Renee looked over at her parents, who nodded to her, and she lay her racket down on the ground and walked haughtily off the court.

"What the hell?" James asked loudly.

"I'm going to go get the umpire," Renee called over her shoulder.

"It was out," Rosie said weakly.

"Someone should have done this a long time ago," Renee's mother said loudly to Renee's father.

James was up in a split second. "What the hell does that mean?" he said, and Elizabeth saw that he was moments away from putting up his dukes. She pulled at the sleeve of his shirt.

"Sit down," she hissed, and Renee's parents got up, so smug and indignant that now Elizabeth wanted to give James the go-ahead to slap them both around, but he had sat down beside her again and waved to Rosie with concern and encouragement. Rosie stood mute, staring down at the court as if a deep shaft had opened at her feet and at its bottom she could see a pile of gold coins, or bodies. The silence was long, fraught with tension.

"Why is she taking it so hard?" James wondered. "*Was* it good?"

"It was out," said Luther loudly, to Rosie.

Elizabeth held her breath.

"I know it was," said Rosie.

"Do you?" he asked, more softly now. He tilted his head slightly, questioning her, daring her; his face was stolid, dark and warm at the same time.

Elizabeth froze. Rosie gazed into Luther's face, considering him. She nodded, holding his gaze, then sat down on the court and retied her shoes. Braiding her bangs, looking around from time to time, she crouched there as if something might be gaining on her.

"This is outrageous," James whispered. "That girl's implying Rosie cheated. God, I can't stand that rich little snot."

"Shh-shh-shh," Elizabeth whispered. A moment later, Renee and her parents returned to the court, this time with the tournament director and a young woman in tennis whites with a stopwatch on a chain around her neck. They summoned Rosie up to the net, and Rosie, now red with shame, hurried forward. She appeared to be concentrating very hard on what the tournament director told her and nodded, obsequious, worried.

"Oh, darling," Elizabeth whispered. She held on to her stomach, which ached with tension.

"Oh, for Chrissakes," said James.

The girls moved back into position, Rosie to the baseline, Renee to serve on the forehand side. Rosie led, five points to three. The lineswoman took her position at the net, and the tournament director walked imperiously off the court and back to his desk.

Renee bristled with electricity and self-righteousness. Rosie stood hunched, dark, hunted; to Elizabeth she looked like an aged French dwarf who might suddenly dart onto the lawn of Renee's service court and steal all the mushrooms. But Renee hit a serve so full of power and spin that Rosie could only whack it back low into the net, where it got stuck in the strings like a small animal.

"Five four," said Renee. "Your serve."

"Breathe, darling," Elizabeth whispered. Rosie was actually panting. Renee sliced the serve down the line for a winner.

Five all. Rosie served well enough, but it was clear now that she was rattled, and Renee easily won the next point. Now she was ahead six-five, set-point. She strolled forward briskly, like a hunter, to retrieve the ball that was still caught in the net. Rosie stood waiting for her to return like a mortified foreigner.

"Renee is going to be a dominatrix when she grows up," James whispered to Elizabeth.

"Shhh . . . " She looked at him gently. He made jokes like this when he was most tense, to cover the rage, the sense of injustice, to cover feeling so exposed. She reached out and took his hand.

"She'll advertise for men to play tennis with, then come onto the court in high heels and a black leather bustier and challenge half their calls." He was quiet for a minute. Elizabeth was aware of the price this was exacting deep inside him, and she was touched and grateful. "This is the Old West," he said. "It's time for Rosie to pull her guns."

Rosie at that moment happened to look toward Luther, who held up his thumb and forefinger two inches apart, to show once again how far the ball had been out, held it up as if it were a slide he wanted her to study. And it was as if all of a sudden a switch were thrown inside

Rosie, and the lights came back on. Crouching to receive Renee's serve, Rosie began to bounce lightly on her feet, slowly at first, stiffly, then side to side in place, taut as a panther.

" 'I'm still here,' she's saying," said James, smiling, and Rosie hit a winner down the line off Renee's first serve. Renee served again, and Rosie hit it crosscourt so hard that Renee could only tap it past the net, where Rosie stood casually, all but tapping her foot with impatience as she waited for it to waft into position. The crowd clapped when she put it away.

"Six-up," she said quietly.

"She's in the zone now," said Elizabeth, flooded with relief.

"Justice has been achieved in Alameda," said James. "It's 'Baby, gas up the tanks; we're invading Poland.' "

And when Rosie won the next two points for set, Luther, on the knoll, closed his eyes, his hands clasped as if in prayer.

T HE phone was ringing when they stepped inside the kitchen. James answered it. It was Simone, still whispering.

"Is Rosie there?" she said, and he put her on.

"Hi," said Rosie, looking nervously at her parents. "Pretty good. I lost to Renee in three sets. How did your appointment go?" Elizabeth happened to glance at her daughter just in time to see a look of bewilderment cross her face. "What?" she said. "Again? Why did you cancel?" Rosie exhaled sharply. "God, Simone. You're totally whacked. What did Natalie say? Yeah? Right. I'm going to call her then. I'm hanging up now, Simone."

She hung up but continued to look at the phone in disgust.

"What appointment?" Elizabeth asked.

"Just with a doctor."

"But why are you so angry?"

"Because she's stupid. Everyone is right who says that."

"And why are you so upset?"

"Because she's ruining her stupid life. And just mind your own business." She stormed out of the room, and they listened to her stomp upstairs.

"Mysteriouser and mysteriouser," said Elizabeth, staring out the window. "I mean, for instance, why would Rosie call Natalie to discuss this?"

"I don't even know who Natalie is," said James. Elizabeth turned toward her husband, who sat at the table holding a knife and fork upright, like *American Gothic,* his eyes even greener than usual, as if they were filled with trees.

H E took a turn for the worse this morning," said the nurse, leading them to Charles's room.

Elizabeth saw the small figure on a huge field of rumpled bed, his eyes closed, his body turning in a kind of spiral. It was as if he were trying to get comfortable in a way he would never achieve again in this world. Rae moaned and pulled up a chair beside him. Elizabeth stood at the foot of his bed, holding his shins through the sheets and thin blanket, barely able to breathe. But she could see that there would be no comfort coming from the outside. The only comfort would be in the ceasing of all this.

"Rae," Elizabeth whispered. Rae looked at her sadly. The room smelled of age and decay and all the efforts to mask that animal smell—lemon swabs, antiseptics, baby powder. The sun shone through the round leaves of an alder outside the window, casting fluttering geisha shadows across the bed.

"Charles," Elizabeth whispered.

She sat beside him across from Rae, who stroked his shoulder and arm, wiping at her eyes with her free hand, waiting. The nurse checked in from time to time to smooth his brow and bedsheets, swab his dry lips with lemony Q-tips, and after an hour or so, to give him a shot of morphine. He stopped turning then and lay still. His breathing grew slower, and the nurse came in more often.

"This could go on for days," she said. "I've seen that happen." But just around two, when the clock in the living room chimed, while Elizabeth was staring out the window at a redwing blackbird in the branches of the alder, hearing somewhere the cry of a mockingbird, cars passing, delivery trucks, children, a radio playing swing, Charles took a long deep breath, and a smaller one, and then he lay perfectly still. His mouth was open, as if something just then had flown out of it and away.

The women looked at each other, astonished. A small cry, like a bird's, escaped Elizabeth's mouth. The nurse came forward. She lay his arm down on the bed, to take his pulse.

"I need you to move for just a moment," she said, and Elizabeth stood on shaking legs and backed away, looking to Rae for comfort. Rae got up and came over to her, and they embraced.

"Come with me," said Rae, and she led Elizabeth away. They settled down on the couch in the living room and held hands. They heard the nurse making a phone call, heard soft talking, watched each other. Elizabeth listened to and felt Rae weeping beside her, while she stared off into space. Her head was tilted and her mouth slightly open, in suspension. She felt as deeply confused as she could ever remember feeling, a dumb animal beside its dead master.

THEY were waiting for Charles's doctor to come by and sign the death certificate. His body looked shocked and abandoned and exhausted in that still, sunny room. His mouth was still open, as if he were crying upward for help, like a deeply sad angel in trouble. So this was his last face. It was terribly stark, Charles empty of life. Rae sat stroking his shoulder and arm, as she had stroked him so often in life, as if to say, You may be gone, but right here and now your arm is beneath my hand.

Elizabeth, exuding a rigidity that looked like calm, tried to sit in a meditative pose and couldn't figure out why she felt so wild, so squirrelly. She got up, walked around, sat back down. There was an enormous hush in the room, as if the air had been sucked out with Charles's last breath. The nurse came in, folded up some stray clothes, gathered up his medicines, and took them away. Rae was crying again, but Elizabeth was staving off everything that was piling up behind her eyes, threatening to wash her away—images of Andrew dead and bloody, her mother in the ground, her father sliding down a chute into the crematorium's fires, Rosie dead behind a bush, Luther zipping himself up, Rosie's mouth open just like Charles's, staring unseeing into space. She, Elizabeth, felt like she was the dam holding it all back.

She slowly looked around the room, trying to catch her breath, until her eyes stopped at the sight of a tiny wooden Ganesh, the elephant-headed god, an amber statue that Charles and Grace had brought back from India fifty years before. It was holding two feather-shaped objects in his hands, like Henry VIII about to tackle a leg of lamb, and all of a sudden she found herself stifling giggles, wracked with suppressed hysterics. A trumpeting snort escaped from her nose, just as it had at Andrew's memorial, and again she pretended to sob, as she had way back then, when four-year-old Rosie had whipped around and glared. Rae wept wetly, quietly. Elizabeth got up and went to the bathroom, where she closed the door and sat on the toilet, pinching her nostrils shut, giggling like a schoolgirl, tears of mirth streaming down her face. She thought of Laughing Sal at Playland at the Beach forty years ago. Sal was a mechanical doll as tall as her father, who welcomed you into the fun house with a soundtrack of endless laughter, bending forward, chuckling, leaning back to howl. Horrible jackhammer noises poured out of Elizabeth's nose, while tears ran down her face. Rae came to the door to ask if she was okay, and she managed through her hysterics to make a noise that sounded like yes, but she knew that she wasn't. She heard Rae's footsteps recede, and then Elizabeth felt grief trying to pierce her or trying to get through to her to save her: it was hard to tell. Crying withheld feels sometimes like dying. Finally when she started to cry, she was so deluged with mucus and tears that she didn't think she would ever again get a full breath.

Rae's eyes were red and swollen. They were sitting in silence, side by side, waiting for the doctor.

"Are you praying?" she asked Rae.

"Mostly feeling this incredible sadness."

Elizabeth listened to the hush like a vacuum in the room. "I can't bear to tell Rosie," she said.

"I know."

"Oh, Rae. Doesn't he look very Japanese right now?"

"Yes, he does. Like something is being sucked in and held, disciplined in rigor. Like something turning in on itself."

"But why does it seem Japanese?"

"Stillness in art, reticence in life."

The doctor came. She was very kind and tender to Charles, stroking his cheek, and to the nurse, to Elizabeth and Rae. Rae did all the talking, filling in the doctor on their shared history, their friendship, Rosie. The doctor listened and nodded kindly, filling out her forms.

"Can we wash him?" Rae asked her, when she stopped talking.

"Of course."

HE had a lot of bruises on his backside, where blood had pooled. They washed his face and legs and arms and genitals and back and bottom with soapy water and did not say a word, although a sound came up inside Elizabeth, kind of an ah-ah-ah, wordlessly, and it was like stroking the air, because that was all there was for her to stroke. She did not feel intimate enough with Charles to caress a body that no longer felt alive, but Rae did. She stroked him, cooing and clucking as you would while washing a baby. Elizabeth longed to let him know how moved and touched she was by his nakedness, lying in that bed, and by his departure, but as she moved the washcloth over his body, her head was filled with images of so many other times—crazy thoughts, memories of Rosie on the tennis court, rallying, running, Andrew in his dark green chamois shirt, pitching a tent in Yosemite, Andrew fishing Rosie out of the river, the biker she had slept with three days after his death. Rae cooing, Elizabeth perfectly silent, they washed Charles's blue nails with red washcloths, one hand each, Elizabeth filled with a sad little voice that she couldn't let out—and that was the deafening sound.

LILY pads floated on the pond in the little park where they held his memorial service at dusk, the little pond where Charles and Grace had spent so many hours with Rosie when she was young. It was a hot summer night four days after his death. Charles's sister Adele had flown in from Austin for the service; their older brother was too sick to fly. Adele and Rae had made the arrangements, letting all of Charles's friends know the time and the place, organizing a potluck for the gathering later at Charles's house.

Rae put star-shaped candles on some of the lily pads, and Charles's nurse brought camellias to lay on others, to consecrate the pond. Both of them asked Rosie if she wanted to help them, but Rosie shook her head no. Everyone kept trying to get her to help them, and she felt they were doing it because they thought it would help her, and she would have none of it. She deliberately stood a certain way, a certain uninviting way she'd seen other teenagers who were being mean to their parents stand, like their body was a card table half folded up. Her hands were knotted against her belly, and her elbows stuck out like, she hoped, a pitchfork. She looked around at the several dozen people who had come, old friends she'd met with Charles over the years, a few distant relatives, waiting around the pond for the service to begin. Lank and James were sitting under a great ponderosa pine, looking very tired. Her mother looked tired, too, and as if she had whiplash. She made Rosie think of a sad flight attendant. She kept smoothing everything and everyone, smoothing away hair from Rosie's brow, smoothing the wrinkles out of James's shirt. Her hands moved like a ballet dancer's hands, like the hands of a waitress at an Indian restaurant. She had brought a tree to be planted here later, a birch, delicate as a deer, with pale green leaves that would drop off every fall and come back in the spring. But she didn't cry, and Rosie didn't either. She felt mean. She looked at all these people, her mother and James, Lank and Rae, with all their words of encouragement, their need to be close to her, and she imagined telling Simone how annoying it had all been. Simone would understand, but Rosie hadn't wanted her here today. She was angry at her for only being a little sad that Charles had died, for still having the tiny baby inside. But Simone would have understood wanting to be left alone. It was like when you were sitting in the shade because that's what your insides felt like or what your insides were needing, cool and dark, and all the grown-ups tried to get you out into the sun.

There was no minister, no program. Adele had brought an enormous bulletin board covered with photographs of Charles—ancient childhood portraits, black-and-white snapshots of his wedding to Grace, color photos of him here on a bench by this pond sometime in the lonely active years since Grace's death. Adele mounted the collage on a tripod, and Rosie stood studying it, mostly for something to do. All these people she didn't know were standing around looking like they were staring at a car wreck. She was worried that she felt so cold and mean. Her mother wandered over. She was dressed very beautifully, in brown silk and linen, with pearls. Rosie was wearing a black T-shirt under a black jumper, black socks, black high-top Keds. Her mother had tried to get her to wear tights and black dress-up shoes. Rosie avoided her gaze, ducking her head down so that her bangs covered her eyes and she had to stare at the photos through thick black curls.

There was a snapshot of Charles in a rowboat somewhere, young and handsome, wearing an old-fashioned T-shirt, like a muscle-man shirt. She almost said out loud to her mother that Charles looked like her dad would have looked if he'd lived another forty years, but if she said that, her mother would just try to make everything come out okay. Rosie wanted to feel these terrible empty held-breath feelings, this extremely sad thing that had happened, Charles dying, and she didn't want her mother to take it away and define it for her and then hand it back. She didn't want a guide. She felt like she had to be mean if she wanted to be herself, while all the grown-ups wanted her to be soft and sad and loving like they were being, and she did not want them to mess with her. She raised her elbows higher, like the turrets of a castle, to keep the grown-ups away. She felt fiercely alone, and she wanted to feel that way.

"They make you sad because they remind me of who he was," she said about the pictures of Charles, and as soon as she said it, she felt angry at herself. It was like something Simone would say.

Rae had covered a TV dinner table with a beautiful silk weaving she'd made for Charles after Grace died—pale blue with egrets, a pelican, poppies, a setting sun. There were candles on this little altar, a small framed photo of Charles, one of his bow ties, a Giants cap. And there were his hiking boots, too, which made Rosie sadder than anything else. She bent forward to breathe them in, relishing the smell of leather.

"The most poignant thing you can see of a dead friend, for me, is their shoes," said her mother. "Maybe because they smell like him. They bore his weight. They touched the ground on which he will no longer walk." Rosie looked over her mother's shoulder at James, who was talking nicely to a group of old people, saying something funny that made them all laugh. She started to think about Edgar Allan Poe, all those stories of people being buried alive, and she thought about how glad she was that Charles had been cremated, so he didn't have to wake up in his coffin and be alive. Cremation meant it was too late for that, although what if you were a tiny bit alive when they sent you down the chute into the furnace, and the fire woke you up? Would anyone hear the screams? She shuddered, saw Charles's body burning, like at a luau. She imagined someone coming by and peering in at the furnace in the crematorium, with a chef's hat and a spatula.

Rae came over and hugged Elizabeth. Then she put her arm around Rosie's shoulder. "I can't hug you, can I?"

"No."

"We're going to begin," Rae said. "We're just going to tell some stories, remembering him. I wrote a small something; maybe you have a story to tell." But Rosie shook her head.

Elizabeth, Rosie, James, and Lank huddled together near the altar. Adele recited the Twenty-third Psalm, several old friends stepped forward and told funny anecdotes. The fog was beginning to roll in, like a visitation. Rosie put her free hand in her mother's. She did not mean to. She felt put down somehow, although that did not make sense—intruded upon, leeched onto—and she wanted all the grown-ups off of her, but without meaning to she had taken her mother's hand. She left it there. Rae, standing by Adele, cleared her throat and looked into the faces of the crowd until her gaze settled on Lank. She raised her eyebrows inquiringly. Rosie looked at Lank, who was wearing the same dark gray suit he'd worn when her mother married James. He looked like a balding angel in disguise as a banker. He shook his head.

"I thought you were going to sing," she whispered to Lank.

"I can't," he said.

A man who was drunk began to ramble on, some story about when Grace was sick and Charles used to sit out in the garden with her for hours at a time in the shade. He read something from the Bible that made no sense to Rosie. She remembered the note in Simone's desk—that in case they were going to bury her, they should shoot her in the head first to make sure she was really dead. She pictured Simone buried in the ground, scratching at the lid of the coffin, her baby floating around in her stomach, waiting to be born. She started hearing the song from when she was little that kids sang about people rotting in the grave: "The worms go in, the worms go out, the worms play pinochle on your snout." She thought about telling the story about how Charles taught her to ride a bike, but she felt too mean, like it was too good a story for them. Pedal and steer; pedal and steer. The sun was going down over the grove of oaks to the west. The candles flickered on the lily pads like lightning bugs. Rae stepped forward and began to read.

"If we were having a religious service here today," she said, her voice very high, "which of course Charles would not have permitted, a priest would be saying that we are committing him to a love that goes broader and deeper than one we can see." Rae looked right at Rosie, from the other side of the candlelit pond, and Rosie looked back with fierce concentration. "And I believe we are," Rae said. "If we can trust love in life, as Charles so obviously did, if we believe that love is the truest, most enlivening fact of our lives, then we admit that love is real in life—and so may in fact be real in death." Her voice was trembly and wet. "I remember when Grace died," she said. "At her service Charles said that we who had loved her in life would not lose her in death. It is true. We didn't lose her. Because death is not what is finally sovereign; love is. And so in this spirit we commit him." A lot of people, including James, were crying softly. Rosie shivered. The evening had grown cold. Her mother was staring off into space, blank as a garden statue. Pedal and steer, Rosie remembered, I won't let you go, I won't let you fall.

And then Lank stepped forward. He seemed confused, like he hadn't picked out what song he was going to sing yet, and her mother reached forward and scratched one of his shoulder blades lightly, the way she did to give you encouragement. Rosie looked into her mother's face and saw how tired she was, too. Everyone here seemed so tired. Lank closed his thin lips to make an instrument out of them, and he hummed one note to himself, like his own little pitch pipe. He began to sing the same song they had sung when they buried Grace. It was a Christmas song, even though Grace had been buried in May and even though it was now well into summer. It was slow and mournful, like a spiritual, hanging in the night as if each quavering mournful note were being placed on a shelf right above him. He was singing with his eyes closed, and Rosie tried to hold her eyes wide open so the tears wouldn't pool and fall. But she felt her meanness and her safety melting even though she did not feel like crying with these people, and her tears did fall as Lank sang.

Lo, how a rose e'er blooming,
From tender stem hath sprung.
Of Jesse's lineage coming
By faithful prophets sung.
It came a floweret bright.
Amid the cold of winter,
When half spent was the night.

Miserable, her back bent forward, she buried her face against her mother's side without meaning to, and finally, past all of that resistance, a quiet mewling sound rose from somewhere inside her, like a small wounded wind.

seven

I N the week that followed, Elizabeth cleaned out and relined every drawer in the house, throwing out little broken things that they were supposed to mend someday, announcements of events that had passed long ago, invitations they had meant to respond to. It was the dandruff of their lives. She hummed little songs as she worked, and listened to Joan Baez. Time passed, and the crazy broken feelings of loss subsided. Rosie was gone so much of the time, practicing, hanging out with Simone, who had all but disappeared from sight, and even with Hallie, who called from time to time. Rosie had some secrets, that was one thing Elizabeth now knew. Elizabeth tried to get her to tell, but her chance had come on the river, and Rosie apparently wouldn't give her another.

Elizabeth had heard her getting up all night, from her little rabbit nest of a bed, up to pee every hour or so, down to the kitchen for milk at midnight. Elizabeth had found the unwashed glass on the counter this morning.

"Hello, love," said Elizabeth. "What are your plans for the day?"

"I don't have any."

Rosie's gaze passed over Elizabeth, slippery as oil. "Can we go up on the mountain?" she asked finally.

"You want to go for a hike? Or do you want to tell me something?"

"I want to talk to you, but not here."

"Okay. Why don't you go pack us a lunch while I finish up here?"

R OSIE packed salami sandwiches, Oreos, a thermos of Coke. She had not actually decided which of the two secrets she would tell her mother today, about cheating or about Simone. But she couldn't go on keeping both of them.

Surrounded by clouds and fog, they drove halfway to the top of the mountain, where they broke through into sunshine. Rosie stared through the window and listened to Elizabeth's pathetic folk music on the car stereo. The foliage was fleecy, woolly, all looking from a distance like a thick green pelt you could stroke or even wrap yourself in. She thought about wrapping her mother in it, like a car blanket, to comfort her and make her feel safe. Then she felt a stab of annoyance; her mother was the one who should be taking care of *her.*

When they'd driven for twenty minutes, they came to a place to park in the dirt by the side of the road. They looked out through the windshield at the nappy hillsides, the wind-sculpted trees, yellow Scotch broom everywhere.

"You know," said her mother dreamily, "I *think* the Muslim holy colors are green and gold."

Rosie's stomach buckled at her mother's oddness. She looked at her skeptically. "Why did you say that just now?"

"I just remembered it, darling. Okay?" Rosie nodded, feeling old and worried. "I asked a woman from Tehran who goes to my meetings why those two colors. And you know what she said?" Rosie shook her head. "She said, 'We like green so much because we live in the desert. And everyone loves gold.'"

Rosie thought this over for a moment; finally they got out of the car. Rosie carried their lunch in her mother's old canvas knapsack, and as they began to walk she felt almost elated; they were away from everything, in the middle of nowhere. This filled her with a sense of lightness, as if she could breathe deeply again. And the smells enveloped her, the sense of life that is not yet fouled. She could smell the salty seaweed smells of the ocean. There were still a few poppies and lupine around, all that blue and yellow, the poppies so sweet and gold, like a Buddhist monk's robe, like little cups you could drink from.

Rosie rehearsed her opening lines. Simone was really starting to show, but big clothes covered her stomach. They walked for a while beneath the cover of trees, Douglas fir and redwood, over moist crunching vegetation. Mama, Rosie practiced saying, I cheated a few times this year. I didn't even really mean to, but that's what Renee's mother meant when she said someone should have gotten a line judge long ago.

Her mother suddenly reached out and put her arm around Rosie's shoulders.

"Rosie? Is it too soon for you to tell me what you wanted to? Or should we just hike for a while?"

Tiny metallic explosions of fear went off in Rosie's stomach. She decided not to tell, rather to make up a new pretend secret she'd been keeping—that Hallie smoked or something.

"Hike for a while," she said.

She tried to think of something to fill the silence with. Under and beside the perfect, magnificent redwoods, she was the size of a ladybug.

"A redwood is a tree you have respect for," she said. It made her feel grown-up to say this.

Now they were in fog again, or a heavy mist, and Rosie stopped. She smelled the wet, springy, primeval softness underfoot, the life, the rot.

"Mommy?" she asked, without meaning to.

"Yes?" Elizabeth looked into Rosie's grim, tight face.

Rosie stared down at the earth and leaves at her feet. She didn't speak for a moment. "I'm trying so hard to tell you a secret. A horrible, horrible secret."

Elizabeth simply nodded, but Rosie felt like the wind had been knocked out of her. Her face began to crumple, and Elizabeth pulled them both over to a great rock at the foot of the slope beside the path, then waited for Rosie to sit down beside her.

Fingers of sunshine now streamed through the trees, the soft-edged shafts inside a cathedral.

Rosie listened to her mother's voice, which sounded very far away.

"Darling, there's nothing, nothing in the world, you could tell me that you've done that will be so bad—nothing, nothing." After another minute, Rosie came back and sat on the rock beside her, and Elizabeth pulled her near, and Rosie folded over sideways with her head in her mother's lap. It was very quiet, except for the sound of a nearby stream.

"There's two things," said Rosie, looking up into the branches above her. Then she said something into Elizabeth's lap that, muffled though it was, sounded like "I cheat."

"What?" said her mother. "What did you say, darling?"

"I said. Oh, Mommy. There's something so bad. I'm just going to say it." Elizabeth peered tenderly into her daughter's brilliant blue, troubled eyes. Rosie wasn't breathing. At this moment she still did not know which secret she was going to say. Then she looked down for a second and off into the distance, and when she looked back at Elizabeth, the terror was gone, replaced with a hushed intent look of surprise.

"Simone," she whispered, "is pregnant." She drew in a deep breath and held it; she felt like she did when they entered the rainbow tunnel on the way to the Golden Gate Bridge and she held her breath all the way to the other side—suspended, bursting, focused.

"God almighty," Elizabeth said. Rosie watched her expectantly. "Jesus Christ," Elizabeth whispered. She blinked as if her eyes hurt, and her mouth hung open and she tilted her head back slowly to stare at the canopy of green above their heads. "Is she going to . . . have an abortion?" Rosie shrugged and after a moment shook her head.

"I don't think so. She's canceled two appointments to do it so far."

Elizabeth buried her face in her hands, shook it from side to side. Time passed. Rosie closed her eyes too, listened to her heart throb in her chest, hard and fast. After a while she opened her eyes. All the greens were almost too bright.

"God almighty, Rosie. Is there really a second one?"

Rosie didn't say anything for a moment. "There was just that."

"You said two, you—"

"Shhhh, Mommy," said Rosie. She felt like when a shot of hers hit the top of the net and then, after a long moment, dropped onto the other side. "The first secret is she's pregnant. The second secret is that she's maybe going to keep the baby. She hasn't decided."

"When is the baby due?"

"Six months."

"God. That's why she's gained so much weight. This is why the big shirts." Rosie nodded. "What does Veronica say?"

"They're not speaking."

"Well, they better fucking well start speaking." Elizabeth stared up through the branches. Rosie felt a stab of pain that her mother was angry at her.

"Actually," she explained, "they only stopped speaking this morning. When Simone told her."

"Simone told her for the first time—today? Jesus Christ, what did Veronica say?"

"I don't know, but Simone is grounded."

"Oh, Rosie! You! Simone! What a secret!" Rosie finally turned around so she could sit in her mother's lap. "Who's the daddy?" her mother wanted to know.

"This guy who's eighteen and plays tennis."

"Can you describe him?"

"He's no one you know. His name's Jason Drake. He's really handsome and stuck up."

"Is he sticking by Simone? Never mind. Don't even bother answering."

"He gave her two hundred dollars for the abortion."

"The abortion she decided not to go through with."

"Yeah."

"I see. And how are you—how are you holding up?"

"Not so good."

Her mother held her tighter then, held on too tight for a minute, but it felt good, like it might hold them all together.

ELIZABETH shook her head, in a daze. "Can we just sit here another minute while I—process all this?"

Images of Simone began to play in her head, scenes of Simone having sex, oral sex, screwing, hugely pregnant, screaming in delivery, Rosie as her birth coach, swabbing her with compresses the way Rosie wiped Elizabeth's forehead when she was depressed. Simone with a baby. Elizabeth rubbed her eyes. Then Rosie nudged her and, when she looked up, handed her a cup of soda. Elizabeth took the cup and a sip, and then stared out at the redwoods until her vision blurred. Pregnant. Simone was pregnant. She was doomed; the light of her future had just gone out. For Simone to have already had sex was disastrous. To have gotten pregnant, to be facing an abortion, would be a catastrophic setback. This, though, was tragedy. This was almost evil. She looked at Rosie and shook her head. Rosie looked back at her with concern and fear, her lips pressed tight together like a worried little child. "Pregnant," Elizabeth whispered, filled with a terrible emptiness. They gawked at each other. Each time she thought the word *pregnant* or

saw an image of Simone with a bulging tummy, something reverber-
ated in the mountain air like a sonic boom inside her.

"Mommy," Rosie pleaded softly, "don't space out on me now."
Elizabeth looked at her daughter intently and tried to inhale a deep
breath of fresh mountain air. The fog was moving into the redwoods,
like there was a wordless relationship between them, old friends. Rosie
was peering into her face as if trying to read a smudgy set of blue-
prints.

eight

THE next day, Rae invited Rosie over to spend the night. She was in the middle of a large weaving, and the smells of the fibers were very strong. Rae was weaving sorrow into a landscape of bottle greens and taupe. The sorrow was a curvy band of muddy purple blue, and the secret she was weaving into it was a ginger-red rayon ribbon. You couldn't see it, though, at first, through all those dull colors.

"You know about Simone," said Rosie. "Right?"

Rae nodded. "I do know," she said.

"What would you have felt like if your best friend had gotten pregnant when you were thirteen?"

"Oh, Rosie. You know, it was so different then. My best friend would have been whisked away and made to have an abortion. Which would have been illegal and maybe dangerous. She simply wouldn't have had the choice of keeping the baby."

Rosie leaned against the loom. The wool in the weaving smelled like animals, earthy, damp, sweaty, more like boys, like men. Silk smelled more like girls, like sweet dreams, but she couldn't smell any now.

"Tell me how you feel." Rae's voice was quiet and kind. Rosie, eyes closed, was mute. Rae made it look so easy to make something beautiful out of her life with little acts of goodness and attention. All Rosie had these days were ugly pieces of yarn—all fear and secrets and hating everyone.

She took a long deep breath and started to tell Rae that Simone had had a little bleeding in her underpants but that the doctor said she was fine, everything was fine, the doctor said. Only maybe she was a little afraid, and Rae said, "Uh-huh," so quietly, and Rosie said it was all so strange because she was afraid that Simone would lose the baby, and she was afraid Simone would actually have the baby; she was afraid she would lose Simone, because she lost everyone—her daddy, and Sharon, and Charles—and she was afraid that their life, her life and Simone's life as best friends, was now ripped to shreds, because how would they be able to be friends when Si-mone had a crying baby around? She said she felt like she was underneath a sort of heavy blanket, and she felt sorry for Simone and also jealous that Simone got to get unstuck from being a teenager. And she felt afraid, just afraid, afraid in every way, and everyone would say her best friend was a slut, and she was afraid because she was so so so glad it wasn't her, and she was afraid because abortion was so horrible and Simone was too far along and she felt afraid because she hoped the baby would die so they wouldn't have to deal with all this. Rae made a whistle with no sound in it, like a little wind. Rosie fiddled with her fingernails, clicking them against each other. She was also afraid of things she couldn't tell Rae, like that every day she expected a letter from the regional sportsmanship committee, summoning her before them about the cheating; she was also afraid she would never get caught; she was afraid because she dreamed about kissing James, and Lank, and Luther—she didn't mean to have those dreams but she woke up with that buzz, that tightening down in her vagina.

Rae stretched out on the floor, and Rosie lay down beside her. "I'm afraid of a thousand things," she said in a very small voice that sounded even to herself like Betty Boop's. Her heart was brimming over with misery, and tears rolled down the sides of her face, falling on the carpet.

"Rae, are you not ever afraid because you believe in God?"

"I am afraid sometimes. But I have company."

"You mean, because you feel like God is with you?"

"Uh-huh."

"I think I'm a Christian," said Rosie. "Except for the Jesus part." She heard Rae give a quiet laugh through her nose. At first Rosie felt worried that Rae thought she was stupid, but then she could tell that Rae was just making that little laugh because she loved her.

THE next night, at the Fergusons, over the sound of James's pencil on paper and the turning of magazine pages came the nebulous hum of

Lank and Rae in the kitchen. They were washing dishes. Elizabeth had decreed that tonight would be a reading night. Lank, lonely and bored, needed company, and Rae needed to get away from the phone, and they had both called Elizabeth to invite themselves to dinner. But Elizabeth had said they were welcome to come over only if they felt like sitting around after dinner and reading. They had both agreed. But when James and the Fergusons had taken up their stations, Rae and Lank had stood around trying to figure out where to sit. They had a brief shoving match over the rocking chair. Then Rae stormed over to the love seat and plopped down.

"What are you going to read, Rae?" Rosie asked, as if Rae were a kindergartner.

"I'm going to read your mother's mind," she said. Elizabeth shook her head and refused to look up.

Lank approached the love seat and tilted his head to peer at the empty space beside Rae.

"What are you looking at?" she asked.

"I'm looking to see if his royal Lordhood is sitting there beside you." Rae blushed a dark crimson.

"You shouldn't tease her about Jesus," said Rosie. "This country was founded on the principle of religious freedom, in case you've forgotten."

"That's right, honey," said her mother.

"And it's sexist of men to mock a woman's deepest feelings—"

"Uh—that's enough, sweetheart."

"God."

Lank sighed. "Rosie, you know me better than that, right?" Rosie simmered. "You know I'm not Jesse Helms, right? You can see the difference? I just want to make sure I don't sit on him, honey, on Jesus. That's all." And so saying, he continued to scout the empty seat on the couch.

Rae patted the space next to her, giving Lank the clearest, kindest look. "He's in my heart, Lank."

Rosie rolled her eyes a bit, but then as Lank sat down next to Rae, returned to her magazine, picking at an eyebrow.

"You don't have anything to read," Elizabeth implored, addressing Lank and Rae. "I just want to have a quiet night here, reading with my family. I was very clear on that." Rosie stared at her magazine, smiling now on the inside. It was so great when other people were getting in trouble besides her.

"You don't want to watch TV with your family?" Rae asked hopefully.

"No," said Elizabeth. "It's a reading night. See how nicely Rosie is reading?" Rosie looked up from her magazine and waved. "See how nicely James is working?" said Elizabeth. James looked up and waved his pencil in greeting, scribbling words on the air in front of his face.

"Is there anything we can do to get out of reading?" Rae asked. Elizabeth shook her head. "Could we do the dinner dishes?" After a moment Elizabeth nodded.

And so Lank and Rae had disappeared into the kitchen.

"She's our sun," Elizabeth heard Lank pronounce. "And we her unworthy planets." James smiled at Elizabeth, who did not notice. She was listening to the sound of water running in the background, the sound of friendly sparring. Memories of Andrew drifted into her head like leaves, Andrew at the sink doing dishes after dinner. She always washed and he always dried, and in her mind she heard, either from the past or from the kitchen, the clink of clean dishes being set down against one another.

nine

Aт 10:30 that night, after Lank and Rae had left and Rosie had gone to bed, when James and Elizabeth were in the living room still reading, the phone rang. It was Simone. "I think I need to go to the hospital," she told Elizabeth, her voice high and tremulous. "My mother's out on a date, and I don't know where."

"Oh, my God, sweetheart. What happened?"

"There's bleeding in my underpants."

"Honey, is it just a little spotting? That's very common."

"No, it seems like a lot."

"I'm on my way, baby. I'll be there in five."

She told James what was happening and grabbed her purse. "Oh, James," she said breathlessly. "Maybe this is God working in Simone's life. Maybe she's having a miscarriage." James crossed the first two fingers of both hands and looked at her hopefully. She almost had him run upstairs and wake up Rosie so they could both come with her, but they decided against it, and she left for Simone's alone.

Leaves rustled in the breeze, an owl accompanied the night birds, the moon was a crescent of white. By the time they got to the emergency room, Simone's eyes were swollen, almost piglike, hurt and scared. It was a slow night, and they were shown into an examination room right away. A kind elderly nurse asked Simone some questions. Upon hearing that she was three months pregnant, though, and planning to keep the baby, the nurse smiled tightly, like someone pretending not to have an opinion. She gave Simone a faded blue hospital gown to change into and suggested she use the bathroom. Then she set about pulling clean paper down over the table, humming a nasty tuneless song. Elizabeth sat down wearily in the empty chair but her heart was racing with a sense of impending salvation.

W HILE they waited for the doctor to appear, Elizabeth pulled up her chair and leaned close to Simone, who lay on the examination table holding her hands protectively over her stomach, scanning the medical posters on the wall. Even now with those swollen animal eyes, open as a baby's, her pale face was radiant, holding the light. Elizabeth smiled at her, reached forward to smooth the blonde bangs away from the scared gray eyes.

"Bleeding doesn't automatically mean you lose the baby, does it?"

Elizabeth shook her head. "Let's wait and see what the doctor has to say."

"Did you bleed when you were pregnant?"

"I think I did a little."

Simone's face contorted suddenly and she moaned. "Oh, I'm having cramps," she said. Elizabeth reached out and took one of her hands, fighting back the awareness of her hypocrisy—comforting Simone with tenderness for having the miscarriage Elizabeth desperately hoped she was having.

T HE doctor was short and fat and adorable, and had Elizabeth sit by Simone's head while her nurse—not the elderly humming one—made a little privacy tent over Simone's knees. Simone flinched when the doctor inserted the speculum and gripped Elizabeth's hand so tightly the fingertips turned purple. "Hmmm," said the doctor, placing her stethoscope on Simone's belly to listen to the baby, and "Umm-hmmm." Finally she sat back and gently took Simone's legs out of the stirrups. "Well," she said. "I can see you've had a lot of bleeding, but your cervix is closed, which means you are not miscarrying. I think I'm going to admit you for tonight, though, because there will be an ob-gyn here very early in the morning, and I'd like him to take a look at you, too. But I don't think the baby is in any real trouble." Elizabeth cringed, her heart sinking, her wonderful hopeful plan pulled out from under her. The doctor continued describing what they should watch for, what she had already ruled out, while Elizabeth, angry and bewildered, fixed a mask of concern and relief on her face, nodding at her words, smiling at Simone as if this were very good news indeed.

"I'm just saying to myself inside, the baby's fine, the baby's fine," said Simone. She was in a bed on the second floor of the hospital. There was, miraculously, a window in the room, and from where Elizabeth sat, she could see the slender sickle moon.

There was still no word from Veronica. Elizabeth had called James to let him know where things stood, and he had groaned when she told him what the doctor had said. She'd glanced over at Simone. "Yes," said Elizabeth to James. "That's exactly how I feel." Simone beamed.

A miscarriage would solve almost everything—except for Simone's broken heart.

"Oh, sweetie," Elizabeth asked finally. "When did you decide to keep it?" As she considered Simone, this child with beautiful baby skin, the peeling nose, the tiny pimples on her forehead, she felt like a wicked stepsister posing as a friend.

"I don't know exactly. But I do know that when I think about not having it, I freak. I mean, I was going to have an abortion. I've made two appointments and then canceled them. I felt like I would die, it would be so awful." She paused for a minute and then went on slowly. "I've never had anything of my own, but this baby is my own. Everything else's always getting taken away from me, ever since I was a kid. I've never met my dad, because he had another family. He belonged to other kids." Simone looked utterly drained, pale as coral.

"Oh, honey." Elizabeth closed her eyes a moment. The room smelled of rubbing alcohol, and she saw herself with a martini glass raised to her lips. She opened her eyes reluctantly and found Simone peering at her, as if she were some distance away. They smiled at each other. This is an idiotic plan, Simone, she wanted to scream, but looking at Simone's limp yellow hair and her terrified eyes, Elizabeth's heart felt heavy with love for her.

"Why don't you close your eyes and rest," she said.

"I need to go pee." Simone got up and toddled off to the bathroom. Elizabeth looked out the window, but the moon had risen out of sight. She got up and went to look for it. She remembered James's face when she had first told him about Simone, how he had scowled, shaken. "That fucking goddamn Veronica" was the first thing he said. In the past, he had said that he could basically handle anything as long as he knew whom to blame, and now he had fixed on Veronica as the problem. "Letting Simone go ahead with this," he said, looking skyward for help. "Letting her have any choice in the matter."

Lank said, when they told him Simone's news, that what life boiled down to was a pregnant teenage girl. Life's only intention was to recreate itself; he remembered some scientist somewhere saying that the chicken was only the egg's way of making another egg. Elizabeth looked over at the closed door to the bathroom. Simone, darling, she imagined saying, we have a moral responsibility not to have children we can't take care of in a really grown-up way. You must not inflict life on someone who will be resented.

But she knew she would not say this. Her heart felt so troubled, her breathing so constricted, that she wondered if she might be having a heart attack. She felt such terrible fear for the baby's future that she realized she was, truly, having an attack of the heart, way down deep inside. She stroked her own shoulder for a moment and remembered Rosie at four or five, crying out that her neck hurt when really she had a sore throat.

The bathroom door opened slowly, and Elizabeth glanced at the moon one more time, as if it might have an answer, might suddenly give off more light, but its silver crescent glow must have been all the moon could manage.

STRAY blonde hairs, wavy and fine, had escaped from the barrette that held Simone's hair back. She had crawled back into bed. "I'm still bleeding a lot," she said. She pulled the sheet and thin blanket back up over her chest and then twisted a patch of the sheet into a spike of cotton. Elizabeth sat back down in the bedside chair.

They were both silent for a while. There was someone else in the second bed on the other side of the curtain, and they listened to her breathe. When Simone finally spoke again, she sounded grim and strangely mature. "I'm not stupid," she said. "I know you'd all be glad if I lost the baby. I know you all think I'm still a little girl. But do you see how the men look at me?" Elizabeth nodded. "Do you see how James looks at me?" Elizabeth lowered her eyes. It was true, it was true. "Can't you just wish for me to not lose this baby? Can't you believe I can do a lot more than you think I can, that just because I look a certain way doesn't mean I'm not smarter and better than you and everyone thinks?"

"Yeah," she said. "Of course I can, baby. We all know how smart and good you are. That's not the issue, though. The issue is that it would simply be easier for us if you weren't pregnant. If you hadn't started having sex yet. Or if you lost the baby."

"But easy's like, who cares? Easy's like, how much is easy going to get you?"

Elizabeth nodded in agreement. "When I got pregnant with Rosie, I wasn't a kid, but I felt like one, faced with the momentousness of that huge a change. And I also felt like no one understood me, but I felt like the baby would because it was of me, like you said."

"You thought Rosie would understand you?"

Elizabeth paused and smiled, surprised that Simone was thinking the thoughts of a mother; she was moved by this unexpected alliance. "I hoped," she said finally. In that moment she understood something about the fragility of borders, her own and Simone's; she understood that Simone believed she might dissolve if she were ripped open by an abortion. If she were haunted by the fear that the world is empty, then this was a way of making meaning, of turning toward life. Elizabeth remembered being fourteen and fifteen, how clearly she saw the nihilism of the world, and how it ate away at all meaning and connection, and so how, in Simone's stomach, a little sprout of utterly misplaced hope was growing.

SIMONE fell asleep at midnight. Elizabeth yawned. Where on earth was Veronica? She must not have come home yet and found Simone's note. Elizabeth looked around the room, desperate for something to read; finding nothing, she closed her eyes and tried to breathe deeply calmly. But she couldn't sit still in her skin; it no longer fit. She reached for the phone and dialed home, but after several rings the answering machine came on. James must have gone to bed, she thought, and she sat there resenting that he hadn't called to check in with her one last time. She hated this, the tedium; it put her smack in the middle of herself, which was her least favorite place to be these days. She'd never understood people who liked to meditate. The concept—that it made sense for her to sit and listen to her head—was ludicrous. Watching Simone sleep filled her with a fearful grief. There was no getting around the truth that Simone was becoming a woman, and suddenly a shutter clicked, and in a different photograph, developing more slowly, she saw that Rosie was, too.

She was shocked by this thought; it was as if it had never occurred to her. Before when she'd thought about the change in her daughter, it was of her becoming an alien, an *other*, a teen. Strange hospital sounds—gurney wheels rolling past in the corridor, talk radio from the nurses' station—ricocheted in the chambers of her mind, tiny pings, buzzes, beeps, as she watched a slightly older Rosie walking away into the future, waving without even turning around. She pressed her hands against her eyes. She saw only a spangly darkness at first, but then she saw Andrew, the Andrew she saw in Foreverland, on yet another beach, turn to wave good-bye to her as he walked toward the gentle waves where she could not follow.

She wrung her hands, like a worried old woman in a fairy tale or a baby. It was as though a new season had come to her of darkness and rain while everyone else had summer and clear bright days. She got up again to look at the sky, hoping to see a shooting star. But she stared out at the night through the window for quite some time without seeing any movement at all.

The door opened not long after, and Elizabeth turned, expecting a doctor or nurse, but there, miraculously, were James and Rosie. A soft cry of happiness escaped from her lips. Rosie was so sleepy that she looked slightly drugged, in sweatpants and one of James's long-sleeved white T-shirts, acres too long, the sleeves rolled up six inches. She peered at her mother, full of both longing and fear, and after a minute walked over to her and into her arms.

"I'm not staying," said James. "But I all of a sudden knew Rosie should be here."

Elizabeth smiled, grateful, and hugged Rosie too tightly.

Simone awoke, blinking with confusion, and then gasped and held her arms open to Rosie.

ROSIE and Elizabeth were still awake when Veronica finally showed up at two, heavily made up, alone. She wore a little black cocktail dress that showed off her breasts, her shapely legs, and big round bottom. She looked like a tipsy call girl stopping by for a visit on her way home—and she looked like Simone probably would in twenty years, like someone who had been around, lived hard, danced hard. Rosie was lying beside Simone, looking very proprietary and wary, and Elizabeth still sat in the chair by the bed.

"Hey, there you are," Elizabeth said kindly.

"I just got home and got her note. I called, but the switchboard's closed."

She walked fearfully to Simone's bedside. "How is she?" she asked. "She was bleeding?"

"Yeah. She'd stopped, though, the last time she checked."

Simone, her lips pouty with sleep, looked like a child of ten or so, flushed now and sweaty as if with fever. Veronica stared down at her and shook her head. "Is she having a miscarriage?" she asked.

"No. The doctor doesn't think so. Her cervix is closed, which means she's not miscarrying. The doctor wanted to keep an eye on her tonight."

Veronica looked exhausted. She smiled the faintest shadow of a smile. "God," she said, looking up. "None of this feels like it can really be happening."

"But it really is."

"Yeah." Veronica turned to Rosie. "And you," she said, "you are a wonderful friend."

Rosie scowled, pleased and shy. Elizabeth could see the genuine affection between them.

"You want to lie down with her?" Rosie said, and after a moment, Veronica nodded shyly. Rosie climbed out of bed, came over to her mother's chair and sat down on her lap. Veronica took off her spiky black heels, stretched out on the mattress beside Simone, and watched her sleep. The little black dress was hiked up past the dark thigh panels of her pantyhose, and her breasts were spilling out, and Elizabeth felt pangs of exasperated fondness: slutty Veronica and ruined Simone, who snored softly. Veronica wiped at the smudges of mascara beneath her eyes. Then she brushed the damp bangs from Simone's forehead and smoothed down the tangled hair, stroking her head, twirling some strands, letting blonde curtains of hair fall through her fingers like sand, all with the most elegant hand gestures, like those of a flamenco dancer, or a baby.

ELIZABETH and Rosie left a while later, when Rosie began dozing in Elizabeth's lap. Elizabeth woke her gently. "I can't carry you, baby," Elizabeth said, smiling as she stood Rosie up on her feet. They went to the bed and hugged Veronica, rubbed Simone's shoulder, promised to check in later that day.

They walked down the hall, waving good-bye to some of the nurses they'd met that night. Rosie appeared to fall asleep standing up in the elevator. Elizabeth took her hand when the door opened and led her out of the lobby, through the parking lot, and to the car. She opened the passenger door and waited while Rosie slid heavily into the seat. Then she buckled Rosie's seat belt and closed the door. Walking over to the driver's side, she happened to look at the moon one more time. The older part of the moon was showing: an eerie circle of shadow at the base of the full moon, as if the shining crescent were holding the missing part of itself in its arms.

ten

SIMONE'S belly grew rounder. Elizabeth had called Veronica the day after the miscarriage scare to tell her that they all loved and supported Simone, but to ask if everyone—Simone, Veronica—was positive that a baby for Simone was really a good idea at this time. What she wanted to ask was, Are you *mad?* Are you fucking *whacked?* Veronica had been drinking and burst forth into a weepy diatribe about abortion, which made no sense until it turned out she was talking about her own, the one she had had when she was fifteen at a hospital in San Francisco, where she had to sign court papers claiming to have been raped. So that was that. And now life went on. Rosie seemed a little more cheerful, was growing taller before their very eyes, while Simone grew heavier, rounder—now bleeding, now not.

Now James was the one full of darkness, secrecy. He disappeared into his study every day and handed her pages to read late every afternoon. He was getting ready to send some of his new book off to his agent, and he needed her unconditional approval. But she only loved some of the book and did not know what to do. For the time being, she pretended to love everything he'd written so far. It was a fictionalized account of a woman he had loved for many years in his twenties. It seemed reasonable to Elizabeth that after having her read such an intense and erotic account of another woman, he might expect some reservations on her part, especially when so many of her own lines and foibles had been woven into a character who clamored for spankings and anal sex.

"Why all the butt stuff, darling?" she asked one night. "Couldn't she be into local politics instead?"

"I just know it to be true."

"I mean, am I crazy?" Rosie had heard Elizabeth ask Rae over the phone one recent morning, and Rae had said no, no. Rosie listened in silence on the extension. There was some beautiful writing, Elizabeth said, James at his best, fragile and askance, his basic American rube humor mixed in with the sense that everything is interesting if you just come at it from a place of wonder. And then there were parts that were so removed from James's experiences, as Elizabeth understood them, of being a lover and a man and a son and a father, that the writing came across as vacant and chilling, and she wondered if she even knew him.

"I think it would help if you could actually tell him what you think," Rae had said.

But it was clear to her that he did not want to hear. He was sullen and defiant.

Rosie, lurking around the house, listening in on the fights, on her mother on the phone, on the silences, felt invisible.

ONE hot summer evening, when Lank and Rae were over for another reading night, Rosie stared at her mother hypnotically until Elizabeth finally looked up, but as she did, Rosie glanced mournfully off into the middle distance.

"Honey, are you okay?" her mother asked. Rosie looked down into her lap. Couldn't they see that she wasn't okay, that she was troubled and lonely and still full of secrets? What did she have to do, go hang herself in the upstairs bathroom for them to notice how sad she was?

"I think I'll go on up to my room," she said, and got to her feet. She really didn't even know exactly what was troubling her, whether it was the cheating, or Simone being pregnant, or if it was loneliness, a huge heavy loneliness. She was afraid people would say she was feeling sorry for herself.

"Shall I come upstairs with you for a while?" Rae asked, putting down her book, but Rosie shook her head. She had been noticing all night that Rae liked sitting near Lank on the couch, being quiet, reading, like James and Elizabeth, like the couple that everyone else was except her.

Simone was a couple with her baby.

"You sleepy tonight, baby?" James asked, and she shrugged.

"I think I'll lie down and rest for a while," she said, and couldn't believe it when all the adults nodded, as if this were a perfectly reasonable thing for her to do and not the oddest thing she could think of to say. God! Lie down and rest? A thirteen-year-old, at 9:30?

She lay on the bed, closed her eyes, and pretended she was in a coffin. She was wearing a white satin nightgown and lipstick. Someone had put one perfect red rose on her chest, beneath her crossed hands. People were sobbing—her mother especially, and J. Peter Billings. Their tears dripped onto her pale, peaceful face. The church was filled with tearful kids, from school and the tournaments, dressed in their Sunday best, holding lighted candles, swaying in grief. It was so sad that she started to cry herself and lay there wiping at her eyes for quite some time, feeling like her heart would break.

After a while she got up and put a Eurythmics tape in her boom box and turned it on loud, waiting for someone to come upstairs and yell at her. But James only yelled from downstairs for her to turn it down, and she did.

She stomped around the room for a moment, until she remembered what her mother used to call when she was younger. "There's the angry clubfoot again," she had heard her say. It used to really hurt her feelings, but they didn't care. They never thought of anyone but themselves.

She sat in her room and thought about cleaning it up, but lay down on her bed instead. She imagined various tragedies, saw herself in a hospital bed in traction, her mother and James and Rae and Simone and Hallie in a circle around her, weeping with relief that she was going to live. She saw herself on a gurney in an ambulance, bleeding nearly to death from knife wounds, smiling a tiny battered sliced-up jack-o'-lantern smile at her devastated mother, winking to say, I've always loved you, Mom. She saw herself with her eyes swollen shut, purple and black, in the wreckage of a burning car, dragging a small child away in her arms, her legs crushed beneath her, clumsy as a seal on dry land. Then she imagined shielding the small child with her body as the car exploded with thermonuclear intensity, felt and smelled her skin blister. She got up and went to the mirror. It was so hopeless. She was so homely, with horrible ropy hair, teeth as big as shingles, and eyes so blue they appeared crossed. She squinted at her reflection to see what she'd look like with her eyes swollen shut, and she practiced small smiles. Then she opened her eyes and pinched her left cheek. A pink blotch appeared. She pinched it harder, until the skin reddened. Her eyes watered, and her heart stirred with a gasp of tenderness for this girl in the mirror, with all her problems and heartache, her dead daddy, pregnant friend—skinny and lonely as a heron. She stared at her reflection, reaching up to stroke some hair off her forehead and then down the side of her face with the back of her hand, softly, gently. Then, as if in slow motion, without being particularly aware of doing so, she made a fist and hit herself on the cheekbone. Tears sprang to her eyes, and she cried out softly. It took her a moment to catch her breath. Then, closing her left eye, she made a fist, turned it all the way toward her so that the knuckle of her middle finger was aimed right at her, and hit herself again. This time she didn't make a sound. She could hardly breathe. She touched her cheek gingerly, felt its heat, felt that it was already swelling, looked in the mirror and saw that her left eye was already closing. She looked up on the bookshelf above her, located just the right trophy, got it down, and used the corner of the base to hit herself on the cheekbone one more time.

WHEN she appeared downstairs, holding one side of her face with both hands, she had to pretend to be crying before anyone even looked up. Then everyone bolted to her side.

"Rosie, Rosie! What happened?"

"One of my trophies fell off the shelf," she said, whimpering. "I knocked against it, and looked up, and it just hit me on the eye."

"In the eye, or near it, on your face?" James said, trying gently to pull her fingers away so he could have a look. And her mother led her to the couch, where she was made to sit while Lank and Rae prepared an ice pack and a cool drink of water. James sat beside her, holding her with one arm, peering at her with enormous concern.

"Wow," he said admiringly, his face creased with worry and love. "You're going to have some shiner."

HER cheekbone was indeed bruised and somewhat swollen in the morning. She assured her parents that she was really okay, and in fact, she felt more like herself than she'd been in weeks. She felt visible, for one thing, and someone deserving special care. Everyone noticed her, everyone was sympathetic. The boys at the club paid more attention to her than they ever had before, and Rosie dropped her eyes and smiled down at the ground, basking in their concern and admiration.

She felt very powerful, like she was really *around,* really somewhere, no longer floating, lost and invisible, but back inside her head, grounded, looking out through her eyes, calm, loved. It was great.

There was still some swelling the next morning when she got up, but the bruises were already fading. So she took a ballpoint pen and colored in a circle on the palm of her left hand, then wet it with spit, as if making a paste, and dabbed a little on her face, lightly rouging her cheek in blue.

"Oh, I think it's worse today," her mother groaned when Rosie appeared for breakfast. Rosie smiled bravely.

"It feels a little better, though," she said.

James invited her into town to do errands that morning with the promise of a hot fudge sundae at the other end, and when the man behind the counter at the hardware store looked up at her and whistled, James said, "Yeah, well, you oughta see the other guy."

The next morning there was only a slight sense of tightness, only the faintest bruise. Rosie sort of wished she could have it forever, or something else like it—a broken leg, for instance. A cast and crutches—people always flocked around the kids who turned up at school on crutches. But still, she felt better than she had in a long time. She and her mother went out to a diner for pie two days later, where they sat in a booth and had to listen to this young mother, maybe eighteen or so, carrying around her squalling baby. "It's like a teakettle," Rosie said, and this made Elizabeth laugh, and they looked at each other and shook their heads, and Rosie rolled her eyes, and Elizabeth heaved a sigh, and neither said Simone's name but they were together in a skeptical, boggled space, and Rosie felt close to her mother again.

THEN James and Elizabeth had a little fight at a tournament.

James had insisted on coming along but could hardly sit still, getting up every twenty minutes or so to check his messages. Elizabeth gave Rosie encouraging looks whenever Rosie looked over. Sometimes James was sitting beside her, watching, pulling for Rosie, other times his seat was empty. Elizabeth was simultaneously annoyed with him and sympathetic. He had not heard from Mel, the producer of his radio essays, in over four days, after having sent him a new piece he hoped to read on the air. He had a short story at *The New Yorker* that an editor had asked to take a look at two months before and a tentative offer of a film option on his first book, and he went off to call in for messages twice in one hour.

"What time is it?" he asked Elizabeth, when he returned a few minutes later.

"Nearly two."

"Then I'm not going to hear from New York at all today."

"Look, as it turns out, at eleven you weren't going to hear. At one you weren't going to hear. You've spent five hours today waiting to hear, when it was not something that was going to happen."

"Elizabeth? Give me a break."

"I hate for you to go through this. It drives me crazy. It's like Rae waiting to hear from one of her possible fiancés. It saps her of her strength. It keeps her stuck in fantasy. I mean, especially with Mel— he's a sadist, James. He's passive aggressive. He's someone Rae would date! Can you imagine having to wait for one of the men Rae would date to validate you as a writer?"

"This is about trying to earn a living. We have a daughter with a very expensive habit. We have bills."

"Darling. This is not about Rosie. It's about your self-esteem. That's all. We'll scrape by however things shake down in New York. Do you want to know what I think? I think New York is the mother you wish would approve of you."

"Spare me the details, darling. Just tell me what to do, O sighted master."

"Fuck you."

"Honestly."

"Just pay attention. Watch tennis. Enjoy my company."

James closed his eyes and let his chin drop onto his chest. Elizabeth resisted the urge to roll her eyes; he looked like he had just found out he had cancer.

"But, Elizabeth, you know how it is. It's like a broken tooth my tongue can't stay away from."

"I think you try to get New York to love you the way you should have been loved when you were little. But New York is huge and in-scrutable and narcissistic; it's so self-involved that your needs and wants are irrelevant. Your needs and wants are funny to New York. It laughs about them. It laughs itself sick."

"I know," he said. "You're absolutely right." And then twenty min-utes later he went to check his messages again.

Rosie did not know that this had been going on until later that night, when she listened in on a phone call to Rae. She went to her room, left the door open, and put on a rap tape, too loudly, but Elizabeth just closed the kitchen door without saying anything to her. Rosie sighed and studied her made-up face in the mirror—the blush, the gloppy black dye on already black lashes. She leaned forward and kissed the re-flection of her lips, closing her eyes, tilting her head, smiling. Then she wiped the pink lips off the glass, or at any rate rubbed it into a cloudy smear, so it made her think of someone's lips who is a little drunk and has been kissing, like Simone that night she got pregnant, when she fi-nally emerged from the boat, her lipstick smeary and askew. Her face had been all—what was that word—sultry, all hot and humid like the weather was now. She'd looked like one of the high school girls who sat in cars with older boys and smoked, and she'd looked at Rosie that night like Rosie was her little baby sister, sent by their mom to make her come home. It did not occur to Rosie to go get a sponge and clean the mirror. It did occur to her to smash herself in the eye again. But as she raised the trophy up she stopped and reconsidered. It was too soon to do it again. People might figure it out. She would have to think of something else. In the meantime, she stared at herself with sorrowful eyes, holding the metal trophy, the gold-plated woman about to serve so confidently. She studied the gold-plated woman, her look of tri-umph, of victory earned honestly; and then she looked back in the mirror, at her own sorry face, the look of sadness, the face of a cheater, and she couldn't decide if she looked more like Mary, the mother of Jesus, or a baby monkey at the zoo.

eleven

ELIZABETH went back out into the neighborhood on the first of August and registered three Democrats to vote. This was about all she had to show for the last two months, but still, presidential elections had been won on less than a vote per precinct, and she came home enthusiastic about the day. She went directly to James's office to tell him how great it had been to be out in the sun, trying to be of help. She had excused herself for interrupting and begun to tell him about all she had seen, but he had looked at her almost wearily, and she ended up feeling that all of her excitement was going into a drain around her feet. She felt hurt and tight, needing an arm around her shoulder, but James was oblivious to this; he stayed near the phone, waiting for the right call.

Rosie and Simone were at Hallie's together, Rosie on the trampoline and Simone, Elizabeth imagined, sitting in a patio chair with her hands folded over her stomach. When Rosie called at six to say they'd both been invited to spend the night, Elizabeth's first inclination was to say no.

"Why don't you guys come home, and we'll go out to a movie?"

"God, Mom," Rosie said, as if her mother had proposed they come over and cut out paper dolls.

In the end, Elizabeth said okay, though the night then loomed ahead of her like a dim cave to be entered alone. James came out for dinner and went to great lengths to be civil and to ask her questions about her afternoon, but it was too little too late. She felt alone. It was not that they were not on the same wavelength—that seemed too linear—it was more that they were not in the same wave field, that wonderful net they could sometimes bounce around in.

She didn't say anything that night, thinking he would pick up on the hurt and comfort her and meet her, but he didn't, and so by the next day she was not trusting him. She realized how lost she was now and how lost everything else was too—the relationship, its harmonies, its ease.

She called Rae.

"Can we go for a walk?" she asked. "Do you have plans for today?"

"Well," said Rae, "I have to finish a couple of weavings by the end of next week."

"Okay," said Elizabeth. Her voice quavered slightly, and she cleared her throat to steady it.

"Come over!" said Rae. "We can talk while I weave."

But Elizabeth said no, no. Rae needed to work. And she had work to do in the garden.

T HE fog rolled in. Elizabeth was glad for the thick mist, through which only a weak and distant light shone. Most people thought of sunshine as being great weather, but sunshine was pitiless. You could see every pore. Fog, though, was a cloak for the psyche. The poor old mind had so much to do all day, all its machinations and things to re-member, its fear, the incessant juggling; God, it was so great to stop.

She began to pull the weeds that grew around the roses. Once she looked up at the window of James's study and saw that he was watch-ing her solemnly. Then he smiled and waved. She waved back. He bent his head, as if in prayer, returning to his keyboard. She studied her suc-culents, with their leathery purple-black leaves. They looked like some-thing you'd find in an S-and-M fern bar. She noticed a little purple guy who seemed a bit dry, and as if pouring an old ancient mariner another rye at the bar, she gave him a little water, imagined him closing his eyes and inhaling deeply with relief.

A LL that day and the next, Elizabeth guarded the words that had re-cently flowed so freely. Her voice got tight first, and then James's fol-lowed, although life went on; the cooking continued, the serving, eating, cleaning. She had learned over the years that you didn't mess with the surface when things were like this, because that was all that was left. So there was no more yelling. All the fluidity that was their life together had hardened; if one of them yelled it might crack them both, leaving shards on the floor to step on. They needed a mutuality, anything that might bring them back into the same world, onto the same side, something to bat around together. But Rosie went off with Simone to the sectionals in Palo Alto, and the heartbeat of the house was more and more arrhythmic.

A belly laugh could have rerhythmed the house. But there wasn't one. The absence of what was supposed to be happening filled the house. They kept skirting this absence, which sat in the middle of the living room floor under a drop cloth; they gave it as wide a berth as possible.

ROSIE checked in from Palo Alto. She had lost in the quarterfinals of the singles to someone ranked higher than she, and she had played great. She and Simone had won their quarterfinal doubles match. This was the first tournament in which Simone had played since her miscarriage scare; her doctor had said it was fine to play, and she was playing beautifully. "How are you?" Rosie asked.

"Fine, darling," said Elizabeth.

But Rosie did not believe her. She could hear something in her mother's voice, a nervousness, but she didn't press because she didn't want to come home. She was having too much fun. She hated herself for feeling this.

ELIZABETH stood at the phone for a moment before hanging it up, and then she walked toward James's study, wanting to reach out and give him some affection. But when she stepped inside, he barely looked up, even though he said, "Hello," nicely. She looked at his back for a minute.

"Whatcha doing?" she said.

He cleared his throat and did not look at her. "Working."

"I'm just missing everyone, James. I feel so lonely tonight."

He began to shuffle things around on his desk, shoving a stack of notes over to one side, gathering loose paper clips together with a cupped hand.

"I'm sorry about what I said. About Mel and New York."

"You know what?" he said, his face pinched and rather cold. "We live together and we're close, and yet you say these things that really undermine me." James shook his head. "I want to talk about this," he said. "But I need to press on right now. I need to get this work done."

It was very scary. She felt once again how fragile their relationship was. There was such fear in not knowing how, when a retreat starts, it will ever end or ever reverse itself. And the hole was so huge, the hole of their discontinuity. Their marriage was a glass mountain, and here they had slid to the bottom, and she wanted to start climbing back up, with him climbing back on the other side, and they would check on each other's progress, and there would be the very gradual getting back together. But no one took the first step uphill. She believed this would happen, because it always had, but two days later they were still sleeping on opposite edges of the bed.

SIMONE was over for dinner after the girls got back from Palo Alto. Rosie looked into her mother's face and tried to feel connected but her mother just looked kind, maybe a little sad. The eggs her mother was serving them from a platter were speckled black with bacon grease.

Simone began flinging herself around in conversation, the way she used to fling her body around. She ate like a horse, like a big fat peasant housewife in the Renaissance, and Rosie sneaked a glance down at her protruding belly, at the baby who was growing inside like a barnacle.

Simone reached for another piece of toast and spread an enormous amount of jam on it with elaborate care, in a back and forth motion like a carpenter spreading cement onto bricks. Taking a bite, she complimented Elizabeth for making such great toast, Rosie for having played so well that day, James for being such a famous writer.

Rosie was grateful for all that energy, which was filling the silences that had erupted in her parents' lives like craters on the moon.

Simone pointed a crisp strip of bacon at James. "It must be fun to be famous," Simone was saying to him, and Rosie saw that he was pleased, although it made him feel shy. "I have dreams of being famous myself," she said. "For being an actress. I would love to win an Oscar. I'm not sure what I would say in my speech," she said. "Because I'm not exactly sure what would move people most.

"I'm going to always make sure I'm not too selfish," she continued, fluttering her eyelashes with indignation at the very thought, and James and Elizabeth exchanged a look of pleasure. Hope or something like it flickered like electricity inside Rosie—oh, they were loving each other again right that moment.

She turned to James and opened her mouth to speak, but Simone spoke first. "If you're an actress, you usually have to marry a slime-ball."

James turned to Simone. "Do you really imagine yourself married to a slimeball?"

"I think it goes with the territory, to tell you the truth, James. He's rich, probably, let's say, but he has affairs and he'll beat me."

In her mind Rosie suddenly saw a man raise his fist to strike Simone, and she cried out, "No!" But Simone studied the candle flame, mesmerized. "Nice people don't marry actresses," she said. "They marry housewives."

THAT night after dinner, when Simone had gone home and Rosie was up in her room, she listened to her parents through the wall connecting them.

"I'm not in the mood, Elizabeth. I'm tired," said James. "I just want to get some sleep."

Here we go again, thought Rosie, lying on her bed with the door open, listening. She picked at her already ragged cuticles, at the tiny bumps on her face, then clasped her hands behind her neck so that her elbows covered her ears.

"So what's wrong with that?" she heard James ask, sometime later. "He's my goddamn *employer!*"

"What's wrong is that Mel's a monster. He's Klaus Barbie. You get blackmailed by him and then you kiss his ass . . . "

Their voices were rising and rising, sliding around the walls into her brain.

"I do not kiss his ass. I just try to get him to let me know if the piece is going to run or not."

"Then why do you always feel disgusting afterward?"

"How do you know I feel disgusting after?"

"Because you always go in and eat too much for the rest of that day. And you always want to have sex—or else refuse my advances— every night until you hear."

"Stop it!" Rosie finally screamed. "Stop it!"

The house was quiet again. "God," Rosie muttered. She scanned her room until her eyes rested on the photograph of her daddy, in the crummy old chair outside, smiling, gentle. He would never have yelled in such a pathetic way. He was always so dignified. Of course, maybe if he had lived to see her as a teenager . . .

She began to cry.

After a few minutes, she sniffled and picked up the book she was reading. It was about a beautiful old dog who'd gotten rabies. She wanted to go in and ask her mother if they'd ever had a dog; her dad had liked dogs, hadn't he? But she knew better than to go into the bedroom now. She looked back at the photo of Andrew.

Rae called the next morning with desperation in her voice, and it bailed Elizabeth out, gave her something to do.

"Come over and garden with me," Elizabeth insisted.

"I can't," said Rae. "I've discovered this little barbecue place that delivers, although unfortunately they won't come more than three times a day."

"Oh, honey. What's the matter?"

"I called Mike."

"Oh, no, no. What did he say?"

"He said he thought about me every day, that he'd been going crazy."

"And what did you say?"

"I asked him to come over for dinner tonight. He said he could come tomorrow."

"See? It's never, never what or when you want. You want to see him tonight? Well, forget it. He needs to be in control."

"But it was such short notice."

"I'm coming to get you. There's thirty-six hours until tomorrow night. And you need to really think about this."

"I just really want to see him."

"I'll be there in half an hour."

"James," said Elizabeth, in the doorway of his study, "Rae called Mike."

"Was he home?" James asked. Elizabeth nodded. "Oh, shit. What are we going to do?"

"I'm going to go keep her company. Maybe we'll go for a walk."

"Okay. Tell her to hold out for cherish." It was their code phrase for Rae. His eyes met hers.

"Okay. I'll tell her."

"I cherish you, Elizabeth."

"I know you do."

"It's just that I have a bad personality."

She came over to the desk and bent down to kiss the back of his head, and he reached behind him to pull her closer so that her nose was buried in his neck, and she smelled the faint scent of sweat, of James. She noticed him sneak a look at the page before him, but she didn't pull away. The smell of his neck soothed her.

"I'm scared there's something wrong with me, James."

"There's nothing wrong with you, Elizabeth. There's nothing that wouldn't get a great deal better if I wasn't such a total asshole."

ELIZABETH and Rae walked on the beach in the fog. Rae would have walked hand and hand if Elizabeth had let her. Neither of them said anything.

"The pain of being alone is so big sometimes," said Rae. "It's oceanic. Sometimes it's dull and doesn't command much attention. But right now it's acute. I feel flayed."

"I know."

"But you don't. You've had two great husbands."

"Yeah, and one died violently, and one is a writer. But I never found a career. You've had this wonderful artistic life and lots of success. Everyone loves you, and they love your work. I envy that so much."

"Oh, Elizabeth. I'm just dying. I want Mike to hold me."

Farther down the beach, walkers turned into dream figures, shadowy and insubstantial.

"Let's look at Mike for a second, okay, Rae? He always looked like he was about to become a giver, right? I mean, that's what he does for a living. Of course, Mike as a professional giver and healer is like Richard Nixon as a Quaker."

Rae laughed quietly.

"You're a moth to the flame, though. Like Lucy with Charlie Brown and the football. Because that kind of inconsistency is always going to remind you in some really complicated way of your childhood. You get to hear 'Home, Home on the Range' playing softly in the background."

"It's better than being empty-handed."

"Rae. It's the call to the grave."

"Maybe so," said Rae. "But it also sounds like the dinner bell." They trudged along the wet sand, the fog protecting them, masking them, as if it were trying to keep them in a dream.

Rosie got on her bike that foggy afternoon and started off down the road not knowing where she was headed. She was dressed all in black, from her black high-top sneakers to James's Giants cap. She thought about going to the club, but it was no fun when Peter wasn't around. He would be back in a week or so, and she fantasized about their reunion. She pedaled aimlessly along the sidewalks of her neighborhood, waving to acquaintances and to people she knew even less well, people she knew by sight but not by name.

Peter always gave her a bear hug when he'd been gone, then stepped back to size her up and see if she'd grown, even if it had just been a couple of weeks. It was one of their little jokes, something a father who traveled a lot would do. She smiled on the bike, peering up into his beautiful baby blue eyes, grinning with shyness and with being glad to see him. But he was glowering back, and she caught her breath. God, what if there was a message waiting for him on his answering machine? "Someone should tell you that one of your students *cheats*," the message would say. "Rosie Ferguson cheats, she cheated against my kid. You shouldn't be the last to know." She pedaled faster and imagined steering the bike in front of an oncoming car, imagined the squeal of brakes, the crash. If she were in the hospital in traction, maybe he would know—maybe everyone would know—that she was sorry.

Her pulse pounded in her ears, hard, the Telltale Heart, and she pedaled faster, riding almost out of control; she still did not know where she was headed. But suddenly Simone's face was on her mind, Simone who'd done something this summer that was maybe even worse than cheating. Rosie slowed her bike down, pedaled along for a moment, then turned in the direction of Simone's house, practicing what she would say, silvery on the inside with panic.

"I NEED to tell you a secret, Simone," Rosie said, standing in the doorway of Simone's bedroom. There had never been and never would be a messier place than this room. Even Rosie's looked relatively together compared to Simone's. It was so bad that it was almost scary, especially when you tried to imagine the person who lived here having a baby. A baby could get lost in here, starve to death under a pile of tube tops. "I can't tell you here," said Rosie. "We need to be outside."

The girls rode their bikes up to the site of the old Miwok Indian village. Now the area was mostly covered with houses, but there was still one side of a low hill that the town had preserved where nothing could be built; in the summer and fall the younger children still slid all the way down the hill on their butts, using sides of cardboard boxes like sleds. Charles used to bring her up here when she was little, and while she slid down the hill, he would find arrowheads and spearheads made of obsidian and scrapers made of antlers that the Indians used to clean the hides of deer and rabbit. He had found a whistle made of bone once but had given it to the museum.

Rosie got off her bike and sat with her back against an old oak tree, gnarled, battered and scarred as if it had been hit by lightning. The leaves were brown now in the summer, round and itchy looking, like moths. The Miwoks practically used to live on mush made out of mashed acorns. Rosie believed that she would have made a poor Indian; she did not actually even like oatmeal or Cream of Wheat. Also, she did not think it was playing fair to use scrapers made from antlers to clean deer hide. She spread her knees so she could study the clearing of soft dirt in front of her. She looked over at Simone, who was using her round belly as a worktable at which she was weaving a tiny pot holder of pine needles.

"So say it," said Simone. "Say what the secret is."

"I can't."

"What could be worse than what I did? Slutty old me?" Rosie gaped at Simone, surprised. Simone crinkled up her nose at Rosie, the way she did at boys sometime, and Rosie looked down. She began to fashion a village in the clearing for the little ants who were scurrying about, a mound of grass and flower petals for the ant children to use as a haystack, a pile of pebbles for cannonballs, a raft made of sticks on which to float down the river.

"What I did was the worst thing an athlete can do."

Simone was silent at first; they could hear the shrill chirp of crickets in the afternoon heat.

"You'll feel better if you just say it."

Pedal and steer, pedal and steer; who would be holding on?

"Simone?"

"Uh-huh? Uh-huh, Rosie?"

"There were some matches this summer, when the people I was playing—Deb Hall once, Marisa DeMay—well, a few others, too, and they hit shots on really important points, like four games all, deuce, where if you won the game, you'd probably win the set. And even though I know you're supposed to give your opponent the benefit of the doubt, I didn't. I mean, all I did was to call these incredibly close shots—I mean incredibly close shots—out, when maybe there was a tiny chance that they were in. And I was sure, I was almost sure they were out—but you know, once or twice the girls acted like I was cheating them."

"Well, that's just ridiculous. I know you would never cheat, Rosie."

"Well, the girls think I cheated."

"That's none of your business what the other girls think. That's what my mother always says. It's just your business what you think."

"Yeah?"

Simone nodded. Rosie was buzzing inside with anxiety. She squinted at Simone for a moment.

"Simone?"

"Uh-huh."

"I think I did cheat."

Simone scowled. "Oh, Rosie. You didn't cheat. That's ridiculous. I'm your *part*ner. Just stop that."

Rosie opened her mouth, about to respond, and then she closed it again and dropped her head back so she could stare up through the ladder of branches above them. There were so many branches and so many leaves that a dozen feet up everything blurred and you could almost believe that the treetop disappeared into the clouds like a beanstalk.

"Does your mom know?" Simone asked after a while, as she wiped at her eyes with the back of her hands.

"Not yet. Hey. Why're you crying?"

"Because I'm sad. And because it's so great to not be the only person who messed up. It's not so bad as when it's just you."

Rosie thought this over, nodded.

"Hey, Simone?"

"Yeah?"

"Do you think you still like me the same?"

"Like you mean before you told me?"

"Yeah."

"I know I do. But I don't actually think you cheated."

An ant walked into a rose petal and then, like a little windup bumper doll, turned and scurried in another direction. "Simone," Rosie said firmly. "I did." She nodded, so Simone could see how solemn and true she was being. "I know just what I did, Simone, and I knew then, too. I could see their balls were in. They bounced in and they were so close and the point was so important to me right that second that I called them out." She raised her shoulders to her ears in a slow shrug, took a long deep breath, and another. Simone looked at her like she was crazy at first, and then awe widened Simone's face, and Rosie knew that Simone was beginning to believe her.

Rosie reached forward and began gathering up all the parts of her village, the grasses, the pebbles, the petals, the little black ants running all over; she gathered it all in the center as if for a giant bonfire. She had a strange feeling of calm, of balance, even as her heart raced. Her whole face was wreathed in apology, in shyness and shame, but she also felt something inside her, patient, attentive, wild, alert, like a wolf who was not hungry, who was not going to hurt anyone.

THAT evening James came into Elizabeth's corner at the window seat and sat down at the far end.

"Is Rae okay?"

"Oh, yeah, sort of. She's going to try and cancel Mike."

"And you?"

"I'm kind of a mess, and I'm also okay. How about you?"

"I'm lonely—I'm missing you and I'm missing me. I'll tell you what

I'm missing most, Elizabeth. I always feel that you know what's important to me and that you will catch me when I fall. But if you don't know what's important to me, then how will you know when I'm falling?"

"I'm falling too, though, James."

"But you mostly don't act like it. That's why I think it's so hard for me to figure out what to do. You have us—me and Rosie and Rae and even Lank. You take care of us. You save us."

"But who's going to save me?"

"We are. I am. But I don't know what to save you from." She reached out to stroke his face and he closed his eyes. "I'm sorry," he said quietly.

She did not feel that anything had changed, but she was glad for his warmth, for his kind attention. He wanted to crawl into her, she could tell, flooded with relief as he was to be on friendly terms again. Sex was the handy way to do it, the punctuation that says, We've come through this again. It wasn't erotic so much as driven by something more mammalian, or maybe more marsupial. She relaxed into his body, and they began making love for comfort, not looking for the transports of sex where you want to lose yourself in the ether of it all. What they wanted was to find each other again and, in doing so, find themselves. Narcotized though she was by the sex and reconciliation, Elizabeth bolted awake from a dream at daybreak. In the endless silence of the neighborhood and the house, she felt weighed down by a blanket of dread and the sense that someone else was there, lurking in the corners, hidden in the blue-gray morning light of the bedroom. James was asleep beside her, but she looked around, gazing at the smoky shadows. She thought she felt Andrew's presence, a gentle ghost the color of rain, standing out in its lightness against the obscurity of the dawn. But then she felt the shape grow murky, change from tall and straight to stooped, and she knew then that it was Luther who had been in the room, if only in her dream.

She saw him leaning against a windowpane, stubbing out a cigarette in the soil of a potted ivy on the windowsill. She could smell the smoke, watched him give her a crooked smile, like he knew something important he wasn't going to share.

She realized with a start that she'd never actually seen him indoors. He was always outside; what need had he ever had to be inside? She squeezed her eyes closed to shut him out, but saw him anyway peering down from above, as if he'd really been there, watching her sleep. Now she suddenly wasn't sure who it was, this phantom, this man who was in their house. Was it Luther, was it Andrew? She wanted the phantom to come back, wanted to see Andrew again, and she opened her eyes to the morning's first light. And in that light she understood that she had been dreaming of Luther.

She could almost see him still, could pick up the dream where she'd left off; she felt him turn and walk away in his well-tended raggedness. Who was stitching up the tears in his clothes for him, who did his darning? She noticed his hands hanging at his sides as he moved away. They were dirty, as if he'd been digging, and he moved with an inexorable slowness that was somehow chilling, for it suggested that he could be moving quickly if he chose.

twelve

ALLIE called the next day, the morning after Rosie and Simone came home from San Mateo with runner-up trophies in doubles. They had lost in straight sets to Deb Hall and Sue Atterbury. They had beaten Deb and Sue twice so far and lost twice. They were tied now for the number one ranking. Rosie was furious; Simone had played the worst tennis of the year, now that she was fatter and sluggish in the heat. On top of this, she had been alternately weepy and mean. So Elizabeth watched Rosie take the phone call from Hallie, sullen, withholding, pigeon-toed, not saying much. Then she began to melt, laughing at something Hallie said, then looking up at Elizabeth and rolling her eyes to show she wasn't really buying it. Elizabeth went to the kitchen to give her some privacy; after a while Rosie came in.

"Can I go over to Hallie's today?"

"Yeah, I guess so. If that's what you want to do. Do you need a lift?"

"No. I'll ride my bike."

Sometime later Elizabeth watched her pedal off, and then she went out to work in the garden, full of foreboding. That goddamn trampoline. Why, after all that Rosie had survived—nearly drowning in the river, all those hours spent on freeways getting to tournaments, all those hours with Luther's eyes on her—did she need to risk breaking her neck at play?

Elizabeth got to her feet, wanting to rush to Hallie's house, drag Rosie home with her, keep her safe. Boing, boing boing, she heard, the springs straining away from the horizontal frame with each bounce on the canvas. And she knew she was nuts, that this was compulsion and therefore about something else, but she didn't know what. She went inside and looked up Hallie's number.

"Hello, Marilyn," she said when Hallie's mother answered. "This is Elizabeth. Just checking in. How are the girls doing?"

"I can see them from here. It's just Hallie and Rosie today. They're having a ball. Rosie's on the trampoline right now—whoa!"

"What?"

"She just did a back flip. All right!"

"How on earth did she know how to do a back flip?" This was how the little girl in *Life* magazine broke her neck thirty-five years ago.

"Well, she's very athletic obviously, and Hallie must have taught her. Whoa!!"

"What!!"

"She just did another."

"Marilyn? Has anyone ever gotten hurt on your trampoline?"

"Not badly."

ELIZABETH, miserable on the couch, wondered if this was what it was going to be like when Rosie started driving. Would Elizabeth sit on the couch every night imagining her daughter dead? Maybe, she considered, she could practice living with the uncertainty. So she breathed quietly, listening. A loud motor: someone in the neighborhood was mowing the lawn; and after a minute Elizabeth's chin was nodding up and down, as if off in the distance she heard, "Boing, boing boing."

Elizabeth got her purse, fished out her keys, and went to the car. "This is crazy," she said but turned on the ignition and put the car in gear. Ten minutes later she screeched up outside Hallie's house and heard the springs and creaks of the trampoline as soon as she opened her car door. She went through the gate and followed the brick path around to the backyard, where her daughter was jumping five feet up in the air with each bounce, up against the cloudy blue sky, the lattice gate covered with ivy behind her. Elizabeth had not seen this much pure joy on Rosie's face since she was a little girl swinging in the park, and she knew her child was safe here. She saw that all these years she could have been jumping with her, risking life and limb for those ecstatic moments. Pain washed over her out of the blue. And then Rosie flipped forward, too high, misjudging, landing on her feet two inches from the edge of the canvas and onto the springs. Hallie screamed, with laughter in her voice, but right away Rosie regained her balance:

boing boing boing. And then Rosie saw Elizabeth, and her face grew dark and puzzled.

She slowed herself down, stopped, glanced at Hallie, and then walked to the edge of the trampoline.

"Hi, honey," Elizabeth said tentatively.

"Why are you here, Mom?"

"Well. I don't know exactly. I guess I've never seen this thing before, and I wanted to see what it was like."

"You should get on it, Elizabeth."

"Oh, no, Hallie, no."

"Come on. My mom does it. It burns off three hundred calories an hour."

"No, no."

Rosie was looking at her with an expression that said clearly that she must not under any circumstances get on the trampoline. But Elizabeth suddenly knew that this was why she'd been called here.

"Rosie?" she asked, pleading.

Rosie looked away in annoyance and disbelief.

"You have to take your shoes off, Elizabeth," Hallie was saying.

"Okay," said Elizabeth, and putting her back against the frame and her arms on its sides, she pulled herself up onto the trampoline. Her arms trembled. Rosie walked to the edge to climb down.

"No—stay with me, honey. Jump with me."

"Yeah, right."

Elizabeth stared into her daughter's face, willing her to look back, and finally she did, the small screwed-up face with the piercing blue eyes as bright as the few clear patches of sky, and that lovely skin, now flushed with red in the cheeks. "Come on, Rosie. Just jump with me."

Rosie felt as humiliated as if her mother wanted to dance together at a tennis club dance in front of the other kids. But Hallie was coming over to actually take her mother's shoes away, the horrible scuffed drug-addict loafers, and she saw no way out. Elizabeth stood unsteadily on the canvas, waiting.

"Well," said Rosie finally. "What do you expect me to do? Pick you up and hold you while I jump? You just start jumping up and down, bouncing, okay?"

"Okay."

Elizabeth began to bounce up and down, jerky and stiff, feeling and—she imagined—looking like Virginia Woolf, with one of her headaches, made to bounce on a trampoline. Rosie bounced beside her, up and down, up against the sky, down with the lattice behind her, and finally Elizabeth got some rhythm going, up and down, higher and higher beside her daughter, bouncing away. Rosie softened, even gently reached for her hands and held them while they jumped. Elizabeth stopped feeling quite so much like a wobbly newborn pony and bounced for a moment with real pleasure. Out of nowhere, though, she almost lost her balance, and then, regaining it, she almost fell over again. She looked up to discover Rosie leering at her evilly, and she realized with dismay that Rosie was taking an extra jump between each of hers, trying to trip her up, the way the teenagers probably did with each other. Elizabeth lost her balance, and fell on her side.

Anger and a deep sense of betrayal flushed through her, as she bounced about clumsily while Rosie kept jumping. "Stop it," she cried, but now Rosie was laughing, and she started laughing too, although she was very mad. It was so hard to get up with Rosie bouncing, and she flopped around helplessly like a turtle on its back. Then she started laughing so hard she was afraid for a moment that she might wet her pants. Rosie pulled her to her feet, but she couldn't find her rhythm again because she kept laughing, even though now Rosie had stopped. And Elizabeth began to feel a shift in her chest, between this now hysterical laughter and a jagged tearing feeling.

Like the sun shining through the clouds, a memory began to show through the veil, distant and then nearer, of six-year-old Elizabeth riding on a seesaw with a boy of ten or so—a mean boy who tricked her, who sat down on the asphalt, lifting her up in the air and holding her there while she begged him to ease her down. She saw him smile with pleasure while she squirmed on her side of the board, high in the sky, afraid she would fall on her head and die, and then finally, finally, the boy bounced up, and she crashed down and hit her pubic bone so hard that her head rang like a gong.

Still she bounced with Rosie, feeling now like a trapdoor might open beneath her and swallow her up. The capsule in her throat filled to the bursting point, and she found herself crying hard. Still bouncing jerkily, she tried to cover her grimace with her hands. "Mom!" Rosie cried in distress and looked over to see what Hallie was doing. Hallie was gaping. Shaking and wracked with sobs, Elizabeth dropped to the canvas, pulled her knees to her chest, and hid her face deeper behind her hands.

Rosie did not know what to do. Hallie pointed to the house furtively, as if perhaps her mother could help. After she tiptoed away, Rosie stood watching her pale wraith of a mother rock back and forth, still crying.

"Mom?" said Rosie, and dropped to her knees, bouncing her mother further about by accident, reaching out to steady her.

"Mommy," she whispered. "Mommy? What's wrong?"

tide pools

one
_____

OH, Elizabeth, Elizabeth."

Elizabeth sat silently on the bed with her eyes closed. She had been sitting like this almost all day. She had spent most of the day before crying about nothing she could put her finger on. James was simply keeping her company. She thought about drinking and she thought about taking an overdose of prescription drugs, although she did not have any. Through her confusion and sadness, she was glad that James was someone who knew about the nihilistic forces out there and therefore forgave her for feeling so pummeled. She wondered if he was having second thoughts about the sickness-and-health part of their vow, the most difficult line of all, yet he did not leave her side.

"What are you thinking about, Elizabeth?"

"Nothing." They sat with their backs resting on the headboard Andrew had brought back from Spain.

"Are you sure you don't want us to find you a therapist?"

"Uh-huh."

It had been five days since the episode on the trampoline, five days of bed rest and crying. Rae had been by every day; Lank had missed only the Friday when he and the other teachers in his school district had had an all-day meeting to prepare for classes, which would begin again soon. No one had been able to cheer her up, so it was agreed that they would all just keep her company until she felt better, until she snapped out of this thing. Lank and Rae had spent one afternoon lying on either side of her, like bookends, watching the TV that James had wheeled in, and watching her sleep. Even Simone was coming by to lie on the bed with her. There had been a strangely lovely hour the day before when Rae had been reading to Elizabeth on the bed, and Simone and Rosie had stopped by. Simone had made a card for Elizabeth, the kind little kids make by ironing crayon shavings between two pieces of waxed paper.

"It's so pretty," said Rae, "and you look so pretty, too. Do you have people to tell you that? That you look wonderful?"

"Well, I'm as fat as a pig," said Simone. "I've already gained fifteen pounds. I've got this weird cellulite all down the back of my legs."

"You're lucky to have cellulite," said Rae, making room for her on the bed. "Ten years ago I had cellulite. I'd kill to have it back. They don't even have a name for what it turns into."

SHE got Rae and James to drive her to meetings almost every day. She didn't feel like driving; she felt too odd. She sat in the meetings and didn't speak, and she left early, but going to them helped her in some low-grade grounding way. It also seemed to make James feel less anxious. She could feel James's worry: that this thing was taking away someone whom he knew—someone so helpful and encouraging and funny, his great listener, his ally—and leaving in its place a millstone and a liability, someone incapable of dishing out joy. James was having to do the work of both partners in this household, and daily life battered at him—dishes and clothes piled up.

He and Rosie grew very quiet, very watchful. Elizabeth had the sense that they were both biting back words they wished they could yell: Get up and fly right! You've always been able to haul yourself up before, goddamn it! You created this; you uncreate it. Instead, they came in and took turns lying beside her, bringing her soup and tea.

ON the seventh day of whatever was going on, she remembered a moment seven years ago, sitting on this very bed with Rosie in her lap, holding a wad of Kleenex to a cut below Rosie's eye where she'd run into a branch and nearly put her eye out. "Why did God make us so soft that we bleed?" she'd asked, and Elizabeth had not had a good answer then, nor would she now.

She and James now sat on this bed, on her first husband's bed, inherited from his parents.

"Life is too sad for me, James."

They had made love in this room so many times over the last five years, a thousand times on this bed, and before James, a thousand times with Andrew. Rosie had lain here as a somber infant, nursing or asleep, considering this or that: her mother's face, her father's hands, long and broad like a doctor's.

Elizabeth thought about her garden, which in mid August was at the height of fecundity, flourishing heartlessly while she was withering up. The good part would be squashing pests, getting to hate and kill something and get away with it. But no one in her family was eating anymore. She'd never had much of an appetite, James was on some sort of a diet now, and Rosie, so rarely home, picked at her food moodily, wanting to be upstairs in her room, listening to her rap music, talking on the phone. All the food Elizabeth's lovely garden produced, all the beautiful basic food she had worked so hard to grow, went bad in the produce drawer of the refrigerator. She was mocked by bounty.

"Shall I take you to a meeting?"

"No, thank you," she said. Actually, she didn't know if she was well enough to leave the house and hang out with all those prickly, self-obsessed people. She thought about calling the woman whom she'd asked to sponsor her years ago, whom she almost never called anymore, but she did not want to have to put up with one of her inspiring little talks. "I'll go tomorrow."

"Do you want me to call Rae and see if she's around?"

"I do," said Elizabeth. "That's what I want." And Rae was home and said she'd be right over. Just like that, she said she'd be right over.

Rae arrived in the bedroom sometime later and lay down at the foot of the bed. She took Elizabeth's feet in her hands, as she had with Charles, and rubbed them as if they were frostbitten and she were rubbing life and circulation back into them.

"Are you okay, honey bear? Do you want to go outside? Do you want to go to Samuel P. Taylor Park?"

"Okay. I think that would be okay."

An hour later they were sitting on an isolated stretch of ground along the bank of the river; their backs were up against the stump of a fallen redwood. As Elizabeth listened to the wet heartbeat of the river, the small woman inside her felt like she was nursing at Rae's breast. The light trickling through the branches and leaves sparkled with flakes of pollen and seedpods and dust, and the two women sat with their shoulders touching, silent. Being here was like being inside a fold in civilization: people up above, in the parking lot and at the campsites, had brought their whole houses along, but down here by the river, no one had brought anything, so this moment was about nothing but the stream. It was about how temporary they were. Elizabeth breathed slowly and deeply, aware of the huge construct of grief she had entered into, the twilight she had entered, abandoned her family to, and wondered what tiny tendrils might draw her back into life.

two

R OSIE watched her mother need to be alone. For the first time in four years, Elizabeth's focus was not on Rosie and James and Rae. James was doing his best to keep the house running, to get Rosie to her practices, but he did this by having Rae and Lank drive her around so he could still find time for his book and his radio gig.

She felt like a ghost. She felt scared of school starting, of everyone finding out that Simone was pregnant. All the kids would shun them, her and Simone; they'd give Simone a very wide berth, like you would around a jellyfish. They would both end up being outcasts, but at least Simone would also end up with a baby. Rosie would be truly alone.

She tried to take care of her mother as well as she could and had almost decided to default in Menlo Park so she could stay home, even though it was the last tournament of the summer. But then out of the blue, Peter had called. He was back! He couldn't wait to see her, to hear about all the matches he had missed, and hoped he would see her later that day in Menlo Park. And so she guiltily said good-bye to her mother and left with Veronica.

She decided to put on a little mascara, the dark blue Revlon she and Hallie had bought in San Francisco earlier in the summer. She wore better clothes than she had been wearing lately, a real tennis dress instead of massive shorts and T-shirts. She felt like she was going to see her boyfriend, but at the club where the tournament was being held, she couldn't find him anywhere; no one had seen him. She simply couldn't believe it—he'd said he was going to be there—and she wandered around the club dazed with disappointment, not hearing the rallies, the chatter, swerving at the last minute to avoid walking into people's backs like an animal with a disease that made it stagger.

She bought herself a Coke at the snack bar, and it woke her out of the trance. She won the first set of her first-round match easily. Martha Allen was young and green and inconsistent. She hit every shot as hard as she could and missed half of them. Rosie won a number of points by just returning the ball a few times in a row. She won the first game of the second set, serving two aces and whacking two backhands down the line for winners. But then Martha, during the change of sides, looked over at her daddy. He was wearing a Panama hat and sitting on the bench that ran the entire length of the ten courts in a row—and Rosie saw him give Martha a sign, to signal her in some way. This is against the rules, Rosie wanted to cry out. Panic started, the jungle drums, movies of losing the entire match to tiny little Miss Martha Allen who couldn't keep the ball in for more than four rallies in a row, who hit puffball serves. Rosie lost the game. That's what the father had signaled: slow things down. Push. Lob. Patty-cakes.

Rosie, her face flushed, told Martha quite firmly, "You know, your dad can't coach you from the sidelines."

"He's not coaching me," said Martha, smiling nicely, flashing her pretty, even teeth.

Rosie won her serve, but Martha served again like the old women at the club who wore wrinkle patches over their crow's-feet and panty hose to play in. Rosie lost three quick points in a row. Standing at the service line, waiting to serve, Martha looked over at her father. Rosie followed her gaze. The father blinked rapidly at Martha and then turned to smile tenderly at Rosie, blinking rapidly at her too as if to assure her that no one here was blinking in code to anyone else; he was just blinking at everyone—a tic in the eye, a blinky tic.

What the blinks apparently meant was that Martha should start serving now with so much spin that the ball bounced off the court as drunkenly as a Mexican jumping bean, and in just a few moments, Martha had won her serve.

Rose felt utterly alone, spooked. Please God, she prayed. *Help.* She remembered Rae saying, We don't always know what God is doing when he or she is silent, but we do know that God can be trusted. So Rosie prayed, Please send me an answer, send me a sign. And at two games each, as her panic mounted, Luther arrived.

He sat ten feet away from Mr. Allen, these two tall men on the benches behind the court—one in the Panama hat, looking like a banker; one with the badly shaved head, dressed in a raggedy black windbreaker, smiling his private smile. A high sound escaped from Rosie's closed mouth, and her forehead furrowed with hopelessness. She served and double faulted, served the next one into the net, pushed the second serve barely over, and then engaged in a cream puff rally that she lost when she tried to change the pace. She knew she was trying too hard, and her mind whirled with advice and blame.

Luther sat watching intently in his slouched bleary way. Mr. Allen sat poised on the edge of the bleacher, moving his head robotically back and forth to follow the rally. Luther was perfectly still. She tried to ignore him, sitting there like she belonged to him, like he was her dutiful master. Still, she found his presence strangely comforting. She lost the game, though, and before too long, the set.

Martha lay her racket down on the court and walked toward her father. They high-fived, beaming, and went off somewhere to talk. Rosie stood staring at her feet wondering, where was *her* mother, and where on earth was Peter? But he *said,* she thought miserably, like a four-year-old: he *said.* Then she looked over at Luther, and he looked into her face somberly. Gently, he beckoned her with a crooked finger to come.

She looked at him.

He crooked his finger at her again. Come. She nodded her head with supreme sarcasm: yeah, right. But there he was, perfectly still, his gaze steady on her face. He crooked his finger. Rosie looked around. No one else was watching. By the other courts, parents sat frozen with concentration. Way down the line of courts, Rosie saw Simone playing the top seed, moving around the court like a chubby clown, with nothing to lose since she wasn't expected to win. Rosie put down her racket, walked to her thermos, took a long cold sip, longing for her mother, not knowing where to go. After a moment, she left the court. She had to pass Luther to get back to the clubhouse.

He smelled dirty, sweaty, male, a little bit like alcohol, like her mother used to smell the morning after she'd been drinking.

"What?" she said to Luther. "What do you even want?"

"Hey, you're too in your head," he said. His voice was as warm and rough as bark. "Change stations."

"*What?*" What did he think—that he got to be her pro? "Peter says to *use* my head," she said primly.

"Look where it's getting you."

Rosie looked into his face, his eyes so brown the pupil didn't show, the iris surrounded by tiny red lines, thick yellow patches in the whites, sleep in the corners, his eyes ringed by black lashes, which were ringed in turn by bags and darkness. She'd never actually stood so close to him before, never smelled his smells so close before, never seen how long and black his lashes were.

"Don't stand there in your head, going 'Look at the ball. Do this, do that, hit sooner.' That's why you're losing." What if someone heard him coaching her, what would they think? Everyone else had these handsome pros, mostly men, all tan, all in white shorts with soft blond hairs on their muscular brown legs, and here was this crazy dark wino . . . "Come back," he said in his rusty whiskey voice, and she tilted her head toward him. She remembered a photograph at school of a Native American medicine man, kind and hypnotic around the eyes inside all those creases, that darkness. *"Frame* it," he said. "Frame the ball on your side as it comes over the net; then frame it on hers. Slow it down. Track it through a frame as it comes back to you." He held up an imaginary camera and took a picture of her.

Click, she hears. Maybe he makes a soft clicking noise; she isn't sure. She sees a frame, a viewfinder around the ball, the ball moving slowly toward her, plenty of time to get into position. And in that moment her mind shimmers with insight, clarity, truth. Click, her mind goes, click, click, coming into focus.

SHE went and bought a bottled water and sat by herself on the bench. Looking down the row of courts, she thought of those drawing books from when she was really young that taught you how to draw perspective—train tracks, for instance, widest near you, narrowing to a point on the horizon. And on each court she saw either two or four children, smashing balls back and forth, bouncing lightly on their feet, mostly grim as soldiers. And her mind shimmered again with the vision of this world, this tournament world, as a factory, cranking out great tennis-playing children, great unhappy tennis-playing children. She thought maybe she might quit playing tournaments, and she wondered vaguely how her mother was doing, if she was still in bed. She saw Rae taking care of her mother, keeping her company, and she felt a sense of warmth, and calm, and quiet. She went back to framing things through the viewfinder: a cypress, a little finch. She framed her hand, and she framed a cloud in the deep blue sky.

MARTHA bounced onto the court as if on a pogo stick, and she continued bouncing up and down lightly on her feet, then twisting side to side, doing some stretches, like she was on some TV exercise show. Rosie felt embarrassed for her. Mr. Allen was at his station on the bench, looking at his watch when Rosie reappeared, and he glanced at her as if he were about to shake his finger at her: shame shame shame. Rosie smiled.

Martha had served the last game before the break, so Rosie now went to the baseline, stared at her feet, took a deep breath. Then she looked up at Martha, who was waiting for serve, bouncing in readiness, tight as a spring. Rosie began her windup, tossed the ball with her left hand, and framed it, framed the ball as it hung in the air, and time hung there in the sky, which held the ball; it hung there in her sights, like an ornament, and then like a cat finally bored with a mouse, she smashed the ball across the court. It was in, way in, and so hard that it knocked the racket out of Martha's hand.

SIMONE lost in straight sets to the number two seed, but they were still in the doubles. They were housing together, and there was a dance that night at the club; tomorrow Rosie would play someone seeded higher than she, so the pressure was on the other girl, whom Rosie had beaten once or twice over the years. She called her mother from the pay phone at the club.

"Mommy," she said. "I almost lost to Martha Allen. Her father was coaching her from the sidelines; he gave her *signals*. She won the second set, six-*two*."

"Oh, God, darling, how awful. But you won?"

"I won six-two in the third. I just cleaned her clocks."

"And that's so hard to do, to win the third when you've lost the second. How did you do that?"

"Well. I'm afraid to tell you."

"Tell me."

She was silent for a moment, hearing her heart beat. "Luther was watching."

There was a pause on the other end; the line crackled. Her mother said nothing.

"After we split sets, Martha and her dad went off together, and I had to pass Luther to get back to the clubhouse, and he said this thing to me—he said, 'Frame it,' like put a movie camera frame around each shot as it came over the net to me and as it went across the net to her. To help me focus. To slow the ball down. And when we went back for the third set, I couldn't *miss*."

"Oh, Rosie! No." She could hear the panic in her mother's breathing. "Rosie, Rosie. You need to *totally* avoid Luther. I need you to absolutely promise that—"

"But, Mom, I had to pass him to—"

"I know. I know, honey. But still! No more."

"I know, but, Mommy?" She took a deep breath. "No one else was there to help me. And none of you knows tennis. Can't you even hear how great what he said was? How much it changes everything for me?"

"Oh, Rosie. I hear that. Of course I do. And *I* will be there for you next time, soon. But in the meantime—"

"I know, I know. You don't have to say it again." There was a long silence. "But you have to let other people be there for me sometimes."

"I know, Rosie. But is Luther next on the list, after me and James? Aren't there any half measures? What about Peter?"

"Peter never showed. And it really hurt my feelings." Elizabeth's heart sank. "Asshole," said Rosie, and Elizabeth laughed very softly. "Mommy?"

"Uh-huh?"

"I need you to be doing a bit better than you are right now."

AND she did feel better, for someone who was crying so much of the time these days. After hanging up the phone, she went outside, weeded and watered. She watched a hummingbird dart into the sage, disappearing into the purple flowers.

Rosie and Luther had talked to each other; Luther had helped her today. How dare he? And what next?

Passing a wisteria bush, she found at her feet a ruby-crowned kinglet, lying dead on leaves and weeds, and she bent to study it. The bird was a male; she could tell by the red crown patch. He was tiny and, except for the ruby crown, drab—until she saw the beauty in the gray and olive feathers, the white on his wings, white round his eyes, and she remembered his high thin notes.

She brought it into the house and showed it to James. He stroked the wings, moved the limp head to look at the crown. Elizabeth leaned in closer to watch him study the bird, and she thought about telling him the latest Luther story, but for some reason she didn't. She remembered Rosie at three years old with her head caught between the slats of Charles's office chair, hot and defeated, saying rather calmly, "I need help with me." Elizabeth, recalling this now, heard it as a prayer and repeated it to whomever or whatever might be listening. She watched her husband gently stroke the kinglet with his finger. "Do you know where you're supposed to bury birds?" he asked. "In trees. High up as you can. So that they're closer to the sky."

three
_____

JAMES had hoped that this was a three- or four-day process, this business of Elizabeth having a little breakdown or whatever she was doing, going to a lot of meetings but not paying any attention, crying a lot in between. But as it went on and on, it began to wear him down.

Rosie was worn out also and bored with it all. But she was watching quite carefully. Her mother seemed surrounded by cotton batting, the kind parkas were lined with; she was focused in on herself. Rosie watched her mother disappear into the bedroom and put sad folk songs on the tape player—too much Judy Collins. She was annoyed with her mother for not snapping out of it but also annoyed with James. She could see that he was still thinking he was at center stage. He was trying to get Elizabeth to react to him with his tiny acts of kindness. Rosie saw him as a mime that no one was watching—acting understanding, and then amused, and then annoyed, just dancing around, day after day, looking guilty and then mad, like first he was thinking, It's my fault, then, It's her fault, then, under his breath, "Women," then to Lank on the phone, *"Mar*riage." But none of it got through to Elizabeth.

It was so hard for Rosie to watch. She tried to describe to Rae one afternoon how offended James was that Elizabeth was lying down so much, how frustrated he often acted. "Women are so much better at hiding despair, aren't they?" asked Rae. "Biting their nails, getting fat." Rosie nodded gravely.

AN old poem began to play in her head, a poem her daddy used to read to her: *James James Morrison Morrison Weatherby George Dupree, took*

great care of his mother, though he was only three. James James, said to his mother,
"Mother," he said, said he: "you must never go down to the end of the town if you
don't go down with me."

But her mother had gone to the end of the town.

One day James was so quietly loving and tender that Rosie's heart was stirred with gratitude. And then the next day he picked a fight. He kept working into the evening, even though he said he was going to make dinner, so he was too hungry by the time he finally got a salad Niçoise made. Then he brought it up on a plate to Elizabeth, with whom Rosie was lying in bed, reading separate books. But when he put the tray over her lap, he jiggled it and the glass of iced tea fell over into the plate of salad, and he shouted swear words as he lifted the tray back up.

"Why can't you just get out of bed and eat at the table with us?"

"I wasn't hungry," she said.

"Well, you have to eat."

"Why don't you leave?" she said, and then she started crying because he did.

Rosie stayed behind, scowling contemptuously at James. "Oh, Rosie," her mother asked after a while. "Can you leave me alone for ten minutes? I just need to get myself together."

The house was a mess, and Rosie walked around looking at the chaos as if she had herself spent all morning cleaning it.

She stood in the doorway looking stern and disgusted.

"James was a jerk," she said. "You'll be fine. He'll be back." She went and got a little washcloth from the bathroom, wet it, wrung it out and dabbed Elizabeth's eyes.

He called from town, full of remorse and love. "I'll come home if you want," he said. She wanted him to come home, and he did. He arrived with French fries and strawberry shakes. The three of them lay in bed—it was still light out—and ate their fries, dipped in ketchup.

Elizabeth had folk music on the bedroom boom box. "Doesn't this music make you sad?" James implored.

"It's what I feel like hearing," said Elizabeth.

"I know, baby, but—"

"Would you stop nagging at her, James? What do you want, for her to listen to your Village People tapes?"

After a moment James smiled.

Two days later Rosie got home early from Simone's to find Elizabeth and James in their bedroom with the door closed, arguing again. School started in a few days. She didn't need this. She needed her mother to get better—soon. She got some cookies and went to her room, where she lay on the unmade bed above the chaos on the floor. After a while she heard her mother's voice rising and looked toward the sound. She lay there thinking about the look on Luther's face right before he told her his great secret, before he taught her how to frame things—his medicine-man face. She sat up on the bed so that her back was against the wall, and she framed the picture of her dad that was on the wall by her bed, and she framed two tiny yellow tea roses in a bud vase her mother had left on her desk, just like the roses she'd given Charles before he died. But at the same time she was straining so hard to hear her parents that she looked like a child with an ear infection.

"Because that is what the truth is," her mother wept.

"You're talking about something that happened five years ago. Something that didn't mean anything to me."

"But why have you lied all this time about it? It meant something to me. That you slept with other women when you were seeing me."

"But even if there were," said James, "it was five years ago! We were dating. You wouldn't say you loved me. Why is this coming up now?"

"Because I finally got around to it. And are you saying you fucked other women because I wouldn't say I *loved* you?" her mother shouted. "I was shy! I was recently widowed."

"Recently widowed? It had been four years! And why did you suck it down? Why didn't you get angry a long time ago?"

"Because then you might have left us."

"But now it's so old, I can't even respond to it . . . I'm sorry! I'm fucking sorry to death! Okay?"

Suddenly her mother bellowed, and Rosie bolted off the bed, sure that James was killing her, choking her—no, then she couldn't shout so loud—and then she heard loud muffled thuds, as if he had begun to pummel her, and Rosie ran toward her mother's room and burst in. Elizabeth was on her knees by the bed, pounding the mattress with her fists, and James was standing a few feet away, gripping a handful of hair on either side of his head as if he were trying to pull it out, and they both turned toward the sound of their door opening and the wrath of God shining on Rosie's face.

"What is going on here?" Rosie demanded. "Get off the floor, Mom."

"Get out of my room," Elizabeth said.

"I thought he was *hurting* you!" She slammed the door behind her and stormed down the stairs.

ELIZABETH and James didn't speak for the rest of the day. Rosie stayed over at Rae's, and James slept on the couch.

All night Elizabeth, in the dark alone, heard a poem playing in her head, as if on a radio whose signal she was suddenly beginning to receive. *James James said to his mother, "Mother," he said, said he: "you must never go down to the end of the town if you don't go down with me."* She remembered listening from the doorway when Andrew, holding Rosie on his lap, read it to her. She remembered the exact sound of his voice, low in timbre, soft and kind, and she remembered hearing the poem again after Andrew died, before she met James. Now she kept turning her head up toward the sound of the poem playing, and then she would realize that it was playing somewhere inside her, but far away.

RAE had come to get Rosie when she called. Driving back to her cottage, though, she disclosed that Lank had stopped over that night and would still be there when they got back. Rosie said, *"Lank* is at your house?" It was such a strange concept, as if Rae had casually announced that Veronica had dropped by.

He'd never been by for a visit before, she said, although they spoke on the phone quite frequently now, like friends, and then tonight she'd been weaving when she heard someone outside call her name. Looking out her front window, she discovered Lank in her garden on an ancient rusty black one-speed bike like the one Einstein tooled around town on. And so she had invited him in for tea.

Rosie felt her eyes squint with disappointment. "What what what?" Rae demanded.

"I was going to ask if it was okay if I spend the night."

"Of course you can spend the night. I want you to. Lank wasn't going to, honey."

Lank's old bike was indeed leaning against the wall by the front door of Rae's house, but Rosie didn't see him when she stepped inside. The smell of the fibers was always so strong when you first walked into Rae's cottage. Sometimes, like tonight, they smelled like grains; they smelled like oatmeal.

Lank banged his head on the top of the bathroom door as he came out a moment later, and everyone gasped at the soft thud. He held up one hand like a traffic cop to stop Rosie and Rae from their worry, and covered his forehead with the other, his brow so broad that his hand did not entirely cover it. "I'm fine," he said, blinking as if he had just woken from a nap, slightly dazed, looking as wise as babies sometimes do.

He was very quiet company. He said that he knew Elizabeth and James were having a bad time because he talked to James every day, but he knew also that it would pass. The three of them sat around and they talked about things for a while—nothing in particular, movies, books, food. There was a Bible on the pillow in the window seat. Rosie looked around the room. There was something new on the loom, much lighter, birds in rich blue and shimmery yellows, cotton and silk, no wool. The colors bounced off the silk and came to meet you.

"What are you making?"

"A shawl for your mother. Fall will be here soon."

"What is the secret you wove in this one?"

"A dried petal from one of her roses. It's a little scratchy; you can get up and feel it if you want." Rosie went to the weaving, held up a hand, and looked to Rae for directions. "There, underneath that first yellow bird. Feel it?" Rosie nodded. " 'The harvest is past, the summer is ended, and we are not saved.' I came upon that in Jeremiah the day I started this weaving. It's a line I read to your mom once that she seemed to like, and I thought, Let's weave in a little sorrow. It seemed like that would make it more healing than just a whole lot of happy colors."

Rosie kept fingering the rose petal. She could feel its crisp edge; it felt like a scab. There was a beautiful clay wall hanging over the loom, of a young Madonna, her head wrapped in an indigo scarf that draped down to her chest to shield the little baby. Mary was only a teenager. How old was she when she had Jesus? Rosie wondered. She looked up into Mary's downcast eyes, crossed her own slightly to blur the vision, to see Simone in the indigo scarf. She felt all this lust inside her. She felt gooey and greasy from longing and confusion. Simone must have too, out there on the boat; she must have known the boy didn't love her, she'd hardly ever even really talked to him before. How much greasier could you feel than to be drunk and have a guy put his penis in you? A phrase came to her: the fruits of sin. Rae never talked like that, but Rosie knew that phrase, the fruits of sin. All of a sudden here's a slut and a beautiful baby, so now the mother looks like a saint, even if she's a slut mother—not that Simone is a slut, because Simone was her best friend and a really sweet person, maybe a little dumb even though she couldn't help it, but still, all she meant was that it was like having all that lust that you're so afraid of, and all of a sudden it's on display, and then you get to be a mother. Out of your sluttiness comes a beautiful baby. It was like what Rae said was the whole point of making beauti-ful cloth—taking some yarn that everyone thought was so ugly and weaving it into a sweet piece of your picture. Rosie came out of the daydream to look back over to where Lank and Rae were sitting.

Lank was starting to tease Rae a little, and she was teasing back, kind of cranky in a light way, and Lank sounded just like James, this friendly complaining banter, and Rae was doing it back, but Rosie could feel the edginess of it, the scab of the petal hidden beneath the silk bird, and Rosie turned to them and said in this tiny voice like Tweety Bird, this little voice that shamed her, "I need you not to fight," and just like that, just like that, they stopped.

THE next morning, James came into their room early. Sun poured in shiny and white through the windows from behind the leafy branches of their trees. Elizabeth opened her eyes. This was the part she hated, the moments of first waking up, of having to come to. The room was so tidy though, and that made her feel safe, and she realized before she saw him that he had been taking care of the house, straightening up, keeping things together.

He looked like hell, so tired. There were more crow's-feet around his eyes. When had that happened? she wondered.

"I miss you," he said. "I feel like something is slipping away from us, and you seem unable to help me stop it. I want us to make up and have a good marriage and be best friends, but I have to tell you some-thing." His words came out fast, as if there were just a moment in which to say them, and he was sitting so close to her that she could feel his breath on the side of her face. "You know, sometimes I feel like I'm married to both you and Andrew—it's as if Andrew is hidden underneath the house in a thick canvas body bag. All of a sudden, sometime this year, I felt like he came back to live with us. And you—*you* won't let anything take the body bag away. And I'm fucked up about having done something wrong—not because I slept with someone else five years ago, when you and I were *dating,* for Chrissakes. To me it wasn't a big deal. It didn't mean anything. But I know I was a total shit to keep on lying about it. It must have felt like *Gaslight* to you; it must have made you feel like you were crazy." He looked up at her for a moment, seeking her eyes, but then he lowered his own. "I did do it. I did it, and I know that it messed with you. I do. And maybe that little secret, that lie, is something in me I had to hold on to, that I couldn't give up. I don't know why. But I don't have it in me right now to do a deep archaeological dig with you. And I can't do the digging all by myself. And I am *definitely* not the person you're going to allow to take that body bag out of this house. I know that, and I don't know what to do. And I'm so tired. I just want you back." He lay down beside her, so they were facing each other, and he put his knees against hers; the soft skin and sharp bones of their legs formed a sort of bridge.

She rested her head back against the pillow and stared at the ceiling. Time moved slowly, silently.

"Thank you," she said. Neither of them said anything for some time. "But if you want me back," she continued finally, "you have to let me go. Maybe that's not what you have in mind. Maybe you just want me to absolve you and to snap out of this thing. But what I want is for you to release me from the tyranny."

"What tyranny?"

"The tyranny of your attention and will."

James continued to lie on his side in silence, knees against his wife's. After a while she reached out her hand and stroked his soft wild hair. Then some familiar brown-bag miracle occurred, one that had occurred before after fights and estrangement, where she began to feel as if water had been wearing away at the stone of their being stuck and that finally there was a little channel flowing through her—of resignation, and a fierce desire for ease.

"Want to take a nap with me?" she asked.

"I'm just going to lie with you a moment. Then I'm going to get to work."

After he left she pulled the covers up over her head. There was no air under the covers, but she did not want to surface. Rae dreamed that marriage would save or fix her, like James dreamed that fame and fortune would fix him. And life with Andrew had felt like that, like she had been saved and whole, like there were few sharp edges. But Andrew had been so easy, unambitious and mellow. They drank together and so were often slightly anesthetized. Things were less real, more like a dream—and there were no teenagers in the family.

She could hear James working in his office. Under the sheets, she opened her eyes and could see that there was light on the other side of where she was.

If marriage was a comforting garment you could wrap around you, a fight could rip it loose and leave you standing bare and alone in a high wind, the high wind of the messes of your marriage, all that was frayed and grubby. Too many harsh words spoken, and too much unsaid, too many compromises snatched at the garment, leaving it grubby and frayed. It was so hard, though, after a fight, because one hardly had the strength or desire even to bend down and pick up the garment at your feet. But then when you did, it would feel warm and heavy and have the smell of your beloved, which is so incredible and familiar and also a little rank, with the mammalian essence of life and the sweat of battle.

four

ROSIE was walking the six blocks home from Simone's one night not long after. Simone had really begun to show. She had pulled up her baggy T-shirt that morning so Rosie could admire the hard mound of belly below breasts that were already swollen. Rosie had been unable to breathe again until Simone pulled the shirt back down. Veronica was talking about taking them to live in Squaw Valley, having the baby there, away from the prying eyes of the people of Bayview. Jason, the baby's father, had not called Simone once, although Veronica had recently gone with a lawyer to visit his parents. It was agreed that after the baby was born, if blood tests proved that Jason was the father, his family would give Simone some money every month.

She couldn't stand that Simone would have a baby to love, that she herself would no longer be needed, although Simone assured her that everything would be exactly the same as before—"except," she said brightly, "we'll have a *baby.*" Rosie smiled. Yeah, sure. A horrible thought crossed her wild mind, an image of Simone bleeding profusely, losing the baby, miscarrying, just being old Simone again with Rosie.

She left, wanting to be alone, needing to walk and to be outside.

She hated to go home these days, her mother so quiet, James always hunched over his desk, working, and there was always the worry that the sportsmanship committee had called or written about the cheating, that they had tracked her down.

Dusk was settling on the town like a spell. San Francisco was coming to light: the lights of the bridges were on, like Christmas tree lights or necklaces; the lights of the buildings shone yellow, and the sky and the water of the bay shone orange, both reflecting the sun going away—orange like the saffron robes of Zen monks you saw around town sometimes. Everything glowed—the bay, the city, the sunset, the darkness of sky behind it. The only sound she heard was her own foot-steps. Everyone was at home eating. James was playing basketball with Lank and the guys tonight. Maybe Rae was around; approaching the Greyhound bus depot, Rosie thought about calling her, so she wouldn't have to go home to an empty house. But she didn't have a quarter. She shouldn't have walked through this part of downtown. It was the crummy part, no little boutiques or cafés, just the depot and a gas station that was closed and a laundromat. The streetlights had just come on, giving the sidewalks a ghostly, metallic sheen. She walked along feeling like she was on a street at twilight in some space station where people weren't doing so well. She kicked a rock out of her path, glanced through the windows of the old bus depot. Her eyes widened with alarm.

There was Luther, sitting by himself on a bench in his raggedy windbreaker and dull black shoes, reading a *Chronicle,* waiting for his bus.

She stopped and stepped backward so that she was no longer in front of the windows. Her heart raced, and she leaned forward to spy more efficiently.

He didn't look up, as she had expected him to. Frame it, she heard him whisper. So now she framed him. The greenish overhead lights in-side the depot shone down, cast a garish illumination on everyone in-side; all the people looked just awful, like they'd just been told they all had cancer, even the little kid in his mother's arms, who was looking up at the propellers of a broken wooden fan, spinning slowly on the ceil-ing. But she bore down on Luther with her vision, so the background disappeared, and she no longer saw the bank of game machines that stood against one wall, two pinball, one Asteroids; no one was playing. And she just looked at him. In profile, from a distance, he was actually sort of good-looking, a little like Paul Newman at the end of *Butch Cassidy,* right before he and Butch step out into the gunfire. She breathed in loudly, exhaled with her mouth pursed, like someone in labor, and she felt a tug in her groin. A feeling she didn't know was there came over her: a tenderness toward him, a sense of his dejection. Darkness was settling in on the street where she stood, and it bathed her, as his creepiness bathed her, as a stirring of maternal love bathed her too, making her feel womanly now, like a person with curves and composure. It made her feel grown up, no longer geeky, and without giving it much more thought, she walked to the front door of the depot and, head high, walked on in.

The stench of ammonia enveloped her as she left the fresh air of the wide street; it was all she could smell at first. And then as she stood inside for a moment, unseen by Luther, she isolated other smells, of high school locker rooms she had changed in before and after matches all over the state, and a stale apple smell of spilled whiskey or wine, like the kitchen and her mother's room used to smell in the old days. Tobacco. An officious metal fan rotated back and forth on top of the cigarette machine, blowing the bad stinking air around everyone's heads, and the men's room opened, sending out a sudden sharp reek of urine that took Rosie by surprise. Luther still didn't look up from his paper. Why should he? She moved toward him. The worst smell of all was coming off his body, coming off his legs, she thought. She cleared her throat. Finally he looked up.

"Hey," she said.

"Hey yourself," he replied; he did not seem particularly surprised to see her. He gave her a shy crooked smile. "What are you doing here? You should be at home."

"That's where I'm going," she said. She looked around at the other customers just for something to do. "Where you going?"

"Home."

"Where's your home?"

"The American. On Mission."

"Oh. In San Francisco."

Luther nodded.

She toed the linoleum. She could hardly breathe. He smelled like sweat and the stale apple smell. She stood with her head tucked down so that her ear almost touched her shoulder. Someone who'd never met her before might have thought this man was family, an uncle perhaps, down on his luck but loved by this loyal lean girl in tennis shoes that cost what this man spent on food in a month.

Rosie chewed on her bottom lip and looked toward the broken fan on the ceiling.

"Do you have anybody in your family?" she asked hopefully.

"Sort of."

"Any kids?"

"Well, not who's still a kid." His voice was low and gravelly, like he had a frog in it, could clear it if he wanted to, but he didn't seem to want to or he knew that it wouldn't help. "I have a grown-up. A daughter in Oregon, maybe your momma's age."

"You don't call her on the phone and stuff?"

"She's probably married twenty years by now."

Rosie lowered her head and raised her eyes. "When d'ja see her last?"

Luther laughed and shook his head. "Thirty years ago? Something like that."

"She was still a little girl?"

"She was twelve. Twelve and a half."

Rosie gasped. "Oh, my God; that's so horrible. I mean, no offense."

"None taken."

"What was she like, your daughter? What was her name?"

"You sure ask a lot of questions." Smiling a private smile, he fished a crumpled pack of cigarettes out of his windbreaker, shook one out, and lit it. He turned his head when he exhaled so as not to blow smoke into her face.

"Her name was Jane. Janie. Beautiful girl. Champion athlete, just like you. Great swimmer, good runner, too. Faster than the boys her age. Good girl, good mommy. Bad daddy."

Rosie considered this. "My mom quit drinking five years ago."

"Isn't that wonderful?" She looked up into his face suspiciously, afraid he was being sarcastic or that he found her self-righteous, but he looked friendly. Even though he was dirty, his skin was nice and dark and he looked sort of wise. She was only a little afraid.

Rosie tried to think of something to say, but Luther spoke first.

"I never seen you play better than you did that third set in Menlo Park. You keep playing like that, you gonna go to the nationals next year."

Rosie flushed with pleasure.

"You gotta bring your serve up, though. You're framing everything now on your ground strokes, volleys, that's good. But your second serve is no good; that's killing you. Can I show you something?" Rosie nodded, tilted her head. "No," he said. "Not here. I need to take you somewhere."

Rosie shook her head.

"I have to go home now."

"You won't be sorry if you let me show you," he said. The swirl of fear began inside her, like she was riding the House of Horrors train, faces coming at her around every corner: her crazy mother up in bed; James, miming concern; Simone swelling up like a sea calf. Luther here, talking soft and low.

She did not look at him, but she stared out the open front door like there might be someone standing there with a card that said, Do it, or Don't. But no one was there because no one ever was these days, and she saw her mother waiting for her at home in bed, mad and worried, and at that moment Rosie felt like a disembodied voice, like the housing for a dead grown-up spirit who looked back over her shoulder at Luther, like he was waiting for her at a soda shop table with a milkshake and two straws, and she shrugged.

THEY walked slowly down the empty street, four or five blocks from the Greyhound bus depot, ambling along like two long-lost friends. She had to tip her head up to see his face. He was much bigger than James, five or six inches taller, maybe the same height as Lank but weighing even more. The air was hot and smelled of flowers and the sea. She heard crickets, a night bird, a dog, their footsteps on the sidewalk, music coming out of this house, a commercial for dish soap from that one, Luther's labored breathing. Boy, she thought, if Mom could only see me now.

She heard the sulfur snap of a match and smelled a new cigarette, and she wanted to tell him he should quit, her mother had, but the silence felt so cool and rich and it had been a long time since she had felt this feeling of really being somewhere in her body, on this earth, walking with this dark crazy man.

five

Rosie and Luther walked up a windy road, several feet apart under the moonlit sky. They had been walking ten minutes now and were already in a good neighborhood where people with money might live, where the lawns were tended to, and TVs glowed blue from inside the old houses, and children in backyards pleaded not to come in, not just yet, and engines revved in a way that made you feel teenage boys were near. Luther was smoking. Rosie glanced at him out of the corner of her eye. He looked like a hobo from a history book, like someone who would come to your front door looking for work in the old days, like a traveling salesman who had fallen on hard times, someone you'd dress up like for Halloween by drawing a beard with burned cork on your skin and tying your things in a kerchief on a stick.

"Did you used to have a job?"

The ember of his cigarette glowed. "I had lots of jobs."

"Like what kind were they?"

"Oh. Sales, mostly."

"But then you lost it or something?"

"Or something."

"Are we almost there, to where we're going?"

"Another block or two. Why, you getting tired?" Rosie shook her head in the dark. It was so strange to hear Luther talking like any man. It had never crossed her mind that he could have regular conversations. Once one of the other girls' mothers had said she had heard that he was quite intelligent, but he always looked so awful, like a jack-o'-lantern, that you couldn't believe this to be true. Maybe he was very intelligent like Edmund Kemper, the serial killer in the Santa Cruz mountains. Her heart pounded. She kept thinking back to his hands under the greenish light of the bus depot, how clean they looked tonight compared with the rest of him—how they looked like they'd been *scrubbed*. Scrubbed too clean. There were no clouds passing over the moon just now, and it shone like a peephole into another kingdom, a kingdom of golden light on the other side of the sky. Long arm branches of the trees reached for them, spindly twigs like a witch's fingers, crisp leaves rustled, and the night smelled yellow black; it smelled like mulch and rotted tree trunks, it smelled like grass turning brown, and the grass of lawns, growing green and tall, and it smelled like a fire somewhere, charred. Tree frogs croaked until Rosie and Luther approached, and then they stopped as if they were scared—as if everything was scared but the crickets.

"Did you ever have any good jobs?" she asked politely.

"Oh, yeah. I had a good job. I was on a roll. You know how sometimes you just get on a roll? And you just keep hitting the sweet spot, without even really trying, and the ball feels as big as a basketball, and you got all the time in the world to figure out your move? And you just can't miss?" Rosie nodded in the dark. "This way," he said, pointing up a hill, the ember of his cigarette describing a right turn. There were not so many houses on this street, not so many cars—more trees, dark, dark. Rosie felt so afraid that she couldn't be sure she hadn't just whinnied. "I was there for a few years, in that groove, until I got into a different sort of match. Then things spun out in a different direction. The ball was tiny again, not just its true size but so small I could hardly see it. The size of a marble."

"Wow." She sneaked a look at his face through the gray mist of cigarette smoke, and it was as dark and old as a hoot owl.

"Then everything caved in, and I felt scared all the time, a cold grippy fist in my guts. I started failing, falling apart."

"So what did you do?"

"I did what you did."

"What do you mean?"

Luther stopped, took a final puff of his cigarette, dropped it to the street, ground it out. "I cheated."

A cold comet of wind raced through her guts, and her heart pounded in her ears like when you're snorkeling and you suddenly realize the tide is carrying you out past the reef, out past your parents, out where the sharks are circling. She thought to run, run for the bushes, run for home where they would take her back and no one knew and no one ever had to know. She heard crickets, frogs. There were no cars along the road, no one to come save her. A thorny spindly branch reached out for her from a gate in a picket fence, and she smelled her mother's roses.

He put his heavy burning black paw, his werewolf hand, on her shoulder, and then he whispered, "Rosie."

She thought he was either going to bend down and choke her to death or kiss her on the lips like a boyfriend, and she thought that she would have to kiss him back. Then he whispered her name again.

Slowly she raised her head, her eyes.

"We cheated, you and me, and someone noticed. I noticed you; someone else noticed me. It hurt us. That's not so bad. So many people cheat. So many people. Everywhere, on every level. Famous people have cheated, paid people to take their college exams, scientists who wanted to be famous have messed with lab results, made them up. Everyone's cheated."

"I don't believe that."

Luther shrugged. "You think it's just you and me? Old awful Rosie and Luther?"

"Why are you telling me this?"

"Because I'm the only grown-up who knows, right? Me, and the parents of the kids you cheated."

"See? You just said I'm a cheater."

"No, I didn't. I said you cheated. You did, right?"

"Uh-huh."

"I'm just saying that you don't need to see yourself as a cheater. Because that's not who you are. You're someone who cheated. There's a difference, and you should try to get that difference, or that's who you'll grow up to be. How many times you cheated so far?"

"I don't know. Maybe five or six matches or so?"

"You're thirteen years old. The time you cheated could be the summer you were thirteen. Mine was when I was almost fifty. I took the summer off. That was ten years ago. I didn't go back. I never worked again, because no one told me that they had cheated too, that everyone had."

Rosie wiped at the spit in the corners of her mouth. She hadn't even noticed that her mouth was hanging open. The moon was caught behind the highest, most skeletal branches of an old oak, and the tree looked like a Halloween crone, like it might cackle and wrap its long bony fingers around her wrist.

"Is that what you wanted to tell me?" she asked. "Because I have to go home now."

"You can go home anytime you want, little girl. Or else you can let me show you something. Your call."

She wanted to bolt, she wanted to tear home. She hung her head and followed.

He took her to the last home on the hill, a small mansion of adobe behind a thick wall of hedge. It appeared whitewashed in the moonlight, a miniature villa with high adobe walls, arches, and domes, even some sort of a tower in back. And yet for all the walls and sense of security, there was an opening in the hedge on the side of the house farthest from the street. All the lights were out in the house. There was no sign of life. They stepped through the opening. Hedge branches brushed her bare arms.

"Where are we going?"

"Shhhhh."

"Whose house is this? Do we know these people?"

"Shhhh. Look." There in the backyard of the mansion, laid out like a glade under the moon, was a tennis court inside a fence. There were no clouds passing over the moon now. Shining through eucalyptus and maples and oaks, it cast long fingers of shadow onto the green pavement of the court, made a lattice shadow where it shone through the net. A breeze rustled the leaves, but otherwise there was perfect silence.

"Whose court is this?" she whispered. Out of the corner of her eye she saw Luther reach into the pocket of his jacket, and fear raced through her; sure that he had a knife or a gun, she stepped away and turned to face him. He had fished out a tennis ball, glowing lime green in the moonlight.

"Huh?" she persisted. "Whose court?"

He smiled at her and then raised his eyes to look at the darkened house, peering in as if he could see something well lit and moving inside. "A family named Parrish lives here."

"Do you know them?" she asked. She knew he could not have such fine friends, people who could own such splendor. "Should we be here? What will happen if they find us?"

She heard him smiling in the moonlight, exhaling through his nose. "It's okay," he said.

She didn't believe him; worry buzzed like flies inside her.

"Let's go," she said, pleading, and still she waited, not able to breathe but hearing the gentle breeze, frogs in the distance.

"The living room ceiling is a skylight," he said finally. A rush of adrenaline passed through her. Jesus, Jesus, she thought, he's been inside that house. She thought of those nurses Richard Speck killed, how they sat around him in a cozy room, bound by his hypnotic powers. She saw Speck's hands around their pretty throats, then thought of Luther's hands, how scrubbed and clean they were tonight. Holding her breath, she wondered if Luther had been inside to rob the place, maybe even that day, and that's why he was headed out of town on a bus. She looked longingly through the hole in the hedge by which they had entered.

"There's a marble floor when you first walk in," Luther was saying. "A spiral staircase. You could lie back on the couch right now and see the moon, the clouds."

"How do you know that?" she asked, trying to make her voice sound stern.

"I had it built," he said. "I had the skylight put in."

It took her a moment to figure out what he was talking about.

"You mean . . . you lived here?" she asked finally. He nodded. Taking out another cigarette, he lit it, inhaled deeply, amused. "I don't understand," she said.

"Why don't you come here?" Holding her breath, prickling with goose bumps, she looked at him helplessly.

"Tell me who lives here now."

"I already told you. A family named Parrish."

"But who are they? How do you know them?"

"Think about it."

"How am I supposed to know?"

He sighed. "My wife," he said. "My ex-wife and her husband, Donald Parrish." The night was still now, except for the frogs.

"And they don't mind if you come here?"

"No. And I hardly ever do." She contemplated his face in profile, how solemnly he studied the night.

"Didn't you hate having to give it up? Didn't it drive you crazy?"

"Stop asking me questions," he said.

"I just want to know."

He didn't say anything right away, and when he spoke, he had to clear his throat first, and his voice was quiet and low.

"No," he said. "It freed me. After it was gone I wasn't afraid anymore."

She looked up at the darkened windows, heard the low whistle, like wind, of him taking a puff from his cigarette. "So now will you come here?" he asked.

She took two steps toward him. He bowed his head, gripped an imaginary racket, stood as if about to serve. She waited for the imaginary racket to come crashing down on her head. Instead, looking up, she found him waiting for her attention.

"Okay?" he said. "What you need to do after the toss is to wait. To wait, Rosie. To hold your left hand up in the air, pointing at the toss for one whole second longer. You need to wait. Just wait, watching; hang with it while it hangs there. You need to do nothing more often. Just watch, calm, friendly. Okay? You try that. You're swinging too soon. You're chasing the ball down. Let it just hang there a moment; you don't need to do anything. Everything's okay. Just wait with the ball." She could not take her eyes off his left hand, suspended in the air in the moment of toss, palm open, graceful as a wing. "Pointing for one whole long second will keep you from closing up too early on the swing," he continued. "Looking quietly, all the time in the world. Waiting. And *then* you swing."

Rosie pictured serving just like he said, her left arm fully extended, pointing to the sky, like the Statue of Liberty, waiting a beat, and then smashing the ball across the net for an ace. She tucked her head down again, then suddenly began to bounce and catch the ball Luther had handed her, throwing it harder and harder against the asphalt. Then she looked up at her opponent, waiting for serve on the other side of the net. She squinted, pointing her racket at the spot on the court she hoped to hit, and slowly slowly dropped both hands for the windup, slow like a ballerina, dropping the racket down her back, tossing with her left hand, pointing to the sky, and holding it, still and poised.

"Now," said Luther, and she swung.

six

R OSIE was an hour late getting home. Elizabeth
had already called Simone's twice, Hallie's once, and was half out of
her mind. When Rosie finally slunk into the house, shutting the door
gently behind her, Elizabeth was so angry she felt capable of violence.
"Where were you?" she demanded.

"Just walking around."

"Every lie you tell chips away at you."

Rosie thought this over, thought over the whole night.

"I ran into Luther when I walked past the Greyhound bus depot."

"You what?"

"You want me to tell you the truth, or lie so you won't get mad?"

"Tell me the truth."

Rosie took a long loud breath. "I saw him when I was on my way
home. And I stopped in to see him for a minute. God, there were
about a thousand people around."

"Why the fucking hell would you want to talk to Luther?"

"Because he knows things; he knows my game."

"I don't even know what that means."

"Because you don't know anything about tennis. He was really good
in college, better than me. In Oregon."

"I'll take you out of tennis to keep you away from him."

"You don't even know what's going on. You just look at what people look like and think you know if they're good or bad."

"Don't you dare talk to me that way."

"Look at Mr. Thackery. Look how good he looked."

She and her child glared at each other, poised on the ledge of pure
will. She looked at her daughter, that face, hardly even a child, un-
cowed, direct.

"You're grounded forever," Elizabeth managed to say. "You'll get to go to Simone's at night when you're about twenty-five. When her kid is almost as old as you are. You understand that, right?"

"Mom."

"You're grounded. Come here." Rosie slouched toward her, head down with guilt, sucking on the cuff of her long-sleeved shirt. "I am very angry. And you have got to start believing me—that you *must* stay away from Luther. But right this second I just need to smell you."

Rosie bristled. "Do you think I've been smoking?"

"I just need to smell you because you're my girl." Elizabeth drew her down into her lap, nuzzled her baby's neck. "You do smell like smoke," she said, surprised. "Do you smoke?"

Rosie shook her head. "No. Want to smell my breath?"

Elizabeth started to shake her head, and then nodded. Rosie groaned and rolled her eyes, then opened her mouth and puffed out a breath. Her mother sniffed it. "Okay," she said. "I believe you." She rocked slightly back and forth. "I'm so angry at you, Rosie. I'm not forgiving you yet, because nothing bad must ever happen to you. I could not go on living; it's that simple." She looked up at Rosie, who was watching solemnly. "I'm really *furious*. Do you understand?" Rosie nodded. Elizabeth gave her a terrible look of exasperation. No one spoke, the air in the room was like a rich quiet broth. After a while, Elizabeth sighed, and looked up. "I'm still mad," she said threateningly, and Rosie nodded. "But anyway. You know what you said to me once, when you were little?" Rosie shook her head. "You bent your face in as close to mine as you could, so your nostrils were against mine, and you closed your eyes and started breathing deeply; then you said, without opening your eyes, 'Let's just sit here and smell each other's noses.' "

Rosie stared off into space, considering this. "Huhhh," she said. She put her nose to her mother's and breathed warm soft air out, onto the tip of her mother's nose, into the nostrils, breathed her mother's air in, and then, raising her lips as if in a kiss, whispered, "Mommy, Mama." Elizabeth felt her child's heart beating faster than it ever had before, as fast as an infant's, a hummingbird's. "Mama." The air was hushed, like in the moments after an echo. "Mommy?" Rosie whispered. "I need to tell you one more thing."

"Tell me, baby."

"It's big."

"Tell me."

Rosie's wide blue eyes never left hers. "I cheat. I cheat in tennis."

Elizabeth drew back as if from a gust of heat; Rosie abided, her head still at a tilt, her lips parted slowly, her eyes now closed, her own nostrils flaring and moist. She nodded.

"Honey," Elizabeth whispered. "What are you telling me?"

"This summer, Mom, this summer I got so afraid a few times, when I was losing to girls who weren't any good, I got so afraid I started calling balls out that were in."

"You called balls out that were *in?*"

"Like, for example, I played Deb, you know, who I hate, and I was seeded way ahead of her, but I was totally tanking a match. And so she hit a ball that landed on the line, and I called it out. And I did that a whole bunch of times this summer."

Elizabeth, sitting in the chair with her huge scared child, gaped.

"Did you win matches that way that you would have lost otherwise?" Rosie sighed and nodded, miserable, sick.

"Oh, my God, sweetheart. I'm thunderstruck."

"I know, Mom. I tried to tell you a million times. The thing is, I'm not a cheater. I'm someone who cheated a few times."

"What does that mean?"

"Mommy, that's what Luther told me tonight; that's what he told me. I thought I was a cheater, but now I know I'm not. And no one could tell me that I wasn't, because no one else watched me so closely, no one else knew, no one who could help me knew."

"Rosie, what are we going to do? Do many people know? Should you turn yourself in?"

"The girls I cheated know. Sometimes their parents were there."

"What about the officials?"

"I don't know. Maybe there've been complaints."

"How on earth, how the hell did Luther find this all out?"

"He just saw me. Almost every time I did it."

"Oh, honey. Oh, Rosie. I don't know what to say. Why do you think you cheat? Rosie, you're such a great player."

"It was because, I guess, I'm just okay. I'm not one of the best. Just one of the pretty good. I wanted to be in the top ten. And I'm not going to be. Not ever again."

"Why?"

"Because the younger kids, the twelve and unders, are great. They take over, they start to beat us. You start to feel like a loser. I don't want James to feel I'm wasting all this money and I'm still a loser."

"Darling, you are not a loser. And anyway, James couldn't care less if you ever pick up a racket again. Maybe—would it make sense if you called someone who was in charge of junior tennis, maybe one of the people on the sportsmanship committee?"

"Oh, God, Mommy. I can't even think about that."

"How come?"

"Too scary." Elizabeth nodded. "I don't want to even tell anyone."

"Well, we have to tell James, honey."

"We do?" Elizabeth nodded. "And Rae, and Lank?"

"Yep. This is a family thing, Rosie. Rae and Lank are family. And this is what families are for. That's just the way it is. But we need to go to bed now, it's late."

But neither moved. They listened to the chorus of night creatures, the pulse beat of crickets.

"Mommy?"

"Yeah."

"Do you think Simone is making a mistake?"

"Yeah. A huge mistake."

"What should we do?"

"What can we do? We're just going to love her, accept her. She's family. And her baby will be family."

"I wish we had a *real* family."

"See, darling, I think we do. Don't you?"

"Not a real family, like the other kids. Like Deb Hall, or Hallie. We're—I don't know."

"We're what? Say it."

"We're like some family you'd get at a garage sale."

seven

T<small>HE</small> Sunday before Labor Day, Elizabeth got up early, even before James, and went downstairs to make the coffee. Outside the sky was a clear Chagall blue. Elizabeth opened all the downstairs windows. She put on Schubert's *Trout,* which had been her father's favorite piece of music, and she walked around the living room dusting with a sock of James's she had found in the downstairs bathroom. She lingered over a lavish dresser of her mother's, slightly battered, with drawer pulls of Victorian leaves. On top, on the plainest blue linen napkin, were tiny framed photos of her parents, her mother as a toddler, her father in his cap and gown the day of college graduation. There were several little paper boxes Rae had made, a stone from the beach, the bigger of the two sand dollars Andrew had found, the tiny one lost now, a picture of Elizabeth's grandmother, a picture of Rosie as a baby. The thing was, you put all the stuff you loved in boxes to shield them, protect them, contain and magnify them and give them a home; and when you put the little boxes on a linen or a doily, it said that this was sacred space. But Elizabeth thought Luther had gotten inside their little boxes, the boxes of Elizabeth's family, and once someone got inside, you no longer had any kind of shield, you no longer even had the illusion of ever having had a shield. You were as vulnerable as a smart little kid.

A memory rose and draped itself like a transparency over her vision. She saw a small girl in the dark listening to a scary radio program, she couldn't remember now which one. And there was a pool of shadows hovering over her, a pool extending from the edge of the bed to the end of the universe; and she huddled there on her bed in the dark, too afraid to get up and turn the light on, even the lamp on the bedside table, and the shadow got bigger and closer, like a cocoon around her, and somehow she crashed through the edge of the circle, through the cocoon, and turned on the lamp. And she sat there, upright in bed, looking around and blinking, seeing her room in the light—there the old radio, there the rug, the rocking horse.

She looked around her living room and felt so much better than she had in a while that she began to cry again, and she sank onto the couch and cried so hard that drool collected behind her bottom teeth and then spilled into her lap. She cried until she heard footsteps upstairs, James's, coming down the hall, and she tried to stop and collect herself but couldn't, and when James came downstairs and sat with her on the couch, she kept on crying. He held her and no one said a thing. Finally when she stopped, he peered down to look into her face.

"Hi," he said.

"Hi," she said tremulously, and smiled.

"You okay?"

She smiled. She thought maybe she was or would be soon; she looked at his eyes, so pretty and green and kind, and she didn't care if she looked blotchy and nuts, because she felt a flicker of something like a candle inside her, a child's birthday candle in the dark cave of her lifelong fear, the fear of her fear and the fear of her grief. It had kept her in a barren, isolated place, kept her away from life. And she wondered, was her grief the way home?

"LANK was over for breakfast," Rae announced later that day over lemon tea in the kitchen.

"He was?"

"Uh-huh."

"Well, that is good, isn't it?"

"He's really great to talk to."

"What do you talk about?"

"You."

"Oh, Rae. Are you dating?"

"You mean in the biblical sense?"

"I mean in any way at all."

"I don't think so. Actually, come to think of it, maybe yes. I mean, I don't really know. Usually by now, after all these phone calls and a couple of walks, I've given the guy a nice blow job. Just out of sheer anxiety. You know, to break the ice. I mean, a girl can get so damn anxious sitting there on the couch with them, hour after hour. I've given guys blow jobs just because I've run out of things to talk about."

"Oh, Rae. Who hasn't?"

Rae laughed, and then Elizabeth joined in, tilting her head back to laugh at the ceiling for what seemed like the longest time. Rae's foamy laughter flowed around her like surf, not washing her away but washing through her, over her, buoying her up. Then they were silent for a while, just a couple of women surfing on near hysterics, alone together in a sunny kitchen. Rae gathered crumbs from the morning's toast into a tiny pile, separated out one big crumb, rolled it around the wood under her forefinger, rolled it over to Elizabeth's place at the table, and deposited it there for her. Elizabeth smiled. After a minute, she covered it with her finger and began to roll it around the table. It felt like a scratchy little ball bearing.

"I remember a few months ago, when I was strung out over Mike," said Rae, "you said something about how I was powerless over the craving to call him. But that underneath the craving were jewels, the jewels of being more intensely inside life, and that Mike was the detour away from them."

"Did I say that?"

"Yes. Maybe I'm paraphrasing a little. I really felt it was true. Don't you?"

"Yes."

"And I keep trying to do what Wendell Berry said."

"What did Wendell Berry say, Rae?"

"Practice resurrection."

Elizabeth gripped her mug tightly and peered down into it, as if trying to read tea leaves. She lowered her nose against the dark brown brim, as if she were going to push her face all the way down inside, as if it were a rabbit hole into which she was trying to disappear. But after a moment, she raised her head, and strained to hear the gray-gold song of a mourning dove.

eight

THE letter from the sportsmanship committee of the
junior tennis league arrived in the mail the exact same day James re-
ceived word that his gig at the radio was over. James brought the mail
upstairs to the bedroom, where Elizabeth was dozing. She had a terrible head cold. He handed her his letter. "It is time to give another local
author the opportunity to have his or her voice heard on the air," it
began. Then he handed her a letter from the junior tennis association,
and they looked at each other with alarm.

"Isn't it too early for the rankings?" he asked. "Should we open it?"
She shook her head.

"It's for her. We have to wait until she gets home from school."

IT was the first day of school, the chaos of teenagers not knowing
where to be when. Eighth grade. The weather was warm and blue;
summer was still here. The hillside behind the school yard was amber
and velvety, dry. Rosie and Simone sat under the great oak in the pasture below the hill, an oak twice as wide as it was tall, where it was illegal for them to be. Kids came here to smoke in the dry grass. Rosie and
Simone ate their lunches and listened to the sounds of the kids hanging out at lunchtime, some in quiet groups on the blacktop, others
shouting, talking loudly, taunting passersby; playing baseball in the
field; younger children, mostly the sixth graders, hitting big red rubber
balls against the backboard. Rosie and Simone were dressed exactly
alike today, in huge blue jeans, T-shirts that hung almost to their knees,
black high-top Keds. They both drank cranberry juice in little glass
bottles. It was their new drink. It was too hot and Jason had left for
college without saying good-bye. Simone had gotten Rosie to call him

at home and pretend to be someone else, and Jason's mother had told her very nicely that he had already left for school two weeks before. Simone's only contact with him was through her mother's lawyer, who was trying to get him to sign a paternity stipulation. His parents' lawyer had informed Veronica that they would arrange for DNA testing at Thanksgiving, to see if their son was in fact the father. In the meantime, the sideways glances of junior high were upon them. A rumor had gotten started, Rosie was not sure how, and Hallie had asked if the rumor was true, and Rosie had said yes. Then everyone knew. The teachers found out; Veronica was summoned. It was decided that Simone could continue coming to this school for the time being. Hallie blended back in with the popular girls, was friendly and distant now with both Rosie and Simone. Their homeroom teacher, Mr. Flemish, was especially kind to Simone, who was the subject of endless whispered conversations. The nice kids didn't know how to respond appropriately and so said nothing. One of the popular boys, during lunch one day, pantomimed jerking off when Simone passed him on the blacktop, and when she retaliated by declaring loudly that he *was* a jerk-off, she was sent to the principal.

ROSIE and Simone had taken to wearing thick black liquid eyeliner, like the hoodlum girls at school who dressed open, as the kids put it, cheap and sexy, and dated high school boys. Rosie loved the eyeliner, was sure it made her look beautiful.

Elizabeth did not say anything about the makeup. So many spikes and arrows had come at Rosie all summer from so many directions, and she had managed to stay open to it all in so many ways that perhaps a little camouflage was just the thing, the lightest possible shield.

JAMES and Rosie sat at the kitchen table while she opened her letter. "Dear Rosie," it read. "This is a very painful letter to write, as we understand that it will be a painful letter to receive. But we have become aware of a number of complaints having to do with your line calls. Our usual policy is to mention these complaints discreetly and to hope that this mention will convince the person that much greater care must be given to avoid even the appearance of dishonesty. Please do not hesitate to contact us if we can help you deal with this situation in any way." She held the letter with trembling hands, aware that James was watching her. She felt humiliation like sirens going off inside her, like a flush and a chill both at once.

"Can I see it?" James said. She looked up at him, handed him the letter, and watched while he read it. "Wow," he said, exhaling loudly.

He did not say anything else. She felt as naked as a baby bird and as cold. She rested her chin in her cupped hand and her fingernails on her bottom lip, and dug her nails into her lip to try and stop the trembling. It felt good, like a sharp compress.

"What do you think we should do, James?"

He reached forward to brush some of Rosie's bangs off her forehead. "I don't know yet," he said.

"Did you ever just want to kill yourself when you were a kid?"

"Honey, look. When I was in eighth grade, I was like . . . like . . . a male version of the little woman in *Poltergeist.*" She considered him. His gaze was level and kind. After a moment she smiled, just barely, and then looked down at her lap.

"Mommy was the tallest eighth-grade girl in the state."

"That's what she says, honey. There wasn't an actual competition."

"And then you two found each other."

James nodded.

"What if the kids at my school find out?"

"About all I know for sure at this point is something Rae says from time to time: that one is really in charge of very, very little."

She picked up the letter and read it again.

"I think I want to go talk to them," she said at last. "I want to tell them certain things, so they feel differently about the whole thing."

"This, this letter, does not require that something outside of you happen. This is about something happening inside of you."

Rosie looked at him blearily. "I hope they don't rank us number two. We should be number one. It would be great for Simone if she got to be ranked number one in the doubles. Because it's probably her last year. I mean, let's face it."

"Oh, sweetheart." They looked at each other in silence. "Let's go play catch in the backyard," said James. "And wait for your mom to wake up."

"I don't want to, James."
"Well, I need you to. C'mon, Rosie."

Lᴀɴᴋ came over the next day and brought Elizabeth a present wrapped in newspaper: a cactus in bloom. It was fabulous, like a strange-looking woman in a fancy hat.

"What's the occasion?" she asked.

"I'm happy you're on the mend. Anyway, it's just a porch present."

"What do you mean?"

"Oh, my aunt Tat in Texas used to always bring little gifts wrapped in newspaper, so you wouldn't think it was any kind of big deal, and you wouldn't get your hopes up like you would if it came in wrapping paper and ribbon. Also, it meant that you didn't have to write a thank-you card, because it was just a porch present."

"So are you my caseworker for today?" she asked.

"I guess. I wondered if you would go help me pick out a great pair of shoes."

Elizabeth thought this over. "Is this a trick to get me outside?" Lank nodded. "Okay."

Bruno was on a blanket in the back seat of Lank's car. Elizabeth made a quiet fuss over him while Lank cleared textbooks and stacks of binder paper off the passenger seat. He waited by her side of the car while she climbed in, and then closed the door for her. They drove along. It was a beautiful warm day and he had some Mozart on the stereo and she didn't feel like she had to talk. A few times she looked over at him and smiled, and he would crinkle up his big nose so much in smiling that a great crease appeared between his eyes, and his teeth looked very long, and she felt that she trusted him entirely. They had not been alone together in a long time, and she wanted to tell him all these memories that had come back to her. She stared out the window, listening to the sound of the car's hum, of the oboe's joyful lament, and her mind floated. And for some reason, in all that peace, with Lank and the woodwinds and the yellowing mountains in the distance, her mind turned to sex. She remembered the night when the Adderlys had agreed to watch Rosie, and she had picked up a biker and brought him home to screw. It was only one week after Andrew's funeral. She remembered the biker's big arms, his long shimmering black hair that brushed her breasts as he moved over her. She remembered that the old woman who used to live across the street had watched the man leave the next morning through binoculars. There were still flower arrangements all over the house, mostly dying now. There was a brown paper grocery bag of rotten persimmons on the front porch that the biker pointed out to her, because they had gone bad, were attracting flies. She did not remember having seen them before he pointed them out, and their presence on her porch filled her with a deep shame.

She and Charles Adderly had kissed very drunkenly one night in the Adderlys' garden, while Grace was tucking Rosie in. Andrew had been dead about a month. It was strange, because Charles didn't usually drink so much. All Elizabeth could remember was that she had taken her shoes off, and the garden was wet, and mud squished through the mesh of her stockinged feet.

"What are you thinking?" said Lank. Elizabeth slowly turned to look at him, his cherubic lips, the downy soft baldness on the crown of his head, his waiting for her to answer, the safety of his face.

"Darling Lank," she said softly. "Let's go get you some shoes."

HE tried on some very plain black walking shoes with laces.

"They look good," said Elizabeth. "How do they feel?"

"They feel okay."

"Do they fit?"

"They fit okay."

"If you're not sure whether shoes fit, they don't."

"Says who?"

"Says Rae. Who worked in a shoe store one summer."

"Well, then, she should know," said Lank.

"Of course, she's still got a closet full of shoes that almost fit but don't. These are pretty cool. Try them on."

Lank held up the pair of black shoes with thick spongy soles so that the salesman could see them. "Can I try these in a ten?"

He put them on, took one step, and said out loud, "Oh, God. Oh, my God. Oh." He walked around the store for a minute with his eyes half closed, moaning.

Elizabeth smiled.

"Look," she said. "You know that I am not a religious woman. But even I know that if you try a pair of shoes on and you say out loud, 'Oh, God,' you should buy them."

I_N his car, she turned to him and said, "Right after Andrew died, I had sex with someone I picked up at a bar, just because I liked his shoes."

"Oh, Elizabeth."

"My husband hadn't even been dead a month." They studied each other for a long quiet minute.

"You must have been heartbroken," he said at last, gently.

"I guess I must have been."

They drove along in silence. He reached into his pocket and withdrew a pack of Juicy Fruit, got out a stick, unwrapped it, and handed it to her. "Here," he said. "Time for your gum."

"You know, Elizabeth, I've done stuff to women that would curl your hair, stuff I didn't think I was capable of doing. I was like those guys in *Deliverance:* in a certain mood, I could see you, see any woman, as something for me to play with." He glanced out the window as they drove along. "Hey, Elizabeth?" he asked, after a moment's silence.

"Yeah?"

"What kind of shoes were they?"

A_T an outdoor café on the water, watching the ferries and sailboats, silent brown pelicans gliding by on powerful wings, he put his chair next to hers and his arm around her shoulders, and they sat quietly together. A stranger watching them, noting their dark clothes, their closeness, Elizabeth's handsome dignity, Lank's cherubic compassion, might have assumed that they were a quiet and creative couple, one who had just buried a cavernous pocket of grief.

L_ATER they ate onion rings with tartar sauce, Lank's favorite food. He looked out of place on the dock among all the sporty tan people, like an undercover monk from outer space. "You and Rae are on the phone a lot these days, I hear," she said. "Can you imagine seeing what it might be like to be really together?"

"You certainly are direct about some things. We talk every day. But tell me, don't you think it's a problem that she's not my type at all?"

"Maybe it's actually a good thing."

Lank smiled. "And there's the Jesus issue."

"Compared to her tender heart, that's such a big thing?"

"I don't know. Actually, I find that her weight doesn't bother me that much anymore. Up at the Russian River that day, when she was standing alone in the water, I first saw how beautiful she is."

"She's a big ripe juicy peach."

"Yes, I know. And to tell you the truth, when James and I were rafting this summer, we saw a couple I had met when they first hooked up together seventeen years ago. The woman, Darcy, had always been thin, and tense, and exciting. But after sixteen years of marriage, Darcy had gained a good thirty pounds. And she was radiantly happy. So I thought, Huh—maybe happiness sometimes weighs a little bit more."

SHE looked at him seated two feet away, peering into her face—and she didn't really hear what else he said. She was looking around the crowded sunny deck at diners in all their guises—men, mostly, some in casual clothes, others ready for tennis, golf, bicyling, running, some in suits and ties. A handsome older man with a Yacht Club cap stood at the railing looking through binoculars out toward the bay, and she remembered Charles the night so long ago when they scattered Andrew's ashes from the sailboat. She wondered what this man was looking at today, and she imagined standing beside him, peering through the twin telescopes of the field glasses. She was startled just then by a flicker of the strangest sensation; as through binoculars, instead of sailboats, seals, buoys, she saw Andrew and Luther side by side, shoulders touching, Andrew faint and fair, Luther darkly chivalrous. But instead of seeing two men distinctly, she felt like she was having double vision. So she squinted to focus the two into one, but Andrew just slid behind Luther and disappeared from sight. Something inside her cried out, Don't go!—but the more she struggled to see Andrew, the clearer Luther became, sharp as if outlined in charcoal. She blinked in frustration, but as she opened her eyes, she suddenly knew who Luther was and why he had come into her life—Andrew's black shadow who had come to take him home.

LANK was calling her name softly, but she was in a basement where Andrew had lain all these years like a mummy. And his body was no longer there. The absence shimmered; it caused her to catch her breath. After a while she entered that empty space and tried it on like a garment. The shock of its cool emptiness caused her to open her mouth, as if to sing. "What is it?" Lank asked softly, but she turned slowly to him in amazement, unable to answer. She practiced bearing the emptiness. It was like riding a bike for the first time, coasting along suspended in space, your feet not touching the ground, scared and thrilled. And for a moment she felt like she had taken out earplugs she'd been wearing all these years, and just for a moment nothing separated her from the sounds and smells and movement of the semen-smelling sea.

nine

O NE early afternoon the following week she sat by the window in her bedroom, waiting for it to be time to pick up Rosie at school. They had arranged to meet with two men from the sportsmanship committee that day, just to bring things out in the open. She glanced at the clock: ten minutes until she had to leave. She stared off into the branches of the tree. Somewhere in the back of her mind, the poem began to play: *King John put up a notice, "lost or stolen or strayed! James James Morrison's mother seems to have been mislaid. Last seen wandering vaguely: quite of her own accord, she tried to get down to the end of the town—forty shillings reward!"* She could not get the poem to stop playing in her head, and she stopped trying to, stopped fighting it. And after a while, as she sat there, she heard outside the window a tiny house finch, singing from what sounded like the highest point around—a long complex Charlie Parker song, rapidly moving, highly melodic, hitting lots of notes. Elizabeth closed her eyes to listen, heard the clear sharp insolent song: Hi! she heard him crying to the other males, I'm exactly this particular bird, and I'm *alive*.

That cheeky aliveness rang in her ears with a piercing intensity; it felt too bright and crisp for a moment, like in the old days when the psychedelics first came on and she felt like she might tip over. Threatened and frightened and overwhelmed, she missed the comforts of her illness. She thought maybe she had preferred being grief-calloused to this new raw immediacy.

E LIZABETH and Rosie drove to their meeting with the sportsmanship committee that afternoon. Indian summer had arrived, just as the leaves were beginning to turn. The rains would be here soon. They drove to the junior tennis headquarters in Oakland, listening all the way to oldies on the radio. From time to time, Rosie wondered out loud: should she offer to quit the circuit; would they kick her out; would this affect her doubles ranking? It was close but she and Simone should be number one. And Elizabeth said, "We're just going to show up and tell the truth. Okay?" Rosie nodded. They were driving past the Berkeley marina, past the pristine sailboats in the harbor, the bay speckled with windsurfers, buoys, a hot yellow sun beaming down on the water. Rosie covered her eyes with one hand.

"Oh, Mommy," she said, exhaling loudly, and Elizabeth took one hand off the steering wheel, ran her hand over Rosie's hair.

"Okay?" she said, and Rosie tried to smile, dipping her head for a moment, like a bird, and then raising her head imperiously, looking from side to side like a jowly empress.

THINGS went pretty well, except for one detail, and it was a big one: one of the two tanned middle-aged men at the huge oak table in the office into which Elizabeth and Rosie were shown was Deb Hall's father. They did not realize this at first. He introduced himself only as Herb, and the other man as Mr. Macete. Herb was the handsomer of the two, big and burly with lots of dark hair and thick black lashes framing his hazel eyes; Rosie's first impression was that his lashes were actually too thick, like he wore mascara. He indicated chairs in which they should sit down, and without a moment's pause asked Rosie how she felt about their letter to her.

Elizabeth watched her closely as Rosie tried to begin.

"Well," she said finally, hanging her head and squirming with embarrassment. "I did cheat." Hunched over, she buried her face in her hands, the penitent waiting for the whip to fall; not feeling one, she glanced up with regret and a strange, almost rapturous look of shame. Her eyes widened blankly, and she looked truly abashed. "A few times this summer, I cheated. I called some balls out that were in on important points. I won some games I might not have. And I did get good rankings, so I thought maybe those matches shouldn't be counted."

"This is all done on computer," said Mr. Macete. "The computer cannot log in cheating." The two men looked at each other. Herb looked grim; his flashing eyes seemed false and expensive.

"Deb told me," he said. "Deb and her mother said she might have won that match except for your calls."

"Deb?" said Elizabeth.

Rosie began to pant; she felt like a little pug who had been running to catch up with its owner. Now it all came back, and she sat nodding at Deb Hall's father, the awful father of awful Deb Hall, and he did have bad eyes, weird eyes, psycho eyes, like Mandy Lee's father kept saying that day when he almost had a fight with him. She turned to her mother. "Deb Hall."

"Ah," said Elizabeth. The room grew quiet. "But surely," Elizabeth continued, "this is not the first time someone has been called in for cheating."

"Actually," said Mr. Hall, "it is the first time anyone has ever wanted to talk to us about it. Certainly we've made the notification before. And how ironic that this time the cheating involved my daughter. Who did mention it to me at the time." Rosie was listening in a daze. Mr. Hall continued. "The usual situation is that someone else mentions this problem to us, and we summon them to us. But because it was my daughter, and I am cochair of the sportsmanship committee, we did not know exactly how to proceed and so chose to take a wait-and-see position."

"So in that case," said Elizabeth, "I would think that it would count for something that my daughter has come to talk about it."

"Of course it does," said Mr. Hall. "It's quite brave of her. On the other hand, of course, it's a deeply dishonorable thing to do, to cheat, to disregard the rules of fair play—to betray the trust of another child. It's the worst thing a child can do on the circuit, the worst thing an athlete can do *period.*"

"Oh, for Chrissakes," said Elizabeth. Rosie looked at her as if she'd suddenly belched, as if she were ruining everything. "I'm sorry, darling. But this is nuts, Mr. Hall. Here she is, with no one making her do this . . ."

"Mom."

"Now, don't get me wrong, Mrs. Ferguson. I think it's quite courageous for Rosie to be here today. It's just that I'm not sure how to proceed. We cannot simply disregard the matches that she won by cheating. Is that what you expected? My daughter would be ranked one position higher if she'd won that match. And then, what if she'd gone on to win the next match, too, and the next? And what about doubles?"

"I never cheated in doubles," said Rosie. "Ask Simone." Mr. Hall gave Mr. Macete a look full of condescending mirth; Mr. Macete looked back at him with absolute neutrality, and Rosie wanted to smile. She imagined getting together with him later to talk about Herb Hall; oh, she would say, he's got *bad* eyes, weird eyes—

Psycho eyes, Mr. Macete would say.

"I just wanted to tell someone," said Rosie. "I just had to do that. I decided that my mom and I would come today and just tell the truth. And you should just do what you have to do." Elizabeth's mouth dropped open.

"Herb," said Mr. Macete, "what if we just start from where we are? Clean slate and all that?"

"Because it wasn't your kid she cheated against, Francis."

"Look," said Elizabeth, standing up. "Like Rosie said—why don't you guys do whatever it is you need to, and let us know. The season is over, except for those late fall tournaments. We'll wait to hear from you. But we have said all we needed to."

"Mom?" said Rosie, getting to her feet.

"What do you want them to do?" Elizabeth asked, ignoring the two men. "You want them to tell you you're a very naughty girl, and you must promise to do better?"

"No."

"You want them to tell you you're expelled from tournaments, that you need to confess publicly at a press conference? Maybe put you in stocks?"

"No."

"Well, look, honey. You wanted to do the right thing. And you have. Okay? So let's let them do what's right for them, and in the meantime, well, let's—"

"We may not do anything," said Mr. Macete. "We often don't." He stuck out his hand and Rosie shook it.

"I may not even play any more tournaments," she said. He nodded.

"I understand," Mr. Macete said. "But don't not play because of us."

Rosie stood considering this. After a moment, finally looking up, she asked, "Do you need to tell my pro?"

The two men looked at each other and shook their heads.

"No," said Mr. Macete. "We don't need to tell him."

Three evenings later J. Peter Billings called Rosie at home.

"I need to see you in my office tomorrow," he said, and blood pumped loudly through Rosie's head. When she got off the phone, films filled her head of groveling, pawing the ground, begging forgiveness on her knees—films of killing him, sloshing gasoline on his pro shop, burning it to the ground, filling the club with the smell of barbecued tennis balls. She called Simone and asked her to come over. And she got a terrible headache. Her mother put her to bed and gave her some aspirin. James was mad, stamping around Rosie's bedroom in his most Napoleonic way, until Elizabeth said gently that they needed him to settle himself. He curled up at the end of Rosie's bed and held on to her shins. Simone came over, round and soft, and sat on the floor with her back against the bed so she could lean her head all the way back and smile at Rosie and Elizabeth. "I just got kicked out of the club," she said.

"You mean for being pregnant?" Rosie asked. "I bet you Jason doesn't get kicked out."

"Of course he won't," said James. "They've got a family membership. It's too much money for the club to lose."

"I wonder if I'm going to get kicked out for cheating or for you being pregnant."

"For keeping bad company," said James, and smiled at Simone. He and Elizabeth looked gently at each other, Elizabeth with her head on the pillow beside her child's, James holding onto Rosie's ankles.

Rosie hardly slept at all that night. She turned the light back on at midnight, tried to read, and finally went to her parents' room. They were sleeping back to back, her mother snoring softly, James silent until he opened his eyes and bolted into a sitting position.

"It's me," she whispered.

She lay in their bed in between them, held by her mother, who dozed. James stayed awake with her in the dark. "Peter had to kick Simone out," he explained. He talked to her like she was a grown-up, trying to help her understand. Peter saw Simone in flower, he said, and felt wild with mixed feelings—betrayal, disgust, a need to protect her, a longing to own her. The prize, said James, from Menelaus on has always been the teenage girl. Rosie did not know who Menelaus was, but she listened to James and was grateful that he was staying awake with her. The last time she looked at the digital clock, it was 2:45. She lay on her back, staring at the ceiling, imagining the meeting with Peter, imagining how disgusting she must seem to him. James gave off a smell of flannel, of coffee beans—a roasty smell. He was lying on his side next to her, yawning, telling her things, trying to stay awake, and she listened to the murmur of his keeping her company.

HE went with her to the pro shop for her meeting with Peter, and he waited while she went inside. He sat on the weather-beaten wooden bench outside Peter's office, underneath a little Japanese maple, its foliage now the color of flames. She gave him one last look before going in, as if she were about to step onto the gangplank of a slave ship.

PETER stared at her, so personally hurt and disappointed that you'd have thought she had scratched his van with a nail. She tried to meet his eyes but couldn't.

"Do you have anything to say?" he asked, and she cringed.

"I don't do it anymore is all," she said.

She thought she might faint. Something inside her was uncoiling, spinning out with a bad burned smell. She thought of those little disks she used to light on the Fourth of July, when she was still a kid, where long cinder snakes spiral out at you.

She listened to him talk about the disgrace that her cheating brought on him, the disgrace Simone's getting knocked up brought on the whole club. Sentences poured out of his mouth like black ash snakes. "You did not resist temptation," he said. "Each of us must resist it every day," and she imagined that he was going to shout, Bad dog! at her in the next breath. He would have to rethink their whole arrangement, he said. Only a couple of kids could have the kind of cheap junior membership she and Simone had enjoyed, had taken advantage of, had stained with their respective behavior. Rosie slowly lifted her head. He was red in the face, and a fat blue vein stood out on his forehead. Why, he asked, should someone like himself, who had worked so hard and so honestly to get to where he was today, teach a person with so little respect for the rules? Huh? She raised her shoulders and let them fall, shrugging to show she had no answer. He was so disappointed in her that he was shouting, and spit collected in the corners of his lips. She thought he was acting a little nuts, like one of those angry preachers on TV, and she had to look away. She scanned the rows of tennis balls; the rackets hung on hooks in the Peg-Board, waiting to be sold or strung; the beautiful clothes on the rack, white as snow, unsoiled.

Then she thought of Simone.

She saw Simone's face up close, her wide gray eyes, the little white flecks of peel on her nose. And thinking of Simone gave her strength. Without looking at him, she got up, and he shouted at her to sit down; serene as a sleepwalker, she left the pro shop.

"Hey!" he shouted at her back. "Get back in here."

"Hi, James," she said. "Let's go." They walked to the car in silence and drove home.

SHE had not played tennis since. Almost a month had passed. She had not decided what she was going to do in general, over the long haul, but for now, she was not playing. She had not yet been kicked out of the club, although she probably would be. Simone had been and said she did not care; neither did Veronica, Rosie reported. Veronica in fact was glad to save the monthly membership dues. James was secretly looking forward to doing the same.

SIMONE was wearing a baby blue smock in mid-October at the Fergusons' kitchen table, eating a blackberry yogurt. Her face was full, brimming with health, her complexion still glowed, sweet and ripe and creamy. She had already added twenty pounds to her frame. But this day her eyes were slitted and fierce. The preliminary rankings had just come out, and she and Rosie were ranked second. Deb Hall and her partner Sue Atterbury were ranked number one.

Rosie was furious. She thought back to the meeting with the committee, saw Mr. Macete and Mr. Hall sitting there.

"You got taken," said James.

Elizabeth squinted at him, one eye closed, and then turned to Rosie. "I have to say, Rosie, though, by the same token, you cheated. I couldn't love and admire you more, but the fact remains—you cheated a bunch of kids out of wins that were theirs. You stole from them. You stole something. So maybe this is the right way for things to have turned out."

There was a guilty, thoughtful silence in the kitchen. Everyone stared at the floor, darted glances at one another, clenched their jaws.

"Nah," said James finally. "You should protest. Herb Hall can't lower your ranking because you cheated, right? It's all done by computers—wins and losses."

"Yeah," said Simone. "But if it's too close, someone has to decide."

"I want you two to play Palo Alto next month so badly," said James. "I'll drive you to the tournament every day."

"You don't even get it, James. You don't get that I feel like I'll have to pay for this my whole life."

"For cheating?"

Rosie was breathing strangely, like a bull getting ready to charge, and Elizabeth felt a force like weather building inside her daughter.

Rosie wanted to scream, What do you fucking think?

But instead, still breathing strangely, she crawled onto her mother's lap and cried for a while. Simone came and sat next to them and took Rosie's hand.

James and Elizabeth exchanged glances.

"Rosie?" said her mother. "I don't know what's going on in you, but whatever it is, you have paid. Okay? You are free and clear."

Rosie sat very still. I am not a cheater, she thought. I cheated . . . After a while, she asked in a small high voice, "I am?" And her mother nodded.

Free and clear, Rosie thought, and could have stood on the table to bellow, I have paid! I am free and clear.

ROSIE and Simone disappeared into the upstairs bathroom just before dinner. Simone sat on the toilet while Rosie studied herself in the mirror. She looked at her reflection, the laser blue eyes, the hateful long straight nose. She gathered her thick black hair into two handfuls, pigtails collected just above her ears, like a child of five, and she practiced smiling the way children do when asked to smile for a photograph, close-mouthed and strained, and she stared at herself this way until her lips began to hurt.

Sometime later, thick with intent, Rosie came downstairs looking for the big pair of scissors. When Elizabeth asked what she needed them for, she would not say.

"Will you tell me later?"

"You'll just have to wait and see."

When Rosie returned with the shears, Simone locked the bathroom door behind her and had Rosie sit down on the toilet.

"You sure about this?"

Rosie did not answer. She appeared to be in a trance. She saw herself as she was tonight, with a towel wrapped around her shoulders, and she saw herself listen to Herb Hall, cringing because of course he was right, cringing again as she listened spellbound to J. Peter Billings—of course they were right, she had cheated—and she saw herself holding a trophy, about to strike her face just below the eye, like someone trying to kill her.

"Well?" said Simone.

Rosie stared at her own reflection. "Okay," she said.

Simone cut off all those shiny black curls. They dropped to the floor, lay in a pile like leaves. Rosie watched in the mirror as Simone hacked, snipped, trimmed, first to the length of a sixties pixie cut, then shorter and shorter until it was cropped and spiky, unevenly so, sheared to nearly a crew cut in places, with one Dr. Seuss sprout near the crown.

It looked pretty terrible in one way, and this made her feel afraid. Without all that extra hair hanging down, she was exposed, all eyes— focused on, like in a mug shot. Like she was guilty, which maybe was true. But at the same time, this face now looking back at her was new, like something that had emerged from an eggshell already looking as if it might be ferocious someday—like a baby dinosaur, instead of a chick. And this made her feel much less afraid.

Rosie stepped into the kitchen. Elizabeth gasped loudly, frightened at first. Rosie smiled proudly, shyly, staring down at her feet in their big untied black high-top sneakers. She looked as strange and spare as someone recently sprung from a concentration camp. Scalp showed in one or two places. Elizabeth could hardly catch her breath. "Good Lord," she said.

"Wow," said James, looking back and forth between Simone, who stood there still holding the scissors, and Rosie, who was meeting her mother's stare.

"God, Rosie. It's so—what's the word, James?"

"Stark."

"Yes," said Elizabeth. "Stark, and beautiful." Rosie smiled rather gently and ran her hand through the feathery bristles. She felt scared to death that she looked like a freak, that she would be ridiculed; what would the popular girls say, let alone the boys? Look, there goes the Shavehead, with slutty old Simone. But it was the right thing to do. She was different now, she was free and clear. The plates of the earth had shifted and settled inside her, and the world should know.

JAMES took them all out for dinner that night, everyone but Simone, who wanted to go home and read her baby books. Veronica had bought her a book called *What to Expect the First Year,* and Simone was studying it every night, as if for a final exam.

He took them to a ramshackle seafood place two towns away that he had always wanted to try. Elizabeth and Rae walked on ahead in silence, James and Lank followed behind, and Rosie took up the rear. In most ways her hair really looked quite awful, all tufts and spikes and patches of near baldness, but Elizabeth was struck by another kind of beauty she was seeing in Rosie for the first time. She shone with the same kind of loveliness so many women develop who have been sick with cancer, when so much excess has been stripped away, and their eyes are radiant. Rosie's eyes gleamed blue as sapphires.

Something Charles had said came to Elizabeth now: that all that fear she'd felt all those years that Rosie would die was really the fear she'd felt as a child that *she* would die; that there was no one she could count on as a child, no one knew how to help her be safe inside her parents' crumbling marriage; and so death must have seemed a relaxing alternative to the tremendous anxiety she felt all the time. Yet curiously, finally seeing her child resemble all those children Elizabeth had noticed with dismay over the years, whose hair was growing back after chemotherapy, somehow lessened the fear.

INSIDE the restaurant were big empty cable spools for tables; the wood was so heavily shellacked that Elizabeth knew it would be greasy. Nets hung from the walls, trapping crabs, a lobster, starfish, floaters, all as if to proclaim to the diner that all the fish served here was fresh: Look! Freshly caught fish! Here are the nets! See for yourself! Above the bar was a stuffed rabbit with antlers, a moose mounted nearby, and hideously, a stuffed giraffe's head.

They were seated, and right away Rosie began doing origami with an empty sugar packet she'd found in the abalone-shell ashtray.

"How you doing, girl?" asked James. "What are you thinking?"

"I don't know," she said sullenly. "I'm thinking about, how could Peter always be such a great pro and teach me so much, and then—fire me? How could he stop liking me?"

"He didn't stop liking you," said James. "He just felt you didn't re-flect well on him anymore. He needs the surface to be perfect, to have all these perfectly successful kids. But we don't need that. We think you're great. I mean—you know—*mostly*. Okay?"

Rosie nodded. "Okay. But I'm going to *totally* show him."

"Yeah?"

Rosie emptied a new sugar packet into the ashtray and carefully folded it into an accordion.

"Because you shouldn't ditch someone the first time they have problems, right? I mean, I never did anything before that was wrong."

The waitress appeared at their table with their sodas.

"Any questions?" she asked.

"How big is the large crab Louie?" asked James.

"Big."

"Big as a bale of hay?"

"No. But pretty big."

Rosie looked around the room, at the statue of a lighthouse, the gi-raffe, a wooden lobster. The life jackets on the wall made her think of drowning, of all the nights she'd lain in bed as a child and imagined her own death at sea, her mother suffocating underwater. She felt a chill blow through her mind, like a breeze of fear, and she ran her hand over her bristly head. "You're gonna be sorry," she said, whispering to her lap, seeing Peter in her mind, hardly moving her lips, hardly making any sound at all.

"What did you say?" her mother asked.

"I said, 'You're going to be sorry.' To Deb and Sue." She glowered. Elizabeth nodded. Rosie looked at a ratty deer's head mounted on a plaque, hanging above the bar. "James James Morrison Morrison," she said under her breath, whispering into her chest, "commonly known as Jim, told his other relations not to go blaming him." She noticed out of the corner of her eye that her mother was staring at her mouth, as if lipreading or straining to hear the murmur of the poem.

"Rosie?" said her mother. "What are you whispering now?"

Rosie pursed her lips. "*Nothing,*" she said, exasperated. "God." But she noticed her mother was smiling with a pleasure that looked like incredulity. This seemed a bit odd. She looked off at the giraffe's head on the wall by the entrance and shook her head. "I don't know," Rosie said forlornly. "But, Mom? Why would anyone shoot a *giraffe?*"

ten

B Y the day the year's last tournament began, in Palo Alto in November, autumn was revealing itself, in the sudden cold and darkness, in the snap, the smokiness. The leaves on the trees bordering the courts and clubhouse had changed to yellow and red, Halloween orange, and brown, and some had fallen to the ground in drifts. Elizabeth couldn't help but think of endings, of curtains being drawn. And then Simone stepped out onto the court, her belly so round now that she looked about to deliver. Her colors were changing, too. Her face was fair once more after a month of cool weather; her roots were growing out darker again, after the natural streaking of the summer sun. Her eyes, ringed in black eyeliner, were grayer, less blue—the gray of whales, of slate. She was dressed in maternity-paneled white shorts, covered by a huge plain white T-shirt. Rosie wore long baggy white shorts, a tiny white tank top, scuffed-up black high-top Keds, and lots of liquid liner. The bald patches had begun to grow in, although she still looked like she was out of the stream of life and into the stream of something else. She kept the extra ball in her pocket and watched her first opponents, whom she'd never seen before, extract theirs from their tennis panties. They wore tiny tennis dresses, their long shiny hair in pigtails tied with matching colored ribbons. Elizabeth was struck, studying the two younger girls, by how much hair describes personality and charm, while Rosie, running her hand over her wispy head, looked recently sprung from some terrible army camp, all of that curly shiny charm gone, pared down to the stuff of which she was really made. A number of people had come to watch them play their first match, Rosie the cheater with the weird punk haircut and her pregnant four-teen-year-old partner. The daddy was at San Jose State, people said, and it was true. He played second singles on the tennis team. One of the older boys had heard from Jason and now passed it along that Jason had not spoken to Simone since early summer. People also came to watch Rosie and Simone play their second- and third-round matches, which they won easily, and they came in droves to watch their semifinals, which they won in three sets. Peter never showed at all, not even to watch his other students. Through all four matches, Simone moved about the court awkwardly, and Rosie automatically began to cover for her, poaching more shots at the net, running back to chase down any lobs that came to either of them. It was her mission now to cover for Simone and the baby, to run interference for them, be their bodyguard, their legs. And at the same time she was aware, or at least imagined, that people were watching her line calls, watching to see if she'd cheat.

She was playing practically anything that didn't actually hit the back fence. She played shots that her opponents hit out, that were clearly out, refusing to risk the appearance of cheating, and in their semifinal match, played one ball that landed at least a foot past the baseline. Rosie stared at where it landed on the red asphalt, at the twelve inches between the ball and the white baseline, and without even exactly meaning to, in some sort of trance, she called out, "Good shot."

Simone studied her for a moment. Rosie winced. Simone closed her eyes.

People arrived for their championship match the next day at noon. Elizabeth, James, Rae, and Lank sat together in the stands. Veronica tottered into sight midway through the warm-up rallies, wearing wedgies and one of Simone's old tennis dresses. She looked worn. She sat on the bottom row of the bleachers, flanked by her salon's manicurist and masseuse, who stretched out their legs in the sun.

Sue and Deb were younger than Rosie and Simone, both much smaller, too, and in their prim little-girl dresses and ponytails got to assume the role of underdogs, even though they were now the number one ranked team. Rosie tramped around during the warm-up rally, killing time, shorn head high; Simone lumbered. Sue and Deb tore around the court like kids inside a pinball machine; Rosie and Simone, with their black liquid liner, plodded about like bored Europeans. Deb, bouncing about while waiting for each shot, darted to each ball with feverish concern. In between shots, she grabbed and tucked extra balls under her bloomers with such industry that it was something like playing against a wired little chipmunk who loved tennis but was, at the same time, preparing for winter.

"Who's the dad?" Elizabeth heard someone call out from the stands, but when she whipped around to see who might have said it, all eyes were on the court, swiveling back and forth. Veronica slowly, slowly turned her head to peer up at Elizabeth. Elizabeth waved and Veronica smiled, then turned to watch her daughter. Simone's T-shirt, wet with sweat after five minutes of rallying, clung to her huge stomach so tightly that even from the stands you could see her big knot of a belly button.

Finally the match began. The girls had been given a referee, a middle-aged woman named Mrs. London, who sat on the lifeguard chair and kept score out loud, leaving the line calls to the girls. Rosie and Simone got off to a bad start. Rosie, serving first, tried to serve like Luther had taught her, but double-faulted twice and missed an easy backhand. Everyone else held serve, and Rosie served again at one-three. She was unable to concentrate. She kept looking around for Peter, who wasn't there, and Luther, who wasn't either. You could hear the crowd gasp when Deb or Sue chased down a tough volley or got to the net for a drop shot; they were yipping encouragement to each other, high-fiving, clenching their fists in victory. The crowd loved it. It was very American. Rosie and Simone, however, in eyeliner that was already beginning to smear, looked dark and ethnic, like gypsies. Rosie was flushed with shame at being rooted against, at playing poorly, but she held serve, sending the second serve over in a little puffball that the opponents had trouble returning. Three games later, there was thunderous applause, as the younger girls took the first set.

They looked like they might curtsy.

Rosie and Simone stood at the baseline conferring, big, crabby, uncute, wiping sweat off their foreheads and eyes with the sleeves of their T-shirts. Rosie looked like a raccoon, Simone like a hooker.

"We've got to slow things down," said Rosie. But within moments, Mrs. London announced, "Game, Misses Hall and Atterbury. They lead two games to one." Rosie felt panic rising inside her. It was her serve, and she was having trouble swallowing. She tried to imagine what it would really feel like to cut through the skin of Mrs. London's neck with a chain saw.

She slowly went into the backswing, and then her left hand, which held the ball, jerked forward so that her toss was flung three feet in front of her, and she had to chase it down.

"Sorry," she said, and went to serve again. The next toss was only six or seven inches from her head, but she swung at it anyway, and narrowly missed hitting herself in the temple with the racket. This produced a crippled little serve that dropped over into Sue's service court with so little force that there was nothing left over for a bounce; it all but stuck to the court like a mud pie. Sue did a double take, and the crowd laughed.

"Lord," Rae prayed in a whisper. "Smite these evil shits."

"Quiet, please," said Mrs. London.

"Doesn't Jesus mind that you hate those girls?" Lank whispered.

"Nah," said Rae. "I don't think Jesus can't stand them either."

It took five minutes to win the game, with a series of spinning, wafting, hunchbacked little serves and an almost equal number of double faults. Rosie's head raced with worry.

Two all.

Poor Rosie, thought Elizabeth, almost unable to watch. It was so disconcerting to feel the crowd rooting against her. Please, Elizabeth prayed, with her eyes closed. Help her not defeat herself. She felt James dig his elbow into her ribs, and she opened her eyes to find Luther in the bleachers beneath them.

He was sitting next to Veronica's manicurist. Elizabeth looked at him, at this person of whom she had been most afraid, who even now studied her daughter with such concentration. And out of nowhere she saw that he was one of the people escorting Rosie over the threshold. She also saw pathos and yearning and after another moment she even finally saw herself in that dark and weathered face.

Later, when she found herself staring absently at the back of his baseball cap, at his badly wrinkled blue oxford shirt, she realized that the shirt looked just like one of James's that she had put in the laundry last week and had been lost ever since. She craned forward to read the label but could not make it out. Please help Rosie not defeat herself, she prayed, and please help her not to be stealing James's clothes to give to Luther.

Simone mouthed the word "Luther" at Rosie.

Rosie looked over to the stands, located her parents, and then saw

Luther sitting in the bleachers at their feet. He was wearing a blue base-ball cap with a white letter F, and he was looking at her.

Rosie was returning serve, filled with projections of disgrace and easy misses, but Luther's arrival distracted her from the attack on herself. She ended up hitting a backhand low and hard that sizzled down the middle of the court, right between the two younger girls.

"Great shot," said Simone.

"Game to Misses Ferguson and Duvall. They lead three-two in the second. Change sides, please."

F, thought Rosie, changing sides. What did it stand for? She did not remember seeing this hat before. Usually if he wore a hat it was an SF Giants cap. Fuck, fart, fat. She went to the net, while Simone hit some beautiful serves, and Rosie put away two volleys at the net. They pulled ahead, four-two.

But Sue won her serve, and Rosie's stomach cramped up with a sense of impending doom, of what it would be like to have been ahead four-two, and then lose her serve, letting the other girls catch up. Deb would serve for five-four, and then all they'd need was to hit a few shots to Rosie at the net, and they'd win the game, the set, the match. And then she realized she hadn't even served yet—had tragically lost all those points in her *head*.

She took a long deep breath. She imagined her left arm going up for the toss jerkily, like the arm of an erratic ball machine, and she closed her eyes. Shhhh shhhh shhhh, she said to herself, the way her mother used to soothe her to sleep. She looked over at Luther, like she used to look back at her mother when she was little, checking in. He was looking at her solemnly, and she turned her attention back to the court just as the thought entered her mind that F stood for frame. Of course: for frame it.

And she did. She slowly threw the toss into the air, let it hang there in slow motion, waiting with it. Then she smashed it down and over across the net. Fifteen-love. Simone turned to give her a thumbs-up. She missed the next serve, but threw up her second toss slowly, quiet inside, framing, framing, saw it frozen in space against the true blue sky, and she forced herself to let it hang there an extra moment, like a nail that she then slammed into, acing Deb on the second serve. Simone turned around with her mouth opened wide in a silent happy scream.

They won the set, six-two. Veronica and her manicurist bounced in their seats, clapping tiny socialite claps. The masseuse, who seemed stoned or perhaps just deeply unclear, clapped as if making tortillas.

Rosie smiled at Elizabeth, shy and proud, as she and Simone walked to the snack bar for Cokes. Elizabeth pantomimed cleaning up the smeared makeup under their eyes. Rosie looked away.

"You're in the zone," said Simone.

Then Simone looked up and pointed. Rosie turned to see what had startled her so, and her eyes flared wide. Peter stood with his back to them, talking to another pro. Rosie looked like she might be about to tiptoe away, all burlesque high step and grimace. Her hands started to reach up and cover her raggedy jagged hair. And then she stopped. She gave Simone a long sideways glance, and Simone patted her mouth, yawning. Rosie smiled, and they walked away from him.

"Hey, Rosie," he called after her. She stopped and looked expectantly over her shoulder, while Simone stared straight ahead like a pointer. "Nice going so far today," he said, and seemed easy and genuine, like an old friend. He studied her with a strange look on his face, like he was proud of her—and something else. He ran his hand over his head. "Too bad about the hair," he said, and winked at her. She felt a blush start in her belly, and she wanted to say, Too bad you're a *rock,* but smiled instead, nice as pie.

Elizabeth saw the girls troop back onto the court, first Deb and Sue, so clean and wiry, and then Rosie and Simone, in their baggy wrinkled clothes, so dopey looking that you couldn't help but wonder if they'd taken short naps during their ten-minute break. Still, momentum was on their side, having won the second set, and Elizabeth expected them to take the third handily.

Play resumed, and everyone held serve until it was Rosie's turn. They were behind two games to one. Elizabeth's stomach ached for her child. One toss at a time, she said silently. Slow down. But Rosie's first serve was out by a couple of inches, and she pushed in her second serve—what Peter called an old-lady serve—and Sue hit a low cross-court forehand that looked like a winner. But it landed an inch out.

Rosie looked at Simone for the call. Simone shrugged; she hadn't gotten a good look. Everyone held their breath, even the crowd, waiting to see what the cheater would do. Rosie looked up helplessly at Mrs. London. It had been close, and it had been out.

"Your call?" asked Mrs. London. Sue and Deb stood waiting, peeved. The air buzzed around her. Out, Rosie practiced saying.

"It was—good," she said. Deb and Sue high-fived. And then Rosie's game fell apart before their very eyes. All she could do was pat the ball back, keep it in play, pat, tap, lob. Elizabeth, watching Rosie's tight frightened face, saw her in dense salty water, having a hard time moving, and each time a wave—winning a rally, getting in a soft first serve—lifted her up to the surface for a moment, she gulped for air.

But Rosie won the game. Two up.

It was a miserable third set, and the air bristled with anxiety. The only person hitting well at all was Simone, so the other team kept the ball away from her as much as possible. But at three games to four, Rosie served the worst game yet, and within minutes, Sue was serving for the match.

She served a hard first serve to Rosie's forehand, which Rosie patted back, and an endless rally between the two girls finally ended when Rosie hit the ball into the net. Simone won the next point, slamming the return down Deb's forehand line. Rosie clenched her fist with the brief victory, and Elizabeth watched Simone give Rosie a look of encouragement. But Rosie patted back the backhand serve, and another long baseline rally ended with Rosie hitting a ball just slightly long. Fear flashed across Rosie's face again.

"Thirty-fifteen," said Mrs. London. Deb and Sue were two points away from winning the match. Veronica had her face buried in her hands. Mrs. London suddenly turned to watch a disturbance left of the bleachers, where Luther was frantically fanning his face with his baseball cap, staring at Rosie. "Ex*cuse* me," said Mrs. London. Rosie was looking at him, puzzled. Luther tugged on the brim of his baseball cap. Rosie turned away. She stood staring down at her feet, eyes closed, lips moving. Everyone was watching her.

She moved into position to receive serve, tense as a cat on a fence eyeing a bird.

Sue served to Rosie's forehand, and Rosie smashed it down the middle of the court, where Deb managed to send back a puffy little lob. Rosie moved into the net like a bored assassin and put it away with a forehand volley.

"She's back," James whispered to Elizabeth. "Finally. When they're two points away from losing."

Then Sue aced Simone.

"Forty-thirty," said Mrs. London. Match point. Rosie turned to Simone, made a fist, whispered something. Simone nodded.

Sue served to Rosie's backhand, and Rosie walloped it back, keeping Sue in the back court, but Sue returned it angled so sharply down the middle of the court that Simone, still at the service line, could hardly get to it. She managed only to lob it to Deb at the net—a short low lob, the easiest shot in tennis to put away. It was over. Rosie turned away from the net to avoid getting hit in the face with the ferocity of Deb's overhead, and Deb smashed it to Rosie's right, jumping up in triumph. But Rosie, with her back to the net, happened to be looking right at her own baseline when the ball landed and so saw, miraculously, that there was red asphalt showing between the spot where the ball had landed and the white line of the court.

"Out," Rosie said with amazement, as much to herself as to the others. She looked up at Mrs. London. "It was out." She looked over her shoulder at Simone, who gaped at her, and they both smiled.

"What?" said Sue, coming up to the net to investigate.

"It was out," Rosie said, grinning, and looked over at her mother: Mommy, it really was out. Elizabeth nodded: I know.

"Out," said Simone brusquely. "Just missed. Sorry. Next point."

Deb's shoulders dropped, and then she and Sue looked at each other with derision. Luther smiled. Rosie went back to the baseline to receive serve.

Veronica turned around and mouthed to Elizabeth, "Was it out?" and Elizabeth suddenly understood that Veronica knew; Simone had told her about Rosie's bad calls. Elizabeth nodded, held her fingers an inch apart. Veronica made fists of triumph.

"Deuce," said Mrs. London, just as Luther stood and turned to leave.

"Wait," Elizabeth said, and leapt to her feet. "Aren't you going to stick around and watch her win?"

"I just did."

Elizabeth studied him as if he were a panorama—a mountain, dark and distant. They looked at each other then, the air between them thick with what the other knew. Then as he turned away from her, he gave her a knowing smile. Her head dipped slightly forward as she strained to read him, like a secret message, but someone hissed, "Sit down," from behind Elizabeth, and by the time she had turned to see who it was and then back to where Luther had been standing, he was gone. She saw him off to the left of the bleachers, walking away, no longer in the hunched position of someone walking into a knifelike wind, just careful and slow.

RALLIES began to last forever. Twice Simone stepped boldly in front of speeding bullets, angled back impossible volleys for winners, and they caught up to five-four, Sue and Deb still leading.

But the younger girls rallied and pushed and lobbed until Simone was serving at thirty-forty, another match point for Sue and Deb. Simone hit the first serve out. Elizabeth covered her eyes, but then heard the crowd clapping again. Simone had not double-faulted; she had served an ace on the second serve. Deuce, ad in, deuce, add out— match point again. Simone, clearly winded, hit the first serve into the net.

"Just push it over, baby," Elizabeth whispered.

But instead Simone slowly wound up into the backswing, *slowly* placed her toss several feet above her left shoulder, and slammed the ball at Deb.

Deb blocked it back into the net.

"This is guts ball," James said. "This is fucking brave serving here."

Deuce.

Simone served an ace. Veronica wiggled with happiness.

Ad in. Rosie put away a backhand volley. Five games apiece.

Twenty minutes later, with various grown-ups groaning, Rosie and Simone having blown their first match point, Deb and Sue another, no one breathing much and everyone in the crowd as tense as rats, Elizabeth with a headache and James's eye twitching, Rae staring at her feet, and only Lank and Veronica watching, Rosie, on the second match point for her and Simone, watched a lob waft gently over Simone's backhand at the net. She watched Simone pause a second too long before moving a couple of feet backward and rising up on the balls of her feet to try for it, and Rosie's stomach buckled with the realization that Simone's timing was off, that the moment had passed when Simone might still leap for it, that now the top of her racket would tick it away; and even as Rosie realized this, her body had begun to turn, and without consciously meaning to, she began to run, run for this ball that was clearly Simone's, that Simone was about to miss, and Simone's eyes flickered away from the lob toward the blur that was Rosie in sudden motion. Simone crouched and backed out of the way into the alley, and Rosie got into position so far over to the left that their entire court was open; they were both in Simone's alley, within a few feet of each other. The ball bounced as Simone dropped awkwardly to the ground, her head tucked down. Rosie looked to make sure Simone was out of the way, and then pointed to the ball with her left hand, poised, swallowing, waiting, and made herself wait another full beat, until the second it began to drop from the sky where it hung, and she stepped forward, smashing it crisply down the middle of the court, so that both of their opponents looked to the other to get it, and neither did. As the crowd began to clap, Simone looked up and over her shoulder at Rosie, whose eyes were closed and whose head was thrown back in a grimace. Simone smiled and pushed herself clumsily up off the court, turning slowly to face Rosie, and they both looked skyward, sweaty and disheveled, mouths open, smears of eyeliner ringing their eyes like bruises, like bull's-eyes. Rosie bent down to lay her head against Simone's big belly, as if to tell the baby they had won, and then looked up again into the sky. "Great playing, partner," she said, finally looking into Simone's blissful face, and they walked into each other's arms.

eleven

"WHERE is the blue shirt you gave me last Christmas?" James asked Elizabeth the following Friday. "I want to wear it to the reading."

Suddenly Rosie appeared to be deeply engrossed in the comics page of the *Chronicle*.

"Why don't you wear the white Brooks Brothers shirt, darling?"

"Because I want to wear the blue shirt. You volunteered to do my laundry last week. This is not about oppression; this is not something we need Gloria Steinem to come arbitrate. You did the laundry, I haven't seen my shirt since. I just wonder if you might help me find it later. Okay?"

When he had disappeared into his office, Elizabeth stared at Rosie until her daughter finally looked up with a face so full of fake innocence and real guilt and defiance that Elizabeth had to smile. Rosie looked down at the comics.

"Honey? We need to get that shirt back. Okay? We'll take him another one—we'll buy him a brand-new dress shirt at Penney's, but we need to get James's back."

Rosie scowled into her lap, sheepish and indignant, squirming on her chair. "Penney's?" she said. "Penney's?"

"Penney's is fine," said Elizabeth.

"It's not good enough for James. You wouldn't buy him a shirt there."

"Rosie?" Elizabeth's voice rose threateningly. "I want you to figure out how to get that shirt back."

"Well, I know where he lives. At the American. On Mission. In San Francisco."

"Oh, God, Rosie, you weren't there, were you? Tell me you weren't in his room."

"I don't even know where the American is."

Rosie called information and got the number of the hotel, took a long deep breath and dialed. "Hello," she said when someone answered. "I need to leave a message for the guy named Luther who lives there? Do you know who I mean? Okay, could you tell him Rosie Ferguson called—what? What?" Her eyes narrowed, as if she were straining to hear. "For good, you mean? Are you sure?" Elizabeth bent forward, peering into her daughter's face. "Okay," she said. "Thank you."

"What?" said Elizabeth.

"He checked out a few days ago. Someone came by to give him a ride somewhere." She seemed stunned. "I bet he went to Oregon. That's where he's from. He didn't leave any way to get hold of him. He's just gone."

"Wow."

"He didn't even say good-bye." Rosie's face clouded over, and Elizabeth reached for her, but Rosie sidestepped her on the way out the kitchen door, and Elizabeth let her go. She listened to her daughter stomp upstairs, heard the door to her room slam. Elizabeth remained at the kitchen table, imagining Luther in James's favorite shirt in the car of a friend, heading home.

Rosie lay face down on her bed, Elizabeth beside her.

"He's just gone," Rosie said into the pillow, in a voice an octave higher than usual. Elizabeth lay facing her child's trembling body. "He's just gone," she said again. They lay on their sides, several inches apart. Rosie's breath smelled like milk. With all that hair gone, she looked like a baby again and, like all babies, closer to the place where she had come from.

Rosie finally spoke. "Mommy," she implored, "the worst thing that could ever happen happened to us," and Elizabeth inhaled sharply. "And you don't even know what I mean, do you? You don't know if I mean Mr. Thackery, or Simone, or Luther, but what I mean, what happened to us was that my *daddy* died. And I don't even know if we cried."

"We did a little."

"But we loved him more than anything. We loved him more than the whole world, and then one day like lightning he was just gone." Elizabeth was trying not to cry, because she didn't want Rosie to be afraid, and because in the face of that wild grief it was all she knew how to do. "I remember being on his shoulders, walking through town with him when I was little. On his shoulders. I remember how huge his hands were, holding my ankles. I remember how everyone loved him and was glad to see us. But you were too shy and people weren't that way with you. But when we walked around, Daddy and me, people invited us in. That weekend before he went away, he took me into town, he was meeting old man Grbac for a drink at the bar, but he had me with him, I don't know how that could be, but that's what was happening. Maybe it was at a restaurant, so I could be there with him." It was autumn, she remembered, and he was wearing the dark green shirt Charles and Grace had given him for his birthday. He had it on over a white T-shirt. She could remember that she could see the top of his T-shirt even though the green shirt was buttoned. "I thought he was a god, Mommy. I thought that's what God looked like," she said. Elizabeth reached out with her top leg and covered Rosie's, and they lay there entwined. "And he walked so fast, remember that?" She smiled.

Elizabeth nodded. "Because he had the longest legs," she said.

Rosie remembered being up on there on his shoulders, how her bottom bumped on the bones in his shoulders, and that he'd just washed his hair because he was going on the trip the next day, but he'd used her baby shampoo. So he smelled like a baby, and he couldn't get it to lie right because it was too clean. "And I remember we passed that old man who used to live in the house the Thackerys bought, and remember, they had that incredible persimmon tree?" Elizabeth nodded. "It was full of ripe persimmons. I can remember the exact color they were, and the leaves were orange yellow, like the color of the peaches in that book of Japanese fairy tales Charles gave me when I was little." Elizabeth held her breath. "And the old guy was reaching up for the persimmons with this contraption he'd made of bamboo. He'd split a bamboo stick and pushed the slats apart and stuffed a small red ball down into it to hold the slats open, like a funnel. So it looked like a badminton birdie. And he could reach up with this thing and jiggle a persimmon so it would drop into the bamboo funnel, and then he'd pick it out gently and place it in a basket. He had a whole basket full.

They looked like a basket of orange tennis balls." Elizabeth exhaled, her chest burning, and when she inhaled again, her breath quavered. "And Daddy stopped so we could watch for a while, and he made such a fuss; he kept telling the old guy what a brilliant invention it was, because it turned out the guy had thought it up himself. And he wanted to give daddy a big bag of persimmons to take home. Daddy tried to explain we were heading into town and that we had to hurry home, because he was leaving on this trip." Rosie's face opened and tears poured down, some running the length of her long straight nose before dropping onto the pillow. "He said he'd come back the following weekend, when he got back from his trip. But the old guy said they might be too ripe by then, and we should take them right that minute. So Daddy did, even though it was kind of a pain in the neck to lug them down to the bar and back." She stopped and covered her eyes with the palms of hands, and Elizabeth felt a wedge finally open her heart, and still entwined they cried and cried and cried for all those years of having missed Andrew, of having loved him more than life.

"We've looked everywhere," Elizabeth told James an hour later, when she and Rosie finally emerged. "And we can't find your shirt."

"Have you guys been crying?" he asked them, looking at their faces, their eyes swollen with tears.

Rosie looked guiltily at the floor and walked off.

"We felt so sad about Andrew," Elizabeth said. He nodded and seemed scared, but Elizabeth took his hand and kissed it. He looked back at her. "But you know what, James? Maybe now I can allow him to go and be what he is. Which is dead. Maybe now I can let him finally die." She looked at him almost shyly. "And—I don't know. Maybe I can even let Rosie go and be what she is."

"Which is what?" he asked gently.

She clutched her neck, as though the words she needed were stuck inside. He took her hand and lay his cheek down on it.

"Say it," he whispered.

"A young woman," she whispered back.

His reading at the local bookstore that night went well; two dozen people showed up. He read beautifully. Elizabeth and Lank sat together, as miserable as tennis parents at the very beginning before any-one had shown up, proud and relieved for him when people finally came. Later in bed James admitted that he was unbelievably grateful that anyone had come at all on a Friday night, yet surprised and ever so slightly bitter that more people hadn't. Then he laughed out loud.

No one wanted to go to the tide pools the day after the reading ex-cept Elizabeth. Rae and Lank were going to a matinee in the city. James was back at work on his novel. Simone and Veronica were at the flea market. Veronica's lawyer had squeezed some money out of Jason's family for clothes and furniture, and they had spent the last few week-ends at the flea market, looking for a crib, a swing, baby clothes. "They're eating it all away, though," Rosie confided with enormous hostility. "They look through one batch of stuff and then they stop for Vietnamese noodles. Then they find one little pair of booties, and they celebrate with doughnuts." Simone had already gained thirty pounds, and there were still two months to go. Two months! Rosie found her-self missing Simone already even though she saw her every day. She could feel her friend traveling away from her like a slow train. It hurt too much to think about. School was hard, the rains had begun, and on this cool winter weekend morning, all she wanted to do was to flake— lie on her bed and read Kurt Vonnegut, watch television, maybe eat a TV dinner for breakfast. So Elizabeth almost had to go out to the Pacific tide pools by herself. But finally she convinced Rosie to come along for the ride.

"Why do you love those tide pools so much?" Rosie asked. "I wish we could go to the water slides instead."

"I love them because of all the life that goes on in them without me. And I love the silence."

They didn't talk much on the way out. Elizabeth looked over at her from time to time.

"You okay?" she asked at one point.

"Uh-huh," said Rosie, nodding.

"Good."

"Mom?"

"Yeah?"

"Can I drive?"

"No."

"Why not?"

"Because you're thirteen and a half."

"But Veronica—"

"Rosie? Stop."

Rosie stared down at the floorboards and smiled.

SHE took off down the beach by herself, walking on the soft wet sand. She wore baggy clothes, jeans big enough for two of her to fit into, a faded flannel shirt of James's, recovered from the ragbag, over a tiny black T-shirt, and lots of liquid black eyeliner. Her hair looked particularly terrible today, still spiky tufts but flattened on one side from sleep. Elizabeth stopped to watch something in a tide pool but noticed out of the corner of her eye the S shape Rosie had gotten her body into, her chest sunk in and her head down and tucked, as if life were trying to propel her forward while her body held her back.

Elizabeth went over to the reef and stood for a while in the bracing spray. Then she slowly hunkered down to peer into a rocky pool the size of their kitchen sink. She was entranced by the color, movement, surprises, by all the same things that monkeys love. She watched a nudibranch crawl slowly out from behind some seaweed, this violently colored sea slug, bright orange with spikes. A tiny porcelain crab that could fit on a dime, frightened by the arrival of the nudibranch, held up its claw threateningly, and then scuttled off. The smell of the tide filled her—rich, salty, the smell of kelp and brine and a hint of decaying meat, the whole chemistry of the earth in solution. Elizabeth studied Rosie, way at the other end of the reef, watching her own tide pool. You couldn't tell from here whether she was a boy or a girl. Elizabeth thought of the cute bouncy kid in tiny tennis dresses, bounding around the tennis court in the early spring, wide-eyed, taking in everything. A light breeze blew in off the water.

Elizabeth felt like God standing there, so huge and alone, staring down at this tiny world at once so mysterious and transparent, its creatures so helpless. Water, returning after low tide, wafted over the tide pool, and everything that was loose in it waved. All that hunting and hiding and frond waving, and all those millions of other things going on that you couldn't even see.

Nearby anemones sat wedged against a corner of the reef, pulpy and skittish, pebbles stuck to their green flesh like gelatinous rubble, spiky white tentacles waving in the water. She had to crouch down to touch one, cause it to retract from a flower to a blob. After a while it turned back into a flower; when she touched it again, it retracted back into a blob. Looking up, she was surprised to find Rosie now looming over her.

They looked down together then at the anemones, the snails, and hermit crabs.

"They're so ridiculous," said Rosie. "Borrowing shells from each other and then wearing them around like huge hats. But I guess I kind of like how they lug them around," she continued, using the toe of her shoe to point at a hermit crab. "Like they're taking their nice new house for a walk."

Elizabeth shifted her weight, and her shadow crossed over a crab the size of a fingernail; it rose up, shaking its claws at her like an old man waving his cane.

"I'm starving to death," said Rosie.

"Are you really?"

"Uh-huh."

"What if we go get some lunch and then come back?"

"Can we buy magazines to read while we eat?" Elizabeth nodded. They headed back toward the car. The soft roar of the ocean, it seemed to Elizabeth, was the sound of the earth breathing; the wind seemed to go just any old way, but the waves definitely had a pulse. She walked along side by side with her quiet rangy daughter—who even half smiled at her once—in the tiny black T-shirt and voluminous jeans, the worn flannel shirt big enough for a lumberjack now tied at her waist, dragging along on the ground. Rosie sang softly. And Elizabeth suddenly saw that Rosie was no longer her mother's golden child but was now her own odd person. For as long as she could, Elizabeth strained to hear the two together, the antiphony of tune and ocean, until she had to stop for a moment and close her eyes with the sudden feeling that something that had dropped was rising on its own.

acknowledgments

It would not be much of an exaggeration to say that this novel, like all my work, is a collaboration.

To begin with, after God looked through His Rolodex and found the perfect little boy for me, He set about finding me a new editor. Robin Desser is *just* the most amazing woman.

Endless thanks to the legendary Elizabeth McKee, my first agent, who always wanted me to write about tennis, and to Chuck Verrill, my ardent advocate and wonderful friend.

Neshama Franklin is so articulate, so clear and lyrical and right, that I can not imagine having written this book without her.

John Kaye is awesome. I wish you could meet him. He's one of the smartest, funniest people on earth.

Father Tom Weston is one of the others. He's a great friend, brilliant, hilarious, greatly rich in spirit. Among other things, he was this book's dogged gardening consultant. Dr. Paul O., who taught me about acceptance, was my medical advisor, and I just love him so much.

Hillary Bendich and Susan Hayes gave me invaluable weaving insights.

Maggie Fine, of Santa Fe, helped me understand the soulfulness, intelligence, and integrity of teenage girls, because she is a person with those qualities in rich abundance. Her mother, Lynn Atkison, was generous beyond words in teaching me about what it means to be the mother of a teenage girl. I owe this family a debt I will probably never be able to repay.

Mallory Geitheim, Judith Rubin, and Anne Huffington are three brilliant women and teachers.

Jim Bedillion was an invaluable source of tennis tournament information and lore; ditto to beloved old tennis friends Darby Morris, Bee Kilgore, and Nancy Chance.

Maggie's friends Alecka Barna, Jolene Butler, and Amanda Mather spent a whole day with me, telling me secret things.

Leroy Lounibos went to a thousand tennis matches with me; and there is no one on earth more fun to travel with. Doug Foster shared his great insight. Charley Carney gave me one of his best stories. Sheila Lopez—the gifted dancer and director—revealed for me the shimmering beauty of a teenage girl's dark side. Claire Barcos and Lindsey Cimino were always there to answer my questions. The mothers of all of Sam's friends took extra care of Sam so I could finish: Judy, Sara, Rachel, Joanne, Sue, Jill, and Mary. And so did the dads. And our life would not function at all without my brother Stevo's help.

Once again, the world's toughest and most insightful copy editor, Nancy Palmer Jones, saved me from myself.

And I cannot imagine life without the unspeakably precious people of St. Andrew Presbyterian Church, Marin City, California. Come join us: services at 11:00.

about the author

Anne Lamott is the author of the novels *Hard Laughter,*
Rosie, Joe Jones, and *All New People,* as well as two works of nonfiction,
Operating Instructions: A Journal of My Son's First Year and *Bird by Bird:*
Some Instructions on Writing and Life. A past recipient of a Guggenheim
Fellowship, she lives with her son, Sam, in northern California.